B…

A BILLIONAI… …SS ROMANCE

SYLVIA HART

Content warning

Please be aware that Bossy Terms has depictions of graphic sex including light bondage and light humiliation dirty talk. There is also swearing, light power play, and semi-public sex.

Contents

One

SERA

Trust yourself.

That was the advice that both of my parents gave me when I graduated from New York University. I don't know what they're worried about, though. I never doubted myself during four years of college, and there's no way that making book covers is going to suddenly make me start.

Well, that's what I thought before I showed up at The Atrium Hotel for my first corporate event. The Loughton House annual Christmas party. I've never seen so many people dressed to the nines. Everything feels extravagant and luxurious. We always had plenty of money, but this… this is different.

I'm trying to blend in as well as I can, even though I don't know anyone here. Dressed in a sparkling red dress, it's like I'm at a senior prom, except I'm the one without a date.

Until I get my first lesson about adult Christmas parties when a man in his late fifties sits down across the table from me. I give him a smile, but memories of this same interaction happening a thousand times in college run through my mind. This is different, though. I'm not at some college bar surrounded by frat boys in Lacoste shirts. I'm supposed to be meeting and greeting.

He's not a bad looking guy for someone thirty years older than me. Obviously professional. He exudes a confidence that tells me that this isn't his first time at one of these Christmas parties, and he's certainly talked to plenty of new people. Maybe he's a manager?

"I haven't seen you at the office. My name's Roger," he says, not giving me a chance to say anything. Even as he talks, his eyes drift toward my cleavage. Maybe it's not all that different from college…

I'm sitting under a crystal chandelier, wearing a beautiful dress, and drinking expensive champagne. My career with Loughton House Publishing is going to start right after the Christmas holidays. Please, please, please do not let Roger be one of those frat guys all grown up.

"I'm Sera," I say, giving him the benefit of the doubt. "Truthfully, I don't even know why I'm here." I'm trying to be funny because that's what you're supposed to do at these things, right? Be personable and interesting.

I flash him my biggest smile, and he grins before scooting his chair around the table. "Well, I'm one of the marketing managers, and if you don't already work for Loughton House, I'm sure I could get you a job in my department…" He doesn't even bother to hide that he's trying to look down my dress. Holy shit, is this really the way things are going to be? Do I slap him? Do I throw my drink at him? I hesitate for just a moment.

"Sweetheart! I told you not to leave our table!" a voice says from behind me. I turn to an unknown man standing right behind my chair. Someone who is probably the complete opposite of Roger. Where Roger had immediately reminded me of the guys at bars in college, this guy makes me want to get to know him. Handsome and in his late twenties, he's got a smile that you can't turn away from. He has that allure that you'd expect from a movie star.

Purposefully messy dark brown hair that covers sharp brows gives him a playful professionalism. Where every other guy here looks like they got dressed up for the event, this guy looks like he was born to wear a tux.

And that smile pulls at me for some unknown reason.

Roger frowns, and my mystery man squats down until his face is only inches from mine, but he's looking at Roger instead of me. "I'm sorry. I thought you'd heard about my fiancée." He runs his hand along my back, and surprisingly, I don't feel the need to pull away from him. "She was in an accident recently."

What the hell is this guy talking about? But seeing Roger's frown, I'm more than a little thankful for my mystery man's interference. Even if I don't have any idea what he's talking about.

"I hadn't heard about you being engaged."

"We've been keeping it quiet, especially with the accident and the amnesia. Don't worry, though, we'll have a big ceremony after she gets her memory back. Forgetting your wedding would be the worst, you know?"

Roger nods, but I'm not sure he's buying it. My mystery man says, "Come on, sweetheart. Let's go back to our table."

He takes my hand, and I let him pull me to my feet. I'm glad to get away from Roger, but more than anything, I want to find out what this guy's doing. Did he really make up that story to pull me away from Roger, or is he the one who doesn't know what's going on?

As soon as we're a little away from where I was sitting, he says, "My name's Andrew, and you can thank me whenever you feel like it."

The smirk matches the laughter in his pale green eyes. He seems genuinely happy, like a kid riding his bike with the wind in his face. It's like this is Andrew's playground, and he's only here to have a good time. Yet, the way his eyes focus on me is unnerving.

"I'm Seraphina, but everyone calls me Sera." Why did I say that? It's been a long time since a guy made me stumble on my words. I give him a smile as I shake his hand. "And thank you, even though I thought you were crazy when you started saying we were engaged."

Andrew pulls me toward a table far away from Roger and grabs two glasses of champagne from a passing waiter. "First thing that came to mind," he says. "Be glad I went with that instead of the second thing."

Don't ask. "Your first instinct is to make up a lie? Is that your way of telling me you're a bad boy, Andrew? Because I happen to be done with that phase of my life."

He laughs, a little rougher sound than I'd expected judging by the expensive tux, but when he pulls out the chair for me, his eyes are still dancing, and that smirk on his lips is even more pronounced. "That's good. Bad boys ride motorcycles and get tattoos while I ride in helicopters and get new suits."

I arch my eyebrow. "Oh, another lie. If you're not an author, you might consider changing professions. Making up stories seems pretty natural for you." Then I glance at the tux again, and there's a glimmer of a possibility that he's telling the truth. There are a lot of very wealthy people in this room. Probably a lot of upper management who occasionally ride in helicopters.

Before Andrew had dragged me to this table, I'd felt a little nervous. Okay, more than a little. But now, I'm getting more comfortable, something that I doubt would have happened if I were still talking to Roger. When Andrew laughs at my comment, I can't help but grin back.

"I wish I could write books. Authors have it easy. They get to sit in their little writing caves and do their thing. Nobody bothers them. They live in their make-believe world for a few months and out pops a book that pays for their lives. The rest of us, you included, have to deal with all the annoying problems of a business that depends entirely on those authors. Seems a little lopsided, don't you think?"

I don't think I'm qualified to talk about authors when I've never even met one. "I think I'd rather be a cover designer than an author. Sure, I have to change out of my pajamas and show up to the office, but I don't have to come up with something from nothing. Granted, I haven't even started working for Loughton House, so my opinion is only theorizing."

Andrew frowns, the smile slipping for a moment. "You haven't started with Loughton House? Then why are you here?"

"I start on the third. David Steiner, the hiring manager who made my offer, suggested I come to the Christmas party since I live in New York."

Andrew's smile returns as he leans back in his chair. "What do you think so far?"

"Well, I've met two people. One nearly got slapped for trying to look down my dress. The other claimed I was his fiancée before I even knew his name. At this point, I'm just hoping my boss is a functional human."

"I'm sure you'll be pleasantly surprised. If you're a cover designer, you'll probably be stuffed in an office somewhere and poked with a stick every couple of days to make sure you're still alive. Like an author who occasionally brushes her hair."

"Ah, then I have nothing to worry about. My childhood dream was to slowly become a troll at a computer, so what more could I ask for? Do I occasionally get to eat, or do I become one with the computer?"

I'd been focused on his smile and eyes before, but now that I'm looking at him, it's impossible to miss how attractive he is.

"You aren't going to fit into this place at all," he says with a sigh. "It's a shame because I haven't enjoyed a conversation at one of these Christmas parties this much in years."

What does that even mean? "Are you doubting my skills? Or whether I can become a cover designing cave troll?"

"Neither. Though, I hope you don't actually become a troll. You're too pretty for that." He lets out a little sigh. "Well, Loughton House isn't known for being full of sass, and I doubt you can keep that locked up. I shouldn't be saying this, but maybe you should look for a different place to work. Trust me, I've been here for what seems like forever, and I think Loughton House is going to smother you."

Andrew's dancing around something, but I can't place it. It doesn't matter, though. I knew that going into a corporate job like this would require me to learn how to work within its culture, and I'm nothing if not adaptable.

"I wouldn't worry about that too much. Fitting in is one of my specialties. As long as there are a few normal humans there, unlike you and Roger."

He chuckles again, and his eyes twinkle in the lights from the chandelier above us. "Good luck with that. I'm still working on fitting in."

He sees someone out of the corner of his eye and almost flinches. "Let's go get a drink," he says and quickly stands up, turning his back in the direction he was looking.

I'm tempted to try to figure out who he's running from but ignore the thought. I decide right there and then that I'm going to tag along with Andrew until there's a reason not to. Maybe he's a liar, but at least he's interesting. I'll get my fill of meeting and greeting new people when I start working for Loughton House. Tonight doesn't need to be about that. Tonight could just be fun.

So I follow him.

Because sitting and staring at a bunch of strangers is far less entertaining than following a particularly handsome one when he's mysteriously running away from someone. As a bonus, I enjoy the view from behind him.

When we get to the bar, both of us still holding half-drunk champagne flutes, I say, "Should I be worried about a secret killer at the Loughton House Christmas party, or is this just someone you don't particularly like? Or maybe it's a scorned lover who's going to make a scene?"

"Now who sounds more like an author? It's someone who will turn an otherwise enjoyable evening into a less than enjoyable one. How about we finish this champagne and get a little stronger drink while we're hiding?"

I grin and finish the champagne before setting the crystal flute on the bar. "I'll have what you're drinking."

He cocks his head with that smirk frozen on his face. "Single malt Scotch is your drink of choice?" A few strands of brown hair slip from their place and fall in front of his eyes, giving him an even more playful look.

"If you were a proper gentleman, you'd order something you thought I liked. Though, if you're dead set on Scotch, that's fine with me. As long as it's good Scotch, that is." I glance at the bartender, who's looking very entertained by our conversation.

Andrew huffs and turns to the bartender. "Fine. Give us some panty-droppers, Hank."

Hank? He knows the bartender? "Panty-droppers, eh? Are you running from someone who drank them with you before?"

"Definitely not," he says, and his smile fades just a bit. Hank mixes liqueurs together in the shaker with a deftness that only comes from a lot of experience. "It's too bad we had to meet here. It's stuffy, and I can't even leave."

"Why can't you leave? Are you on… party arrest? Does Loughton House install ankle monitors?"

He chuckles. "I'm required to be here, and the door guy knows who I am, so there's no way out of it."

Immediately, Andrew became even more interesting. Why would he be required to be here? And why's he important enough that the door guy knows him? The bartender knows him, too. I'm missing something.

"What exactly do you do here, Andrew?"

For a half-second he pauses, and then he says, "Oh, we always host parties at The Atrium, and I manage enough people that it's mandatory that I come to all the parties."

I arch an eyebrow. The very first thing that came to mind when he said he wanted to leave was that I could get him out of here, but do I want to tell a manager that I can help him break the rules? Maybe I could leave it up to him?

"I mean, I could get you out of here if you really wanted to leave. I'm not entirely sure why you'd want to go since the drinks are free and where else would you go? But if you really want to leave, I could make that happen."

Andrew looks like I offered a three-year-old a bucket of candy and told him I'd keep his mom away until he ate it all. Truthfully, I kind of feel like that, too. I'd thought that my days of chaotic adventures were over, but maybe becoming a professional doesn't have to be the end of the chaos.

"I think you might be an early Christmas present, Sera. You have no idea how much I want to leave this party."

I chuckle and take another look around the room, looking for opportunities. I hadn't thought of how to escape the place, but I've always had a knack for doing things on the fly. There's a part of me that's screaming to stay professional. Don't be that stupid college kid. But how often do you get to plan a daring escape from a place like this?

There's a massive Christmas tree like every Christmas party. There's a Santa sitting on a gold chair next to it, and a woman dressed as an elf stands next to him for no reason since there aren't any kids here. My instincts kick in, and I compare the Santa standing against the wall to Andrew and try to decide how similar they are.

"I guess we get to find out whether you're a liar or actually fly around in helicopters," I say.

Andrew arches an eyebrow. "What are you talking about?"

This is going to be one hell of a night. For a half-second, I consider changing my mind and instead, enjoying my free drinks and the pretty atmosphere. I could do a little meeting and greeting. I could even make a few connections that I'll probably need in the coming months. But Andrew's smile calls to me. The possibility of adventure. The chance to have a story to tell and a memory that I'll never forget. All the same things I've sought out my entire life are too tempting.

"If you're really that rich, then you're going to buy a couple costumes…"

"This is awesome," Andrew says as he steps out of the bathroom in a full Santa costume. He looks silly with that fake beard and stuffed coat.

I glance down at myself and feel a little less enthusiastic about my outfit. I hadn't thought this through quite as well as I should have. The elf skirt was not made for someone with an ass, and I have to keep pulling it down. "Where'd you stash your tux?" I ask.

He arches an eyebrow. "There's a big pocket inside the suit." He pats his belly and lets out a terrible impression of a jolly old Santa laugh.

I have to pull up the top, cursing the person who invented strapless dresses. As I reach behind me to pull down the back of the dress again, I catch Andrew staring at me. "Should I call you Roger?" I ask with a grin. I try to make light of his stare, but it's unnerving in a way I'm not used to. I'm already feeling more than a little uncomfortable, not because I might show a little extra skin, but because I might do it at such a professional event. Yet, the way my body reacts to his stare surprises me.

Instead of making me want to cover up, like when Roger stared at my cleavage, my skin flushes and my heart races. I catch his gaze when he looks up, and he's grinning. "Sorry. There are some things that a man can't help but stare at, and you in that costume is definitely one of them."

Blood rushes to my cheeks. Great. "Well, hopefully everyone's looking at me when we walk out the door, because then they won't see you."

Andrew gives me another glance and grins. "There's no doubt who they'll be looking at." I don't know if it's the champagne or the atmosphere, or if it's just what happens when this complete stranger looks at me, but every fiber of my body is on high alert right now. When he brushes past me, his hand barely grazing my hip as he moves to lead us out of the Christmas party, it's electric.

And for the first time in my entire life, I wonder if this little adventure is more than I can handle. Or, more truthfully, if the guy dressed in a Santa suit is.

In for a penny, in for a pound, as they say, and I'm not one to let a little nervousness ruin a chance at chaos. "Where do I put my dress?" I ask before he gets away from me.

He pauses for a second and grins. "Give it to me." Andrew takes the dress, and after looking around, he stuffs it down his coat, wedging it in with his tux. "This is such a wild night," he mutters. He takes my hand in his and drags me away from the party. Away from the place I'd planned to be for the night. Away from everything I'd expected.

Two

SERA

"YOU'RE FREE TO GO," I SAY AS WE STAND IN THE lobby of the Atrium Hotel, still dressed in our stupid costumes. "I have successfully helped you to escape the prison of a fancy Christmas party, and no one will be the wiser."

"You have my eternal gratitude," he says with a grin, but his eyes don't dance as much as they did earlier. There's a mist of thoughtfulness in them which contradicts the success of our prison break. "What are you going to do now?"

I hadn't thought that far ahead. In fact, as I glance back at the hallway we'd come from, I kind of want to go back into the party. "I don't know. I mean, it's your prison break, not mine."

Andrew's grin fades behind the silly Santa beard. "Right, but are you sure *that's* how you want to spend tonight when the world is your oyster? Drinking and hanging out with Roger? Remember, I won't be there to save my betrothed now."

I chuckle at the comment. He's right, I wasn't having fun, but what else is there to do? I don't have any other plans. "Do you have something else in mind?"

He dramatically strokes his fake beard. "I don't know. I hadn't planned that far ahead." A grin crosses his face, and he says, "Have you ever gone dancing with Santa?"

"Dancing?" In these outfits? That sounds ridiculous. Then again, pretty much everything since I met Andrew has seemed a little over-the-top.

Before I can respond, we're interrupted by another stranger. "Jesus fuck man, you're twenty minutes late." I whirl around to see a guy in his twenties wearing a cheap suit approaching us. "The party's already throwing back shots, so if you want any tips at all, you'd better get in there."

Andrew arches an eyebrow at me, and I give him a little shrug. What the hell is this guy talking about? Then I realize that we're wearing these stupid costumes, and he's getting us confused with someone else.

Andrew says, "Traffic, man. Took me an hour to go two miles."

The guy ignores the excuse and says, "Come on. Let's get you up on stage." On stage? It's only then that he seems to recognize that I'm here and grins. "Oh, you brought a naughty little elf to help the act? I've never seen anybody do that before, but I've got to hand it to you for finding a sexy little thing to work with you."

An act? A *naughty* elf? What the hell are we getting roped into?

We walk a little behind the guy as he leads us to somewhere else in the Atrium, and Andrew says, "I guess our Christmas party Santa was moonlighting as something very different. No wonder these are tearaway pants..."

I whirl around to look at Andrew as he grins at me. "Tearaway pants? Like, the kind you rip off?"

He nods and his hand goes to the red pants, where he flips a little tab open to reveal buttons running up the sides. "There are only two times people wear tearaway pants, and I'm not dressed for basketball."

Did I really run away from a corporate Christmas party to get on stage with a guy I've never met and watch him strip? Andrew asked what I wanted to do tonight, and I didn't have an answer for him. But is this what I want to do? Is this what any sane person wants to do?

Is this what Sera from college would have done? Maybe. It depends on what I'm going to have to do because there's no way I'm stripping.

"Are you sure you want to do this?" I whisper to him. "I know we snuck out of that Christmas party, but we're not hiding from the law like criminals. We can tell him he's got the wrong people."

Andrew chuckles. "We said we were going to have a little adventure, and I think being a male stripper for the first time would count. I mean, we can always leave if either of us wants to. I'm not taking off my hat or beard, so it's not like anybody'll recognize me."

But what about me? I'm wearing a slutty elf outfit, and now I know why. At the same time, I remember the way Andrew had looked before he'd put on that Santa costume.

And I can remember how I'd wondered what he looks like under that silk shirt.

The only question is whether I'm worried about people recognizing me. No one from Loughton House will be there, and if it's a male stripper they hired, then that's who they'll be looking at. I chew my lip. Is the juice worth the squeeze?

Is having an adventure and getting to see Andrew without some of those clothes on worth whatever repercussions come after this? This could be my last adventure for a very long time. I'm supposed to be a professional now. My reputation is important, and I need to worry about climbing the corporate ladder.

Will I regret turning this down? Yes. As a wise man once said, "You'll find the only things you regret are the things you didn't do."

"Fine. No question if either of us wants to back out of it. Just walk off the stage and the other person follows."

It's not a question. It's a statement of what's going to happen, and Andrew nods to me. "Deal. And just so you know, I'm a terrible dancer, so we'll probably get booed off the stage."

I chuckle at my partner in crime. "Well, I'm not. Maybe I can help a little after all, because this slutty little elf costume isn't coming off."

He winks at me as we walk into a room filled with thirty women in their early twenties making more noise than a frat party. They're wild, yelling absurd things. As we walk to the stage, I hear one of them scream, "All I want for Christmas is Santa's dick!"

And I thought that I'd seen some wild parties in college, but I've never been to a bachelorette party before. The guy we'd been following leads us to a miniature, curtained off area in the "wings" of the rickety stage. He turns to us and says, "You were supposed to be the big finale, but you were late and all the other dancers have already left. Once your song is up, you're good to go."

Andrew's gone along with everything, but he stops the guy now. "Should I expect any of them to get on stage?"

The guy shakes his head. "Doubtful. They've been pretty loud, but none of them seem like they're drunk enough to do anything that stupid. And if they do, I'll handle them."

Andrew nods to the guy and reaches into his suit. I watch as he pulls his tux and my dress out of his coat. I'd almost forgotten about it, but now that my gaze goes from the red dress to the elf outfit, I question how I ended up here. My chaos years are supposed to be behind me, and I should be embracing a more professional lifestyle. Less like Dad and more like Mom. I guess that'll have to start tomorrow because now I'm excited.

"Ready?" Andrew asks, and I nod, no longer nervous. *Santa Baby* begins to play from the speakers, and a grin crosses my face. His expression matches mine as we walk out onto the stage. Covered in fake snow with a cheap Christmas tree in one corner, the stage is small, but I doubt that Andrew's going to need much space.

A candy-striped stripper pole is set in the very center of the stage, and Andrew goes directly to it. Someone in the audience yells, "Santa baby? More like Santa Daddy!"

Andrew faces the pole and starts shaking his ass while I

stand near him, and I can see him laughing. I don't know what he expects the audience to get out of it since the costume hides his entire body, but he keeps doing it, and I get a very terrible idea.

I guess that it's a night for terrible ideas, though. Because I decide to go with it. Instead of dancing by myself, I strut over to Andrew and put my hand on his stuck out ass. He whips his head around, and surprise is written all over his face. I give him a grin and a wink. Then I slap his ass. His whole body turns, his back pressed against the pole, and the surprise has turned to shock.

My hand connects with his ass, and it's a sensation I hadn't expected. Before, I'd been excited to see him with his shirt off, but now I'm thinking about other body parts. "I thought you wanted to do this?" I whisper as my hands go to his coat, undoing the buttons one at a time as Christmas music fills the air, occasionally interrupted by explicit shouts from the crowd.

"Yeah, but I didn't know what you were going to do." He pulls away from me, slipping past me and facing the audience as he pulls the coat open. The last buttons on the coat snap and fly into the audience. There's nothing under the coat. Except his chest and abs, which are definitely stripper worthy.

Mouth-wateringly delicious. He pulls the coat off and tosses it onto the stage. Then he does a few quick thrusts. Maybe it's the music that's gotten into me, but I walk up behind him and put my hands over his hips. "Do you want to leave?" I whisper.

He doesn't answer as my hands slide up his hips and run over his abs. I feel like I'm the one in control of this madness, and it's insanely hot. As I run my fingers over his chest, he turns around and takes my hands, raising them over my head. It's his turn to touch my body. He holds my hips, his fingers digging in just enough that my body begins to react.

No one's ever held me like this. I feel so freaking vulnerable as Andrew's hand slides upward over my ribs. "Do you?" he asks. Then his hand brushes against my breast, and I pull away.

Andrew faces the crowd again, and in a single movement, he rips the Santa pants off, and the crowd goes wild. This time, when he makes thrusting motions, the women in the audience are standing up. The woman in a tiara even stands up in the chair, looking extremely wobbly.

I don't blame them. The boxer briefs he's wearing do nothing to hide what he's packing, and it's certainly something to celebrate. Once again, I approach him from behind, and this time, when my hands go to his hips, they don't go upward.

Sliding down his thighs, my fingers brush his bulge, and it swells. Fuck me. Every inch of my body knows exactly what I want to happen tonight. All the while, Santa Baby plays in the background.

And again, Andrew whirls around, but this time, he doesn't tease me. He picks me up and pulls me to him. When I wrap my legs around his waist, his bulge presses against me in all the right ways.

"How long is this song?" he whispers and that warmth inside me swells at the same time that *he* swells.

I ignore him as the bachelorette gets out of her chair and starts walking toward the stage. "We've gotta go," I say, and push away from him. He sounds surprised, but then he sees me staring at the woman who looks barely out of college, doing her best to climb the railing.

"Oh fuck," Andrew says. Our guy is nowhere to be found, and Andrew doesn't wait around for some crazy drunk chick to get to us. He grabs our clothes and runs. I follow him, laughing the whole way.

"Santa Daddy! Where are you? I want you to trim my tree, Santa Daddy! With your cock!" Andrew grabs my hand and pulls me toward a door. He opens it and pulls me into what's basically a closet. The room is pitch black and so tight that I'm pressed up against Andrew, who isn't really wearing any clothes.

"What are we doing?" I whisper into the darkness.

Andrew shifts. I don't know what we're pressed up against, but that movement ends with his crotch pressed against my stomach. The music isn't playing anymore. The crowd isn't begging Andrew to show them his dick. We're all alone in a very dark closet like we're playing heaven or hell in high school.

"I don't know. I kind of panicked. That lady seemed crazy, and the last thing I need is to have to deal with some kind of wild mob trying to hump me. I doubt I'd be able to hide the fact I broke out of that Christmas party if that happened."

A giggle escapes my lips. "That's what you're worried about? Not the cock-hungry mob you'd imagined trying to rip what little clothes you have on off?"

Moments pass and Andrew shifts again. It's hard to think in the silence when his body is throbbing against me. Jeez, he really is hot, and my body is thrumming in response to his heat.

"What got into you on that stage?" he asks, his words coming out barely louder than his breath.

I don't know. Maybe it was the drinks at the party, or maybe I let the whole adventure thing take over. "I thought we were doing a stripper performance? And you said that you were a terrible dancer, so I thought I would help you out a little."

"Well, I don't think I've ever met any woman who was as ready to 'help me out' in a public place. Do you do that for all the men you spend a couple of hours with?"

Absolutely not. I may be very go-with-the-flow, but I'm not really a wham-bam-thank-you-ma'am kind of girl. "I don't spend a lot of time with part-time stripper Santas, so I don't know. Maybe you've unlocked a hidden kink. What do you think about that, Santa Daddy?"

All of our whispering is wasted when he cackles. Not just laughs. No, he cackles like a hyena with something to prove to the rest of the pack.

"Santa Daddy?" a voice calls from outside our hideaway.

"Let's go," Andrew says, all laughter gone, but then the door opens, and the very drunk bachelorette stares at us. Without hesitation, Andrew bends down and presses his lips to mine. I'm in shock at first, but then I forget about the fact that I'm kissing a stranger. Or that a different stranger is watching us.

It's like our lips have known each other for far longer than the two hours we've spent together. And my hands move on their own accord, caressing his body as though they were as intimately familiar with him as any boyfriend I ever had in college. Except that something's stirring inside me that no boy in college ever woke up.

Because I forget about the bachelorette. I'm focused on the way his tongue dances with mine, with the way his body radiates heat. The way he presses himself against me even more than he did before.

His hand goes to my neck and slides upward until his fingers tighten in my hair. "I think she's gone," he whispers as his lips kiss the crook of my throat. I glance at the door and see that it's empty, but when he pulls back on my hair, I don't care. His lips press against my skin hard, and there's a sharpness to his kiss.

He tries to move down my neck, but there's not enough space. He gives me one more hard kiss that leaves me gasping before pulling back. "I have a room," he whispers...

Three

SERA

My back slams against the hotel door hard as my mostly naked Santa runs his card through the key card reader without looking. His lips haven't left mine since we got out of the elevator. My body's going absolutely crazy, and I'm kind of surprised hotel security hasn't kicked Andrew out of the hotel since he never put on any of his clothes.

"I need to rip that little elf outfit off you," he whispers as the door slams open.

We're one step inside the room, and my back is against the open door when he turns me around, pressing me against it. I'm panting, the only sound in the room, until I hear the zipper on the back of the costume coming down. Cool air rushes into the costume and gives me goosebumps all along my bare back.

"Then why are you taking your sweet time getting me out of this thing?" I say back, not knowing how he'll react.

His lips brush my ear as he presses up against me, his hands still on the bottom bit of the costume. "I was trying to be a gentleman, but I guess that's not what you want." There's a sudden jerk that threatens to throw me off balance except that Andrew's pressed against me.

And the costume opens all the way up. He tore it. Ripped the damn thing in half. It goes to show that those muscles aren't only for looks. When he runs his hands under it, all the sensations I've been feeling are heightened.

There's a bit of fear there, too. I've never been a one-night-stand kind of girl. Tonight is different, though. He's different. One of his hands finds my breast still covered by my bra, and the other hand goes between my legs. He presses himself against me, every muscle in his body tensed.

"Are you just going to hold me like this? Two half-naked people in the door of a hotel room?"

I can hear him chuckle, and then he releases me, his hands sliding out of the ruined costume. Stepping away from the door, I turn around as it shuts. I take a good look at Andrew. Even in the darkness of the hotel room, the full moon's light streams through the open window and illuminates his features.

He's been nearly naked for more than thirty minutes now, and this is the first time I've looked at him without any of the chaos. Andrew is a beautiful man, but he looks ridiculous in the beard and hat. I smile and knock off the Santa hat, letting his messy chestnut brown hair out. "Take off the beard. It's creepy."

"Oh yeah? You can sit on Santa's lap and tell him what you want for Christmas."

That sounds even weirder. "If you don't know what I want, then you haven't been paying attention. And part of that is for you to take off the stupid beard."

I run my finger over his abs, and he gasps as my hand moves to the waistband of his boxer briefs. I hesitate with the tips of my fingers under the band. "The beard?" I remind him.

And he rips it off, throwing it onto the floor. "Much better." His lips look so fucking kissable, but I want more than kisses. The throbbing between my legs knows exactly what it wants. My fingers slip further under the waistband, and I finally feel him. God, he's so hard.

"Now it's your turn to take things off," he growls. The look he gives me is molten, and it's like I can't help but do what he says. I don't want to let go of his cock, but my body knows that I won't get what I want until my clothes are off.

The elf costume is on the ground almost immediately, split nearly in half. I'm left in my bra and thong. "Fuck, you look good," he says in barely a whisper. He steps closer to me, and this time, it's him that explores my body. He traces the curve of my breasts and moves up to my throat.

His fingers curl around my neck, never tightening but reminding me how much larger he is. How much stronger. He bends down and kisses me again. My arms wrap around his back, and in an instant, I feel my bra clasp release.

His kiss becomes more intense, more desperate, and both of his hands move to my ass. Like in our little strip tease, he lifts me into the air, and I wrap my legs around his waist instinctually, all my focus on his kiss. I don't even realize we've moved until he lays me on the bed. Without hesitating, he pulls my bra off and tosses it onto the crushed velvet of my elf costume.

I'd thought he was hard before, but I can visibly see him growing, straining at the fabric. He doesn't take the boxers off yet, though. No, he climbs on top of me, his lips going to my breast as his legs wrap around mine, forcing them together. His hands go to my wrists, pushing them against the bed.

His lips find my nipple, and I can't help but moan. When I move to run my hands across his chest, I realize that he's pinned my hands to the bed. My whole body feels caged, and for some bizarre reason, the throbbing between my legs grows exponentially.

"You're fucking beautiful," Andrew whispers when he releases my nipple. Even as he compliments me, a shiver of something different runs through me. There's a part of me that wants to push him away, to escape the cage of his body on top of mine. Yet, those green eyes hold me in place. His hand holds mine while the other lightly brushes my cheek. And I decide to relax, to go down this lust-filled rabbit hole.

Andrew's muscles are taut, but it's not from holding himself up or holding me down. The harsh lines of his muscles flare as his body stiffens when his hand moves to my breast. For only a moment, it's like he's frozen, not wanting to move. But then he releases me. He lets go of my wrists and rolls off me. Immediately, I pull my arms back to my sides and breathe. My heart's racing as I watch him stand up, but it's not at seeing his nearly naked body.

It's the way it felt to be held down like that. It's how it felt to be captured, to lose all semblance of control. Stretched out and unable to move a muscle while Andrew had free access to my body. Those green eyes watching as his fingers left goosebumps on my skin.

My eyes follow him as he pulls his boxers off, and his cock springs into view. He takes another look at me as his hand goes to it, slowly stroking himself a few times before giving me a grin. When he bends over to dig in the Santa coat, my eyes are drawn to his ass. Round and firm enough you could bounce a quarter off it.

He pulls his wallet out, slips a foil package out of it, and tosses the wallet to the ground, and all the while, his eyes stay on my body. My hand slips between my legs. His hand boes back to his cock, slowly sliding up and down the shaft.

"I want to watch you finger yourself," he says. His voice has become more of a growl, and his words are less of a suggestion and more of a command. When I slide my middle fingers inside me, I imagine how it's going to feel with his body pressed against mine as he slides in and out of me.

He rips the package of the condom with his teeth as he steps toward the bed. He's watching me as he rolls the condom down his cock. "That's it," he says. A shiver runs through me when he crawls onto the bed. Instead of getting on top of me, he bends down and kisses my inner thighs. His lips are hard and hungry as he leaves a little trail of kisses going from my knee toward my core.

Before he presses his lips to my pussy, he stops and pulls my hand away. With our gaze locked, he puts my hand to his lips and sucks my middle finger. His tongue swirls around it, tasting me for the first time. "You taste fucking amazing, Sera."

My hips instinctively rock back and forth. My body knows what it needs. "Fuck me," I beg. He smiles and doesn't hesitate to spread my legs a little wider as he lines up with my entrance. As he leans down to kiss me, he thrusts. His lips press against mine, and I can taste the desperation that he's hid behind that smile.

"You feel like fucking heaven," he whispers. I can barely think, let alone talk, as he fills me. My body has wanted this since I saw him without that coat on. The first time I touched him on the stage, I knew that this was where we'd end up. The pressure has only been building since then, and it's like a wave of bliss rolls through me.

His hand runs up the side of my body, fingers gripping and pulling as he takes me. He kisses my neck, his teeth grazing my skin, and I wrap my body around him. My legs pull him harder to me. My arms keep his chest pressed to my breasts. I need his weight and his warmth to surround me.

I don't know if I've ever needed it so badly, and I can't explain why.

His thrusts are hard enough that I'll be aching tomorrow. It only makes me want more. His breath is hot against my skin, and it comes out as a shadow of a growl. There's something about Andrew, a harshness hidden behind the mask of a smile. And I want more of it.

"Harder, Andrew," I whisper into his ear. He does not disappoint. Instead of trying to fuck me harder, he pulls back to where he's sitting on his knees. His hands dig under my ass, and he lifts me into the air. He moves like a machine, holding my hips in the air as he slams into me repeatedly. The same taut muscles that held me in place only moments before are keeping my hips suspended in the air, and there's nothing I can do to stop him. My legs wrap around his waist, but it's like I'm trying to hold on to a bull by the horns. Pointless.

Once again, I don't have control. He's taken it away and somehow, my body can't get enough. That pressure that's grown with every touch is getting close to the breaking point. I don't know how much more I can take before the orgasm rips through me.

"That's it, Sera. Take it," he says as those green eyes pierce me. My moans explode as his words, not his touch, are what send me soaring into an earth-shaking orgasm.

Before I'm even done convulsing, he repositions me, turning me onto my stomach. His body covers me, most of his weight holding me down as his cock slides into me from behind. He isn't gentle about it, sliding balls deep inside me while I'm still moaning from the last orgasm.

His arms wrap around mine, and he pins them against my sides. Like before, I'm caged. I'm helpless.

And I love it.

His body pistons into me. Sweat drip from his chest onto my back, but I barely notice it. I barely think of anything except how good it feels. His arm slides under my collarbone as he presses himself even tighter against my body, and I can't imagine anyone ever feeling more constricted and helpless than I do right now.

Another orgasm rips through me, and my body can't even convulse. I can't do anything except take it. Somehow, Andrew knows, though. He repositions himself so that he can pull me up onto my hands and knees, finally giving my body the freedom to move. All without letting his cock slip out of me. I glance behind me and see a very different expression on Andrew's face.

His entire body is covered in a thin sheen of sweat that I can see even in the dim light of the moon. His jaw is clenched as he stares at my ass while he thrusts into me. God, he's the epitome of masculinity right now. One of his hands moves to my waist, his fingers digging in at the same time that he slaps my ass with the other.

A resounding crack fills the air of the hotel room, and that's the final straw. "Harder," I groan. His hand comes down again, and my ass stings, but it's too much. I scream, and my arms give out on me. I collapse in front of him, and he keeps fucking me, every thrust harder than the last as wave after wave of bliss flows through me.

And he finally groans out his own release. I watch him as his face slowly transforms from the intensity of only a moment ago back into the playful man I met at the party. He's panting from exertion, but now he's smiling.

"Holy shit," he says between breaths.

He pulls out of me, and I smile at him, the aftershocks of all of those orgasms still rolling through me like ecstatic waves. "Yes," I say in agreement. "Holy shit is right."

When Andrew stands up, I catch a glimpse of his legs shaking for a moment, and he has to grab the bed to stabilize himself. He grins at me before pulling off the condom and tossing it into the trash.

"I don't know if I've ever had sex that good," he says as he takes a deep breath. "Ever."

I chuckle and roll onto my back. "I would normally ask if you're ready to go another round, but…"

"But you can't move?"

I nod my head, the smile cemented in place. "You know, I didn't mean for tonight to end up with me in your bed, but I think I'm glad you convinced me of it."

"Me convinced you? You're the one who was trying to fondle me on a stage."

Fondling. What a funny word for what happened. "The details don't really matter, do they?" I say it with a grin.

"So the record is clear, I didn't mean to end up in bed with you either. Though sometimes, I'd rather be lucky than good."

I arch my eyebrow as he crawls into bed and wraps his arm around me. His hand immediately goes to my breast, and I can feel the shadow of what it felt like with him on top of me. It's a peaceful feeling now rather than the desperate one earlier.

"Well, I think we both got lucky tonight," I say, knowing full-well how punny it is.

His hand moves from my breast up to my collarbone, and his finger traces the curve. "You're funny," he says, and as his finger grazes my skin, the excitement fades, and I'm left with exhaustion. My eyes get heavy as Andrew's hand drifts over my skin, exploring my body.

"That feels so good," I whisper. When his hand moves to my stomach, it moves a little faster, a little harder, yet it doesn't tickle. It's the most soothing sensation in the world. Who would have thought that the touch of a stranger could put me at ease like this?

Then his hand moves between my legs, running over my inner thigh, ever so gently. Ever so slowly. Instead of getting worked up, I'm calm and relaxed. As I let myself fall into sleep, I'm left thinking that this is how I'd like to go to sleep every night forever.

When I wake up, the moon is low in the sky, and I can see the hint of sunlight turning the horizon golden while the rest is still black. I stretch out and look over at the man that rocked my world last night. I know nothing about him. Not what he does or where he lives or even his last name.

But I'm infatuated with him already. I've never met a man who could make me feel the way I did last night, and I'm not even talking about the sex. No, he turned an otherwise awkward evening into something out of a fever dream.

He's sprawled out, taking up far more than half the bed. Even sleeping, he looks like he's grinning, and there's no doubt in my mind he's the kind of man who finds humor in everything. Someone who could make anyone laugh. He certainly made me laugh plenty last night.

I'm tempted to climb on top of him and have a repeat of last night, but my bladder says that I have to make a quick trip to the restroom first. I sneak out of bed, tiptoeing across the room until Andrew stirs, and my eyes move to him instead of where I'm walking.

My feet catch Andrew's pants. As I stumble, the wallet he'd dropped last night goes flying. Luckily, when I glance back at Andrew, he's still snoring. Even though my bladder feels like it's going to explode, I move to pick up his wallet and see that it's open, his driver's license on display.

Sunlight peaks into the room at that instant and flashes across the picture of the man that I may have developed feels for in a single night. And I see the name. Andrew Loughton. Loughton. As in Loughton House.

This is not my boss. This is the boss's boss's boss's boss. If that weren't enough, a piece of paper is sticking out of the wallet, and I recognize it immediately. It's a plane ticket. My need to pee is forgotten as I slide the paper out and see that the date of the ticket is today. For London. And it's a one-way trip.

That son-of-a-bitch. Not only is he someone I definitely shouldn't have had a roll in the sheets with, but he's also leaving with no intention of coming back. I glance back at him. Andrew fucking Loughton.

"I guess we aren't going to have any second rounds," I mutter as I put my underwear and red dress on. "At least you were a good lay…"

Four

ANDREW

It's the first time I've been to New York in three years. My mind waxes nostalgic on my last night here, one that I haven't forgotten. The last time I had time for anything other than work and rest. A night spent with a crazy new hire named Sera that ended with a night of mind-blowing sex. And when I woke up, she was gone. The only thing proving she was ever there was the sexy stripper elf costume she left behind.

I never came home for Christmas or Thanksgiving. Not even to visit. There was always a reason I needed to be in London. Something that my dad was sure would bankrupt the company if I left, even for a weekend.

Anyone else would have been happy to have his family home again. Not Russel Loughton, though. Not the man who disowned my brother Mason or the one who forced my brother Phillip to spend nearly his entire life learning to run the family business.

But now, Phillip isn't running anything. He took vacation or something, and now dear old Dad expects me to run two branches at the same time, something that literally no one has had to do before. Awesome. At least I'm home, though. I've missed this place. There's something about the hustle and bustle of New York that no other city in the world can compare to.

London's a big city, but it's different. There are plenty of things to love about that place, but it's… nicer? Is that a thing? Does anyone else actually prefer places that are grungy and loud and smell bad? I like the constant sound of traffic. The way the air smells like exhaust and hot dog stands. There's no place in the world like New York.

And it's home.

Taxis and Ubers honk as I walk down the sidewalk. Road work has cut off one lane, so the drivers are especially annoyed right now. It makes me smile as I go inside The Atrium Hotel. I don't have a room here since I own a house on the East Side, but it's the only good bar within walking distance from the office.

I need a drink before I look into everything that I'm in charge of now that I'm here. Running an entire branch was rough. At least sixty-hour work weeks. More meetings than I could ever care about. And all the while, I knew I was doing less than my dad or brother.

Now Dad expects me to run two branches at the same time? I'm looking at an insane amount of work ahead of me. But at least I'm home. At least I get to see my family again. Well, most of them. Mason's still in the Mediterranean, the black sheep of the family after Dad disowned him.

I sit down at a table in The Atrium and order an Old Fashioned and watch as the bartender makes my drink. Even though I know I'll have more work than I can handle, I'm so relaxed right now. There's something about being home after so many years. Is this what it's like for people who go off to college?

I don't know how many times I've had a drink at The Atrium, but it's almost like I've grown, and this place has stayed the same. Like it was stuck in time while I grew up. It only makes the nostalgia of that last night I was here worse. Especially when I see the place that Sera and I were standing when we were propositioned to do some stripping.

It only makes me smile and wonder if she's still working for Loughton House. I don't have time to reconnect with her right now, but the thought sticks in my mind.

The bar is busy at this time of day. Six o'clock on a Tuesday, and there are plenty of people laughing and talking, drinks in hand. I lean back in my chair and do a bit of people watching, one of my favorite past times. Unlike most men in my position in the world, I stopped putting bars and chasing women into the same basket.

There are times when a man needs a good drink and some solitude.

Which is why it's so annoying when a woman sits down at the table with me….

Five

SERA

Sitting in The Atrium's bar after work isn't exactly my perfect Tuesday evening plans, but sometimes, I don't want to stay at work, and I don't want to go home. It feels like it happens more and more these days.

I've been with Loughton House for three years now. At first, it was really nice. I got to dive headfirst into my career, and there was never a lack of ways for me to practice my art. I met quite a few awesome people who I've begun to think of almost like family.

But they have their own lives, and I feel like I'm stuck in a loop. The same thing every day at work. I'm nobody, and though I enjoy what I do, it never changes. My free time is no different. Sure, I go to concerts and events, but I don't have anyone to go with.

Maybe that's the way it is for single women in their late twenties, though. My mother's voice runs through me, the angel on my shoulder, "If you want something, don't wait for it to fall in your lap. Reach out and take it."

But what is it that I really want? Is it a group of close friends I can have adventures with? Is it work that gives me that sense of fulfillment? Or is it running off to live in a hippy commune in Arkansas? Okay, I can probably cross that last one off the list of possibilities.

I need something more than what I have, though. Growing up, I was a force to be reckoned with. I worked with my mom at her law office and toured with my dad in the summers. I was at the top of my class in High School, and in college, I did what both of my parents suggested. Work hard and play harder was my motto.

But now? Now I'm treading water, and I don't know where to go or what to do. I need something more, something to throw myself into.

As I sip the slightly oversweet mojito, I notice a woman who looks like a trophy wife in the making. They're not unusual here since The Atrium is known for its high-profile clientele. If I were looking for a rich husband with a prestigious job, this would be the place I'd go.

I see her home in on her target. A man in an expensive suit sitting all alone. Like a wolf going in for the kill, she circles around, taking him in. I pause for a moment, the mojito resting in my hand, waiting to see how he reacts. I don't know how many times I've watched this exact scenario happen in the past. Every time, there are two possible reactions. Some men love the idea of a beautiful woman talking to them. They smile, and whether or not anything happens, it's like those women have made the man's day.

Or he gets flustered. Tries to push them away. They're relentless, though. Flirty words, compliments he can't ignore, and the far too common soft touches. Those are the times I feel sorry for the guy. I've been in the same position plenty of times, when unexpected men ruin my peaceful evenings. Sometimes a girl wants a stiff drink and some peace and quiet.

I watch as the guy smiles at her, and I'm about to go back to ignoring them, but then I see his face. A face I don't think I could forget any more than I could forget the way I craved him that night. The way he made me feel things I've never felt since.

Andrew Loughton. The man who accompanied me on the wildest night I've had since I hired on with Loughton House. He was off-limits, and we never should have done any of the things we did that night.

Here he is. The way he rescued me from that creepy old guy flashes through my mind, and I grin. One good turn deserves another, right?

There's a sane part of me hidden deep inside me that's probably screaming to ignore Andrew Loughton and leave the bar. Let him be a forgotten memory. I've never been good at listening to that part, though.

One more sip of my mojito, and I take a deep breath before going into full acting mode. Andrew may not remember me, and I wouldn't even blame him. We only spent one night together, and he's probably had a girl in his bed every night since then. That's what billionaires do, isn't it?

But I spent too much time thinking about that night not to remind him of it. Of me.

I can hear the prospective trophy wife trying to win him over. "You're so handsome. Are you a model or something?"

"Nope. Just a guy in town to do a little business. It's about time for me to go, though…"

She flashes Andrew a smile and licks her lips. God, she really is a wolf. "Are you sure? I've got a room and a bottle of wine if you're in the mood to get to know me better…"

"No thanks. I actually have an appointment."

She runs her manicured nails over his arm. "Are you sure you can't call in sick?"

I'm fully confident in my actions now. For a second, I'd hesitated. Maybe he was enjoying it since he was smiling. But from what I remember about Andrew Loughton, I don't think he knows how to frown. He doesn't want to be here anymore than an elk wants to be circled by wolves.

So I'll rescue him.

"Oh my God! I can't believe you!" I scream, drawing every eye in the bar. I throw my drink in his face, the mint leaves catching in his eyebrow as the clear liquid drips down his face and into his lap. Shock rushes through him as he blinks away the drink. "Our daughter has been desperate to see you. You've been gone for two weeks, and instead of coming home, I find you at the bar with this… *woman*. You may have been broke, but at least you were broke and honest. Now? Now you're going to be broke and fucking divorced, you piece of shit."

He stares at me for a few moments, and then he recognizes me. I can see it in his eyes when the lightbulb clicks on. When I turn around to walk away, he jumps out of his seat, leaving the woman.

"Sera?" he asks as his hand touches my shoulder.

I look back at him. "You can thank me whenever you want."

He laughs, and I turn around to face him. "You looked better as Santa than as a cheating husband," I say as I pluck the mint leaf off his eyebrow.

"You know, you didn't have to throw a drink in my face. You could have just made a scene."

I shrug. "That's true, but I enjoyed this way a lot more. It was good to see you, Andrew."

There's a part of me that wants to stand here and talk to him, to see how he's been, to find answers from that night we spent together. But I don't really want them. That night was so long ago, and though I've thought about it since then, I know it was better that I left.

"Wait," he says as I turn around. "Let me buy you dinner for rescuing me. I owe you."

I shake my head, and without turning around, I say, "No, we're even now. Thanks, though." I walk away, leaving him staring at me.

I'm not the naïve twenty-two year old girl that met him at that Christmas party. I know who he is now, and there's no way I'm going to waste any time on dinners with men I could never date. It's bad enough that we spent that night together, but there's no way in hell I'm going to get roped into falling headfirst into lust with Andrew Loughton.

Six

ANDREW

My father is sitting in his office when I get there. Russel Loughton is like the sun, and everyone else in his world is like planets orbiting him. He knows he is the most important person in his universe, and the way he looks at everyone tells them how little they mean to him. Myself included.

"Morning, Dad," I say as I close the door behind me. He's staring at his laptop, a serious expression etched into his face. He doesn't acknowledge me as I sit down across from him. I see him scroll down the screen, and I wait patiently. This is how it always is with us.

I was never my father's favorite. Truthfully, I'm glad I wasn't, because being his favorite meant that every ounce of his attention would be on me, and I don't think I'd have survived that growing up. My oldest brother, Phillip, had that honor and misery.

And at the same time, I was not the hated son, either. Mason had that terrible position. I can't remember a single time that Mason and my dad got along. It got so bad that when Mason turned eighteen, my dad tried to tell him what he was going to do for college, and Mason hit him in the face. That was when dear old Dad disowned him and cut him out of the family money and company.

I don't expect Dad to rush over to hug me, even though it's been three years since I've seen him in person. There's no need to praise my accomplishments or hard work. It just would be nice if he acknowledged my presence when he's the one who asked me to come to his office.

After a few minutes, my dad shuts his computer and finally turns to me. "The London branch isn't doing as well as expected this quarter." It's a statement, not a question. I don't respond, waiting for his criticism.

"Do you have connections with the top agencies there? Are you missing opportunities with the smaller booksellers?" The tone is not curious or trying to be helpful. It's dismissive and patronizing. As usual, I smile and accept that there is nothing I could ever do to be seen in anything but a negative light by my father.

I give him a nod and say, "I have very solid connections with all the top agencies. I've got most of my top sellers in window displays already. We're just in a bit of a summer slump, and I'm sure that we'll pick things back up next quarter."

Dad narrows his eyes at me, but he doesn't respond. "I need you to find someone to handle the day-to-day operations in London while you stay here for the next few weeks. Keep in touch with them, but the priority needs to be New York. Phillip is having a fucking midlife crisis and has given up his job and connection to the family along with the family money for the next month, and he can't be counted on to handle the New York branch."

He shifts in his seat, leaning back ever so slightly, which means he's no longer in "chastisement mode". "For now, he's working as a junior editor, living on barely enough money to survive on the street, and I will not put up with you giving him any handouts. The purpose of this is for him to realize that he's not capable of surviving like that, so unless you enjoy the prospect of running both branches permanently, I suggest you let him fail."

Phillip gave up his money? What the hell? More than that, though, I consider what this means for me. Is this changing the things we've all accepted since childhood? Is Dad thinking of handing the company to me instead of Phillip?

He doesn't ask if I can do it or if it's too much. I mean, I've been running the London branch for three years, but it's a tenth the size of our New York operations. That should have been a question, though. I'm not familiar with anything happening here. "Why don't you?" I'm genuinely curious. It's not like my dad to give up control, and letting me run the entire company even for a couple of weeks is definitely giving up control. Could this be a test?

"I have other things to take care of," he says as dismissively as when he didn't respond to me walking into his office.

A laugh escapes me. I can't help it. What the hell is there to do other than run the fucking company? I'm sure that he thinks he's doing something important, but truthfully, I don't even know if he remembers how to run Loughton House's day-to-day operations. Phillip's had that job for a decade. I've run London by myself. And Dad? He's "supervised" like a parent forcing his kids to clean up their room while he plays on his phone.

The door swings open and Phillip walks into the office. What the hell has happened to my brother? A midlife crisis? No, this is something different. Is that shirt made of polyester? And when did he start growing a beard?

"And I thought I was the crazy brother." I stand up and walk toward Phillip, whom I haven't seen in three years. "But giving up the family fortune for a month is something only you'd do." I give him a hug.

My hand touches his shirt, and I know I'm right about it. "Where the hell did you get this shirt? A dumpster? Is that polyester?"

He grins at me, wider than I've ever seen. "I went thrift store shopping yesterday. My nine-hundred dollars a week doesn't go very far."

I'm currently wearing a suit that costs half a year's worth of that salary. It makes me take a second look at him. The Phillip I grew up with wouldn't be smiling. He'd be pissed. Furious. He's a nobody right now. But he looks happier than I've ever seen him. Immediately, I know that there's more to this story than I've heard from Dad.

But that doesn't mean I can talk to him about it. At least not right now. "Fucking Castaway over here. Next, you'll tell me you're rubbing sticks together to make a fire for warmth. Jeez, Dad. You're really letting Phillip live like this?"

Dad grins, just a little. Just enough to tell both of us how much he's enjoying this. If there's anything about my dad that everyone knows, it's that he thoroughly enjoys punishing people for mistakes. There's no doubt that he considers Phillip's decision a mistake, but I'm not so sure it is. There's a reason behind it because he wouldn't be smiling like that if he was unhappy. My brother is not a *cheerful* man.

"He chose this. Not me. He can come back to the fold anytime he wants. Which brings me to why I called you up here, Phillip. I'm going to spend the next two weeks in Beijing to deal with permitting issues for that expansion. London's running well currently, so Andrew will have to manage both the London and New York branches simultaneously. Unless you're ready to be done with this nonsense..."

Dad was always one for the theatrical, and he lets those words sit in the air like a looming threat. Or maybe a promise of misery. I want to sigh, but then Dad would turn that anger toward me. Instead, I arch my brow at Phillip.

But Phillip doesn't seem fazed at all. "I'm sure he'll manage. I have complete confidence in my little brother."

Dad's glare is venomous, and I'm more than a little shocked at Phillip's response. He knows he needs to watch himself, but he's being careless. Why would you poke the bear? "You're shirking your responsibilities, Phillip, and you know that."

"No. I'm taking a break." Oh God, Phillip looks pissed. I scoot back a little, so I'm not in between those two. Is this going to be like what happened with Mason? Is Phillip going to hit him? Or is Dad going to hit Phillip? "I've spent every moment of my life making sure I took care of my responsibilities. I'm not a machine, Father. I want to do things that make me smile for once instead of worrying about this damned company."

The vein in Dad's throat pulses like an angry snake living inside him. Fuck. What the hell is happening here? Phillip's always been so ready to be the obedient son and do what he's told. This isn't him. Not at all.

"And so you're aware," he continues, staring straight at Dad without an ounce of fear. "When I come back to run Loughton House, there will be changes. I will delegate, and I *will* have time to do as I wish. I'll continue to run Loughton House to the best of my ability, but I will also enjoy my life alongside running the company."

Dad stands up, more furious than any time I can remember, other than when he disowned Mason. "And what happens if I disapprove of those changes?"

Phillip smiles as calmly as if he were ordering a Pina Colada on a beach somewhere. Not getting into a pissing match with the only person in the world that could take everything he has away. "Then you can either fire me or get the fuck over it."

Then he turns to me and says, "See you around, little brother," before he walks out the door.

Dad glares at the door for a moment before turning all that anger toward me. "This is what I'm talking about, Andrew. He is worthless to me, to the company. It's time that you stepped up and learned to take charge of things in case Phillip isn't capable of doing his duty. Your old office is ready for you, and everyone has been informed to report to you."

I'm left more than a little flustered, but I guess Dad doesn't care because he opens his computer and promptly ignores me completely.

I take a breath and don't bother trying to tell him goodbye. He'd ignore me even if I did.

I guess it's time to get to work. I have a multi-billion dollar company to run.

Seven

SERA

I LEAN BACK IN MY CHAIR AND STARE AT THE GRUNGY guy on my screen. Long, bleach-blond hair drips with sweat, part of it covering his face. He's the perfect model for this book cover. Rock star romance covers are a personal favorite, but I can't help laugh thinking about the actual books.

See, I know what rock stars are like since my dad has been one since I was in diapers. And not a small-time, dive-bar kind of rock star. No, he's played at all the biggest venues, many of them with me hiding in the wings as people screamed his name.

I paint a bit of smoke onto the cover behind the model, a canvas for the real art on this cover. A music staff hides in the smoke, light blue with a hint of glow. It's the little things that make an otherwise plain cover stand out and sell books.

I smile at it and close my eyes. A rock star is just a man. When I was little, I didn't understand. I thought my dad was the coolest person in the entire world. If he wasn't, why did so many people scream his name?

My parents got divorced when I was about six. I barely remember them together, but they always did the co-parenting thing right. No badmouthing each other. No arguing over who got to spend time with me. No lawyers or lawsuits. They were wonderful parents. Just… very different.

My dad, well… he likes women. Not in a typical rock star style, though. He wasn't spending every night with a different girl. No, he fell in love with women. Over and over and over again. I can't count how many serious girlfriends he had. He married six of them.

My mom was a workaholic, but even she had had three failed marriages after my dad. I'd guess that was because she cared more about her work and me than she ever cared about them. I don't blame them for wanting to walk away. She was the best mom I could imagine, but I doubt she was the best wife when she was married to her work.

Phillip walks into the cubicle. Phillip Loughton is a strange man. He was like a walking billboard for the ice-cold boss until he decided to see what it's like working at the bottom of the totem pole. And he didn't do that half-assed, either. He did a full swan dive into that role. Hell, he was living in a freaking storage closet for a week.

Now… well, now Phillip seems like a pretty decent guy. Though, I still have my reservations about how much of it is an act and how much is the real him.

"Somebody left the coffee pot on all morning and the break room stinks like burned coffee," he mutters. "How am I supposed to edit all day without an afternoon cup of coffee?"

Addison, the newest junior editor and my cubicle-mate, turns around and grins at him. "You could always clean the coffee pot and make some more?"

"Clean the coffee pot? With what?"

I chuckle. It's fun to watch them bicker. I don't know if I'll ever be as easy around Phillip as Addison is, but that's probably because my mom's voice is always in my ear. He's not a friend or colleague. *He's the boss, and he decides your fate.* Maybe he's a nice guy right now, but when he's done with this little experiment, he'll probably go right back to being the guy he was before.

"The sponge, Phillip. Like you do with any dishes. Did you think that burned coffee pots were magically cleaned?"

He chuckles and stands up, nothing like the boss of three weeks ago. That guy would have snarled at her. Not laughed.

"I thought that work would be the one place where nothing would be new." He walks away to clean the office coffee pot, and it's hard to reconcile this man with the guy who scared the living shit out of everyone at the office for the past three years.

"Phillip sure has changed," I say.

Addison looks at me with a grin. "Everyone says that, but I don't understand it. I mean, he was a little grumpy when I first started, but that's only because he was unhappy. I guess being a billionaire doesn't suit everyone."

Right. Because being broke is so much more fun than being rich. "I think that maybe there's more to it than that." It's obvious that Addison is the one who brought some happiness to him.

That's when Trish shows up. "You will never believe who I just saw."

"Who?" I ask.

She gives me a grin. "Andrew fucking Loughton. Whatever is going on with Phillip is making things change around here. I can smell it. Andrew hasn't been back since they opened the London branch, and now he's here and Phillip is editing? The times, they are a changin' is all I'm saying."

I glance at Addison, who's frowning. "Someone has to do Phillip's job, right? What if their dad needs someone to cover for him? That's not so strange, is it?"

Trish glances around her. "Yeah, but the thing is that with Andrew at the helm, who knows what's going to happen? He's always kind of been the fuck off brother. We all know what it was like with Phillip running things. And Daddy Loughton. But Andrew?" She shrugs. "I've been here for seven years, and for the first time, I feel like this entire company is on shaky ground. It might be time to brush off the resume, you know? Just in case."

That thought bothers me more than I'd like to admit. My hope had been to move up, not leave Loughton House. I've been doing a lot of thinking since seeing Andrew the other night, and it's time I started focusing on where I want to be. There's no reason I shouldn't be climbing the corporate ladder. My mom did it faster than anyone before her, and she was a partner at one of the biggest law firms by the time she was forty. My dad became an international sensation before the age of thirty. If they could do all of that, I can too.

And the best place to do it is at Loughton House where I know the business and understand the hierarchy.

Phillip steps into the cubicle, a fresh cup of coffee in his hand, and I notice a coffee stain on his red polyester shirt, yet another oddity about this experiment of his. "Loughton House is going to be fine under my brother's command," he says softly as he sits down at his desk and opens his laptop. "He's only filling in for my father while I'm doing this. Remember, he may be new to running New York, but he's been completely in charge of London since its inception, and they're very profitable."

He doesn't pay any more attention to us as he gets to work editing whatever book he's working on. Addison does the same, and Trish gives me a look that tells me exactly what she's thinking. *I'm going to brush off my old resume.*

I sigh and nod to her. Instead of thinking about brushing off my resume, I make it a point to go home and start brushing up on the responsibilities of the positions I could move into. If things get shaky, I'm going to need to take advantage of any openings.

I look back at the rock star on my screen. Sometimes I wonder how my parents see me. They were both so damned successful, and here I am painting smoke on half-naked guys. It's time I started living up to my potential.

Eight
ANDREW

I LOOK OUT THE WINDOW OF MY OFFICE AT THE night sky. It's different from London. Fewer clouds and more skyscrapers. I've enjoyed being home again, seeing this skyline again, but it's almost over. I know it as well as I know my job.

Phillip may be the best at running Loughton House. He was born to do it. There's a reason people referred to him as the Prince of Publishing. Well, now he's become king, and truthfully, that's a good thing.

But it also means that I'm going to be forced to go back to London.

My fingers drum on the arm of my chair as I think about what happens next. Dad gave the company to Phillip, and since he finished his little mid-life crisis, he's been focused on fixing everything he saw wrong in his life. Especially our broken family.

He's going to convince Mason to come back to Loughton House. Now that Dad's not there to stop him, Phillip will want to reconnect. Phillip and Dad may have stopped talking to him all those years ago, but I never have. We've even visited each other occasionally. That means that I'll do the reconnecting.

I know him better than anyone else in the world. He's going to come back. I don't know if he'll sell the resort he's running or if he'll have someone else manage it while he works with Loughton House. Either way, Phillip will have him here where he can watch him and spend time with him.

Which leaves me going back to London. That suits me just fine. With all the turmoil and Dad being out of the picture, it leaves me with my first chance to do something important. Something more than follow orders.

Taking Vanguard to London is going to be why he sends me there. Vanguard, the only real innovation in the publishing industry in decades is our ticket to securing our future. Instead of going through agencies who find new authors from submissions, we're actively hunting down self-published authors who have the stories but not the marketing chops to succeed. We're becoming less a traditional publisher and more of an independent publisher. How exactly we go about succeeding with that is still a little up in the air.

If we don't get Vanguard to succeed, it may signal the death of Loughton House. The entire industry is slowly starting its death spin. Fewer readers, competition with self-publishers, and competition with other media has slowly taken bite after bite out of the market as a whole.

We have to right ourselves or in thirty years, the family business will be a shadow of what it is now.

That's Phillip's pet project, though. He came up with the idea, and he's pushing it. Hard. I have other ideas on what we should be doing, and while Vanguard isn't a bad plan, I think we should be focused on innovation instead of maintaining profits. We should be leading the way in publishing *of all types*. There's no way that he'll go along with it, though. Not while his pet project is still in the works.

This is my chance to prove to my brothers that my ideas are valid, and I'm not just the baby. For the first time ever, I have a chance to make a name for myself within the family, and I'm going to take it.

I just don't know how I'll have the time to start anything with the workload. London's suffered while I've been in New York. I'll have to do everything secretly or Phillip and Mason will weigh in, and most likely tell me to stop. "Only have one expansion at a time," was always one of Dad's sayings. I'm sure that's been carved into Phillip's brain at this point.

Yes, I'll have to do it in secret while keeping London running at better than expected numbers, *and* instituting Vanguard. There's simply no way I can do it. Not alone.

I frown as I look out at the city. But there won't be a better time. Maybe I could find someone to help me. A clever employee looking to move up. Someone who can keep a secret. They'd have to be smart as a whip, though, since they'd be walking into a whole new world they've never dealt with. And they'd have to excel at it with very little training.

The first person who pops into my head is a terrible option. Absolutely the worst. There's no way that Sera Wylder could ever help run an entire branch of Loughton House. She *is* trustworthy, though. I haven't heard any whispers of what we did at that Christmas party. And she *is* looking to move up.

But she's only a cover artist. Who understands how to manipulate people. The frown only deepens. Who else would work? I run through lists of names of upper management and even lower management. None of them fit the profile. Maybe someone in London?

"Fuck it," I whisper and turn around in my chair to open my computer. Maybe Sera isn't a terrible option. I'd have to teach anyone the position, so maybe I can teach her. Probably not, but I'm going to kick myself if I go with someone else when she could have done it.

I pull up her file and frown even more. But for different reasons. It doesn't make sense. Top scores at NYU School of Fine Arts. A very solid portfolio. A slew of amazing covers. Every single review is outstanding. Why didn't she ever move up? Why did it take me coming to New York for her to get a chance?

Then I see it. A single comment in one of her later reviews. "Does not focus on time management, but gets her work done, regardless."

I chuckle. That would have set the old Phillip off. No one with that in her reviews would have ever moved up. In my opinion, that's a highly sought after trait. It means that she's confident in her ability to get things done faster than expected.

I dig deeper and go through her college transcripts.

Holy shit, she took business classes on the side. Not the basics to get a minor in business, either. She seemed to ignore the requirements for a business minor and took classes that interested her. What kind of college kid does that?

Sera Wylder is a confusing woman. Everything points to her being a corporate climber, but she's sat at the same entry level position for three years. Now, I hear that she's looking to move up for the first time. What changed? And how badly does she want to move up? And how high?

The more I dig, the more I wonder if maybe she *is* the right person for what I'm looking for. Maybe she has what it takes, but I've never rolled the dice on an employee before. I'm going to need to know everything about her before I trust this project to her.

More than anything, I'll have to accept that once I bring her in on it, there's no changing what she is to me. A tool. That night, all those years ago, will have to be a forgotten memory. The last thing I want is for either of us to further complicate an already very delicate situation.

I won't get another chance like this, and I'll need to move quickly. The longer I try to hide things, the more likely it is that they'll find out before I have all my ducks in a row.

This is a crazy thing I'm going to do, but I'm fucking tired of being the forgotten brother. Sometimes, you have to put all your chips on the table and let the cards fall where they will. The biggest thing influencing those cards is the person who I recruit to help me.

And that's looking more and more like it'll be Sera Wylder.

Nine

SERA

Why the hell am I riding the elevator up to Andrew Loughton's office? Other than an over-the-top temptation of a night at Addison's, I've managed to steer clear of the man that sends my libido into overdrive every time I see him.

Over the past month, a lot has changed. Trish was absolutely right, and I'm glad I decided to step up. Instead of keeping my head down and doing my job, I've been dropping hints about the thought of moving up and getting more responsibility, and maybe that's where this is coming from.

But Andrew isn't running anything at this point. Overnight, Russel gave the entire company to Phillip and retired. Then they sent out a big email blast telling everyone that we're going to have to work more hours. It's been a madhouse, but I'm doing exactly what my mom suggested. *Be ruthless. Be invaluable. Be everything they didn't know they needed. And let your boss's boss see it.*

I didn't think it'd be Andrew who would be noticing.

I'd thought he'd be going back to London now that it's Phillip's company. When I decided to make changes in my life, I also decided that I'd do whatever it took. I just hope that this little visit is work related. The Slack message was simple, yet it told me absolutely nothing about what to expect. "Come to my office ASAP." What the hell could it be about?

Even worse, there's a part of me that can't separate Andrew, my boss, from Andrew, my mysterious stranger from three years ago, and that part of me is going absolutely crazy. A night I can't forget with a man that blew away every other person I've dated since then.

Andrew says, "Come in," as soon as I knock on his door, and when I step into the office, I'm a little awestruck. I've never been in one of the senior managers' offices. It's enormous. Like an entire hotel room, except the entire back wall is a window that looks out over the city.

Andrew's L-shaped desk sits in the middle of the room, a very modern-looking thing made of steel and glass, with a massive monitor to the side of him next to his laptop.

There are small shelves that are littered with weird trophies. There's one that might be for swimming. Another stands above the rest with a giant bowling ball on top. Is that one with a dog on it…?

"Thanks for coming so quickly," he says and stands up. My attention is pulled away from the trophies as he walks around the desk. He pulls a chair around to his side of the desk in front of the monitor. I get a good look at him again after what seems like forever. God, he's so much different from Phillip. It's not fair to have billions of dollars, plenty of brains, and the looks of an underwear model.

"I've got an author that's been nothing but a headache for his pre-publishing team. He wants a cover that won't sell, and for some idiotic reason, the issue got passed all the way up to me. We want to keep him on with us, but he's not being sensible. I don't know how, but he managed to retain the right to refuse a cover in his contract."

I frown at Andrew and at the computer, and a tingle runs through me as his eyes roam over my body. I should have remembered how it feels to have him focus on me. "So why am I here? Can't you convince someone to use a suitable cover instead of a terrible one? Isn't convincing people to accept things they don't want in Chapter Six in the *How to Be the Boss* manual?"

Andrew chuckles, but he doesn't stop setting things up in front of the screen. "Well, Chapter Seven is delegation, and I'm delegating today. I think you can convince this guy better than me since I don't have any idea what his book is about. I've got the files for you to skim through real quick. Then you can deal with him in the meeting I have scheduled in ten minutes."

Ten minutes? What? "That's impossible. I spend more than ten minutes thinking about a cover for an author I've worked with before. I may not even be familiar with this author's genre."

This time, Andrew stops and looks at me. "I think you're wrong. I think you'll do fine, and we'll have an author willing to work with us when you're done. But in a worst-case scenario, we won't publish the book. I won't waste money on a book that won't sell. So come sit down, skim over the information, and then we'll get on the call."

I take a deep breath and go to the seat Andrew's positioned in front of the monitor. A file is already open on the screen. This is what I wanted, wasn't it? A chance to do something other than make covers every day. Maybe this is my opening. Maybe this is how I do exactly what my mom said. *Be ruthless.*

"Fuck it," I whisper and start opening documents. It's an urban fantasy book, and he wants it to be a picture of a… that can't be right. I read it again. He wants the cover to be a duck in a fishbowl.

I blink and look at Andrew. "Is he serious?"

"He wants a red duck in a gold fishbowl. The title is Feathers of a Phoenix, and I guess there's some kind of duck symbolism. I don't know, and truthfully, I don't care. He needs to dial back the artsy bullshit and let us do our job."

I've seen some bizarre cover requests and thoughts before, but this takes the cake. Or the entire dessert buffet. "Okay, so you want me to convince him that he's an idiot without telling him that he's an idiot?"

"Yes." Just one word. Andrew's sitting inches away from me, the closest we've been since that Christmas party. I can tell that he's changed since that night. He's still got that silly smile on his face, but there's more to it now. Maybe someone in his family told him the same thing my mom told me. Maybe he's learned to be ruthless.

He's got an aura of confidence that verges on arrogance. No empathy, even though he wants me to do something very complicated with no warning.

That confidence is sexy. Mature in a way that only experience and responsibility can give a man. I need to get back to the point of this meeting, though. Seeing Andrew may remind me of our night together, but right now I'm trying to start my upward climb, and I need to be focused. "Fine. I've never talked to this guy before, so I'm going to have to feel him out. Don't get in the middle of it unless you really think I'm screwing it up."

His smile comes out then. "I'm not going to get in the way at all. I want to see how you do. If you tell him to go fuck himself, then we'll scratch him off the list of authors. It's not like his books are going to make or break Loughton House."

I nod to Andrew and take a deep breath as he sets up the call on the computer. A man in his late forties connects for the Zoom call, and I know what I'm dealing with. The kind of person I've dealt with so many times in the past.

"Good morning, Mr. Cooper. I'm Sera Wylder, one of the lead cover designers with Loughton House."

He doesn't try to be pleasant, and I'm sure he's had this conversation multiple times with other account managers. "I thought that my issues with my previous cover designs had been escalated further up the chain than a lead cover designer." He's got an attitude, but I put on a smile. The same one I learned from my mom at an early age. *It doesn't matter what you have to say, make sure you say it with a smile.*

"I am as far up as the discussion will go, Mr. Cooper. By the end of this conversation, I'm sure we'll have everything straightened out."

His eyes open a little wider and his bushy eyebrows raise. "Oh, is that right? You're going to try to push me around like that weasel of a manager did?"

I purse my lips together, never losing the smile as I shake my head. "No sir, Mr. Cooper. I'm going to make whatever cover you decide on. If you want a duck in a fishbowl at the end of our conversation, I will make it, and we will print it."

I glance at Andrew, who has his own eyebrow raised. He's already said that he wouldn't publish a book with that cover on it, but he hasn't interrupted me yet. He's testing me. I resolve myself to not screw this up. *Be ruthless.*

Everything Mr. Cooper does on the screen seems a little more animated than necessary, and he grins. "Really?

The last person I talked to said that you wouldn't publish my book with the cover I'm describing."

I nod. "Your contract states that you get the final say on covers, so we're going to go with whatever you decide. It certainly doesn't hurt me if your book flops and Loughton House drops you after *Feather of a Phoenix* loses money. I'm just a cover designer." I say it with as much nonchalance as I can muster. It's important that he thinks I don't care, even if every muscle in my body wants to tighten with nervousness.

"Wait." He pauses. "Why would it flop? Sure, it's not exactly a normal cover idea, but I don't want it to get lost. Urban fantasy has been growing so much in the past few years, and my last book didn't exactly knock it out of the park. I want to get back to my debut numbers."

I shrug. "Look, Mr. Cooper. Your job is to write books that readers fall in love with. I'm not going to try to tell you what your next outline should look like. My job is to take what's in your book and make a cover that will convince as many of your current and potential fans to buy it as possible. I've spent the past four years doing that every single day. Loughton House is the number one publishing house for urban fantasy, and everyone agrees that your idea of the cover will sell fewer books than mine."

I give him another big smile. "But if you're sure that you know more than dozens of people who've spent their careers selling books, then I'll get started on your urban fantasy book with a duck on the cover this afternoon."

For the first time, he looks worried. "You really think Loughton House will drop me? I've published six books with them."

"I've had confirmation that if you insist on your cover and it does not do well, you will be dropped with no intention of ever considering another one of your books again."

Mr. Cooper takes a deep breath. "You think you can design a stand out cover? One that's not the same as everyone else's?"

"I'm very good at my job. And if you don't like it, let me know and I'll rework things. But I promise you that any cover I make is going to sell more books than the idea you have insisted on."

I glance at Andrew again, and see him grinning off-camera. "Fine," Mr. Cooper says defeatedly. "Make the damn cover. You win. I don't want to be dropped."

I feel like I should reach out and pat him on the shoulder, to tell him it's going to be okay. But he's not here, and I don't think patting the monitor would work quite as well. "I'll get a mock-up to you sometime next week. I think we're going to work well together."

He doesn't respond, simply ending the call. I turn to look at Andrew, who's grinning from ear to ear. "That was fucking amazing. And to think you're only a cover artist with no training in dealing with customers."

I can't help but smile a little, even though I'm feeling sick to my stomach. "If you think cover artists don't deal with clients, you probably need a lesson in what our job entails. Now, why didn't you have that meeting? I bet you could have had that conversation in your sleep, and you were sitting here with me, so you didn't save any time."

Andrew leans back in his chair, getting comfy. "Well, to be honest, I needed to know if you could do anything other than make pretty pictures. I needed to see how you dealt with assholes. We're looking for someone to head up the cover side of things in Vanguard, the new indie division of the company, and you're one of the possible names on the list."

Suspicion runs through me. If this had come from Phillip, I wouldn't doubt it, but from Andrew? Is this one of those "quid pro quo" scenarios? I want to climb the corporate ladder, but not like that.

"How closely does this position work with you?"

He chuckles, and I have a stray thought of kicking the bottom of his chair. How funny would he think it was to tumble onto the floor? I don't do it though. My mom would be proud.

"I'd be your direct supervisor. Don't worry. This isn't me trying to have a little inter-office fun, Sera. You really are one of the most qualified people, even though you don't have any management experience. A little birdy told me you were looking for a change, and things are changing around here. We want young and adaptable people to get the ball rolling with the indie department. It's the best time to make moves if that's what you're looking for."

It sounds like exactly what I've been wanting. The only reason I'd push back on it is because it's Andrew making the offer. "Okay. I'm listening…"

Ten

ANDREW

He's going to change the way the whole office works. From the ground floor to the top. Just like I expected.

"No. That's fucking insane." I say from across the table. Phillip's got a very determined grin, and I'm smiling on the inside even though I've got a serious look on my face. He may be the best at running a publishing company, but he's never understood people as well as I have.

"You're right. It is. Absolutely insane. And we're going to do it, anyway. Don't worry, you'll get to play with plenty of things soon enough, but right now, I'm still the one making the calls."

Now I have to string it out. Dangle the line that makes him think I'm not ready for it. "Dad would set you on fire if he were here. You know that, right?"

"I don't think he would," he says. Which is more than a little crazy because he absolutely would have a year ago. Though, Dad's different now, too. Maybe he wouldn't today, but a year ago, my brother would have been sent to start a new division in Antarctica for even thinking about this stuff.

"What about you, Mason?" Phillip asks, his eyes turning to the man sitting next to me at the table. "Do you have opinions?" Mason's grinning. He's always been a mixture of me and Phillip. So serious like Phillip, but he hides it behind a smile like me. Right now, he's got nothing to add to the conversations since he only started with Loughton House a few weeks ago and hasn't had time to get his feet under him. That won't be the case when we reconvene for the end of the year meeting, though.

"You know that I'm only here because I couldn't turn down the paycheck. I have no idea what's going on, and even I think it's a little crazy. Then again, I've been living on a beach in the Mediterranean for the past decade, so even wearing this suit is a little nuts to me."

He's only working here now because I called him. He wouldn't have taken a call from Phillip or Dad, but I've kept in touch with him ever since he moved to Europe. Realistically, it wasn't the smartest decision, but regardless of my plans, my brother needs to be part of the family. He's an ass, but so is Dad.

"Well, those are the plans. I need you two to get things moving, and once everything is finished up here, I'm going to need you to go to the London office and do the same thing. Rebuild it how you feel is in line with the new vision of Loughton House Publishing."

I hesitate and glance at Mason. Phillip took the bait. Now I need Mason to do the same. A few little hints over the past few days. Nothing straightforward enough that it could somehow get back to Sera. Just enough to leave Mason puzzling things out.

I sigh. "I don't want to go to London for the same reason you don't."

"But you're single." The words come out flat, but they come with a frown. He doesn't understand, but he's trying to figure things out. And he's trying not to act like Dad, trying not to force me to do anything.

I shake my head. "No, I'm not." *Come on, Mason. Jump in like you always used to. Come on.*

"Alright. First, I'm not Father. You don't have to hide shit from me. Two, congrats. And three, why can't you bring her with you? I'm sure most women would love to take a trip to London. She can explore a new country while you disassemble and rebuild our office there."

Mason doesn't wait for Andrew to say anything. "It's because she works for you."

Thank all that's fucking holy for Mason being so predictable. Even after all these years. It takes everything in me not to grin.

Phillip takes a moment, and I can see that he's put two and two together. He knows who I'm talking about. There's only one person it could be.

He nods, the carefully laid pieces clicking into place. "Take her if she wants to go, and I assume she will. Hell, get her to help you out. There'll be plenty of design choices to make, and she's good."

This is exactly what I'd hoped for. It's too bad that she can't be anything more than someone I use to get what I want, though. Everything I've found out about Sera Wylder is that she is the perfect co-conspirator in my plan, even if she doesn't know it yet. The only real wrench that could be thrown into this plan is if one of us catches feelings. I have to make sure that the only woman I've never been able to forget never gets close to me.

Mason pushes his chair back so he can stand up. "Are we done?"

Phillip looks at me before nodding. He knows nothing about Mason at this point, so he's trusting me to be his filter. I guess he didn't see any kind of frantic look on my face because he says, "Yeah, we're done. Do you have somewhere to be?"

"Anywhere but in here. I don't know how you two sit around and talk all day. Don't you have any actual work to do? Or do you simply enjoy doing it in the middle of the night? I'm pretty sure that's what your dream girl was complaining about, wasn't it?"

I can't help but laugh a little. That's Mason. Straight and to the point. The exact reason he and Dad never got along. And the reason he could run an island getaway by himself.

He nods to us and leaves. I'm having trouble even thinking about anyone or anything else, though. Everything is set for me to cement my place in the family as something other than the baby brother. But the charade has to continue on.

"I know you and Mason haven't always seen eye-to-eye, but he's going to fit in well here. It's not like he's been lazing about on a beach."

Phillip shrugs. "I know he'll do fine," he says as he stands up.

I lean back in my chair and look up at him. "You're doing a hell of a lot to win a girl back. You know that, right? Normal people wouldn't do this. I certainly wouldn't."

"Addison isn't just 'a girl'. She's the woman I'm going to spend the rest of my life with, and I'd burn Loughton House to the ground, if that's what it took. Lucky for you, I doubt that's what she wants."

I know exactly what Addison wants, and it certainly isn't for him to burn the place to the ground.

As Phillip walks out of the room, I take a deep breath. The setup for my plan is in place. Now, there's only one dice roll left. Getting Sera to go along with it.

And that might require a little kidnapping…

Eleven

SERA

THE TAXI SITS IN TRAFFIC AS I WONDER WHAT NEW hell I'm in. Not only did my new position start a few weeks ago, but now I get to have my first insane meeting with an author. One who refuses all technology, including cell phones. Because that's totally normal, right? According to Andrew, he hand writes his entire novel and pays to have it typed up.

I don't even know what the meeting is about. Is he trying to describe what he wants? Or does he require that he meet every person who touches his book?

Jeremy McDermott. A name that does not ring even a single bell, but who also has a private jet, and an author that Andrew assures me, is a top priority. Which is weird because I've never seen a book with his name on it. Maybe he's using a pen name?

I don't know, and truthfully, I don't even care. What I care about is the fact that I'm spending my entire afternoon dealing with this instead of the work that's sitting on my desk. I guess that's the hard part about being the Cover Design Manager of Vanguard. That and the fact that I have absolutely no direction.

I report to Andrew right now, but that's been all business, thankfully. No weird vibes or anything. Just work, which is perfectly fine with me, but more importantly, no solo talks in his office. Sitting inches away from him. Thinking about how good it would feel if he ran his hands across my lower back. His fingers slipping under my skirt's waistband…

What the hell are you even thinking about? I need to be focused. Everything's so confusing right now, but I need to remember that this doesn't have to be where I stop in my climb, even for the short term. I need to keep my eyes to the sky because Loughton House is still very much in turmoil.

Not thinking about what Andrew's hands would feel like.

Traffic is at a crawl, and I'm left to think about everything that's happened in the past few weeks. A chaotic flurry of upward motion at Loughton House after half my friends left to work elsewhere. It's exactly what I want, but there are still so many rungs in the ladder before I'll be living up to my potential. This position is barely more than a glorified cover artist who also has to deal with frustrating authors.

To climb that ladder, though, I have to be the best at what I do. Normally, that'd be simple, but Vanguard is anything but simple. Everyone's still trying to piece together the right way to do anything, and even Andrew is a little lost in how to approach problems because we have fewer resources, so our market is distinctly different.

It leaves me having to do a lot of thinking and theorizing, which isn't something I've done in a long time. My efforts are working, but it's all happening too slowly. I need to make people take notice of my success better. I can't simply keep my head down and focus on my work anymore.

This is not the first private jet I've been on. Both of my parents have rented them, but this one is different. For one, it has the Loughton House emblem on the side. *I didn't know Loughton House had a private jet. And why did they fly this guy to New York?*

The jet is motionless on the tarmac, but the engines are still idling. There are removable stairs leading up to the door in place. It feels strange to walk out to the jet all alone, but this is what Andrew told me to do. What a weird freaking author. Couldn't he have met me in a car outside the airport? Or a hotel room? Literally anywhere more reasonable than the jet he arrived on? Is he really going to take off immediately after I talk to him?

I guess that if he's bringing in as much money as Andrew insinuated, he's worth the hassle. At least he's not a weird rock star. Then I'd be walking into a plane full of groupies.

The hair on the back of my neck stands up straight, like someone's watching me. Something's wrong, and I don't know what it is.

Or maybe I'm just crazy.

I take a deep breath and walk up the stairs into the jet. Where commercial airlines have gray hard plastic and worn out carpet, this thing feels like someone stuck an old library into a jet. Hard wood paneling, deep brown leather, and a vague sense of formality fill the space. The seats aren't arranged in the most efficient way. Instead, it's been made to look like a sitting room. Several pairs of chairs are spaced around bolted down tables. It's luxurious in a way that even a car couldn't be.

This is something pulled from times gone past and forced into the present.

A flight attendant gives me a smile and ushers me into the main area of the plane with all the seating. Then she slides the door closed behind me. There's only one person in the cabin, and his back is to me so that the only thing I can see is the top of his head, the chestnut brown hair which is a bit of a mess.

I can feel the trap snapping shut, but it's in slow motion, and I can't quite believe it's happening.

I walk around to the opposite side of the man, and there's no more doubting that I've been trapped. The man in the chair is *not* Jeremy McDermott. It's Andrew Loughton with a grin on his face.

"What the hell is going on, Andrew?" He just grins and sips Scotch from a crystal tumbler. "You said I was supposed to meet Jeremy McDermott here." My voice rises along with at least a brief panic. There's no reason I should be afraid, but that animal instinct inside me is going absolutely crazy.

This is Andrew, though. He's not dangerous. Well, not dangerous in the serial killer way. Just the "I can convince you to make bad decisions" way.

He takes a deep breath and lets it out, almost like he's savoring the taste of the air. "Sit down, Sera. I have a proposition for you. One that could change both of our lives forever."

Oh God, this is too much pomp and circumstance. Is he part of the mob? Am I about to receive an offer I can't refuse? I don't answer, mostly because I'm a little freaking terrified.

"I want you to come to London with me and learn to do my job."

That's not very Godfather of him. "You want me to learn to run an entire branch of Loughton House?"

That's a ridiculous thing to suggest. There are a hundred, no a thousand, more obvious choices than me. I know nothing about business. Not really, at least.

"Yes. Not officially, mind you. See, I have plans, and none of them are plans I want anyone to know about. I can't take care of them while also running the London branch *and* building the London branch of Vanguard. There's not enough time in the day to take care of it all. I need you to oversee the core Loughton House operations as well as introduce Vanguard to London."

He smirks a little and sips the Scotch again before continuing. "But don't worry, it's not nearly as bad as it sounds. Unlike my brother, I do a lot less active work in London than Phillip ever did. It mostly runs itself, and I only supervise it. Your primary goal will be to institute Vanguard over there, and you're already doing a fantastic job with it in New York. It should be easy."

My father's and mother's voices echo in the back of my mind. *Never trust something that's too good to be true. Everyone has an agenda.*

"Why me?" I ask. I'm sitting up straighter. My shields are up. I'm back to the woman who was about to have a strange conversation with an eccentric author. The woman who grew up watching her mother destroy her opponents in the courtroom. The one who knows what it was to be powerful.

Not the woman who's been overwhelmed for the last month.

Andrew sits forward. "Because you can do it, but also, you aren't a little tattletale. We spent a night together, and no one knows about it. Phillip didn't know. No one had any idea. I'm sure you could have said something to someone in the past three years, but there are no rumors about me, and that's the most important part of this whole thing. I need you to pretend to be me while you're doing everything."

Okay, that's a little more Godfather of him, but it's hardly an offer I can't refuse. Impersonating Andrew will be impossible. I don't even know him. I don't even think I read an email from him until I was promoted. And if I'm caught? This is between family, and Phillip won't punish Andrew for being sneaky. That won't stop him from punishing me, though. This could be career-ending at a time that I'm finally starting progress.

I shake my head. "No thanks, Andrew. There's no way that I get out of this without losing my job and probably my career, and we both know it. Maybe you won't have any repercussions, but somehow, I doubt that impersonating you is going to end up good for me."

"What if I make it worth your while? I could give you a very significant bonus for it."

I stand up, shaking my head again. "Nope. Andrew, I don't need a big payday. I'm not living paycheck to paycheck. You know what would mess me up? Losing my job or maybe getting arrested. There aren't any contracts sitting around, and I doubt there will be an official job titled 'Fake Andrew'. I think I'll go back to work and try to forget this conversation ever happened."

I put my hand on the door, my fingers digging into the little handhold so I can slide the door open. When I try to open it, though, the door doesn't move. And I *feel* the vibrations from the engine getting louder now. The door is rattling ever so slightly.

My eyes open wide as I realize what's happening, and I whirl around to face Andrew, who's standing up, a wide grin on his face. "Might want to sit down. It's a smooth ride, but takeoff can get a little bumpy."

"No, Andrew. I'm not flying anywhere. I'm going back to the office."

He shrugs. "You can try, but the cabin's locked, and if you look out the window, you'll notice that there aren't any stairs going to the ground anymore. We should take off in about a minute. You may want to find somewhere to sit down before we get to the runway."

The ground moves underneath me. It's a familiar sensation. The plane is moving into position to take off. He's serious.

That son of a bitch. I move to the seat in front of Andrew, and my fingers tighten on the armrest. If this was a stranger, I'd have done everything I could to get off the plane. But I'm not scared of my boss. I'm just pissed.

There's no way in hell that I'm going to let him get away with kidnapping me.

Twelve

ANDREW

God, I'm taking a risk with this. It may not be a real kidnapping. Not really. I mean, I'm sure there could be some consequences, but it's only a day of inconvenience for her. Nothing too serious.

But she could blow this out of proportion if she wanted to. Which probably isn't as big of a deal as it would have been a week ago, though. I'm now officially one third owner of Loughton House. In an effort to reduce his responsibility, Phillip has split the company three ways with Mason and me each receiving a third of the company ownership. He did that right after I was told to go to London which makes things easy. Now, I have just as much of a right to start projects as Phillip did when he was owner. It'll just be *frowned upon.* So I'll get a hand slap.

But looking at Sera, it's hard not to be a little worried about what she'll do. She's so pissed, and there's the distinct possibility she'll be just as pissed when the jet lands, but I have to take the chance. This entire plan comes down to a dice roll, and I'm hoping that Lady Luck is on my side today. I've gone through every record we have for her with a fine-tooth comb. Every report, every cover, every email. I know her history better than she does, and she's perfect other than the lack of experience.

More than that, though, I remember what she was like at that Christmas party all those years ago. She was wild. If there was anyone who'd be ready for an adventure, it'd be that girl. Throw in the obvious ability to succeed in nearly any environment, and there really isn't a better choice. If I have to roll the dice, she's my choice.

"You know that as soon as this fucking jet lands, I'm getting a ticket back to New York, right? I'm not staying a single night in London, and as soon as I get back, I'm going to sue you for every dime I can get."

I keep smiling, though. She was going to be pissed. I was ready for that. Luckily, I think that if she sits down and hears me out, she'll accept my terms. Because I'm desperate. I need help, and I can't trust anyone in my family, so I'll sweeten the pot as much as I need to. Being a billionaire comes with a few perks.

"You don't have to do that. The jet's going to refuel and come right back home. It's merely to give us a bit of time for some completely safe and secure negotiations. If, when we land, you still want to sue the pants off me for this little trick, I can't stop you. But I don't think you'll want to."

She keeps glaring at me. I remember when she looked at me with the same intensity before. The way she'd been both turned on and ready to do insane things that night. The way she'd laughed when I got on that stage to strip for a bunch of strangers. How things have changed…

"Well, I guess I'm stuck here for the next however many hours. You might as well tell me your plan so I can explain it to my lawyer when I get back home."

I try not to let her threats get to me. This isn't supposed to be something terrible. I knew she'd leave as soon as I suggested it, so I had to force her to stay and hear me out. It's a bit of sneakiness. Not anything illegal like she thinks.

"Okay then, to business. I'm in a bind, Sera. I'm currently making a huge negotiation mistake telling you that, but I need you to understand the complete picture."

"Oh, did you try to kidnap someone else, and it didn't work out?"

I sigh, my smile breaking a little. "No. It's much more complicated than that. It's… Look, I know how to make Loughton House more profitable, but my brothers don't listen to me. To them, I'll always be their little brother, and that means that my thoughts don't count as much, regardless of how valid my opinions are. I want to change that."

Sera's eyes are intent on me, and I can see her processing what I'm saying. She's listening. She may be pissed enough to really sue me, but she's listening to what I'm saying. There's a chance.

"If I said that I was going to train you to run London, they'd want to know why. That can't happen. This is a win-win scenario, Sera. I'm able to give you pretty much whatever you want, and all I ask is for your discretion and your wholehearted enthusiasm."

Her glare softens a bit as her thoughts turn inward. It's interesting to watch her process what I've said, and unlike most people, she doesn't hold on to the emotions and preconceptions she had before.

"What happens if Phillip or Mason find out that I'm impersonating you? What happens to you, and what happens to me?"

The jet takes off then. The roar of the engines invades the quiet for a short time while it gets up to speed, and then we're in the air.

My smile fades almost completely as we continue the conversation as though nothing had changed. "If they find out, which is highly unlikely since they don't pay much attention to London, then they'll probably step in and stop what I want to do. They'll be pissed at me. What will happen to you? I would assume nothing, and we can try to figure out how to better safeguard you, but you're Addison's friend, and you're at least on good terms with Phillip."

"And you would take complete blame for it, right?" she says. That statement could never have been construed as a question.

"Absolutely. Look, I don't know what your particular needs are, but I'm sure I can help you achieve them. I'm a co-owner of Loughton House, and I don't think you'd ask for anything too difficult."

And she smiles. Without missing a beat, she says, "I want you to teach me everything I ask you to teach me. That's my requirement. When this little adventure is done, I want to be able to run the London branch on my own."

I open my mouth for a moment and close it before I say something stupid. If she'd wanted a few million dollars, I would have done that. If she'd wanted raises or promotions, I could have swung that. But this is only supposed to be six months. It took me five freaking years in New York to understand the business enough to manage London, and I had a rough time of it for the first year or two.

"I will answer any questions you have during this transition period," I say with as little emotion as possible. It's like half the things I say to Sera are wrong. I haven't done anything to make her think I'm not to be trusted.

Her fingers drum on the leather armrest as she thinks. "I'm going to need signed documents stating that you're requesting me to impersonate you. It doesn't need to go through any formalities because I doubt it's even legal. And it doesn't matter if it's legal or not. I need something to prove to Phillip and Mason that I wasn't doing anything underhanded. My boss pushed me to do this, and it's not my place to argue."

I nod to her, very excited at the prospect. "Done." Maybe this is going to work out just fine.

"And I'm going to need a bedroom and bathroom."

Now it's my turn to be confused. "Yes, I kind of thought that would be an assumed part of the package. I don't really want you to be homeless while you're running a multi-billion dollar business."

She grins at me. "No, Andrew. You're not understanding. You told me you'd answer any questions during this transition. I would like to get the most out of my time, so I require a bedroom and bathroom wherever you're living. In the same house or apartment. You're not only getting a partner in crime, but you're also getting a new roommate."

What the hell have I done…

Thirteen

SERA

WAS THIS THE WORST MISTAKE OF MY LIFE OR THE best one? I don't think I'll know that until it's all said and done. In the back of my mind, I hear both of my parents' voices pushing me to follow this rabbit hole through to the end. Any time they would both agree on something, I can usually trust it to be worth following up.

My dad would tell me about how much of an adventure it'll be. I've been stuck in a rut for almost two years, and there's no doubt this will be different. A new place. A new job. New possibilities. And I've never met a man or woman who brought out that need to do something different as much as Andrew Loughton.

My mom's voice would whisper about how many possibilities this opens. Andrew has information and experience that I can learn from. He has connections. He'll owe me. There's no downside, and all the upsides.

Those are the logical reasons that I told him yes, the logical reasons I'm standing in his apartment in London when I had expected to be home for dinner right now.

But they're only reassurances. Sure, I can tell myself that it's the right decision to get in close with a powerful man and make myself valuable to him, but the truth of the matter is that I gave in because it's Andrew, and this is an adventure. Maybe he was the bait for the trap he set, and he knows that, but I have a tough time telling that man no.

"This is home," Andrew says as we stand in the entryway of his penthouse. It's not exactly what I'd expected. I'd imagined something special, but this is… not?

I guess he can tell that I'm not particularly impressed because he quickly says, "I don't normally spend very much time here. Running Loughton House when you barely know what you're doing is a lot more time-consuming than most people realize, even if it's only the London branch. This is pretty much what it looked like when I bought it."

I believe him, but I stay quiet as I look around. The furniture is upscale, but it's simple, meant to sell a place. Beiges and tans with little bits of wood and metal in places. Very neutral in tone and style. There's not really any opulence. Nothing that defines it as his. It's just furniture.

"That's fine. It's not like it's a dump or anything, Andrew. It kind of surprised me you don't have a massive fish tank or a robot that asks us if we want a Scotch when we walk in."

He chuckles. "That's fair. I think if I'd ever planned to live here permanently, I might have gotten a robot or something, but I was always waiting for my dad to call me and expect me home the next day. This was only a place I slept while I wasn't working, so why put any genuine effort into making it mine?"

That's so strange. He lived in London for three whole years and never thought of it as his home? How do you have such a distance between the place you live and yourself? Maybe that's a romanticized idea, though. I'm sure there are plenty of people that don't care where they live.

"Well, show me to my hotel room, and then you get to take me shopping. If I'm going to live here with you, I'm going to need some clothes and necessities since you didn't really give me a chance to pack a bag."

Andrew gives me a sideways glance and the corner of his lips turns up. "I didn't expect you to be quite such a forceful personality. First, you demand that you get to live with me. Now you're assuming that I'm going to buy you a new wardrobe?"

"I'm a forceful personality? I think you take the cake with that one, Andrew. You're the one who kidnapped me, after all. I think a new wardrobe is the least you can do since I'm not calling the police."

He chuckles, and I wonder whether my "forceful personality" actually bothers him. I don't think many people would say that about me, but the moment that he took control of my life by flying me to London with no options, I think a switch flipped inside me. This isn't a situation where the best course of action is going with the flow.

Andrew leads me to a bedroom with a Queen-sized bed in the middle of it. It's a respectably sized bedroom, but it really feels like staged furniture. I wonder if anyone's ever slept in this bed.

I take a glance around the room, and Andrew says, "So we're clear, from this point on, no more comments about going to the police. You've agreed to everything, and if you're unhappy about the situation, I'll happily book you a flight back to New York. You can go back to your job at Loughton House as a cover artist. We'll draw up contracts tomorrow when we go to the office stating all our expectations."

That's fair. It's a little strange to see him so serious, though. "I was only kidding," I say. "But yes, we're both in this completely at this point. There was no kidnapping. It was all a happy accident, as Bob Ross would say."

Andrew nods and walks back to the main living space. I stare at him as he goes. It's a strange thing knowing that I'm going to be sleeping in the bedroom across from him. More than any boyfriend, he left a mark on me. I can't look at him without seeing that Santa outfit. The memory of running my hand over his abs on that stage. More than anything, I can't help but think about the way he made me feel when he was on top of me.

No one else has ever brought that out in me.

He can't be more than a stepping stone for my future, though. We had our fun, but I need to remember that there's a goal at the end of this adventure. I don't know exactly what it is, but I know that there's a purpose here. The longer I spend in this unusual position, the more I'll understand what I can do with the experience. Maybe it's using Andrew to propel me upward in Loughton House. Or maybe it's realizing that there's nothing at Loughton House for me, and I need to go elsewhere.

Or maybe it's even to take my experience and start a small publishing house of my own. That thought is like a lightbulb clicking on in my mind. I *could* do that. I could take what I learn with Andrew and what I've learned in the office from every bit of gossip I could gather, and I could start my own publishing house. What Loughton House is doing works, and it works on a small scale, too. I could tap my trust fund…

I sigh. It's an interesting thought, but not one I should necessarily cling to. The one thing this whole situation *isn't* is a random adventure. It's not a time for fun and games. I won't get another chance like this, and every piece of information I don't get is one I'll need in a year.

I take a deep breath and let it out slowly as the weight of the situation settles on me. Yes, from today until the day I move back to New York, I need to be focused. A smile crosses my face as I accept the facts of my situation.

Andrew is nothing more than a tool.

This position is nothing but a chance to set up my future.

It's going to be the hardest thing I've ever done.

Fourteen

ANDREW

WHAT THE HELL WAS I THINKING? I SHOULD HAVE talked to Sera in the office or a restaurant or even the parking lot. Literally anywhere but the jet. Then, I wouldn't have had to take her shopping. I am positive that any risk of talking to her about my little plan would have been well worth never having to take her shopping.

My shoulders ache as the door to the penthouse door swings open. I drop the bags on the floor two steps inside and immediately go to the fridge. It doesn't matter how much I spent today. I'm sure that Sera's fully aware of how much it was, but it's the least important thing in my mind right now.

The beer lets out a refreshing hiss as I pop the cap and flick it into the trash. Sera hasn't said a word since we left the last store. She was fucking driven this afternoon. How can anyone be so goddamn serious about shopping? I'd expected it to be like the movies or even other times I've brought women shopping. I even joked that I'd be happy to tell her how the lingerie looked.

She ignored me. Every single time I tried to make it somewhat pleasant, she handed me another blouse or skirt. Then, when I thought I was done and would get a chance to enjoy myself while she tried all those clothes on, she didn't even come out for me to look at her.

I was, without any doubt, not her friend or even a roommate. I was her boss, and she was at work.

That's probably a good thing, however miserable it was for me. I'm supposed to be treating her like a tool. Manipulate her. Use her. Keep my distance.

But the worst part of the entire shopping trip had nothing to do with the fact that she was so driven. It was how close we were, how easily it could have been fun. Yet, she was as cold as ice about the whole thing.

There are sounds coming from behind me as she carries the entire wardrobe worth of clothes to the guest room of the penthouse. I don't turn around to look, and I certainly don't ask if she needs help. No, I'm going to drink my beer in peace.

I walk out onto the balcony overlooking London. It's certainly not New York, but there's a niceness to London that home doesn't have. It's old even though everything is as modern as New York.

And it doesn't stink the same. It's not as loud. London seems less a city and more a bunch of big towns smashed together.

As I'd told Sera, it's not home. All of London feels like it's work. I'd hoped that when I came back, it'd be better. I'd hoped that maybe Sera would make being at the penthouse less of a job. But she seems even more serious than I am.

I take a sip of the beer and let the frothy bitterness roll over my tongue. I may not like London as much as New York, but I can get behind European beer. It's one of the few amenities that I haven't been able to find in New York.

"Is the refrigerator a free-for-all, or do I need to go down to the store to get some beer for myself?"

I finally turn around to see Sera leaning on the doorway to the balcony. Her skirt suit is gone, and she's wearing a simple band t-shirt from the eighties and a pair of shorts. The fading sunlight shines on her in a way that makes her smile almost sparkle. Keeping my distance from her is going to be a difficult task. There's nothing at all risqué about what she's wearing, but seeing her as a normal person instead of the ice queen she's been has me wanting her. "You can get a beer if you want one."

"Thanks. And dinner?"

"We'll order in if that's okay with you," I say before turning around to watch the sunset. I want to stare off into the distance, to let my mind wander a bit. But all I can see is Sera. Wearing that same outfit, walking around my penthouse with a smile on her face. Teasing me with that sexy little body. A scene that can't happen. God, why can't I be like Phillip once in a while? Be the robot that's completely focused on the task.

I hear the refrigerator door open and close. The hiss of the beer being opened. Then she's standing next to me. "It smells different," she says. "I don't remember that the last time I was here."

I take a deep breath, expecting to smell London, but instead, I breathe her in. Almonds and lilies. Like that night three years ago. My cock is standing at attention even as I try to ignore her scent. I nod my head. "It always smells different. When was the last time you were in London?"

"When I was fourteen. I spent the summer with my dad on a road trip. Saw pretty much every major city in Europe."

She's staring out at the city as she leans over the railing. Even though she's treated me like her boss ever since the jet landed, right now she feels human. "Did you like it?" I ask.

She shrugs. "It was a place like any other. Bad food. Old buildings. All that mattered back then was spending a summer with my dad. I was a kid, though, so I don't think I was looking at it quite like I am now. It's quieter here, too. Like there's a hush over the city."

"That's because the Brits are nicer people. They don't scream and honk as much as we do."

The corner of her lip turns up as she chuckles, and I turn to face her. "Well, I should order us some dinner. Are you good with Pad Thai? I know a great little place."

We're going to be roommates. And coworkers of the closest kind. I won't have any breaks away from this woman, and normally, that'd have terrified me. I've never been that close to anyone before. If things don't work out with us, she could ruin all my plans. I'm trusting her, and that's not something I do easily.

Maybe there really is a hush over the city. Like the world is holding its breath while we look at each other.

I'm not terrified. I'm not worried at all. For the first time in a long time, I'm calm. It's not because I have a plan to make my mark on the family business, and it's not because I'm back in a quieter lifestyle where everything makes sense again.

No, there's something about being near Sera that relaxes me even when she's obviously seeing this arrangement as a professional decision. Even when I can't stop thinking about her in completely unprofessional ways.

"Pad Thai sounds great. Let me know when the food gets here. I'm going to go put my new wardrobe up. By the way," she says with a grin. "Thanks for the clothes and everything. I know it's kind of necessary, but I appreciate the fact that you took me instead of just giving me a card and wishing me luck."

Her words, those little pieces of appreciation, wash over me, and some of the frustration I had for her shopping trip fades. "You're welcome. I hope the closet is big enough." I give her a wink before she walks back toward her room.

As the last bit of light falls over London, I turn toward the city and take another sip of my beer. Something about this is so right, but I can't put my finger on it. For the first time, I wonder if London really could become home. And I have a sneaking suspicion it has everything to do with Sera.

Fifteen

SERA

Andrew's so close to me. If this room was cold, his breath would fog up my computer screen as he leans over me. One hand is on my chair. The other pointing at the screen. "Okay, now go here," he says, pointing at one of the dozens of icons on the screen. "This is the upper management's SharePoint. You need to go through the daily updates section every morning."

There's so much to remember. I've got a pen and paper out and am jotting down notes as fast as I can, but I'm terrified he's going to walk away after today and I'm going to be completely lost.

I click the icon and pull up the SharePoint page. Andrew continues to walk me through his morning process, explaining each of the various projects and what's expected from them. I don't understand how he could think that I'll be able to impersonate him. There's so much.

"Stop. Just stop," I say as I get lost for the umpteenth time. I take a deep breath and he takes a step away, giving me a confused look. "Look, I can't understand everything in one day. That's impossible, and you know that. How about I look through the seventy-two things you've already explained since we got here an hour ago and actually get a feel for them? Tomorrow, I can try to play with some other things."

He frowns for a moment, a look that's still surprising to me. In my mind, the man doesn't know how to frown. "Okay. Let's compromise. You can spend the rest of the morning looking over the stuff I've shown you, and after lunch, we can look at some more."

"Okay. That could work." I know I need to soak up as much as I can as fast as I can, but skipping five rungs in the corporate ladder and then being expected to pick up everything instantly is a tad much. It's going to take me at least a few days before I even understand the terminology.

He gives me a nod and walks around to the other side of my desk. I still haven't seen his office, and every time I suggest we go there, he's quick to dismiss the idea. It's weird. But maybe that's just Andrew. It's not like I really know anything about the guy. That'll change quickly enough now that we're living together, though.

I explore the SharePoint site while Andrew opens his laptop up and props his feet on the desk while leaning back in the chair. He looks like an insolent teenager the way he's sitting. Not like someone who manages hundreds of millions of dollars.

I click on a project. Each one is actually a book. Well, the book, audiobook, eBook, and all the marketing that goes into it. There's a calendar specific to this project with expected drafting deadlines. Brief comments fill the spaces such as, "George is notorious for being late with his drafts. Contact on the 23rd, but don't expect it for another month."

There's a cover for this book, and, as this is the only thing I really know, I click it. George O'Hare wrote a middle-grade adventure book. The cover is a silhouette of a teenager looking over a cliff. My mind immediately goes into critiquing mode, and I run my hand over my cheek.

"Don't you do it," Andrew says, his voice firm.

My brows furrow. "What?"

He sits up, his feet and the chair legs hitting the floor at the same time, and he looks over my laptop screen. "I knew it. Leave those covers alone. It's not your job, and it certainly is not *my* job. Which is what you're supposed to pretend to be doing right now. Close the file and go back to reading schedules and expectations. Pay close attention to the marketing side of it. Let the editors and cover artists hash out what they're doing with the details. You need to focus on where the money is going."

I sigh. Ignore everything I know and pretend to follow the pages of nothing but numbers. "Okay." I know I'm annoyed, but he's right. I'm not stupid enough to think that this job is going to be easy. It's time to suck it up and figure things out. Even if it means ignoring covers and understanding the spreadsheets. When I was fourteen on tour with my dad, I really doubt I'd have believed that the most important six months of my life would be learning to love spreadsheets.

"Good." He gets comfortable again, and I can't help but chuckle as I imagine what would have happened if his foot had gotten stuck on the desk when he jumped up like that. He would have leaned forward, his feet still stuck to the desk, and that chair would have gone flying out from under him.

"What's so funny?" he asks, his eyes sparkling like normal. He really is a happy person, unlike Phillip. I still haven't met Mason.

"Oh, I was imagining you falling on your ass since you sit like a lazy teenager."

He gets a confused look on his face. "What?"

I shrug. "It's just something I do. Like the opposite of an intrusive thought. Instead of having a flash of what would happen if I opened the car door while we're going down the road at sixty miles an hour, I see how something could have turned out terribly wrong for another person. Like your foot not quite coming off the desk, and it ending with you lying in a heap on the floor, your laptop crashing down beside you. And me laughing at my boss looking like an idiot, all because he sits like a very lazy teenager."

Andrew blinks. "Okay… That might not be completely healthy."

I shrug again and grin. There's not anything unhealthy at all about imagining how things could go wrong. I like to think of it as a superpower. Like my spider senses or something.

He doesn't seem to think as highly of it because even though I'm just going through the SharePoint to look at the Excel files, he keeps glancing at me. After a few moments, he takes his feet off the desk and sits up straighter.

It makes me chuckle, and even though Andrew glances at me, he doesn't say anything. I'm sure he'd make up an excuse the way most men would say they got dust in their eye at the end of The Notebook.

Looking back at the spreadsheet, I try to ignore the fact that Andrew is in the room with me. I try to give the work a hundred percent of my focus. I think I've done pretty well separating myself from the *very* inappropriate thoughts that keep popping up. It'd be so much easier if I didn't already know what he looks like naked or how he could make me scream his name. I cannot let myself take even the smallest step down that slippery slope because I'm sure to fall headfirst into it.

Instead, I focus on the work. I think about spreadsheets instead of tangled sheets.

The information is hard to understand, and I don't have any references. What is a normal expense for a three hundred page book being printed? What does it cost to ship it? Are those costs negotiable? Is that what I'm paying attention to? Or is it a standard that I should ignore?

I'm very lost, and even though Andrew is right there, I know that if I ask him those questions, he's going to stop me from looking around and really getting a good understanding of anything beyond the yes and no questions I have. Instead, I flip to another book's expense sheet and compare them side-by-side.

It looks like they've got similar pricing for a lot of things, so maybe those printing and shipping costs are fixed. Then I notice this one has an entire section about travel expenses. For a Middle Grade author? That's unusual. I can't figure out why it would be there. What kind of travel expenses would a Middle Grade author have?

"Hey Andrew," I say, and it's like he's been waiting for me to ask him something. He automatically closes the laptop, sets it on the desk, and walks behind me.

"What's your question?" he asks, completely focused on me. I don't know if keeping my distance from him or learning how to run an entire business is going to be more difficult.

Then he puts his hand on the back of my chair and leans over to look at the screen before I've even said anything. "Oh, old McGregor." Fuck, his hand is so close to me. My heart beats a little faster. *Focus on the work, Sera!*

McGregor? The author's name isn't even shown. The title isn't shown either. He knows the book from the expense sheet?

"Yeah, I was wondering why he had travel expenses. It doesn't seem like a normal thing for Middle Grade authors."

Andrew grins. "He's unusual. And also one of our most solid authors. Part of his contract requires him to have those travel expenses, and I'm happy to indulge him because he spends that time visiting libraries across the UK and hosting readings. He was part of a national reading campaign a few years back, and he never really stopped. It's great for the kids and great for sales since everyone knows who he is."

"Interesting," I say. After a momentary pause, I ask, "Andrew, how'd you know that this was McGregor's expense sheet?"

Andrew stands up and walks back around to his seat. "Because I know all the major current expense sheets. I see them every week. Sure, I could ignore them and let the account managers deal with the gritty details, but nothing tells you what's happening with a book more than the expenses. And when I talk to management about them, I need to understand those things. It's not about trying to cut costs or make more profit. It's about knowing the books we're publishing. And the expense sheet is at the heart of what's happening. Numbers don't lie. People do."

I slowly nod, not entirely sure that I'll ever do as good of a job as Andrew at knowing hundreds of books by their expenses. Then again, I won't be talking to people outside of emails, so I'll be able to reference their expense sheets. I just need to figure out how to understand what's happening based on a bunch of numbers in Excel.

"Do you only pay attention to changes?" I ask.

"It's more than that. I wouldn't worry about it too much, Sera. It's kind of like covers. Even if you have a background in art, you can't simply make a perfect cover.

You have to understand the books it's competing with. You have to understand the book. You have to…" He pauses for a moment and shrugs. "You have to be in it, you know? Covers are an art, and understanding a book by its expenses is just as much an art."

I nod to him. Okay, that makes sense. Completely. "You're an expense artist. Got it."

"Pretty much. Now get back to reading those expense reports." He's chuckling, but I know he's serious. We both have a deadline. Granted, I don't know exactly when that deadline is, but it's there. The point where Andrew gets tired of sitting next to me and answering all my questions, and finally expects me to do the thing he brought me all the way to London to do.

So, I get back to trying to learn the art of expense reports. I ignore that smile. I push away the shiver that runs through me when he stares at me with those piercing green eyes. I try not to let the images of him doing very dirty things to me take any purchase in my mind.

Expense reports are now the most interesting thing in my life. Far more interesting than the sexy billionaire sitting across from me.

Sixteen

ANDREW

SERA LOOKS LIKE SOMEONE DRAINED EVERY OUNCE OF life out of her when we leave the office for the day. It's early. Only seven pm. I guess that's late for most people, but it's been a long time since I left the office before eight. The only reason I packed up this early today was because she couldn't handle another minute of staring at the screen.

"This is not what I'd expected," she says as we get in the car. Even my driver seems to be surprised at the early hour, but like a typical Londoner, he doesn't say a word. All he does is raise his eyebrow when we get to the car. Then again, maybe he's not thinking about the hour as much as the fact that I'm taking an employee to my home. Yeah, now that I think about it, that's probably the reason.

"What do you mean? Did you think that learning how to run an entire branch of Loughton House was going to fit into a nine to five?"

She shakes her head. "No, I knew that, for the foreseeable future, I'd be working nearly constantly. Hence, the suggestion to live with you. But I didn't think it would turn my brain to soup by lunch. How am I supposed to understand it all as fast as you need me to?"

"You'll get it. I have faith. Well, that's not true. Your work history tells me you'll get it. You have a quick mind, even in new environments and new expectations. All you're missing is exposure, which you're going to get in spades over the next few weeks."

"Andrew, did you know that I have almost no history with numbers and figures? I've got a great art background, and maybe even some management skills. But numbers? They've never been a thing for me."

What she doesn't know is that I looked into her transcripts. I may have been desperate for someone to help me, but I couldn't take a chance on her not being capable. She may not have focused on math and science in college, but she couldn't have made it through those business classes without having a grasp of numbers.

"Don't worry about it, Sera. I don't make mistakes when it comes to hiring people. I already told you that most of the London branch is nearly automated, but it's not because there are machines and robots doing the automation. It's because I chose the right person to do the job I didn't want to do, even if those people didn't think they could do it when they got hired."

She sighs and looks out the window. "How do you have that kind of confidence?" she says after several moments have passed. "How do you know that you're right this time?"

"Because I have to. I make too many decisions to let myself linger on them. I do all the planning and considering that I can before I make a decision, but once it's made, I don't question it. Otherwise, I'd spend my life completely paralyzed. I'd never trust myself. How many million-dollar decisions could I mess up this week alone? The money isn't even the important part. It's the people below me that would be hurt. My dad doesn't run Loughton House anymore, but I grew up in the role while he was in charge."

I have to take a breath thinking about those first few months in London. It was fucking terrifying. Sera turns away from the window and looks me in the eye as I continue. "I knew what happened if I made the wrong decisions. I wouldn't be punished. No, that's not the way my dad worked. He'd 'fix' the problem by cutting costs. By firing people who had done nothing wrong. By making everyone else work harder to compensate. He'd make their lives harder because I had fucked up."

Sera frowns as she listens. "But no one can be expected to never make a mistake. It's impossible."

"You don't know my dad. He's not exactly an understanding man. And nothing matters to him as much as success in business. Well, nothing except family. Not us being happy, but us being successful. It's kind of hard to separate business and family, though. I guess he was trying to make some kind of dynasty or something."

Thinking about those first months is hard. I've tried to forget them for so long. I watched as he cut hundreds of people after I'd missed the first quarterly target by a long shot. He'd told me that if I wanted to hire them back after I could justify it financially, that was my decision. It took me six months to do it, but I eventually hired every single one of them back. I stayed at the office until far after eight in those days.

But it was worth it. Just like the next few months will be. There's a solid plan, just like I had then. I know what I have to do, and the only question left to answer is whether Sera will be able to play the role I need her to.

I'm confident that she will be, but I can't be sure. It's going to be a hard road for both of us. I'm used to it, but is she? Is she motivated enough to push through the long nights and early mornings? Will she be able to do it all fast enough?

I don't know, but I'm willing to risk it because there's no other option open to me.

"Well, I'm glad you're not like your dad," she says. That's all. Her eyelids are drooping already, and part of me wonders if I'm right to hinge my plans on her.

"I guess we won't go out for dinner tonight. Want to order some pizza instead?"

She nods and leans her head against the window of the car. It's silent as the car speeds along on the road to my penthouse. Sera's eyes close, and I let out a soft breath. She looks so fucking worn out, and at the same time, so beautiful.

Sera's working as hard as I did when I first moved to London, and she doesn't have any of the training that I did. She's got no idea if she can do this, and she's still giving it absolutely everything. It's kind of incredible to watch.

Maybe it's not that, though. Maybe it's that I've already seen her naked. Already had my hands on her skin. That night together is probably one of the strongest memories I have of New York, and it's impossible to see her as anything other than my naughty little elf.

Maybe it's both.

What I'm sure of is that I don't think I've ever been more attracted to someone before, but she's off-limits. When I'd come back to New York and saw her at The Atrium, I'd thought we could have some fun together. Even when I'd been her boss, it had been possible. Hell, even Phillip had broken that unwritten rule.

But not while we're doing this. It's too important to muddy with emotions. I have to remember that she cannot be anything more than a tool to get what I want. She'll be compensated with nearly anything reasonable, but at the end of the day, we *both* need to remember that we're using each other.

I don't know how to get this close to her without giving into that same draw that pulled us together at that Christmas party.

Seventeen

SERA

Another day, another new item on the never-ending list of things I don't know. Today's big thing is the monthly sales report, namely how to tell when something is wrong.

Andrew's sitting in my office, like he has every day this week, explaining how we should expect book sales to do. I'm starting to think that he doesn't actually have an office. He's propped his feet up on my desk like that very first day.

Then we're interrupted by Marie, his assistant. She knocks on the door and walks in without us saying a word. "What's up, Marie?" he asks without turning around to see her. I guess he's used to this, but it surprises me. In my world, a closed door means knock and come in when the person invites you in. Not this.

"Your office is almost cleaned out, Mr. Loughton. Who knew that you had this much elf paraphernalia? I filled four entire boxes."

In an instant, his laptop is on the desk, and he's staring at Marie. There's a confused look on her face for a moment, and then she seems to understand that she made a mistake. "Where do you want the boxes put?" she asks.

Why does Andrew have four boxes of elf paraphernalia? And why is he upset about her asking him about them?

It takes almost no time for it to click for me. I chuckle and stand up. Andrew turns in his seat to watch me as I walk toward Marie, and, more importantly, the door. He's on his feet as soon as I pass him.

"What are you doing?" he asks, and I can hear the urgency in his voice. It's on the verge of cracking, and I know that I'm right. I have to be right.

"Going to find your office. I'd like to see it before all your elf stuff is gone."

"You don't need to do that." His voice rises higher. "Really, it's a bunch of stuff people have given me over the years as gag gifts. I don't know who decided I had an infatuation with elves, but that's what everyone's decided."

I give him a grin. "Come on, Andrew. I'm supposed to *be* you soon enough. I might as well understand the little inside jokes. Just show me."

His face turns pale, and he looks defeated. He knows as well as I do he can't tell me no. He can't hide this weird obsession with elves from me. I have to know if it's an inside joke because eventually, it'll be brought up in an email.

"I told her not to talk about it," he mutters. Then he lets out a sigh, like he's lost an argument. "Fine. Come look at my office, and I'll explain the elves."

He leads the way, his shoulders slumped, and it's getting hard not to laugh. I guess that this is why we've been working in my office instead of his.

As we walk, he explains. "So this goes back to my very first day in London. I flew in, and immediately went to work because I wasn't supposed to get the keys to my penthouse until that evening. I brought everything with me into the office since I didn't have a driver or car yet."

He stops in front of a door that looks almost the same as mine, and he takes a deep breath before opening it. The lights are on, and it's nearly empty except for a monitor and four boxes set against the wall.

He doesn't stop talking as I go to the boxes and open them. "I might have taken your elf hat after you left that morning and stuffed it in my luggage. I was busy looking things over when Marie came in to drop off some paperwork. She knocked the luggage off the desk, and the hat fell out."

Andrew walks up behind me, still trying to explain away the weird elf obsession. There are so many elves. Hundreds of little ones and big ones and even some little garden gnomes. I look around the room, trying to imagine all of them.

"Well, I guess that someone asked what you get the boss for Christmas when you don't even know him, and she said I had a thing for elves. So literally everyone in the office started bringing me any elf they found. It's become a thing now."

I'm amazed at the assortment. The first one I pick up is an elf riding a unicorn with a pistol in one hand and an American flag in the other. "I'm sure they *found* this one at the local corner store?"

He chuckles. "That one was custom ordered. Like I said, it's a running joke now, and I don't even mind. It makes me more human and keeps me far from the image that Phillip had for all those years. Now, when someone walks into my office, they're not intimidated. They think I'm a weirdo and can't help but laugh. Then I tell them how they can do better, and we all go on about our business."

I look up at him. "Why would you try to hide that from me?"

He doesn't say anything, but the smile fades. Instead, he walks around the desk and opens the bottom drawer. Then, as though he's picking up something that's going to hurt him, he pulls out a green crushed velvet elf hat. The one I wore that night.

"It all started with your hat. From a night I don't really want to forget."

I start to interrupt him, but he stops me. I don't want to find out now that he's been fantasizing about me all these years. Just like I'll never admit to having wonderful memories of that night.

"I'm not talking about the sex. Granted, that was amazing, but the way we didn't have a care in the world. I… We had fun. We had an adventure."

He sighs as he shakes his head. "Look, Sera. I grew up thinking that I was going to have to act like Phillip and my dad. I thought I wanted to be like them, to run the company like them. They were successful in ways no one else is, and I thought that was the only way. But I woke up that next morning, and I knew I couldn't. I wanted to be fun and a little chaotic, and I didn't want anyone to be miserable when they were working for me. Including myself. That hat, and these stupid elves, remind me I'm not Phillip or my dad. And I never have to be."

It's my turn to sigh. This was not what I expected from Andrew. I don't know what I'd been expecting, but the office turning him into a weird elf collector, and me turning him into the "cool boss" isn't it.

"I guess that makes sense," I say. "Though it is a little creepy."

He's so freaking serious, but when I grin, it seems to break the tension. "Come on, would you rather work with me or Phillip," he says, but the seriousness is mostly gone.

"You. Phillip doesn't know how to make good coffee." That seems to further break the tension. "Okay Andrew, put your weird elves back on the walls. I won't make too much fun of you and your old woman collections. Though, if you suggest I wear an elf hat to work, I'm going to slap you, okay?"

He chuckles. "Fine. But I do have to let you know you look spectacular in green…"

I give him a very serious look even though the thought of wearing an elf outfit makes my heart skip a beat. The way he'd looked at me in that costume isn't something I could forget. What it felt like for him to rip it off me is etched into my mind forever.

He pauses before saying, "You know, you keep giving me these mixed signals. One moment, you're this hardass business woman who doesn't want to think about anything else, and the very next, you're cracking jokes."

If you only knew, Andrew. If you only knew. This week, I've spent nearly every waking moment thinking about work. It's about as intense as my childhood. Everything in my life until I started working at Loughton House has been dominated by the idea of work hard and play harder. Maybe there's a little less playing right now, but that's temporary, and I know that.

Every single moment with Andrew at my side has been more difficult than I'd ever expected. Not because the job is harder when he's there. No, it's because looking at him, hearing him, or even thinking about him draws my attention away from the work. Like right now, I don't want to go back to looking at excel sheets. I want to steal that elf hat from his hands and put it on. To see what he'd do, how he'd look at me.

Andrew doesn't seem to understand that dichotomy, though. "That's called being interesting, and I don't mind showing you a few pointers." I give him a quick wink. "Right now, my priority is figuring out how to tell when a book has a problem based on its sales. So why don't you come back to my office and show me?"

He cocks his head, smiles, and steps toward me. "We can do that, but I think it'll be nice to have time to explore the 'interesting' side of you soon." He reaches for the elf in my hand, and his fingers brush mine. For a moment, he pauses. I've spent the last week doing everything I could to keep from touching him for this exact reason.

A shiver runs through me, and I can't stop my heart from racing. His gaze catches mine, and for that split-second, we're both thinking the same thing. We remember what it felt like to touch each other. We remember how good it felt.

His fingers move to only touching the elf, and I let go. My body's throbbing when he pulls the elf from my hand and sets it back in the box. I take a deep breath, but it's shaky. Damn it, why did I have to worry about looking at his elf collection? Why did I have to care? We're supposed to be keeping our heads down with our noses to the grindstone. Not playing.

And even though we don't say another word, when he walks beside me, he feels closer. Like something happened in that moment that we can't take back. It was only a momentary brush of fingertips, but when I look at him, I wonder if it could have been more.

Eighteen

SERA

"No days off is a recipe for disaster," Andrew says without an ounce of doubt in his voice. "This is not a sprint, Sera. You need time to sleep when you're working fourteen-hour days. Sure, I could probably do it since I've worked twelve-hour days for a long time, but you? You're used to forty-hour weeks, and your brain muscles aren't used to it."

Brain muscles? "We're already short on time, and you know it. We need to keep working."

Andrew leans back in his chair on the balcony, looking as comfortable as a cat lounging on a laptop keyboard. "Nope. I learned that a long time ago, and you can thank your elf hat for reminding me of it, even in my most intense periods. I'm the boss, and I'm saying we're taking Sundays off. Every Sunday. If we don't, I end up acting like my dad, and you'll turn into a very uninteresting woman."

I sigh. There's not enough time to learn everything. The idea of taking a day off every week is hard for me to comprehend. I set a goal, and now I'm being forced by my boss to ignore it for a whole day every single week. It goes against everything inside me. Should I tell him I'm used to those kinds of hours?

No. I'm not used to it, even though I'd like to think I am. I may have worked *and* played hard for more than fourteen hours a day for years, but it was never purely work. Maybe he's right. "Fine. Then what do you plan on doing on our day off?" I ask.

He shrugs. "We'll see when we get there. It's not like we have to make reservations or buy tickets in advance. We show up, wave some money in someone's face, and they let us do the thing. Pretty simple and pretty non-committal. Just the way I like it."

I arch an eyebrow at him. *I bet he likes non-committal…* "Oh, get over it, Sera," he says when he notices my look. "It's not like either of us planned to end up playing Bury the Weasel that night." *Bury the Weasel? What the fuck….* "At what point should I have stopped you? When your hand was literally on my dick while we were on stage? Hold on, everybody. Pause the music. Me and this woman I met an hour ago need to discuss my intentions… No. You were just as into seeing where the craziness would lead us as I was, and it was wonderful. Hell, I still think about it. Plus, you're the one who snuck off before I woke up. Not me."

I huff a bit, but I know he's right. It's not like I can really blame him for any of that night. I was pissed the next morning, sure. That's only because I wanted more. Not because he did anything wrong.

"Fine. I'll drop it. I mean, I kind of dropped it a long time ago, but it's hard to completely forget it. You aren't the only one who thinks about it. The adventure, not the sex, mind you. That was only mediocre." I give him a wink to make sure he knows I'm joking. At least, I think he'll know I'm joking. Hopefully. Maybe?

He's the one who arches his eyebrow now. "Mediocre? Do I need to remind you of how many times you came? How many times you screamed my name in the dark?"

My smile turns into a grin. "I think you're confused. Yes, I came plenty of times, but that's because I knew what I wanted, and I used you like a big, warm sex toy. Exactly how it says in the *How to Actually Climax with a Man* handbook. Oh, wait. You didn't know about that book, did you?"

The glare he gives me only makes me laugh. "I'm only playing. Jeez. I thought Phillip was the one with the stick up his ass."

He gives me a little chuckle and leans back in the chair again. "You're a fucking trip, Sera. Once again, you're being 'interesting'. One moment, you're all work, no play, and the next, you're telling me you used me like a sex toy. Which, on that note, is not exactly something any man wants to hear. I don't know if that was in your little handbook or not, but for future reference, I'd steer clear of that commentary if you ever want to get laid again."

"See, that's the thing. We're never going to see each other naked again, so I can say whatever I want to you. If I was desperate for a human sex toy, I'm sure there's a Brit who'd be happy to indulge me even if I read him the whole handbook."

The glare comes back, but this time, there's more to that look. Like what I said upset him. I've realized something about Andrew. He always smiles, but I'm not sure whether that's because he's always happy or if it's a mask to cover his actual emotions. I spent an entire month with Phillip as my cubicle-mate, and he was simple. He wore his emotions on his sleeve, but Andrew is complex. I see glimmers of other emotions, but then they're gone.

"Maybe that's how you should spend your day off then. Banging Brits. You could treat them like Pokemon. Gotta bang 'em all."

I sigh. That one must have struck a nerve for him to respond like that. I wonder what it is. Did it really piss him off that I verbally put him into the work partner basket instead of the possible sexual relations one?

"Funny. Does it bother you I said I could go find a cute British guy to fill my Sundays, and me, with?"

He takes a sip of his beer and sets it down on the table. While he stares out at the skyline, he says, "Nope. Have fun. Like you said, we're never going to have a repeat of that night, so it won't hurt my feelings any."

Somehow, I don't believe him. His jaw clenches and the smile on his face is the least believable one I've seen so far. Part of me hates I had to say that, but it's extremely important that I set boundaries. I'm not falling into bed with anyone while I'm here, but that includes Andrew.

I take a sip of my beer and lean back in my chair to look out at the London sunset. "You know, I never imagined working with you would be so… not miserable."

He chuckles and raises an eyebrow. "Oh yeah? After that shopping trip, I was positive that you were going to be a very unpleasant person to be around, so I guess I could say the same. You're a fairly decent roommate, and I enjoy having you as my partner in crime. Whether or not you're good at it is still up in the air…"

The quiet sounds of cars passing under us are a mere shadow of what it would sound like back home. The laughing of a group of people leaving a bar is like a chiming bell when I'm used to the sound of gongs.

He stands up, finishes his beer, and says, "I'm going to get another. Do you want one?"

I shake my head, and he walks inside. This calmness is strange. This comfortableness. I wasn't lying about how I feel about our arrangement. How am I living with a man I barely know, doing a job I know nothing about, and yet, I'm almost calmer and more at peace than I was last week? I'd expected to be on edge constantly.

But I'm not.

I should be stressed and worried about failing. What kind of crazy is Andrew Loughton going to bring to my life *other* than kidnapping me? How am I supposed to do a job that's well above my experience level? And isn't he eventually going to get tired of me not picking it up fast enough?

Yet, none of that seems to weigh on me.

I take another sip of the beer as the sun falls below the horizon, leaving us in that beautiful orange twilight.

"You're doing well. You know that, right?" I turn to see Andrew looking at me, his shoulder resting against the sliding glass door frame. "This whole thing is a lot, but you're handling it better than I expected."

I shrug. "I'm not any closer to being able to run a company than I was on Monday. The only difference is that I wake up in the middle of the night because of Excel nightmares."

He lets out a laugh. "Then you're obviously getting the hang of things. It took me a solid month before I started having them. And let me tell you, they never go away. Nightmares about losing a document or adding an extra zero to some random number and causing the entire company to collapse have been my constant companion since I moved to London."

"That sounds like PTSD from office work. I don't really think that's a thing."

He shrugs and goes back to his chair. "Maybe not. But PTSD from stress is. I don't think there's a cure for that, though."

We sit in silence and watch the orange fade into true twilight. It's beautiful. Maybe as beautiful as the New York skyline.

Or maybe it's because I'm watching a sunset without worrying about what I'm doing with my life for the first time in years. Probably since college.

When the streetlights come on, and all the light is gone, I take the last sip of my beer and stand up. "Thanks for bringing me to London," I say softly.

Andrew cocks his head. I expect a sarcastic bit of banter, but instead, he says, "You're welcome. Thanks for not having me arrested. I don't look good in prison orange."

I give him a smile. "I'm going to see if I can think happy thoughts and hopefully dodge any Excel nightmares. See you in the morning."

He gives me a nod and turns back toward the city as twilight turns to night. Looking at him, it's hard to think of him as the carefree man I met at that Christmas party. I'd thought he had become more like Phillip and Russel, had *grown into the billionaire*. But that's not it. He's been beaten into it.

Yet, he still keeps that smile on his face. The long days and heavy weight on his shoulders have taken away a lot of his wildness, but it hasn't taken away the smile. And that's more important than I think most people understand.

Of all the things that someone could admire in Andrew Loughton, I think the fact that he still smiles almost ceaselessly is the one that means the most to me.

Nineteen

ANDREW

Saturday at the office is my favorite day. It's mostly empty. There aren't very many emails. No project updates. Just me working on my own little projects. It's how I set up our workflow. During the week, everything is about making sure that things work on the day-to-day level, but Saturdays are when you make progress.

It's strange today, though. Sera's sitting in her chair, looking over all the things we've talked about. Normally, I'd be working harder than any other day. My focus would be at its highest since there are almost no distractions.

But today? Today, I'm having a hard time not trying to convince Sera to do something other than work. I know she needs these days to learn and grow into a role she still barely even understands, but for the first time since I moved to London, I don't care about work.

"I think I'm getting some of this," Sera says as she sits back in the office chair. "You're not actually checking to see the income at a book's peak since that's almost all based on how your marketing is. It's the tail that matters.

Each month, a good book will drop a little in income, but a bad book will fall off fast."

I nod to her. "Yep. That's when we take a good long look at whether we'll be buying more of that series from the author. Sometimes, it makes sense to do it. Sometimes it doesn't. Either way, we know to pay extra attention to the next series. Sometimes an author does great with their first book, but they can't nail the next ones. Other times, the author can't hit the ending. Or maybe they're a one-hit-wonder. Whatever the case is, we need to know."

She's getting it faster than most people. It's not only that she's understanding one concept and then the next. She's putting the pieces together so that when something strange happens, she'll realize that it's strange. That pause where you don't know why something happened is the most important bit of instinct anyone in the business world can have.

She sighs and leans back in the chair, her eyes closed. I can't help but watch her. My focus should be to looking over the options for different short story authors to pick up for my pet project. I should be on point like I normally am. But I can't sit with my own thoughts here with her.

I know I've told her it's like I'm talking to two different people sometimes, but it's more than that. I'm me all the time. Whether I'm having a meeting with the senior managers here or I'm sitting on the balcony drinking a beer. Sure, the topic and level of seriousness may change, but my personality comes through constantly.

Sera isn't quite like that. She's got a work mode and a play mode. Ninety percent of the time, she's in work mode, and it's hot because she's fucking focused. She's as intense as Phillip or Dad. The thing is, that underneath that focus and intensity, I still see glimpses of the other side. I see her wanting to play, to banter, and maybe something else.

Then there are the few times she actually lets herself go into play mode, granted none of them are like that Christmas party, but she's a ball of laughter and jokes then. And at the same time, you can see the bits of seriousness leaking through.

I don't know anyone like that. They're not masks. They're different gears or mentalities. Drastically different from each other.

"Okay, Andrew. What's next? I think I have this under control. At least enough to answer an email or two."

I grin at her, and instead of standing up like normal, I close my laptop and leave it on my lap. "Now we talk about the reason everyone thinks you're here. Vanguard."

She cocks her head. "What do you mean?"

"Everyone at the office thinks you're here because you're going to help me set up Vanguard in London. We're supposed to copy the way things are done in New York. We'll be contracting an agency to treat self-published authors like their slush pile and find the diamonds in the rough. Then we offer them contracts."

She frowns. "Okay. So what does that mean for me?"

"You get to make some decisions. Truthfully, I'm not all that worried about most of it, so I'm going to leave it to you. We need to send out emails explaining the process to the employees. We need to give them a chance to decide whether they want to become work-from-home or have their own office space, and we need to figure out how to accommodate that."

Her body tenses and her eyes get wide. It's like the thought of actually making decisions instead of only learning is crazy, and maybe it is. Just a little, though. "I'll send you the list of major changes and walk you through how you are going to tackle them. Don't worry about it too much. You won't be re-inventing the wheel. We already did it in New York. Now we're simply doing it again here."

She takes a deep breath before letting it out. "Okay, I can do that. Send me the list and you can give me some pointers on the first few things."

I shake my head. "Nope. It's Saturday at eleven o'clock. We're going to have a long lunch at a nice restaurant. When we get back, we can go through it all, but for now, we're going to let our brains rest a little."

She visibly relaxes before she nods. "That sounds nice. A lot better than I'd thought it would. Maybe you know what you're talking about with this whole take it easy approach."

I arch my eyebrow at her. "I doubt anyone would consider fourteen-hour days, six days a week, the 'take it easy approach'."

Her shrug looks exhausted. There aren't any rings under her eyes yet, but she could be hiding that with makeup. "It's easier than what I was planning." She pauses for a second before closing her laptop. "So, where are we going for lunch?"

"Luciano's," I say without any explanation, and I prepare myself to ignore her. No one should know what they're walking into before they go to Luciano's because it's not only a place to get food. It's an experience, and explanations only ruin it.

Ferdinand, my driver, opens his book as soon as we walk toward the unmarked building that only a handful of people support. The owner and chef, Luciano, isn't some glorified TV personality like so many of the famous chefs in the US. No, he is a chef. That's all. He manages his business, but when it's a single person running a building that was given to him, it's not a very complicated business.

He's spent his entire life and career doing one thing. Making food that is worth paying an astronomical amount of money for.

As we walk to the door, Sera tries to ask about the restaurant. "What kind of food is it? I don't really like Greek food. Why isn't there a billboard or even a sign on the building? Am I going to get kidnapped for real this time?"

Silly questions I refuse to answer.

The door in front of us is boarded up, one more unique piece of Luciano's. Like so many other places that the elite of London visit, this restaurant is hidden. Not because normal people shouldn't eat the food, or even because something is illegal. No, it's much simpler than that. The payment system wouldn't work for the average person.

Because Luciano works only for tips. All the food is free.

We walk down an alley that runs beside the building, and if you pay attention, you'll notice that there's absolutely no trash or debris. It's not instantly noticeable, but after all the times I've come here, it's one of the things I've noticed. Even though it's an alley, he comes out and sweeps it every day.

Propped up against the building is a dented piece of sheet metal that's slightly bent in the middle. It's an enormous piece of steel that no normal person would want to try to move on their own. I pause for a moment, and I give Sera a grin. She's very confused, and I like it. I like that hesitancy, that bit of nervousness. It doesn't make sense, though. I wouldn't get this much satisfaction out of another employee being confused or nervous.

"What the hell are we doing in an alley?" Sera asks. I ignore her and put my hand on the edge of the metal. An edge that you'd expect to be razor sharp, but it's been ground down so that it's completely smooth and doesn't have an actual edge. I give it a little push.

The metal slides along a hidden track, revealing an entryway. "We're going to eat lunch. Like I said."

Her face is a mix of shock and excitement as I walk into the entryway and say, "Are you coming?"

I hold the secret door open for her as she slips inside next to me. When I let go of the door, it rolls back into place silently. "What kind of crazy world do you live in where you go through freaking secret passages for lunch?" she whisper-yells at me. "Is this really the thing that sets you apart from normal rich guys?"

I don't try to keep the laughter in. Maybe I do enjoy the fact that I know of several secret restaurants in London. "There are a lot of secret places in England, and especially London. It's really, really old. There's supposed to be a whole network of hidden tunnels under the city, but I haven't found any of the entrances. Maybe if I hadn't been so busy, I'd have had time to ferret more of them out."

"Okay, as long as I'm not brutally murdered here, this is officially my favorite restaurant already."

I don't take her bait because I am *not* ruining this lunch date with Sera. And I stop mid-step. I realize then that I've never taken a woman to Luciano's. I've definitely never taken anyone from work here. It's always been my little secret. But I'm taking Sera here, even though I barely know her.

I could blame it on the fact that we live together or the fact that we haven't really left each other's side since we got to London. But that'd be a lie.

The truth is that I *want* to show her this place. I want her to experience it in all its glory.

What does that mean?

"What?" she asks. "Is everything alright? We're about to be murdered, aren't we?" She's got a grin on her face, but I can see a bit of fear there, too.

"No murders this afternoon," I say, and without thinking, I take her hand to escort her inside. We both pause and look down. I don't know why I did that, why I took her hand like we were on a date. It was impulsive and almost instinctual. Which only means one thing… I feel like I'm on a date.

I let her hand go, but I don't say anything. What is there to say? It felt normal to hold your hand? Definitely not.

The hallway ends in a glass door. Etched into the glass is the simple word, "Luciano's". No frills or decorations. Especially none that would mark it as a place the elite would eat. I open it for Sera, and she walks in. I know what she expects. A secret basement where villains plan out their evil schemes. At least that's what I imagined the first time someone showed me this place.

It's not at all what's actually there. The silver tinkle of a bell rings as I open the door into a small café. There's no wall between the kitchen and dining area, and I can clearly see Luciano sitting on a stool in the kitchen, slowly stirring a massive pot. The soft sound of an Italian voice plays from an old cassette player on the table next to him.

The room is lit by small lamps arranged on four simple tables set against the walls and two bright ceiling fans in the kitchen. Barstools that look as old as Luciano himself sit in front of the bar, facing into the kitchen.

There are two people sitting at the bar, people I've never met, which is a little strange with how few people know about Luciano's. They talk quietly over their bowls.

"Oh my God," Sera whispers from beside me. Her eyes are on Luciano, but I'm pretty positive that it's not what she's seeing that surprised her.

"That smell… What is it? What is this place?" I give her a grin. "This is Luciano's. A simple man cooking the best food you've ever tasted."

She shakes her head. "I've had a lot of good food in a lot of places. This… It's different."

"It is." I take her hand, and this time I don't let go. She glances at it for a moment, but doesn't hesitate when I lead her to the bar. "What are we having today, Luciano?" I ask.

"Lamb stew with Boule de Pain. Like sourdough for you Americans." His Italian accent makes him sound pretentious, even though he's the humblest man I've ever met. "It'll be a minute before the next loaf is done." Said like that, it's like anyone could make it. Maybe anyone could. But they don't. Well, they don't make it like Luciano does.

Sera whispers, "But what if I don't want that?"

I chuckle. "You do. I promise you want anything that he makes."

She raises an eyebrow but doesn't say anything. I'm sure the heavenly smells of baking bread, the herbs in the stew, and the still lingering scent of braised lamb convince her it's not worth questioning my statement.

We sit quietly watching Dante as he opens an oven and pulls out a steaming round loaf of bread. There's something so uniquely relaxing about watching an expert cook. Unlike all the professional kitchens, Dante doesn't rush around. There's no yelling or frantic movements.

It's slow, and the soft sounds of the Italian singer's voice fill the silence, creating a soundtrack to his movements. The singer's voice is lilting and semi-repetitive, but the music behind her voice dances in pitch, telling a story that needs no words.

"Why do I feel so relaxed here?" Sera asks. "It's like I'm back home watching my mom cook a Thanksgiving dinner."

And for the first time, Luciano addresses Sera. "Because deep down you know that food brings us together. It makes us feel at home."

She cocks her head as he continues. I don't interrupt. If there's anyone who understands what food means, it's Luciano. He uses a wooden ladle to fill two porcelain bowls as he says, "Since the beginning, people have gathered together for food. One or two people cooked, and the rest waited. They watched. They smiled and laughed while their food was being prepared. Making food is like making art. Even using the same recipe as someone else does not make the same food."

He puts the bowls in front of us, steam billowing off the stew. Pieces of lamb float with turnips and carrots and some kind of leafy vegetable in a thin broth. The spices assail our senses, and I can see Sera's body visibly relax at the scent.

He gives Sera a smile as he picks up the loaf of bread. Instead of cutting it, he rips a chunk off and hands it to her. "Food sustains you. Not only physically. It sustains the soul. Each bite is a memory, a remembrance of another time. A time when things weren't so hard, when things weren't so complicated. Focus on the simplicity of good food with a good friend."

Sera can't help but smile, and Luciano winks at me as he hands me a chunk of the bread. "Now, I must go back to my stew, or it will get too hot on the bottom, and the lamb will become tough."

He turns and goes back to the pot. Sera glances at me, and I can tell that she's almost embarrassed as she takes a bite of the bread. I can't remember a time that I saw her embarrassed, and I wonder what it was about what Luciano said that makes her feel like that.

But when she bites into the bread, her embarrassment evaporates. "This is… heavenly? Wonderful? Why are there no words to describe it?"

"It's Luciano," I say. "That's the only description you need to use."

I can see him grinning at us from his pot, but he's used to people having conversations he's not part of. "The stew is better," I say.

I dip my bread into the broth and let it sit for a moment before taking a bite. God, it's something special. Like what I imagine children experience. I've had stew hundreds of times before, but this is like I'm having it for the first time.

And like Luciano suggested, nothing else really matters. Not Loughton House or my future in the family.

Not Sera's workload. Not even what we're going to do when we leave here. Just the food and the girl sitting next to me.

You can't simply eat and leave when you're eating food like this. Maybe that's the real magic of this place. Maybe it's that you have to experience each and every bite, savoring it like a man who hasn't had a bite to eat in days. Where every ounce of food nourishes the body and the soul.

"Now I understand why this place isn't open to the public," Sera says. "No one could cook like this for hundreds of people every day."

"He used to. For twenty years he was a professional chef in Paris, but then he retired and started this place. He knew plenty of wealthy people that set it up for him. I don't think he spent a dime, and everyone was happy they could continue to eat his food, regardless of the cost."

Sera nods as she slowly chews a piece of the lamb. My bowl is nearly empty, and even more than when we're sitting on my balcony, it doesn't feel like we need to talk. Yet, it's almost like we're closer because we're sharing this experience together. As Luciano said, it's like we're watching a play, except that it's our taste and smell that are experiencing the performance.

And somehow, that makes it more intimate.

A simple lamb stew and hunk of sourdough with Sera may be one of the most intimate things I've done with anyone. She smiles at me, and I smile back. The song of an Italian woman is all the noise we need.

I scrape the last bit of broth out of my bowl with the last bite of bread and then push the bowl away from me. I always feel this satisfied after I eat here. Like I can go back to my life with a fresh outlook, almost like the things that had weighed on me for all the months in New York don't matter the same way.

There's no reason to say anything about the way I feel, and when Sera pushes her bowl away, she takes a deep breath before letting out a soft sigh. She doesn't say anything, either. "Thank you," I say to Luciano, who's eating a piece of the bread he tore our chunks off. He nods and gives me a smile.

I reach into my wallet and pull out five hundred dollars that I leave on the counter before standing up. It's nothing to me, but it's how I can help him continue to do the one thing he loves. And the thing that no one else can do as well as him. It's a donation to make sure he never has a financial reason to stop cooking for us. That's the way everyone treats this place, and if they don't, then there's something wrong with them.

Sera stands up and follows me out the same way we came. It's only when we step into the alley that either of us says anything.

"That was not what I'd expected from a lunch," she whispers.

"No. That's because it's not only lunch."

She smiles at me, but the smile almost turns into a frown. "How do you go back to eating normal food after that? How do you eat anywhere else?"

"Well, the answer is simple, really. Do you think you can go back to work and actually get anything done?"

Sera looks confused for a moment and sinks a little. "No. I mean, I *could*, but I don't have the same drive to do it. That probably sounds crazy. I still want to do all the things, but I'm not quite as rushed. It's like I'm not as scared that everything's going to fall apart anymore."

I nod to her. I feel the same way. "Never come to Luciano's if you have to get anything else done for the day. Nothing really matters as much afterward. Well..."

"Work doesn't matter as much," she says in agreement. "Lots of other things do. But not work."

She understands. "What do you want to do with the rest of the day?"

"I hadn't thought that far ahead."

Her grin grows into something that might look a little crazy. "How would you feel about meeting my dad?"

Twenty
ANDREW

FERDINAND IS SILENT, AS ALWAYS, AS WE RIDE PAST the old buildings in Chelsea. Sera, on the other hand, is furiously typing away on her personal phone. We're going to see her dad? In London? Why didn't she say anything about her dad being in the same city, an ocean away from her home? Why didn't she try to visit him earlier? And if she was going to visit him today, why's she bringing me along?

I'm trying to imagine who I'm about to meet, but I can't put the pieces together. What kind of man raises a daughter like Sera? Strong and independent, focused but wild, and absolutely unpredictable when she decides to be. She refuses to tell me anything about him. When I asked her, she said, "He's kind of like Luciano's. It's better to experience him without any expectations, you know?"

What the hell does that even mean? I'm guessing he's not going to cook us lunch and listen to Italian music.

I'd expected today to be relaxed after lunch. Maybe we could go for a stroll down the river or visit one of the hundreds of tourist areas. You know, do the things that most people would do in London. That's not in the cards, though.

"Why did you want me to come along?" I ask, since trying to puzzle things out on my own isn't working very well.

Sera chuckles and keeps watching the buildings we pass by. "I don't know. I didn't plan on visiting him at all. There's been so much going on, so many things to learn and understand, and he understood that. But today, I think I need to see him. I'm dragging you along because, well, we've spent damn near every moment together. You could use a break, too. My dad has a way of helping people feel a little freer, and I think we could both use a bit of freedom."

What? Is he a therapist? "I'm going to have to trust you on that. I haven't met a lot of women's parents."

She pauses for a moment. "Oh… well… I didn't really think about it being like *that*." She shrugs and gives me a grin that, for the first time, reminds me of the girl I met at the Christmas party all those years ago. That "damn the torpedoes" look. The one that had me up on a stage in my underwear.

Like that night, instead of thinking about the right decision, I let the adventure play out. The last time she took me on an adventure is one I didn't regret, right?

"He lives *here*? Sera, if your dad lives in this neighborhood, there's no reason you should even be working."

She huffs and, in a terrible impersonation of me, says, "Andrew, if your family owns Loughton House, there's no reason you should even be working."

I shake my head. "That's different. It's a family business, and I'm paid a lot for what I do. You're a cover artist. Your dad could give you an allowance, and it'd be more than your salary."

"I wanted to make my own way, like my mom and dad. Neither of them had anything handed to them. They didn't have a family business, so I didn't inherit my position. Plus, what am I supposed to do if I don't have a job? My parents won't fund my adventures forever. They worked hard for their money, and they deserve to be the ones to spend it. Not me."

"Yes, but you could have done so much more. If you wanted to work, why didn't you borrow money and start a business? How does someone that comes from a place like *this* end up barely breaking six figures?"

The grin she gives me tells me there's more to this conversation than I'm seeing. "Maybe all I wanted was to be a cover artist? Or maybe I'm using you to teach me the business so I can go start my own publishing empire? Who knows? Maybe twenty years from now, we'll be fighting over authors?"

The thought is laughable. "I guess I'll have to be a little more secretive if I'm training my competitor."

"Maybe you should. Loughton House is doing some very experimental things, and I'm right there in the middle of it."

The corner of her lip curls up, and for a moment, it occurs to me she might do exactly what she's saying. Then I remind myself that even if she has some starting capital, it's not enough to compete with Loughton House. There's no way she could *actually* do what she's suggesting. Plus, why would she suggest it if that was her plan?

The door opens then, and I stare up at a man that I've seen pictures of since I was a kid. Terry Evans. The lead singer of Sweet Delusions. A man who has stood in front of crowds that would dwarf small towns. He was the rock and roll idol of my childhood. No one was cooler.

"Uh…" I mumble and stare at him. *Get it together, Andrew. He's just a guy.*

Sera doesn't even seem to notice as she runs up the stairs to give him a hug. "Hey Dad," she says. "It's been too long."

Terry hugs his daughter, but his eyes are on me. The black hair and dark glasses that he had in his prime are still there. His hair's short now instead of the long, almost eighties style haircut he had back then. The glasses are more modern. But the man looks the same.

"Who's your friend?" Terry asks as Sera steps back.

She grins at me. "That's my boss, Andrew Loughton."

Terry pulls his glasses further down his nose, and I can see his eyes. They're intense. Like he's judging everything about me in a glance. "Nice to meet you, Andrew. Why don't you two come inside? I didn't expect you, and the guys are coming over for an afternoon session."

Sera seems right at home with this, but I'm still more than a little shocked. I'm going to meet the entire band? I memorized every line of every song of theirs. *Snap the fuck out of it, Andrew. They are people that are good at their jobs. Just like you.*

But they're not. They're creators. They make music that people cling to, that gives them emotions that no one else does. Like Luciano said, music can take you back, and that's the last thing I want. The early 2000s were not a good time for me.

"You coming?" Sera asks when I just stand there.

It's like my body snaps to life again, and I give her a grin. She turns to follow her dad and I close the door behind us. What the hell is wrong with me? I've met senators and even a president, and I didn't lose my shit like this. I've talked to members of Parliament and owners of some of the biggest businesses in the UK.

Terry Evans is simply an artist. There is no good reason for me to act like some kind of teenaged star-eyed fan. Sure, he caught me off guard, but I need to pick my jaw up off the floor and be a normal human being.

"Do either of you want anything?" Terry asks as we walk into the kitchen. "Beer? Wine? Water?" He opens his fridge and pulls a beer out.

"I'll take a beer," I say with a touch of hesitation. *Just don't mention that I know who Sweet Delusions is.*

He tosses the bottle to me, and I catch it. He tosses the bottle opener to me after. "And you?" he asks Sera. "The normal?"

She chuckles. "Maybe put a splash of vodka in it."

"Done," he says as he pulls a glass from the cabinet and fills it with orange juice. "You know, Andrew, it's the strangest thing watching a kid grow up in front of you. It wasn't that long ago that Seraphina tried a sip of a screwdriver and spit it all over my face. She told me, and I quote, 'Daddy, I think your juice went bad. Don't pour it Mommy's plants or she'll ground you from your guitar.' Now she's telling me she wants that exact drink."

Sera grins at her dad and says, "I remember that. I think I was six or seven, and it was my birthday. Mom was not very understanding of your attempt at a childhood toast."

Terry laughs as he gets his own beer out of the fridge and kicks it shut. "No, she was not. That's what makes her a good mom, though. I think we did a pretty good job together. All the brains from your mom and all the fun from me. I'd hate to see who you'd have grown into without your mom being on the other side of the table, though."

Sera looks so at ease here. So completely at home around her dad. It's obvious her parents got a divorce, but it must have been a pretty amenable one. "I'd have been like you without the voice. I'd probably have started a girl band and played bass. Could you imagine me with all black makeup in fishnets and a short skirt?"

My mind immediately goes to that image, and I would definitely approve of the look.

"No, but there's probably a thousand boys out there that don't realize how much they missed out on that alternate universe. Have you been playing? I've got a spare bass you could use when the guys show up."

She grimaces, and I'm entranced by the exchange. I can't imagine having a dad like this. One who was simply a friend. Terry pours a little more than a splash of vodka into the tumbler and grins at his daughter. "You're a busy woman these days. Maybe you need to knock some of the rust off those fingers and have some fun."

Then she glances at me, and Terry follows that glance. "Oh," he says.

“Do you play any instruments?” he asks as he hands Sera her drink. “Or sing? Like I said, the guys are going to come over and we’re going to play for a bit. I think I’ve got at least one of every instrument ever made in the studio if you want to join in.”

I shake my head. “Never learned how to play anything. But I’ll be fine just listening.” I’d say more than “just fine”, but the last thing I want is to act like I was a huge fan of theirs.

“That’s too bad. It’s always more fun with a few fresh voices and sounds.”

I pop the cap on the beer bottle and toss it into the trashcan. That’s when the doorbell rings, and I can already hear voices coming from the door. That’s when it hits me. What does spending the afternoon with a band entail?

Terry goes to the door, and I move to Sera, who’s grinning from ear to ear. “Why didn’t you tell me your dad was fucking Terry Evans?”

She shrugs. “How was I supposed to know that you’d recognize him? Not many people do these days. He hasn’t been a big name in fifteen years, but I guess I forgot how old you are.”

I glare at her. “I’m not old,” I mutter.

“Ancient. Decrepit. I’ll probably have to get you a walker instead of an elf for Boss Appreciation Day. You’d probably want a little scooter, though, and my poor cover artist's wages aren’t paying for that.”

I can’t help but laugh. “You know, you’re a little shit, right? Just this morning, you were the diligent employee, working her ass off. Now you’re bringing me to your rock star dad’s house so we can drink and you can call me old.”

She glances at my beer and says, "If you're smart, you'll pay attention to how much you're drinking, or tomorrow, you're going to feel *really* old. My dad has a way of convincing people to do very stupid things like try to keep up with him."

That's one thing I'm not afraid of. "Sera, you do know that the children of billionaires are raised on Scotch, right? We go straight from breastmilk to Scotch and never look back. You might want to tell your dad not to get alcohol poisoning trying to keep up with *me.*"

Her eyes open wide. "I… It's your funeral, boss. Though, if you throw up on me, I will never let you live it down."

I give her a grin and go to the door where the coolest band of my teen years are standing around. All of them are well past their prime, but they're still them. They're still the guys I wish I could have met when I was fifteen. The ones that filled the radio waves when I was learning to drive. I'm about to watch the heroes of my childhood hold a mini-concert with me and Sera as the only audience.

This is a dream come true. Now, all I have to do is pretend like it's no big deal.

Twenty-One

SERA

My boss is about to get himself into a world of trouble. Yes, he probably has drank more than his fair share of liquor, but compared to rock stars, literal rock stars, he's a child trying beer for the first time.

I sigh as I see him staring at them. My dad and his best friends, my adoptive uncles. I spent far too many summers with them not to realize how enamored Andrew is. He grew up listening to them. Probably had a poster of them on his wall.

And here he is about to make a fool of himself. I can't decide whether to protect him or let him act like a complete fool in front of them all. I take a sip of the screwdriver and sigh. It's probably in my best interest to make sure he doesn't do anything too terribly stupid. At least I'll have something to talk about tomorrow.

I walk in front of Andrew and Barry catches my eye first. "Oh good Lord, you've grown up. Fucking Seraphina, looking like a proper businesswoman over here, guys."

The rest of them see me then, and I'm assaulted by them. It only makes me laugh as they pile on top of me to give me hugs. The band mates of Sweet Delusions were my entire summer every year. I toured with them, was the official band mascot in so many ways, and really grew up with them as part of the family.

When they've all had their hug, they step back, one after the other. "It's been what, ten years since we saw you?" Stephen, the drummer, asks.

"Six. You all came to New York to see me the summer of my freshman year in college. It feels like a lifetime, though."

"Lordy, lordy, lordy, you look like your mother in that business outfit," Jared, the bass player, says.

"Better her mother than her old man. Be thankful you didn't end up looking like that ugly bastard."

"That'd be better than looking like you, you hairy son-of-a-bitch."

"If she looked like me, Terry'd have dropped me in the River Thames already."

"What about that concert in Chicago back in '90…"

This is how it always is with them. Once they start, it's a river of nonsense. I love it. It's like three younger brothers fighting at Thanksgiving. And my dad is over there watching them to make sure they don't end up throwing the turkey at each other.

"I thought you were coming over to play, not talk about Tabby," he says with a grin toward me. Then I see him glance at Andrew, who's got a frown on his face. What's going on with Andrew? I'd thought he'd be star-struck with the whole band here. But he's frowning?

"Guys," I say. "This is Andrew Loughton, my boss. Maybe you could remember that and not embarrass me?"

"Hey Andrew," they all say together, and immediately, they're back to the chaos. They're in their fifties, but they've never really had to grow out of their twenties and thirties. All of them are stupidly wealthy, and life is a giant playground for them all.

It occurs to me then that I could have been like them from birth. I could have run around, causing trouble with every step. Even now, maybe Andrew's right. Maybe I could walk away from this whole publishing world. Never do another cover again. Never have dreams of anything beyond fun. I could be like my dad and his friends, retired at the ripe old age of twenty-five.

Except I would get bored. I don't want my life to be about trying to find something more insane than yesterday. I want to do something with my life. I want to make a mark on the world.

And I think I know how I'm going to do it now.

"Guys, take your stuff to the studio," I say a lot louder than normal. "I haven't heard the band play in a decade. It's time." They all turn to me with grins on their faces.

"Alright Princess Seraphina, we'll serenade you with some of the classics." Barry's got that faux servant look on his face like he did when I was little and would go on tour with them.

Princess Seraphina. What a title. I guess it was cute when I was eight and went on tour with them the very first time. That was when I saw him on stage for the first time and finally understood why he always had to leave.

Dad didn't raise me when we were on tour. I was raised by the village, and Dad was the king of that village and of the world that we lived in. He was larger than life, and I was his princess. The only reason he never truly got lost in that world of madness so many other people did. Instead, he lived it up, but he knew his limits.

I never saw my dad lose control. Even with all the parties and all the women. He always knew exactly how close he could toe the line.

"That's right, Barry. Princess Seraphina wants to hear 'Behind the Mask' with the guitar solo."

Barry, the lead guitarist, grins. It's always been his favorite song since the guitar riffs are complicated, and he wrote them all. "As you command, Your Highness."

Everybody else laughs and starts picking up their stuff to carry it into the studio. As they pass, Dad stops beside me. "They've missed you. When I told them you were in London, I had to keep them from going and visiting your work."

He gives me a hug and says, "We've all missed you, Princess Seraphina. I feel like you've been gone ever since you went away to college."

I look up at him. The face I know so well. The man that was my idol for so many years. "Maybe I'll be able to visit more often. I'm going to be in London for six months, so we should spend more time together. I don't think I'll work many Sundays, and we should be able to get together."

He nods. "That'd be really nice, but I know you're going to be busy. You're as driven as your mom. Hell, the boys were right. You look just like her in that fancy skirt-suit. But you've got my eyes, and that's what matters, right?"

I chuckle as he walks down the hall, leaving me behind with Andrew. "Are you going to talk to them at all?" I whisper.

"What the hell am I supposed to say? Yes, Princess Seraphina, let me fluff your cushions? I don't know how I fit into this. It was one thing when it was only your dad, but Sera, this is like a family reunion. How are you this close to your dad's band mates?"

I chuckle. "I lived with all of them every summer for like ten years. They toured in the summer and fall and worked on albums in the spring. It was a busy life for all of them, and the only way I could see my dad very much was to tour with them. You know how they say that children are raised by a village? Well, those three guys and my dad were that village every summer."

"That's insane. A little kid on tour with a rock band? You must have been exposed to so much stuff that's not okay for a little girl to see."

I shake my head. "You don't understand. They all really treated me like their kid. None of them have wives or children, so it was just me. Sure, I saw some crazy stuff at the concerts, but afterward? They partied some, but nothing too wild, and never too much for a kid to see. The line of what was acceptable was clearly drawn, and if they got too close, my dad would rein them in. They knew that he'd drop the band instead of lose those summers with me."

He doesn't look like he believes it, but he doesn't argue. Thankfully.

"It'll be better now that they've got their excitement out and they're going to play. Just watch. Once the jam session starts, you'll be as included as me."

He sighs. "Okay, Princess Seraphina, lead the way. At least I'm finally getting to see Sweet Delusions in concert. I always wanted to see them when I was a kid."

I knew he was a fan!

Twenty-Two

ANDREW

THE ROOM IS A TYPICAL STUDIO. SOUNDPROOFED walls. A glass viewing booth with recording equipment on the other side. Simple, yet effective.

The only difference? They aren't recording. This is where they come to fuck off and do the thing that they've loved for years.

"This one's for you, Princess," Barry says with a grin. He looks around the room before plucking a chord. Then another. The drums pick up the beat as the entire band slowly walks into the ballad. "Behind the Mask" was not one of their big hits. It was too slow for the time. Too melodic when the world wanted speed.

"She paints her face in black and white," Terry sings, his eyes on his daughter as he smiles. The bass picks up the rhythm as the drums fade out. "A mirror of the way she felt…"

A song of introspection. Of being split in two ways. That was Sera's favorite song as a kid? The rhythm catches a bit of speed, and Sera grins. She looks happy. Not that satisfied feeling we had at Luciano's. I'm torn between watching the band I loved as a teen and watching the woman that has become such a huge part of my life.

She may be my partner at work, but we've been inseparable for a week now. It's impossible not to think about her. The look on her face pulls at me. What is she remembering? What memories does this song bring her back to?

"Still like the winter, she looks at herself. A ghost of two sides. Not the woman she was born to be. Not the woman she wants to be."

The guitar solo explodes slowly, a slow burning fire that climbs in tempo. I remember listening to this song as a kid, the way it was so haunting. Hearing it live is even more powerful, and I know this is her song. I know it was written about the little girl whose father and mother pulled her in two separate directions.

The crescendo is a complicated guitar riff that would make even the most skilled players stumble, and Barry does it flawlessly, making it look easy. Stephen's bass picks back up, and Terry begins to sing to his daughter. Probably no different than when she was eight. There is no doubt that he was the best father he could be.

And it tears at me. I can't help but compare him to mine. The man who could do anything, who had built an empire with an efficiency that no one could match. The man who doesn't even look at me when I enter the room.

Sera's dad wrote her songs. Not fairy tale lullabies. No, these were songs that could only be written by a man who understood his daughter, a man who cared about her more than anything else.

And when they see each other, it's like everything in the world is right.

"But she knows she can't be two people," Terry sings. "She'll have to choose a path and give up the past."

Sera bobs her head in time to the ballad, the smile etched on her face as she closes her eyes. She's truly happy here. I wonder what it would be like to feel like that. To relive moments that filled your heart up. To have ever experienced moments like that.

The song closes as slowly as it began, and she doesn't act like a princess. "Oh my God, guys. That was amazing. I haven't heard *Behind the Mask* in so long. It's like I was watching that concert in Atlanta for the first time all over again."

"Oh, that was a good one," Stephen says from behind the drums. "Didn't Terry get you to come out on stage and sing the next song with him?"

"I think I did," he says with a grin. "You were nine, and the crowd went crazy. I bet you've gotten a little better since then. Why don't you come up and give it a try? We can even play *A Haunting Wonderland* just like that concert."

Her eyes go wide, and she looks at me. She'd definitely have sung with them if I weren't here. Well, she's not the only one who can be a little pushy about things. "Come on, Sera. If my dad had a band, I would join in. Think about it like karaoke, and you'll be fine."

The look on her face is priceless. I know about her ragtag karaoke group from the office, and from what I've heard, she never turns down a chance to sing there.

"This isn't exactly the same as karaoke," she says.

"Right," Terry says. "We're playing good songs here. Plus, it's not like you're the only one singing."

She's quiet for a moment before standing up, her long brown hair bouncing as she moves with more than a little frustration in her body language. "Fine. But we're not doing *A Haunting Wonderland. Devil May Care* is more how I'm feeling right now."

Terry chuckles. "As Princess Seraphina commands."

She glares at him, the same look she gives me so often, and now I know where she learned it. That's her Princess Seraphina look, and I will never let her live it down.

That doesn't stop them from starting the song. I guess they realized that if they wait too long, she'll back out of it. Jared, the bassist, starts in low and slow for the intro, and Sera's body is moving with the beat.

I don't particularly remember this song. It's been a long time since I listened to them, and several of the albums are a little blurry in my head.

The drum beat picks up, breaking the bass's rhythm, and Sera and Terry begin to sing. "Broke down, wore out, with the world on your shoulders," they sing in harmony. Him going low, and her going a little higher than normal.

It's beautiful to watch them sing together. There's no doubt they've done this too many times to count. What would it be like to have a dad who spent his life having fun like this? She spent her summers on tour with the hottest rock band on the planet. She probably had more wild adventures before she could drive than I've had in my entire life.

And I'm the one who was born with the silver spoon.

It puts things into a different perspective. Almost like my whole idea of trying to get my brothers to see me as an equal instead of their little brother might be a little pointless. Why would I devote myself to doing all of that when I could spend my days having fun?

Isn't that what Phillip figured out? But he didn't leave Loughton House. He's got a different perspective now, but he's still willing to do what it takes to win in business. He's still focused on making sure that Loughton House never gets swallowed up by all the little upstarts and changes in the market.

But why? Terry and Sera seem like they could do this all day long and never tire of it. But she didn't decide she wanted to be a rock princess. She went into the business world just like me.

Why?

The song continues on; the beat alternates between a fast-paced chorus and slower verses. Terry seems to dominate the verses, but Sera nearly screams out the chorus. All the band members are grinning at her. It's not like they have to pay attention to what they're doing. They've played these same songs over and over again for the last ten years.

No, today, they're having fun with their adopted niece.

She's theirs. And they're having fun playing with her, no different than when she was seven.

A part of me wants to be upset, to be jealous of Sera for this strange family she has, but I really can't. It's too wholesome. The same people that I'd always imagined being hardcore partiers are the people who spent their summers taking care of a little girl, so her dad never had to miss time with her.

It makes me smile to see the entire group like this, and when the song ends, Sera puts the mic back on the stand and walks over to her seat next to me. "Happy?" she asks.

I give her a little chuckle. "Yep. Now it's time I hear you play the bass. That's what your dad said, right?"

"You can go fuck yourself, buddy. That's not going to happen." She turns to the group of guys and says, "How about we take a break and have a few more beers? We can talk about your last tour or something. But I didn't bring Andrew here to force him to listen to a bunch of old music. We were supposed to drink and have fun."

There's some muttering from the group, but when she looks back at me, she's smirking. Like she's somehow caught me in a trick. Little does she know, I'm ready now. I've had time to understand the group dynamics.

And truthfully, I think that it's important for me to have seen this. It's one of the things that you never see in someone's files. Their parents and everything that pushed them to grow into the man or woman they've become.

Terry takes charge when the band acts a little disgruntled about calling the jam session after only two songs. "We can come back in a bit after we've had some drinks and talked. We can play anytime, but Seraphina doesn't come by every day."

There's some huffing and puffing, but everyone puts down their instruments. Sera whispers to me, "I hope you aren't scared of a little poker."

"Poker?" I whisper back.

She just smiles and walks out of the studio. This fucking girl…

Twenty-Three

SERA

I GROAN AS I TRY TO OPEN MY EYES. THEY'RE SORE. Why are my eyes sore? I look up at the ceiling and don't recognize it. White plaster that's been painted with fleur-de-lis, it reminds me of a European church.

"Morning, Princess," a voice says from beside me. I don't recognize the rough and gravelly voice, and I nearly fall out of bed trying to get away from it.

"Who the fuck…" I pause as I see who was talking to me. Andrew is in bed with me in a room I don't recognize, and his shirt is off. "What the hell are you doing in bed with me?"

He chuckles and runs his hand through his chestnut brown hair, making it stick up. Nothing at all like it normally is. "You had a few too many drinks last night."

I glare at him. What the hell happened? I remember singing with Dad at like two in the afternoon. Then he pulled out the poker chips. And the tequila…

Oh jeez. I look down and realize that I'm wearing a shirt at least. Not mine, and I'm not entirely sure whether that's better or worse than no shirt. But I don't think I have bottoms on. I have to run my hand down and realize I'm still wearing my thong. At least there's that.

"Are we still at my dad's?" I ask, trying to get my bearings. It's been so long since I drank with my dad and his friends. I think the last time was when I turned twenty-one. I've become a lightweight, and they have not.

He nods and gets out of bed. He's wearing a pair of boxer briefs and is not at all worried about me seeing them. It seems a little strange until a terrible possibility crosses my mind. Oh my God. "Umm… did we…?"

Andrew chuckles and shakes his head. "No, but not for your lack of trying. Sera, you might need to remember that tequila should never be drank straight from the bottle. Ever."

What did I do? I'd thought that Dad would push Andrew to drink too much, but I never thought I'd be the one to black out. Even on my twenty-first birthday, I maintained some amount of sanity. I'm my father's daughter, and I never lose control. But since I started at Loughton House… I only drink occasionally, and never more than a few. I'm not the same girl that they all remember. I've changed.

"But don't worry, Princess Seraphina, I did not—what'd you call it? Oh right, I did not spend the night giving you my big fat worm. I'm guessing it had something to do with the fact you couldn't find the worm in the tequila bottle. And for the record, I do not appreciate that terminology. Not one bit."

He grins and looks down at me sitting on the floor beside the bed. "What?" I ask as he grins. "Did someone draw a dick on my face?"

"No. I never got to see you the morning after that Christmas party, and I always wondered what you'd be like."

I haven't thought about that night nearly as much as I'd expected since we came to London. We've been too busy. Now it's different. He's standing there in only a pair of boxer briefs. His muscles are on full display. The outline of his cock is *very* noticeable, exactly like when we were on stage together.

He chuckles and walks to the bathroom. "I think I understand you a little better now, Princess." He closes the door behind him, and I try to jump to my feet, but the hangover hits hard, and my body doesn't do what it's supposed to do.

I end up falling onto the bed, face first into the white duvet, after I trip on the sheet I'd wrapped around myself. Trying to hurry, I stand up and look around the room for my clothes. I can't remember where I put them, and when I bend over to shake out the blanket, that's when the door to the bathroom opens, and Andrew walks into the room.

"Now that's a view I could get used to," he says.

"Andrew Loughton, go back into that bathroom so I can get dressed." The knowledge that I tried to get into Andrew's pants last night mixed with a terrible hangover and the fact that I have no real understanding of what happened has me very short-tempered. I need clothes, coffee, and food, in that order.

He doesn't say anything as he goes back into the bathroom and shuts the door behind him. Where the hell are my clothes? I get on my hands and knees and look under the bed, but there's nothing under there. They're not on any surfaces. Are they in a drawer?

Did I leave them somewhere else in the house? Did the whole band see me take off my skirt? I feel like I'm going to be sick thinking about that. I'm a grown woman, and my dad's always been very accepting of "having fun" as long as I'm safe, but that's too far.

"Are you looking for your clothes?" Andrew says from the bathroom.

"Yes! Do you know where they are?"

The door opens a crack, and he slides them through. "Thank you," I say and breathe a sigh of relief. I look down at them as I pick them up. Neatly folded, something I doubt I did last night. It makes me pause for a second, and then I push it to the back of my mind. There will be time to figure out what happened last night when I am dressed, have coffee in me, and am eating something greasy.

I get dressed as fast as I can, still not knowing where the hell that shirt came from. "You can come out now," I say, and Andrew steps out of the bathroom wearing his suit as though we were going to go to the office.

"Thank you again," I say, and he gives me a grin.

"Your dad texted me earlier to let me know he was leaving for most of the day. Coffee's in the pot, and there are eggs and bacon in the fridge if you want some food."

Why did Dad text Andrew instead of me?

"Food would be good. Coffee would be better."

Andrew nods and opens the door. I follow him as he leads me to the kitchen. My dad moved to London after I went away to college, and I've never been here. I guess Andrew knows the place better than I do, and when he reaches into a cabinet to pull two mugs out, it surprises me.

"What do you want in your coffee?" When we first woke up, he was making a real show of picking on me, but now he's being quiet, which I'm thankful for. But why? I'd assumed that he would keep up the jokes all day long.

"Just coffee. No need to complicate things."

"I think today's a no complication kind of day," he agrees. I doubt that's true. Losing control and acting like a drunken idiot always comes with repercussions. And those repercussions almost always end with complications.

He hands me my mug and sits across from me at the island. The swivel barstools remind me of the ones he had when I was a kid. He always talked about how a barstool was the best coffee spot because you could turn to talk to anyone else, and you didn't have to turn your head.

"Do you remember anything at all from last night?" he asks after he takes a sip.

I shake my head, and I immediately regret it. "Brief flashes. I remember Barry telling me I couldn't reach the bottle of tequila since it was on the top of the fridge and pushed against the wall. He thought I was too short, so I climbed on the counter to reach it."

Andrew nods, a half-smile on his lips. "You don't remember falling, though?"

"Falling? Nothing hurts…"

He chuckles. "That's because I caught you."

Typical. "Well, thank you for saving the idiot drunk girl." I take a sip of the coffee and relish the hot bitterness as it burns away the taste of last night. "How bad was it? Really?"

He shrugs. "You're a different kind of girl, Sera. You were probably one hell of a party in college. I thought that our little Christmas party adventure was about as crazy as you got, but I must have been wrong. I assume you get it from your dad?"

"That's what Mom says." I don't know how many times she told me that after hearing about what I'd done. She also always said that I got my survival instincts from him. "It always works out, though," I continue. "I need to know. Why did I wake up in a shirt that wasn't mine?"

It takes Andrew a moment to answer as he sips the coffee. The sunlight streams in from the garden windows, illuminating little motes of dust in the air. They drift through the air completely unfettered, with no purpose or direction.

"Your dad suggested you might want it instead of a stuffy suit to sleep in. He was right. As soon as you walked into the guest bedroom, you started complaining about how trapped you were. I never expected the lead singer of Sweet Delusions to be such a smart guy."

I do hate feeling trapped once I've had a few drinks in me. Maybe I always hate that feeling, but it's unbearable after I've been drinking. "So I didn't end up embarrassing myself too much?"

"Not in front of your dad and his friends. Just in front of me, but that's okay. I won't hold it against you. Though, if you ever call it a big fat worm again, we might have to rethink this whole living situation."

Now it's my turn to grin. "Well, thank you for not… You know."

"No problem. We've all been there." He looks very thoughtful this morning, not at all his normal self. It's like he's thinking hard about something.

"What's going on in that head of yours?" I finally ask, breaking the silence.

He shrugs. "I don't know. Yesterday was a weird day. Last night was weird in a different way. It was all fun, don't get me wrong, but it makes me think that maybe I need to re-evaluate some things in my life."

I don't know what he's talking about, so I settle into the silence. The only sound in the room is the soft sipping of hot coffee. Finally, Andrew sets his mug on the island and stands up. "How do you like your eggs?" he asks.

I arch an eyebrow at him. "You cook?"

"All the time. Okay, not all the time, but occasionally when I'm not working fourteen-hour days."

He gives me a grin and starts looking in the cabinets for a pan. "I'll eat eggs and bacon however you want to cook them. Though, I'd rather that we weren't here when my dad gets back. I think that conversation would be better over the phone instead of in person, if you know what I mean."

He chuckles and stands up. "I guess we're eating breakfast somewhere else?"

"I think that'd be better." The thought of talking to Dad about how badly I lost control last night is not a conversation I want to have with Andrew here.

He shrugs. "Your family, your call. We'll catch a cab since my driver has the day off on Sundays, and I don't want to deal with finding someone else."

Yes. Escaping this catastrophe as fast as possible sounds like an excellent idea right now. Some greasy eggs and bacon and maybe a blueberry scone at a diner. Then a shower and maybe a nap. That sounds like a wonderful way to recover from last night.

"I think that's a brilliant plan." I give Andrew a big smile, but the one he returns isn't quite as bright as normal. What the hell happened last night?

Twenty-Four

ANDREW

"STOP FIGHTING IT, ANDREW. YOU'RE BEING AN IDIOT, and we both know that night was the best one either of us has had in years. That's why you brought me to London. That's why you're spending all this time with me. Why wouldn't we repeat that night every night?"

Her words echo in my mind as the taxi flies down the street. I remember everything that happened last night, and though everyone knew she was drunk, it was fun until she decided it was time to go to sleep. Then it got… confusing.

Because she's right. I kept that stupid hat to look at when I wanted to think about the best night I can remember. The sex was amazing. She was amazing. Everything about that night is burned into my mind, and last night only reminded me how much I enjoy her when she's like that. When she's completely carefree.

That's what being drunk with her is. The side of her that's obviously been influenced by her dad is out in the open. Wild and ready to have fun. Damn the consequences. The same crazy girl I got on a stage with.

She's a fucking employee, though. An employee that I need to be focused on her job. I have goals and plans that she could ruin if something happened between us. As long as everything stays strictly business, then there's no chance that she'll get sidetracked or pissed enough that my plans get ruined.

That's all they are. Plans. I haven't made a move yet, haven't had time between training Sera and starting the Vanguard expansion.

After yesterday, I'm not even sure if I want to follow through with those plans, though. After seeing her and her dad together, just playing and having fun. Seeing what it would be like to have a past that's built on laughter and smiles instead of work was eye-opening in a way nothing else has ever been.

I'd thought Phillip was crazy when he walked away from the family business for a month. Now I understand. He eventually came back, but that time away changed him in some amazing ways. He, and the business, are better for it. Should I step away? No, I don't think so. I had fun in college. I had plenty of time being wild and crazy, though I doubt it was anything like Sera's.

"How bad is the hangover?" I ask.

She grimaces. "Like I got hit by a truck. I think my eyelids are bruised."

"What you need to do is eat some breakfast and sweat it out. Hot tub, sauna, or a long run."

The look she gives me makes me consider asking the cab driver for a bag. "Addendum. I will not consider any form of exercise currently."

"Well, that leaves the hot tub or sauna. A bottle of Gatorade or six and a lot of sweating will fix you right up."

The cab pulls onto a side street as our destination comes into view. A classic American diner in London. No British food to be found. Just good old eggs, bacon, sausage, hash browns, and pancakes. Maybe some waffles.

Sure, we could have gone to a place where it's fifty dollars a plate, but truthfully, when you're hungover and look as rough as you feel, nothing beats some cheap diner food.

"I can smell it already," Sera says with a grin. "Salt and grease. That's my love language right now."

"You and me, both." When we get out of the cab, she leads the way into the diner, and I can't help but look at her ass in that tight skirt. How many times did I have to cover her up again last night? How many times did I look at that thong and have to turn away? My dick is still hard thinking about it.

Everything about last night makes me want her. It was a reminder of what it'd be like to be more than coworkers. I've done my best not to let things go beyond professional, but there was nothing about last night that was professional, even discounting our lack of clothes this morning. Why couldn't we have fun at least some of the time? Why couldn't we enjoy ourselves while still getting our work done? Am I really so scared of losing a little control? It eats at me, and I know that every ounce of logic is getting lost.

When we sit down, my mind is still trying to deal with the way I'm being torn. I've ignored the way I felt ever since I convinced her to come to London. I'd been able to forget that Christmas party and the freedom I'd felt. The whole reason I'd stolen that stupid elf hat. I'd been focused.

Now? Now I want to take her back to the penthouse and throw her bed out the window. I don't want to go to work tomorrow. I want to spend weeks getting to know every inch of her body.

"A dip in the hot tub is the answer," she says, breaking me out of my thoughts. "Saunas are nice, but relaxing in a hot tub sounds like heaven right now."

Instantly, I think of her in a bikini. That's not something I should do when I'm trying to get control of myself. "Oh, yeah?" I don't know why I suggested either of those to her to begin with. I should have said a nap or long walk or literally anything other than "let's take off our clothes".

She picks up a menu and says, "Doesn't the penthouse have a hot tub as an amenity?"

There's no way to get around the topic now. "It does. Actually, it's a private hot tub that has to be reserved."

"Reserve it for an hour, then." I'd have thought that she was being commanding, but the corner of her lip curls up, and for a moment, my mind goes to the possibility of her *not* wearing a bikini. Which is the opposite of what I need right now. Those tits and ass... That tight little waist.

Fuck.

"I'll reserve it for you," I say as I pull my phone out of my pocket. "I think I'll take a nap instead."

For a second, her smirk fades into a frown before she shakes her head. "Nope. You're coming with me. I may be hungover, but I feel refreshed. Tonight, I'm going to have real questions for you, and I want you to be as refreshed as I am."

Why's she doing this? Why's she pushing me to get in the hot tub with her?

A nice soak sounds wonderful. I may not be feeling as bad as her, but it'd be nice to get rid of this pounding headache. The only reason I *wouldn't* go is because my resolve to keep this strictly business is cracking. It seems like she's doing it on purpose at this point. Doesn't she realize how terrible that could turn out?

"Fine," I say and call the front desk to reserve the room. Our waitress brings our plates, gives us a smile, and lets us eat our food.

Salt and grease are exactly what I'd wanted, and judging by how Sera is focused on her food, I guess she feels the same. The table is quiet as we eat, both of us focused on the thing that's making us feel better. It's been a long time since I got that drunk. Sera wasn't joking about how much her dad and his friends would drink. I guess I should have expected that from professional rock stars, though.

When Sera scrapes the last bit of eggs and hash browns into her mouth, she leans back in the booth with a smile. "I almost feel human again." She pauses for a moment as she watches me finish the last of my plate. "Did you have fun last night?"

I chuckle and use the paper napkin to wipe my mouth before answering. "It was not what I'm used to. That's for sure. And I don't think I'll ever forget getting to see Sweet Delusions play. They were my favorite band in my early teen years. I don't know if I'd call it 'fun', though. More like stressful. You were a bit of a handful, and your dad asked a lot of uncomfortable questions as the night went on."

Are you really only working together? I see the way you both look at each other. You don't take your eyes off her, and she looks to you every time there's a question…

That was the beginning of the questions. I can't even remember half of them, but every one was more and more pointed. Not like Terry was trying to be threatening or even trying to protect his daughter. When she told me there was no way in hell I was sleeping on the couch, he raised an eyebrow but didn't seem fazed at all. He simply wanted to understand things.

Luckily, I was taught by the best on how to evade questions. A little truth here and there to satisfy the questioner, and then a few jokes. Terry might be able to out drink an elephant, but he's probably not used to someone so used to protecting his weaknesses even after too many shots.

"That's too bad. They really are fun to spend time with. I guess we all got a little carried away, though. I kind of forget how normal it is for them to drink a bottle or two when they get together. Someday, his liver's going to give out on him."

I chuckle and say, "Well, I'm not worried about his liver right now. I think that maybe he's immune to alcohol at this point, and it's us that have to be worried."

She grins and nods. "Very possible."

There's a new tension between us. A strangeness where our conversation sputters out when it never has before. It could be the hangovers, but it could be something else. Maybe she *does* remember things from last night. I know I can't stop thinking about it.

The waitress comes with the check, and I pay it so we can leave. As we walk across the cobblestone sidewalk, her heel catches in a crack. Her momentum carries her forward, and my body reacts instinctively. Like last night. Reaching out with one arm, I catch her, but it's awkward. The muscle in my shoulder strains at an angle that's completely wrong.

Sera grips my arm, and though her weight is only there for a moment while she gets her balance, I know it's more than that muscle is used to. "Fuck," I mutter under my breath as pain shoots through my shoulder.

I don't pay it any attention, though, and help Sera stabilize. "Are you okay?" I ask.

She nods and uses me to step backward so she can get her heel out of the crack. "Well, that's a first. I don't know how you moved so fast. You're like a ninja or something."

There's only one way that I could have caught her. Like Terry said, I don't take my eyes off her. Even when I probably should be focused on other things. It's not like I've been doing it on purpose. It's almost instinctual. Like my eyes are drawn to her, and it didn't start when we came to London. No, from the very beginning, my attention has always been partly on her anytime we're together.

"I don't think ninjas would pull a muscle catching a damsel in distress, so I'm not quite there yet," I say with a grin. I roll my shoulder and hear the soft clicking.

Sera frowns, but it goes away almost instantly. "Well, it's a good thing we're getting in the hot tub, right?"

"I guess so," I say, rolling it some more. If only the hot tub was as simple as it sounds. No complications. No feelings. Just slowly cooking in a concrete pot until the hangover and headache are gone.

As Sera waves down the cab, I can't help but recognize the fact that there's never going to be simple with her again. That we've managed to have a strictly business relationship until now is kind of crazy to begin with, and I think it's because we've never had time to slow down.

But now that I've had that moment to breathe, I know that nothing's going to be the same.

Strangely enough, I don't think I'd change anything even if I could.

Twenty-Five

SERA

My body is throbbing as I walk into the private hot tub area wearing only a bikini. Nothing risqué at all about it, but I don't think I've felt this exposed in my entire life. It took me a while to start remembering things from last night.

It was all fun and games until I climbed on that counter. The flashes of memory seem to surround that moment when my foot slipped. I immediately looked to my dad, like I'd have done when I was a kid.

But it wasn't his hands that caught me. It was Andrew. Just like today when I nearly fell outside that diner.

After that fall from the counter, when he had his hands on me, I remembered what it was like at the Christmas party. The way his hands had felt on my bare skin. It's embarrassing now to think about how I'd acted around him last night, but I'm not ashamed of the feelings that are rising inside me.

I grew up as a rock star's kid. I've seen parties since I went on a tour with them for the first time. And no one catches falling drunk girls. They just fall. They hit their heads, and everybody laughs. But Andrew caught me.

How is it that everything seems to have changed since that moment? How can one stupid mistake have changed my thoughts about my boss?

I know that I'm about to walk into a hot tub that could very quickly turn into our first tumble in the sheets in almost four years. I know that it's going to complicate everything from here on. It could ruin my chances of learning everything he has to teach me. I may never know enough to start my own publishing house now.

But I am not my mom. I can't be completely focused on my career. I have to live a little, have to experience the things that make life worth living. And Andrew is one of those experiences.

I walk down the steps into the bubbling water and sigh. Well, regardless of what else happens, at least this is going to help with the hangover.

Leaning back against the concrete, my messy bun is like a pillow. I close my eyes and put my arms on the edge. It's like every drop of sweat that pours from my body is taking a little of the poison I filled my body with last night.

"You look comfortable," Andrew says as he steps into the pool. I look up at him, see his naked chest, the hard muscles that make it hard to believe he's anything but a model. "All you need is an oversized pair of dark sunglasses, and you'd look like you belonged on some Hollywood set."

I grin at him, but it's hard to take my eyes off his body. "Is that a good or bad thing?"

"I'd say good. After this week, we both need some relaxing. I'm glad you pushed me to join you instead of taking a nap. Though I might still take one after this."

The image of him getting out of bed and stretching in nothing but that pair of boxer briefs flashes through my mind. Fuck, he looked good. He still looks good.

"So, what's up with you taking off your pants last night?"

Andrew leans against the opposite wall and sighs. "I hate sleeping in pants. It's not like you haven't seen me naked before, so I didn't think it was a big deal. Plus, what's the difference between boxers and shorts?"

Nothing except that I could nearly see his cock through those boxers. Not exactly typical boss-employee relations. I guess sleeping in a t-shirt and thong isn't either, though. "Well, it scared the shit out of me."

"I could tell. It's not every day that a girl falls out of bed when she sees me next to her." He grins and I catch his gaze go down to my half-submerged breasts.

I have another flash of last night.

"You're too drunk," he whispered, his breath hot on my neck. His hands grip my waist, tight enough to hurt. Tight enough to send lightning through my whole body.

His gaze drifted down to my blouse, the silk pressed tight against my breasts. "Maybe another time, but not tonight."

I remember what it felt to have his lips that close to my skin. The way his breath tickled me and made me quiver at the same time. The way my entire body was desperate for him.

"What are we going to do?" I whisper, not talking to Andrew. I need to say the words out loud, to finally vocalize the question that's never been asked.

"What do you mean? We're going to relax and recover so we can go to work tomorrow."

I shake my head ever so gently. "Andrew, you know what I mean. You remember last night."

He turns his head to look past me and sighs. "You remember?"

"Yes. Not everything, but enough."

He shrugs and stares at the brick wall behind me. It's the same look he's had all morning, the same seriousness that I didn't understand before.

I stand up. I know that there are two options. One, I can either try my damnedest to forget about every bit of lust I've had for him, to ignore every image I've had of his naked body, and I can try to be the professional businesswoman that my mom would applaud. Or two, I can mix business and pleasure. I'm not naïve enough to think that people fall in love and get married and have happily ever afters.

But why am I fighting a good time? Why am I turning away from repeats of that Christmas party?

I know why Andrew isn't. He needs me to do a good job and stay focused. He needs to use me. But I need him just as much. We're using each other for business. Why can't we use each other for fun as well?

Andrew's eyes run over my body, and I already know what he's thinking. I can see the lust in his eyes. It's brazen, not turning away or hiding the fact that he wants me like he has every other time I've caught him staring.

"What do you want, Andrew? I'm not asking what we *should* do. I'm asking what you *want* to do."

He huffs, and his eyes return to meet my gaze. "You know what I want, Sera. The same thing I wanted the moment I saw you. To rip the clothes off you. To make you scream my name in the middle of the night. Or the middle of the day."

It's my turn to grin now. "Then why haven't you done it already? I didn't drag you to the hot tub to spend quality time with you."

His expression hardens. There's a battle going on inside him between lust and logic, and I know which is going to win.

I take a step toward him, the water running down my nearly naked body in little rivers. I'm only inches away from his legs. He stands up slowly, that expression never changing. "Last night was a mistake," he growls. His body is so close to mine that I doubt the water below me is as hot as the air between us.

"Was it?" I whisper back, and my lips move closer to his neck like his did last night. I can smell him. The same cologne as he wore the night we were together. The same scent that I woke up to this morning.

"We have important things to do, Sera." His hand moves as fast as lightning, gripping my jaw between his thumb and index finger. He turns my head to look at him, moving me away from his skin. "We can't let our emotions get involved when we're already short on time."

"I never said anything about emotions. I don't want your fucking emotions, Andrew. I need your brain for work, and I need your body for fun. Fuck your heart."

His jaw tightens so much that I swear I hear his teeth grind together. But then his other hand moves to my waist, just as tight as last night. His fingers grip bare skin. "Is that really what you want?" he asks.

"Yes." The word leaves me as a whisper.

He stares into my eyes for a moment before he finally lets go of my jaw, his hand moving to my breast as he kisses me. I don't think I've ever been kissed this hard. I've never felt a man need me this badly.

And I drown in it. It was inevitable from the beginning. Like taking the chains off that had been holding me back for so long. My hands find his back, his naked skin against my fingers, and I hold on for dear life.

The hand holding my breast moves, slipping under the flimsy piece of cloth, and the hand on my waist pulls me to him. I don't put up any resistance. This is what I've craved since the very beginning, since the time I saw him in the bar. Whether I knew it or not, there's no doubt now.

Andrew Loughton is the only man I've ever fantasized about, and there's no way in hell I'd ever have been able to hold myself back.

His kiss moves to my neck, and there is nothing soft about it. I look up at the ceiling and revel in the sensations. The sharp bite of his lips on my skin. That ache in my breast and hip. The way my body throbs in time to my heartbeat, which is racing.

"I should have done this as soon as I came back to New York," he hisses.

"Yes." No other words are necessary.

I've had so many questions and worries and doubts about my desires, but they fade under his touch. My hand moves to the back of his head, pulling it lower toward my untouched breast, but he resists, finally pulling his mouth away from my body.

"No. Not here," he says through heavy breaths. "Not the first time."

This time, it's my jaw that tightens. I don't want to wait. I can't give him a chance to think. I need him, and he certainly needs me.

"Fine…"

When I look at him, he's still breathing hard, and I realize that, unlike me, he's still clinging to some bit of control. His body is shaking ever so slightly. "You're too fucking tempting," he says.

"As if you were any less?" I respond as he finally takes his hands off me. Then he seems to think better of it and pulls my bikini down to cover my breast.

"I hope you're ready to moan my name all night," he says.

I smirk and walk out of the hot tub. His eyes are on my ass, and I sway my hips a little extra. "Are you just going to tease me, or are you coming?"

Twenty-Six

ANDREW

WHY DID I WAIT SO FUCKING LONG TO KISS HER? LIKE my fantasies have become my reality, my hands slip under her bikini to grip her ass in the elevator. My lips press against hers, and her hand runs through my hair, tightening in it as her nails scratch my scalp.

I breathe her in, the taste of her lips, the scent of her skin. I need her. I need to touch, to hold, to consume her. "That feels so good," she whispers as my fingers dig into her ass even harder.

The elevator dings, and the door opens to my penthouse, but we don't move. Our entwined bodies are like people starving, and the only nourishment they can find is the other's touch. Until the door shakes again as it begins to close. I lift Sera into the air, her legs wrapping around my waist, and stick my foot out to keep the elevator from closing.

I let out a moan as she kisses down my neck. My cock is straining at my shorts, and every time Sera moves, she grinds against me. I dig my keys out of my pocket and in a moment, we're inside. She never even thinks about what's happening around her. Everything revolves around her lips on mine, her body pressed against me.

And I want to feel the same. I want to forget the world for once. As the door slams shut, I begin to let go, to focus on the sensations that are coursing through me. I drop the keys on the ground and run my hand through her hair as I hold her up with the other. My fingers tighten in the sandy brown hair, and my lips go to the crook of her neck, kissing even harder than before.

She lets out a moan as I pull her hair back. Her eyes are wide open and staring at me as I lay her down on my bed. God, she's fucking beautiful. Every fiber of my being wants to do exactly as I'd said. To rip her clothes off her body, but I have to pause for a moment to stare at her. I've fantasized about this moment for far too long not to bask in it.

But the urge to see her naked body again is too much, and with both hands, I grip the tiny piece of fabric holding the bikini top together. Sera gives me a confused look, and then I pull it apart. The little piece of fabric tears in two, and I reveal both of her breasts at the same time.

She shivers under me, and after only a glance at her breasts, I move my hands to the bikini bottoms. I pull on the string, and the knot comes undone. Then I untie the other side and reveal her pussy. She's watching me, her chest rising and falling faster than before. I press my palm against her swollen lips and let my eyes run over her body.

She gasps as a finger slips between her lips. "You're fucking gorgeous, you know that, right?" I ask.

A smile appears, but as my finger finds its way inside her, the only answer she gives me is a moan. "I could play with your body all night long. I *want* to play with you all night long. You have no idea how desperate I've been for you."

I'm talking, but it's not really directed at Sera. The words need to be said. I need to make it real. All my desires and emotions have warred with logic since Sera came back into my life, and those words cement the fact that I'm choosing her over logic.

She runs her hand over my chest and up my shoulder until she's squeezing my neck ever so softly. But it's enough to break my trance. It's enough to remember that my cock's straining at my shorts, that she's desperate for more than a finger, and that I haven't just fantasized about *seeing* her.

I'm leaning over her, but now I stand up. In a moment, my shorts are on the ground, and I'm naked. She licks her lips, and her hand moves between her legs, her fingers spreading those beautiful lips. Her fingertip taps her clit, and my cock gets even harder.

Part of me wants to dig a condom out of the nightstand and start fucking her immediately. I know that will be a short-lived experience after how badly I've wanted this. Instead, I run my hands under Sera's ass and slide her to the edge of the bed. Before she can hang her legs over, I spread them and kneel between them, letting them rest on my shoulders, her wet little pussy right in front of my face.

As soon as my tongue slides between her lips, her legs are quivering around my neck, pulling me tighter. "Oh fuck," she groans. "I…" Whatever comes after is garbled as another loud moan fills the room.

She tastes so fucking good, like her scent has been distilled and turned into liquid. I could drink it forever, and for a moment, I consider never leaving this spot. My fingers wrap around her hips where her bikini bottoms were tied. My thumb finds that little indention between her hips and the beginning of her mound, and my tongue finds her clit. Each flick of my tongue makes her body tense, and I'm barely teasing her.

And then I move lower. My tongue finds her entrance and makes circles around it before finally pushing inside. She goes crazy, and I pull her body to me. I breathe her in, and the world around me fades. Just like she was lost in our kisses, I'm lost in her scent and taste.

"That's it. Oh my fucking god," she moans. My right hand releases her hip and moves to her breast, my thumb and index finger finding her nipple, and they squeeze it ever so slightly while the rest of my hand tightens around the rest of her tit. Soft and full, I want to squeeze harder, to use her tits like handholds while I fuck her.

To make her scream while I stretch this little pussy out.

"I'm going to…" she mutters as I tongue-fuck her. In and out, in and out. Then I move back to her clit, and her body convulses hard enough that I have to hold her down if I want to keep licking her. And I definitely want to keep licking her.

She's panting as the orgasm recedes, but she manages to say, "No. I want your cock, not your tongue."

I've thought back on that Christmas party so many fucking times, but none of those memories or fantasies compared to this, and I haven't even been inside her yet. Her legs release me, and I stand up. Her eyes don't leave my body as I turn to my nightstand.

"Not yet," she says, and I hear her shift on the bed. When I turn to look at her, she's getting off the bed. And getting on her knees. "Give me the condom," she says with a grin. "And I'll make sure it's on before you're inside me. But first, I want a chance to play, too."

My hand moves without me looking at it. I'm staring at the woman I've lusted over for weeks as she kneels in front of me. I grab a condom and take a step toward her. Her lips are barely parted, and her tongue slips out as she licks them. "Condom?" she says as she puts her hand out.

I don't hesitate to put the foil package in her hand and take a step forward. My fantasies were based on memories, but her lips never came close to my cock that night. I don't have a memory to think about.

But now…

She drops the condom and wraps her hands around my ass. I bend my knees a little as she maneuvers her mouth to take my cock in it. As soon as her lips envelop the tip, I know this is going to be something different. She looks up at me as she slowly pushes herself down the length. Her tongue slides along the bottom, and there's resistance at the back of her throat.

Then it's gone, and she keeps swallowing my cock. A shiver runs through me. No, not a shiver. My body shakes as lightning courses through me. My hands grip her hair as tightly as when I was kissing her, and it's like she doesn't even notice.

Her hands grab my ass, and she bobs her head as her throat massages my cock. There's no way I'm going to last long with her doing this. I'm struggling to maintain any control as I watch her perform magic tricks on my dick.

The whole time, she keeps staring up at me. Her hands run up to my lower back as she finally pulls her mouth off me. She catches her breath for a few moments as she grins. "Fuck, Sera…" I mutter, and then she runs her tongue along the bottom of my cock.

I'd thought I was desperate for her earlier. I'd thought that nothing in the world could make me want to be inside her more. Seeing her on her knees like this after having nearly my entire cock down her throat is like the only aphrodisiac that's ever made sense. I was so very wrong.

She lets go of me and picks up the condom wrapper. "I hope you haven't forgotten how to use that thing," she says as she rips the foil package. "You don't have any idea how many times I've played with myself thinking about you fucking me."

"I haven't forgotten." She rolls the condom down my cock, something I've never experienced a woman do before, and then she stands up and gets on the bed.

"Then come show me."

Twenty-Seven

SERA

THE TASTE OF HIS COCK IS ON MY LIPS. MY BODY'S thrumming with need as I lay down on the bed, legs spread wide and pussy soaking. It's a good thing he let me swallow his cock, or I'd be screaming. After he made me come with his mouth, I would have been far too sensitive to have him fucking me.

But now, it's all I can think of.

My fingers find my clit, and I make lazy little circles over the sensitive bud while he positions himself between my legs. Flashes of our first time together run through my mind. How he moves me from one position to the next. How each thrust he made only brought me higher.

The way I screamed his name hours after meeting him.

He kneels between my legs with his knees on the bed. For a moment, I wonder if he's even going to fuck me. Leaning forward, he runs his hand down my cheek until he gets to my neck. When his fingers trace the lines of my collarbone, I shiver. His hand is so big, so strong. He could wrap those fingers around my throat and hold me still while he did whatever he wanted.

But he doesn't. He puts his other hand on my hip and lifts me, his gaze never moving away from my eyes. Then his cock slides inside me. It's so much bigger than I remember. My body tightens as he pushes past any resistance. "You fit me," he whispers. "Perfect."

He bottoms out, and his balls press against me, a shiver running through me. Perfect. As though we were made for each other.

"You're too big," I whisper.

A tremor runs through my body as he says, "No, I'm not." The certainty.

He's right. When he starts to move in and out of me, there's no doubt how right he is. I'd felt consumed by him when we'd gotten to the penthouse. Like everything else had faded.

But this is more. Like there's a curtain around us, draped over us and blocking out anything else. My mind can't comprehend the world beyond his body and mine. His lips find my breast while his hands move over my body, claiming it with every touch. "God, you feel so fucking good."

Every thrust is like heaven, and when his teeth press against my skin, pure ecstasy races through me. Already, pressure is building inside me. I run my hands over his back, my nails leaving white lines in their wake, and up to his neck. When they reach his hair, I pull a little, nothing like what he's done to me.

A fire lights up in his eyes. His hand grips my breast harder, and he snarls as he thrusts. Like I'm pushing the gas pedal down. I pull on his hair even more. He resists, his other hand moving to my breast as he glares down at me.

And I know I'm not staring into Andrew Loughton's eyes. It's something harder, something more primal. I don't let go of his hair as he does his best to fuck me hard enough to bruise me. It only makes me want more. His balls slap against me in time with my moans and whimpers.

I wouldn't change a thing, and when one of his hands moves from my breast to my hair, yanking it hard enough to hurt, I know that the dam holding back the pressure inside me is about to burst. My muscles are tensed from head to toe in anticipation.

Then he bends down and presses his lips to mine. His teeth take my lip in them, and it's too much. I scream out the orgasm that erupts inside me. Andrew inhales, sucking the scream from my lips along with the air.

He's consuming me. Everything I am. My pleasure. My pain.

And he growls in payment for those screams. His hands move back to my hips, and he lifts them in the air. My convulsing body tries to escape the lightning shooting through it, but he has a steel grip, and when he uses me, I know he was being gentle before.

He only ever hinted at this side of him. It only lasts for seconds as I constrict around him, but those seconds feel like days. Like I'm being electrocuted by pleasure, and I don't know if I should moan or scream. And in the end, I'm silent as I watch him.

He's covered in sweat. His muscles quiver with exertion, and gaze is locked on my naked body.

And then he groans. It's a sound I'll never forget, a sound that will forever make me feel calm and relaxed. And wanted.

He takes a slow, deep breath as he gently releases his grip on my hips. "Holy shit, Sera. That was…"

"Amazing? The best sex of your life? Yeah, I agree."

He opens his mouth to say something, and then he simply grins. "Yeah. That about covers it."

He's probably the hottest guy I've ever been with. "I guess you haven't forgotten how to use that thing," I say as he pulls out of me and stands up.

He turns around to toss the condom in the trash, and I get a good look at his ass. Yeah, I don't regret this one bit. I take a deep breath and lay back in bed. I'm still laying the wrong way, and I don't know exactly what will come next. What I don't expect is for him to straddle me.

"I can't believe we did that," he says, as though he doesn't notice me jerk in surprise. "You're a fucking temptress. You know that, right?"

I look up at him, but I can't help noticing the way his cock rests on my stomach. "I'm the temptress? You're the one who suggested we either get in a hot tub together or get naked in a sauna. Plus, I was drunk last night, so you can't blame me for being horny. You took off your shirt and pants and slept with me even though you *weren't* that drunk. I'd say you're the temptress."

He chuckles, and like it's not weird at all, leans forward, his hands going to my wrists and holding them down. I don't have to move to know that this is the same steel grip he had on my hips only a few minutes ago. He leans down until he's only inches from my ear, and says, "I'm glad you convinced me to."

His breath runs over me like a teaser of what we've just had… And what we might have many more times in the future.

"I'm glad you convinced me, too." He moves both of my wrists over my head and holds them with one hand. I feel more vulnerable right now than I've ever felt even though he just finished fucking me like an animal.

With his other hand, he brushes a few stray hairs away from my cheek. The weight of his body is resting on my wrists, pressing them deep into the comforter, and he's watching me as his hands move down my neck again.

"I like this," he says. "I enjoy having control of you." The feather-light grazes of his fingertips leave goosebumps in their wake as he wraps those fingers around my throat for a moment. "Have you ever let someone play with you like this before?" he asks.

His eyes don't follow his hands. Andrews not noticing the little trail of goosebumps or the way my nipples are as hard as diamonds. He can't tell that my pussy is already throbbing again, ready for another round. He keeps looking into my eyes as he talks.

"No," I say. It's the truth. I may have had some rough sex in the past, but I've never watched as a man explored my body like this. "But I like it." That's the understatement of the year.

My body is going crazy, and when I notice his cock is getting hard again, my body gets the memo. Everything inside me is ready for round two. Especially if he's like this.

"That's good." His voice is so low that if the entire penthouse wasn't so quiet, I don't know if I'd be able to hear him. "Because I think I'd like to do a little more of it. We're going to spend a lot of time together, so there's no reason we shouldn't make it a little more interesting."

That sends a shiver through me. What does that even mean? Sure, today's a day off, but what about tomorrow? Is he going to want to do things after fourteen-hour days at work?

The thought is crazy. Hell, he's running this entire branch, and we've been so freaking busy since the moment we arrived in London.

Yet, I can't deny how hot it sounds.

"What do you mean?" I ask. I need to know. My mind is going crazy thinking about what he could be thinking.

He grins and leans forward until his lips find my neck. God, I don't think my body's ever been this sensitive. His teeth brush the skin ever so gently, but it's like lightning shooting through me.

Then he sits back up, that grin still on his face, and he shrugs. "You'll just have to find out."

Okay, that's the most terrifying statement anyone could say. I try to pull my hands free, but he doesn't let go. "You expect me to go along with that? Would you go along with it?"

Instead of answering me, he lets go of my hands and lays down beside me. His hand moves just as fast as it goes to my pussy, and he slips a finger inside me before I have a chance to close my legs. "No, I wouldn't go along with it, but it doesn't turn *me* on. You're soaked, Sera, and it's not from the sex."

My jaw tightens, not wanting to admit that he's right. I don't want to accept that his finger inside me right now is nothing compared to the feeling of his hands holding my wrists down and his body forcing me to stay still.

I push his hand away from me and stand up. My eyes go to the wall in front of me, staring at the white plaster as I take a deep breath. "I don't know, Andrew," I say. Just this morning, I was kicking myself for even considering letting us move to something other than professional. Now he wants to do… what? Tie me up at work?

I don't hear him get up, but before I know it, his hands are on me. His hard cock is pressing against my lower back, and as his arms wrap around my arms, pinning them to my body, I can't stop the shiver that runs through me.

His voice tickles my neck as he says, "You can always tell me to stop, Sera. I only want to have a little fun. We can work hard and play harder." *Damn that phrase. And damn me for loving it.* One hand moves between my legs while the other holds my breast. "And if you ever want me to stop, I will. Say the word, and we'll go back to being coworkers."

Fuck. His arms tighten around mine, his muscles pinning my arms to my body. His fingers press against my skin. I know that if he wanted to hold me down and do what he wanted, he could. There's no way I could overpower him. And yet, somehow, I feel comfortable being held like this. I feel safe.

"I don't know." The entire idea is terrifying. But maybe he's right. Maybe we can have fun and work at the same time.

"Remember that you can say no anytime you want." He kisses my neck delicately, in drastic contrast to the amount of pressure he's putting on the rest of my body. I let out a little moan, and he says, "I'll take that as a yes."

Then he lets me go. All the pressure is gone in an instant, and I'm left feeling alone. I don't know how the hell I've gone from pushing him away to wishing he was holding me down in the past couple hours.

I can finally turn around, and I see Andrew walking to the bedroom door. "You coming?" he asks.

"Coming? Where are we going?"

"I need a snack. So, unless you want to miss one of the few times I cook, I suggest you come sit in the kitchen with me. Pretend I'm Luciano on a bad day."

I can't help but grin, but that feeling of being alone, of being vulnerable, doesn't go away. Something shifted inside me when he climbed on top of me and held my arms down. And when I look at Andrew, all I can think of is how he felt when he was playing with me. If someone had tried to explain it to me yesterday, I'd never have understood how anyone could get drawn to someone controlling them like this.

But that look in his eyes… That feeling of safety and vulnerability at the same time… Andrew got his hooks in, and now I don't know if I want them out.

Twenty-Eight

ANDREW

I'VE STRUGGLED TO BE FUNCTIONAL TODAY. SERA'S wearing very professional clothes as always. A cream skirt-suit, her hair up in a purposefully messy bun. If I didn't know any better, this would be another normal day at the office.

But I do know better.

Yesterday opened Pandora's box of desire, and there's no way I'm going to stuff it all back into the box unless Sera specifically tells me to stop. She's focused on her computer, going through my emails and doing her best to answer them. I'm reading what she writes and correcting word choices as she goes. This is week two, and already, I think she's going to handle the job.

"You can ignore the rest," I say. As usual, I prop my feet up on the desk, and my laptop is resting on my lap. "They're not important enough to deal with this morning."

She takes a deep breath and lets it out, finally relaxing after forty-five minutes of focused attention. "How'd I do?" she asks.

"Pretty good. If your job was to answer emails, then you'd have done flawlessly. But you're supposed to be me answering emails, and you still sound too much like yourself. Not enough humor. Not enough inside jokes. You'll get there, though."

She nods. There was no doubt that would be her struggle. We have very different personalities. "Okay, now what?"

"Now you take off your underwear," I say, as though it were any other task.

She blinks for a moment, and I see her body tense up. But then she relaxes. "Okay. Whatever you say, boss. Want me to take them off here or in the bathroom?"

The tension between us is so thick, you could cut it with a knife. I stare at her and wonder where exactly she's going to draw the line. Is she playing along, waiting until I try something more than a little tease? Or does she want me to do all the things I hinted at yesterday?

Then I see how fast her chest is rising and falling. Her heart's beating like crazy. She's nervous, but she's trying to play it cool. "Here's fine."

She glances at the blinds that I shut this morning when we came in. Then, after a deep breath, she stands up and reaches under her skirt. Bending over, she pulls her panties down and steps out of them. With no hesitation, she picks them up and tosses them to me. "I assume you want to keep them?" she asks after I catch them.

"Absolutely," I say with a grin.

"Anything else?" The look on her face says she expects more, but I don't want to give in this fast. I want her to simmer, wondering what's coming next. I want her to be a little nervous about how I'm going to add some more "fun" to our working environment.

"No, that's all. Now we can look at the earning statement on *Black Rabbit Run*'s first week of sales."

She turns her chair back to the computer and starts pulling up files. I can't stop staring at her, thinking about what else I'm going to do today. What else *we're* going to do.

My cock is already straining at my pants. This little arrangement may be a fucking fantasy come to life, but I'm going to have one hell of a time trying to get anything done once she's able to take care of her job without me.

I do not relish the day that I have a reason to go back to my office.

For the first time since coming back to London, I'm sitting in the conference room. Sera's sitting across from me with her laptop open. Her underwear is still stuffed in the inside pocket of my suit jacket, and we haven't said a word about it since. After the meeting, though…

But first, we must deal with my brothers. This will be the first time she interacts as part of the team rather than only training.

"How are things coming along across the pond?" Phillip asks. "Have you found any agencies willing to work for Vanguard?"

I pull up the info for the agency that we recently signed as a third-party contractor. "Sharon and Sullivan are who we're going with. They've got serious contacts in both romance and fantasy, but they're small enough that it's not costing an arm and a leg to keep them on contract."

It's strange. I barely even knew Phillip for most of our adult lives, but after spending so much time with him in New York over the past six months, I can almost hear him nodding. Mason's reaction surprises me, though. He's only been working with us for a few months, so I expected him to act like Sera, mostly listening.

"I had imagined you'd pick up Trinity instead," he notes. "They're smaller, but they've always focused on more unknown authors while Sharon and Sullivan tend to do a lot of thieving of clients. Sure, Sharon and Sullivan have a better list of authors, but that's because they stole them from agencies that actually found them. Is that what we're looking for? Or are we still focused on finding the diamonds in the rough ourselves?"

Damn it. I'd completely forgotten about Trinity. "Trinity would be better." I'm shocked to hear the words because they're coming from Sera, who's sitting up straight now. "They even started hunting self-published authors already. They know what they're doing, and they're doing it well."

I glare at her. Damn it. She's supposed to be supporting me, not telling my brothers that I'm fucking up. "But," she continues, "they're not large enough for what we're looking to do. Our plan was to start with Sharon and Sullivan, and if they failed too much, we would pull Trinity in to work beside them. Basically, let Trinity teach them while S and S do the heavy lifting with their numbers."

Phillip and Mason are both quiet as Sera's words sink in. They knew she'd be here, but they were unaware that I'd be essentially bringing her in as a partner. I've already been putting some of the weight of it on her shoulders, but that was only between the two of us.

And I'm shocked at how well she's handling it. Especially now. I hadn't thought of that plan, but it's far better than either of the other ones. She's barely been in this position for a week, and she knew which agencies I was considering. She made alternate plans? When did she manage that? I've been with her from dawn 'til dusk.

"It sounds like you've got things under control," Phillip says. The tone of voice is very business-like, but I can hear the surprise in it. I'm sure that he'd expected to have to micro-manage London even though I'm now officially thirty-three percent owner of Loughton House. Just like him.

"I think so. It's a smaller office, so things are a lot smoother over here." I don't know if I'm pulling off the confident attitude I'm trying to exude.

Mason's not quite as convinced, though. "Have you worked out how to incorporate new offices for the people who don't want to work from home? I know it was a challenge for New York, and you have an even smaller office than we do."

"Almost no one wants to work at the office. New York's vibe is different. The managers already had offices here since Dad didn't really worry about how I managed London, so we're going to end up with extra space. I'm thinking that we'll change some of that extra space to conference rooms for meetings at the beginning of each phase of projects. We've lacked that possibility for a while."

Again, the line goes a little quiet for a moment, and Sera raises an eyebrow in my direction. I can hear the question she isn't saying. *"What are they talking about with us on mute?"*

I give her a slightly disheartened look and shrug. "That sounds great," Phillip finally says, breaking the silence. "Keep us abreast of any additional issues, but it seems like you've got a good plan in place."

"Will do," I say, and my finger hovers over the end call button. "Talk to you again in about a month when we have more concrete things in the works."

Then, I hit the button and take a deep breath. My fucking brothers. I don't blame them for their distrust since it's the very first time that either of them has had any responsibility for London, but it makes keeping things secret more difficult.

"What the hell was that about?" Sera says, standing up and walking around the conference room table until she's standing next to me. "Does Phillip think you're not capable of running London or something? You've run this branch since it opened. He's never touched it. Why would he suddenly be trying to run it for you, or worse, to criticize your decisions?"

I shake my head, and she sits on the table. Completely unprofessional, she spreads her legs a little as she leans forward, her elbows on her knees. "Is it because you're the youngest? Or is Phillip always like that?"

"More than likely, it's because we're trying to co-operate both branches. No one is specifically in charge of either, and I should probably pay more attention to New York. Then again, it's probably also because Mason's working with Phillip."

When I glance at her skirt, I can't see all the way up it. Just a little bit of extra thigh. I want to run my fingers over the soft skin. To touch her and remind myself of how good a day I was having until this conference call. "Phillip and I got over *most* of our issues when I was working with him in New York. He's taking a little more of a hand's off approach than he has historically. Mason, on the other hand, is as fierce and demanding as ever. And it's a new business for him, so he's full of ideas and overconfidence."

Sera squints at me. "But he's got less experience than I do with it. Why the hell should he think he can suddenly doubt you when you've been in charge of literally everything in London for three years?"

I shrug again. "He's just Mason. It's the way it's always been. Generally, it's a good thing. It's how he built a thriving business with no real startup or experience after Dad ex-communicated him. But it's annoying when I'm the one he's focused on. I'm the little brother, and that's the way it'll always be. Even if I stuck it out and learned the business while he couldn't simply get along with Dad."

A grin flashes over the annoyance as I sit up straighter. "But that's why I'm doing what I'm doing. That's why I'm being sneaky and clever instead of having open discussions with them. Sure, I could probably do whatever I want without their agreement, but I don't want to deal with their arguments. I know what I'm doing, and I'm going to do it."

She gives me a little chuckle. "Well, I'm on board with that. I trust you, Andrew. You're smarter than you act, and you care a hell of a lot more than you pretend to. Don't hide stuff from me, okay? That's the fastest way to push me away."

"I'm the same way," I reply. "No secrets, Sera. And you did one hell of a job coming up with that alternate plan for the agency. How'd you come up with that on the spot?"

She runs her hand over my shoulder, her fingers digging into the suit jacket. "Mason's not the only person who's a little more intense than you're used to. You put Vanguard in my hands, and that's been my plan from the beginning."

When she says that, the pieces finally fit together. "You've been working on that after you say you're going to bed?" I say, more than a little shocked.

"When else was I supposed to work on it? It's not like there's any time to deal with Vanguard plans while we're at the office. How else did you think I always had opinions on something I have literally never dealt with before?"

I shake my head. That's nuts. I'd expected Sera to do well and work hard, but this... This is more than I'd ever do. This is Phillip level dedication.

"I guess I picked the right woman for the job," is all I say.

She smirks and slides off the table. "Come on. Time to get back to work, boss. I've got emails, and at some point, you're going to have to actually start this whole secret operation you've been planning."

My body stiffens up at the thought. Not yet. Not now that we're finally having some fun together. I had so many plans for what I'd do with her in the office.

She turns and glances at me, one eyebrow raised in question. "You're worried about starting this, aren't you? You've never made big changes all by yourself, have you?"

"Go take care of your emails," I say, pulling away from her hand. "I'll be in my office."

She stares at me, and I know the way I'm acting is confusing, but truthfully, I need a few minutes to process what she said. Am I really procrastinating? I'd thought that I was making sure she was ready, but maybe it's more than that.

Something inside me is pushing me to find new things to think about and worry about, namely Sera and our newfound physical relationship. Maybe sex with her is something I've been missing for longer than I knew. Or maybe it's that I have a mental block, and I need to push through it.

Either way, Sera can answer some emails at this point. It's time for me to grow a pair and do the thing that I've set out to do.

Even if I'd rather be balls deep inside my assistant.

Twenty-Nine

SERA

God, I can't believe I convinced Andrew to go work in his own office. I've been desperate for him to do something other than tease me all day. Then, after I rocked that meeting with Phillip and Mason, I was ready to jump on his dick.

I guess I pushed him a little too hard with that realization about him being out of his element. I didn't mean to do that. It occurred to me right there, and I accidentally said it out loud. One of those terrible curses I was born with.

Now I'm sitting here with a very insistent throbbing between my legs. My panties are in Andrew's pocket, and I'm looking around the room for a phallic shaped object. You can fuck anything if you're brave enough, right? *What the hell is wrong with me? Has it really been that long since I had good sex?*

Actually, yeah. It has been. I lean back in the office chair and close my eyes. I should have fucked him more yesterday. Really worn myself out.

For the first time since getting this office, I kick off my heels, scoot my chair back, and prop my feet on the desk like Andrew does every day. I let out a deep sigh and try to relax for a few moments, but even then, the image of Andrew over me is insistent.

I'm tempted to slide my fingers under my skirt. Just a little teasing would scratch the itch, wouldn't it? *It definitely will not!*

Maybe I should try to think about what else I need to make progress on. I know there are emails stacking up that I need to get to. Now that I've been doing the job Andrew wanted me for, I realize half his day must be spent answering pointless emails. I can't answer all of them yet, but I can filter them. I can answer the ones that are simple and let Andrew handle the complicated ones, most of which are from Phillip or Mason.

There's the floor plan redesign that needs to be done by Friday. I've only put a little thought into it, but we already had an interior designer give us a suggestion which we'll probably only tweak. There's the first suggestion from S and S, the agency we've contracted to find self-published authors we can make offers to.

But that's not what I *want* to do.

Fuck it. I stand up and move through my office. I will not get any work done with my mind in the gutter like this. Isn't that what this whole arrangement is about? Having some fun and scratching an itch?

Andrew's office is two doors down, and when I pass the little window next to the door, I see him on the phone, and an idea pops into my head.

Without knocking, I slip into the office. Andrew gives me a confused look, but he keeps talking to whoever is on the other side of the line. I lock the door and close the blinds, and when I turn around, Andrew's look is sharply confused. I don't pay any attention to what he's saying. Or even what he's doing.

I stand in front of him, a smirk on my face, and I slowly unbutton my blouse. One button at a time. Andrew's eyes grow wider with each button as my bra comes into view. When I shrug off the blouse, he inhales sharply.

My bra is off a second later, and I drop it to the floor. I want Andrew to want me like he did last night. Leaning forward over his desk, I let my tits hang, and his eyes don't leave them. His hand goes to his crotch, slowly rubbing it through his slacks. Then I stand up and walk around the desk. After pushing his chair away from it, I get down on my knees in front of him.

His eyes open wide. I brush his hand away from his crotch and undo his belt before undoing his pants. God, I'm fucking soaked. Doing this is turning me on more than playing with myself in my office ever would have. When his cock springs out of his pants, rock hard, I lick my lips and look up at him.

Gripping it by the base, I wrap my lips around him. He smells like he's been turned on all day, and he should have been. I've been walking around without underwear for his pleasure, and it's been more than a little unproductive, so tasting that desire on him makes it all worth it.

He pulls the phone away from his ear for a moment as he lets out a sigh. That's it, Andrew. I want you to be desperate to be inside me. He runs his other hand through my hair, his nails scratching at my scalp, and I melt at his touch. Something about this whole thing has me acting a little crazy. Maybe it's the fact that I've got my boss's cock in my mouth in the office. Or maybe it's because I instigated it. Or maybe the sex last night still has my body going crazy.

Whatever it is, I want more of it. When Andrew's fingers tighten in my hair and pull my face further down his cock, I do my best to relax and let him control me. All the while, he's still talking on the phone. Even when I feel tears well up in my eyes.

He releases my hair, and I nearly fall backward, trying to catch my breath. Andrew looks down at me as he slowly strokes himself. Still slick with my spit, his hand slides along the shaft effortlessly. I run my fingers over my breast, remembering how he'd explored my body yesterday. His hand speeds up, and I hear him say, "Alright. I'll get back to you tomorrow with a contract. Thanks, Joe."

Without taking his eyes off me, he ends the call. "You look fucking good with my cock in your throat. You know that, don't you?"

I don't know what to say, and he doesn't give me much of a chance to figure anything out. His hand goes back to my hair, and he drags my face to his cock again. I open my mouth, and when he starts to fuck it, I don't struggle at all. Even when it hits the back of my throat. The only part of it that bothers me is that I can't see him, can't see the way he looks at me.

"That's it," he says before pushing me down harder. "That's a good little slut. *My* good little slut." Something inside me cracks a little at those words. Even while I'm choking on his cock, I start moaning. I'm sure he thinks I'm trying to be sexy, but it's not something I can control.

I'm running out of air, and Andrew has somehow brought me to the edge of orgasm with fucking words. When he lets me go, I don't pull back so I can breathe. No, I guess I lost any kind of survival sense when he claimed me like that. My mouth moves to his balls, and I stroke him, my fingers squeezing him tight as I lick his balls.

"Holy shit," he mutters, and his hand goes right back to my hair. Not to drag my mouth back to his cock. No, he's guiding me up higher. Forcing me to stand. "If you kept doing that, I'd have come, and I'm not letting myself come anywhere but inside you."

A shiver runs through me as I consider what those words could mean. *Inside me.* No one's ever come inside me before. Condomless. Skin to skin. Him filling me up… Fuck. Part of me knows I should tell him to stop, that we need to be safe, but something makes me pause for a moment. Yep, every survival sense has gone out the window.

I hear him rifling through his pocket and he pulls out his wallet. Oh, he didn't mean it like that. Part of me is relieved. We obviously shouldn't be fucking bareback like that. But when I see the condom, I know that without one would be better.

For a moment, I consider telling him about the birth control. I ignore the thought and spread my legs and lift my skirt. I'd thought I was soaking before, but this is something different. Andrew notices it, too, and runs his finger over my lips, sending lightning through me. Then he brings his finger to his mouth and sucks it clean. He leans forward and whispers into my ear, "You sure taste good, slut. I think I might tie you to a chair and lick you until you pass out. How does that sound?"

I close my eyes for a moment, and when I look down again, he's already rolling the condom down his shaft. He runs the tip against my pussy, and my entire body tenses.

I let out a moan as I feel his cock slide inside me. "But that will have to be another day. Today, I want to fuck you until you're begging me to stop. Right here in the office. I want you to be sore and swollen for the rest of the day. When you close your eyes, you should imagine me thrusting into you, stretching that tight little pussy."

How much I needed this is beyond words. It's not that I need to get laid. I'm not just looking for an orgasm. I needed to *feel him,* to *hear him*. I need… *him*.

His hands go to my ass and squeeze. "I love your ass. The way it bounces when I fuck you. The way it tenses when I…" Then he slaps my ass. I fall forward a little, barely catching myself on the desk as my body registers the sting. "…spank it."

My body knows that I'm getting everything I want. This might look rough or painful from an outsider looking in, but it's decadence to me. He reaches around and grips my breast as he slams his body into mine, shaking the desk under me.

"And these tits have kept me up at night." His thumb and index finger find my nipple and slowly twist it, causing a complex combination of pain and pleasure to radiate through my breast. All I can do is moan. "Fuck, Sera. You make me wonder if there's anything in the world, I wouldn't give up to play with your sexy little body whenever I want."

I can feel the pressure building inside me, but I don't want it to end yet. I don't want my body to squeeze his cock for all its worth. "You have it," I whisper. "You'd better use it."

His thrusts speed up, making it even harder for me to keep from coming. "You're right," he whispers. "I will not go a day without having my way with you multiple times. I hope you're ready for that, little slut."

It's impossible to be quiet as the dam finally breaks. His thrusts are too much. His words are worse. "Fuck, I'm coming," I moan, and that seems to only push Andrew to fuck me harder.

"Good girl," he snarls, and his hand tightens even more on my breast. The other hand comes down hard on my ass again, and I don't jump at all. Instead, I push back against him, wishing he'd get even deeper.

"Please don't stop," I mumble. My arms are shaking as I hold myself up on his desk. The orgasm isn't even over yet—the aftershocks are still racing through me—but I can already feel that pressure building again.

The hand on my ass moves to my other breast, and he uses his handholds as leverage. Each thrust is hard enough that I wonder whether he's trying to make me come again or trying to hurt me. Because he might just do both.

"Fuck," he groans, and his rhythm shifts. Short, hard thrusts instead of the full, deep ones. He's coming. Part of me wishes he wasn't done, but mostly, I'm completely satisfied.

Unlike most men, he doesn't relax. No, his cock slips out of me, but his hands are just as rough. They let go of me, but then they grip my hips and spin me to where I'm facing him.

One hand goes to my hair, pulling it back and forcing my head up to look at the ceiling. His lips press against my neck as he kisses me. The other hand goes between my legs, and three fingers slide inside me.

My whole body tries to escape, but he doesn't let me. His thumb presses against my already over-sensitive clit, and he whispers, "We're done when I say we are."

Fuck me. What have I gotten myself into…

His lips move down to my breast, and he takes my nipple between his lips as his fingers play with my pussy. God, every inch of my body feels like it's about to explode. I'd felt satisfied before. The craving sated. This is different, though.

His lips leave my nipple for a moment, and he says, "I can't wait until we do all this work so that we can spend days and weeks in bed. I want to explore every inch of your body."

Instead of going back to my breast, he kisses his way back to my mouth. His lips press hard against mine. His fingers press against my G-spot while his thumb makes circles over my clit, slowly applying more and more pressure. When our lips meet, it's like that's the key in the lock holding everything back.

The pressure explodes inside me, and I moan out from the pleasure. His lips don't leave mine as he inhales my breath. "That's it," he whispers. "Give it to me. All of it. All of you."

My body shakes in his hand. Convulsing around his fingers. My lips finding his, and even while I quiver, they latch onto his. As though his lips could steady me.

As he withdraws his fingers, he pulls back. We're inches away from each other, and it's like the world is still closed off to us. Like we're not in his office with dozens of people that could knock on his door at any moment.

No, for this moment in time, we're two people secluded from the rest of the world. "I wasn't expecting that," he whispers. The growling and snarling are gone, and in their place is the smile that caught me in the first place.

"Me neither. I just thought I'd get a little afternoon delight. Not… that."

He steps back, and his eyes trail over my body. He's seeing the little marks he's left behind. The tiny, nearly unnoticeable bruises that dot my breasts and hips. He says nothing about them. They're his marks, after all. Ones I asked for.

"I don't know that we can have 'a little afternoon delight' based on our history." There's a touch of concern in his voice, but there's still all that desire in his eyes. Like he'd only need another little spark to start it all over again. And maybe I would want that another day, but I'm about to pass out as it is, and we're barely through half our day.

I give him a grin and finally take a step away from him. God, it's hard leaving that little bubble we were in.

I've never felt like that with another man before. Is it because of the intensity of the sex? Or is it something different?

I start to walk around the desk, but he stops me. "You're gorgeous, Sera. You know that, right?"

I turn to face Andrew. He's standing with his pants around his ankles and a suit jacket over his shirt. He's not exactly looking like the billionaire he is, but he's still one of the most handsome men I've ever met.

"You're not too bad yourself," I say.

I pick up my bra and blouse, and Andrew pulls his pants up. By the time I look even semi-professional, he's already sitting in his chair again. But he's not going back to work. He's staring at me.

"What?" I ask.

He shakes his head. "Nothing. I meant what I said, Sera. You're the most beautiful woman I've had the pleasure of spending time with, and I enjoy looking at you."

Those words send another shiver through me. Damn him. It was one thing for him to compliment me and say dirty things when he was balls deep inside me, but now? Now when he says things like that, it makes me question my resolve. Mixing pleasure and business is one thing, but anything more than that is out of the question. We're not here to get involved with each other.

We're here to accomplish our goals. At some point, I'm going to have to walk away from Loughton House if I want anything more than what I've already earned. I can't go back to being a cover designer. Not now.

"Well, get your work done so that maybe I'll have a reason to let you look at me again." He gives me a smirk, but I know there's more going on behind those eyes than flirting. Because as I'm turning around, I catch him glance at me with eyes that scream everything other than sex.

I can't let myself lose sight of my goals, though. Andrew may be doing all of this for some family pride thing, but this is my career on the line. You cannot get into a messy relationship with someone who's having you impersonate them, is the owner of the company, and who you're probably going to be competing with in the next year.

So, I walk out the door. Andrew Loughton may be the best fuck I've ever had, but his brain is more valuable to me than his dick.

Thirty

ANDREW

"Are you sure you want me to take the lead on this? It goes against what Phillip did in New York." Sera asks. Her chest is rising and falling far faster than it would be in a normal meeting with me, but that's probably because of the timer.

I nod to her. "Sera, I trust you. I don't give a damn what Phillip did. He's smart, but he can't break away from the way my dad ran Loughton House. He's still stuck in the same mentality that all the other publishing houses are running things. You're not, and I can't find a flaw in your logic."

It's crazy how much has changed in a month. Sera barely needs my input anymore, and I don't even know if Phillip or Mason could do as well as she's done with Vanguard. I'm still watching everything she does, but half the time, it's me trying to understand her decisions rather than me second-guessing them.

The timer on her screen makes little chirping noises, and whatever she was going to say is cut off. She looks at the timer and swallows hard. I walk around her desk and stop the beeping.

"Unless you've got questions, it's lunchtime." She knows exactly what I'm going to have for lunch today.

She shakes her head. "How do you want me?" she whispers.

"Skirt and underwear off." Instead of saying anything, she just stands up and removes them before sitting down in the leather office chair again. I dig into her drawer and pull out the fluffy handcuffs I'd put there this morning.

Kneeling, I run my hands under her ass and pull her toward me. When she's on the edge of her seat, I smile up at her. "Remember, you can always tell me to stop."

She swallows hard again and nods, and I wrap the handcuffs around her wrists and then around the arms of her chair. The chains are short, and when she pulls against them, I can tell that she's more than a little terrified.

Over the past month, I've realized that Sera's biggest turn-on is losing control. Hence, the handcuffs at lunch. I turn her chair around so that it's facing the floor-to-ceiling window behind her desk, and I push her chair against the desk.

Her legs have to spread all the way, and her ass has to be on the very edge of the chair for her ankles to reach the handcuffs I've connected to the legs of her desk. When I lock her ankles in place, she tries to pull against them, but there's no way for her to move, at least not when I kneel in front of her.

"You smell so fucking good," I say as I look up at her.

She's drenched. This morning, I told her what I was going to do. I'd put those handcuffs in her desk drawer while she watched. There was no doubt what was going to happen, and I made her go through half a workday with that knowledge.

She begged me at ten to fuck her, to let her have some relief, and I'd told her no. She tried to tempt me by stripping in my office, by playing with herself on my desk, and I smiled and told her she had work to do. I've made her simmer in desperation all morning.

That's about to change, though. Her eyes are on me as I flick my tongue across her clit. Her body tenses, and I'm sure she's already overstimulated. My hands run over her thighs and up her blouse. A part of me wishes that I'd told her to strip completely, but I know that playing with her breasts would be too much for her.

I have to walk a fine line taking complete control. My tongue moves back and forth over her clit, teasing her but not really pushing her towards the edge quickly. Her body and mind have to be manipulated. If I push too hard, she'll start being more terrified and less turned on. If I don't push enough, she won't get as much out of it.

She lets out a soft moan. "Andrew, please don't tease me anymore. I'm going crazy."

I know she is. It's hard to keep myself from giving into what I want to do. I've been as desperate for her as she's been for me. Probably more because I could have had her anytime. I could have thrown those handcuffs in her desk drawer, turned her around, and fucked her senseless as soon as we walked into the office.

But she wouldn't be begging me right now if I had.

She'd be smiling and enjoying herself instead of battling the need inside her.

My tongue moves to her entrance and makes a lazy circle around it. Her hips try to buck, but the restraints hold her still. Fuck, she tastes so good. My hands find her waist, and my thumbs dig into the little dimple between her hips and her mound. I don't know why, but I love that spot on her.

There's a river flowing between her legs, and my tongue moves to lap it up. Sera shifts, desperate for more, but she already knows that I'm going to do what I want, not what she wants.

"Please, Andrew. Please, let me out so you can fuck me. I need you inside me."

When she begs, it makes it so much harder to stick to the plan. I look up at her, and her muscles are straining against the handcuffs. She's panting, and her eyes are closed. Time to really get her worked up.

My tongue moves back to her clit, and I press my lips around it. My tongue moves as fast as it can while I gently suck. Sera's entire body goes taut. "Please! I'm begging you. Use me!"

I'm a little worried that she's going to get so loud that people in the hall can hear her, but I don't stop. There are some things that are worth the risk. Fucking your assistant into oblivion is one of them.

I slide two fingers inside her, and all the chains on the handcuffs go tight at once. "I'll do whatever you ask, Andrew. Please, just fuck me like your little office slut."

My cock is straining at my pants. I don't know if any woman has ever turned me on this much, and all Sera's done is beg. My fingers slide in and out of her in a "come here" motion, and the whole chair shakes.

That's it. Exactly where I want her. I pull away from her pussy and stand up. She's like a wild animal when she looks up at me, and again, a part of me wishes that I'd had her strip before sitting back down in the chair.

With quick motions, I click the quick release on the handcuffs, letting her go free. "Bend over the desk, slut," I say as calmly as though we were still talking about expense reports. She doesn't hesitate at all.

I don't even bother to take off my shoes. I undo my belt and unzip my pants as she gets into position, spreading herself wide for me. "That's a good girl, Sera," I say as I run my hand over her ass, my fingers sliding between her legs and finding her clit. She moans when I open her top drawer to get the condom.

"I want you to watch me while I fuck you," I say. She turns her head to look at me while I open the condom and roll it on. Her eyes are glazed over, completely lost in her need. I step behind her and raise my hand. She watches it, knowing I'm about to slap her ass, and doesn't move an inch. Her hands grip the edge of the desk, and she licks her lips.

I thrust, filling her in a single movement, and there's a spark in her eye. This is exactly what she wanted. It's exactly what I wanted, too. She squeezes her pussy around me, and I have to pause. I've been inside her every day for nearly a month, and she still makes me wonder if it's all real.

My hand comes down on her ass, and she groans, her body relaxing. Her gaze doesn't waver, though. I grip her waist hard and start thrusting. "You feel so fucking good, Sera," I say, but I don't think she can hear me.

Her body convulses like it did while she was in the chair, but this time, her pussy clenches around me while she lets out a low moan. Fuck, that feels good. "That's it, slut. Come for me. Show me how bad you needed me to use you."

"Thank you," she groans. "Thank you, thank you, thank you…" She only stops when I slap her ass again. It's taking everything I have to keep from coming already. Sera's pushing back with every thrust, and I don't know how much longer I can last like this.

But I need her to come at least one more time.

I pull out of her, and she lets out an audible groan. I don't give her enough time to beg me to keep going, though. Instead, I reach under her and pull her into a standing position. I'm sure that she's still feeling aftershocks from the orgasm, but that doesn't matter.

I turn her around to where she's facing me and guide her onto the desk. Her legs are spread immediately, and I pull her ass to the edge. My hands hold her hips completely still as I do my best to fuck her into oblivion.

I need to come. I think Sera can tell because she bites her bottom lip while she moves her hand under her leg. Instead of playing with her clit like she normally does, she cups my balls and gently squeezes.

Fuck. I've never had anyone do this before, and there's no way in hell that I'm going to be able to hold back. "That's it, boss. Use my little pussy. Does it feel good to stretch me out like that?" She lets out a little moan, and her core tightens around my cock.

I'm so close, but I keep fucking her. Feeling what little bit of control I've maintained fraying, I lift her ass into the air and slam her body against mine with each thrust. I can't hold out any longer.

As I let out a low groan, Sera pulls a little harder on my balls. For a moment, I imagine what it'd feel like to be deep inside her with no condom on.

And then the thoughts gone as I orgasm. All the hours of pent-up need are gone, and I feel sated. Like there's nothing in the world that could be wrong right now.

"Fuck," I whisper when I let her body go back to the desk. I feel exhausted and wonderful at the same time. Like there's this simmering fire inside me that only she can stoke.

"Fuck is right," she says with a grin. "I don't think I've ever been that desperate for dick in my life."

I chuckle as I step back and let her sit up. I feel like my head is under water and the universe is throbbing. It's not a feeling I'm familiar with. Sera takes a deep breath and hops off the desk. When she looks back at it, there's a small puddle on the wood. "Well, I guess it's a good thing I took the skirt all the way off this time. Who'd have guessed that being handcuffed would be such a turn-on?"

I did. I understand Sera in a way that I've never understood anyone before. I feel like I know her better than she knows herself sometimes, and I only want to know more about her.

Part of me wants to push back on those desires. I went into this thinking that we couldn't have anything other than a work relationship, and I've done a hell of a lot more than step over that line. Learning about her, though, that's how I end up crossing the next line, and that's not something I can accept.

Fuck buddies are one thing, but a relationship would ruin all the work we've been doing. Once people catch feels, there are so many things that can go wrong. I can't risk that.

As I bend down to undo the handcuffs from the desk and chair, I look at her. There is not another person in the world that I want to see more than her. Even after spending nearly all day with her for a month, I still get excited to see her, to talk to her.

Isn't that the definition of catching feels?

Thirty-One

ANDREW

Every day that I hide my actions from my brothers, the more likely they are to realize that I'm funneling money into this venture. I've already spent five hundred thousand on retainers and contracts with everyone involved on the ground floor. We're halfway through our six-month deadline, and it's not just an idea at this point.

I finish up proofing the current contract, one with a journalist who will be one of our first. Loughton Media is going to be a drastic step away from Loughton House's classic traditional publishing business, but it's still all based on the same principles. The only difference is that this will be entirely web-based.

The idea came to me when I was working on the original Vanguard idea with Phillip. That initial idea that we had during Loughton House's lowest quarter. Sure, we sell eBooks along with physical books, but it's all based on the idea of a book bringing in revenue. Loughton Media will be its own product, and each publication will simply be a piece of the product. One more draw for prospective consumers.

I'll be hiring journalists, artists, critics, and various types of fiction writers under contract rather than salary. They'll be paid based on how many readers they get, and paid well. Unlike similar platforms, this won't be a free-for-all space where anyone can publish whatever drivel they deem valuable. Since every author will be chosen by hand, the process will take a great deal longer. But the quality, something that Loughton House is known for, will be there. I won't dirty the family name with a cheap cash grab like so many other places. Eventually, we will have an entire group dedicated to what I'm doing so that we can scale.

The list of interested writers is getting longer by the day, and my slowly widening inner circle is doing a hell of a job grabbing up new ones daily. All we're really waiting on at this point is for the infrastructure to be built. Well, that and the market research so that I can show Phillip and Mason. I started this project with no actual proof of concept that would be acceptable to major businessmen or investors because deep down; I know that it'll work just like Phillip believed in Vanguard before it was fleshed out. But Phillip and Mason will want to see the numbers and the unbiased data.

I flip over to my emails and see one that Sera flagged for me. From Phillip. Clicking it, I raise an eyebrow.

Are you coming home for Christmas or staying in London? Mason's going back to the island, and I'm trying to make plans. Let me know when you get a chance.

I frown. It's not even Thanksgiving yet, and Phillip is making plans? How the times have changed. A year ago, he wouldn't have even realized it was Christmas until he showed up at the office and no one was there.

I shoot him a quick, "We'll be there," response and feel the noose tightening around me. There's no fucking way this is all going to be ready by then. But it must be. By the first of the year, they're going to run through the numbers. They're going to see all of it, and they're going to have a lot of fucking questions.

I lean my head back on my chair and sigh. They'll be happy with Vanguard. S and S already has a dozen new authors signed, none of which would have been found without them, and all of whom look very promising.

The core business is still struggling a little, no different from when Dad criticized me about it when I was back in New York. None of our big authors have released anything in a while. Maybe New York can maintain that consistent production of new releases, but England's so much smaller. We have big ups and big downs.

None of it matters, though. Everything is running as smoothly as it can, except for Loughton Media. That's the big hiccup, and I need to get it moving faster, but there's no way to get programmers to hurry. At least none that I know of.

I'm left feeling very lost. It seems like it's been a long time since I wasn't swamped, but now there's nothing to do except wait. With Sera here, I don't have that many responsibilities, and it's giving me too much time to think. Even though everything's going reasonably well, it's hard not to question whether this whole thing is what I should be worried about.

Because Sera is all that I really want to think about. We've worked together and fucked nearly daily for almost three months. Yet, we still claim to be nothing more than coworkers with benefits. She still usually sleeps in her own bed. Neither of us has broached the topic of what happens after these six months is up.

Other than the Sundays she spends with her dad, we're nearly inseparable. Even at work, we're in constant contact. I've never had that before.

I know Sera, and she knows me. Backwards and forwards. Sure, I've found out what kind of flowers or food or entertainment women enjoy plenty of times, but how many times have I spent time trying to understand their stories? Especially the ones beyond the funny and entertaining.

Sera spent last night telling me about the time her dad took her to Paris when they were on tour. How they'd had ice cream under the Eiffel Tower and talked about what she wanted to do with her life. She'd told him she wanted to make her own way. When he'd asked why she didn't want to start a band like him or become a lawyer like her mom, she'd stood up and told him she didn't need help. She could tie her own shoes and she could make her own money when she was a grown-up.

It's those little things that I've never witnessed secondhand before. They're the things that make Sera real to me where other women have just been flings.

Sighing as I stand up. I shouldn't do this. I should enjoy a little bit of a breather. Maybe I could take a walk or even a nap.

No, I want to go see what she's doing. I want to help her get through her workload faster so that we can leave early and maybe spend some real time together. Because I want to hear more stories.

I walk out of my office, and I hear her voice. Strange. She shouldn't be talking to anyone. No one in the office should even really know she's here. A tickle runs up my spine as I stop to listen.

"It's hard, Mom. There's still so much to figure out, even after three months."

There's a pause as her mom responds, and I can't help but wonder if anyone else has heard her talking. Why didn't she close the door to her office before talking to someone on the phone? I don't care if she tells her mother what's happening, but damn it, I can't have the senior management hear her.

I take a glance down the hall, and everyone's doors are closed like normal. They all stay busy most of the day, and unlike New York, they do most communications through Slack or phone calls. It's the culture that I pushed from the beginning.

Maybe I lucked out. "I'm okay. It's not too much, but it's a lot. Yes, I've been spending plenty of time at Dad's."

She's interrupted for a moment, and I wonder what her mom's telling her. Does it have anything to do with that night we spent at her dad's house?

"No. It's not like that. I still have my eye on the prize. Andrew does, too. This isn't a romantic thing at all. You told me to be fierce, and I am. I'm not some princess waiting for true love. I'm just blowing off some steam with him. You know how it is. Remember that I'm basically running a company at this point, and I'm not doing too bad of a job. Can we please leave it alone?"

I glance through her window and see her with her feet propped up on the desk. Look who's being the lazy teenager now? The thought barely lasts an instant because listening to her explain our arrangement strikes a nerve. I don't know why since she's not wrong. We're both working hard at trying to accomplish things, and this whole arrangement started because we wanted each other physically. But it still pisses me off.

"Yes, I'll be home for Christmas. That's what Andrew said to his brothers, so I assume he's taking me with him."

Part of me wants to sit and listen to her conversation, to understand her relationship with her mom, and maybe understand her a little better, too. But the other part knows that if I hear her talk about us like that anymore, I'm going to get more than a little frustrated.

Deep down, I know that there's more to this than two coworkers scratching an itch. Even the most mind-blowing sex wouldn't have me wanting to spend more time with her. In fact, with all the time we spend together, I should want some alone time. But I never do.

Which is why I walk into Sera's office with a grin on my face. She looks a little shocked to see me, but when I reach behind me to lock the door and close the curtains, her eyes get even wider. She knows what I'm going to do.

It wasn't my first instinct to make this brief visit sexual. Hell, we've already played once today. But seeing that shocked expression and hearing her talk about our arrangement that way makes me want to remind her of what she asked for.

She certainly hasn't been bothered in the past when I was on the phone. She's struggling to stay in the conversation as I walk past her desk and stand behind her.

"Yeah, I already figured out what I'm getting for Dad," she says, and I hear her breath catch when my fingers touch her throat. Ever so lightly, barely more than a feather. Her chest is rising and falling far faster than before, and when my fingers move to the button on her blouse, she shivers and tries to look up.

I undo two buttons before I slip my fingers under the satin and follow the curve of her breast until I find her bra. That doesn't stop me, though. I slide under the lace and cup her breast. My fingers tense, and she bites her lip, knowing what's supposed to happen next.

God, I love playing with her like this. With how often she starts things, I'm sure she enjoys it nearly as much. Yet, there's that itch in the back of my mind. The frustration with how she talked about our arrangement.

She lets out a gasp and then seems to remember that she's still on the phone. "Hey Mom, I've got to go. Remember, I still have a job to do."

There's a pause, and she says, "Love you, too." And then she ends the call right before a low moan escapes her lips. I'm tempted to do more than tease her, to have a second round before we even get to lunch.

But I know that she, at least, has things to do. When I pull my hand out of her shirt, she frowns. "What are you doing?" she asks.

"Nothing. I thought you needed a little teasing, is all. How's your mom?"

She blinks in confusion, and I give her a grin. Yes, this is unusual for our arrangement. When we start something, we tend to finish it. "My mom's fine." She takes a deep breath and lets it out slowly, but it's a shaky breath. She's trying to control herself, and I'm sure that if I ran my hand up her inner thigh, I'd find her soaking wet. "Andrew, what do you mean that you're just teasing? That's not the way this game is played."

I shrug and walk around her desk. "I was bored, and you were on the phone. I thought I'd get your attention since you obviously weren't hard at work."

She leans forward, her movements still shaky. "How are you bored? Aren't you starting Loughton Media? Aren't we on a time crunch?"

This is the first time she's been in this position, so I'm not surprised that she's unaware that there's a lot of hurry up and wait at this point. "Well, I'm used to running all of London by myself, and now all I have to do is get things rolling for Loughton Media."

She chews her lip for a moment, and I can't help but think about how much I'd enjoy those lips on my body. But we're having a genuine conversation, not a teasing one. "I guess that means you have some time?" she finally asks.

I nod. "What do you have on your plate that you're not in the mood to do?"

"Deal with the invoice for the floor remodel. I've been putting it off for days because I don't have any past invoices to go off. And maybe deal with the contract for *Tales from a Starship*. That one makes little sense to me. I've run through the file, and I have absolutely no idea why we're offering him any money at all, much less the advance that's being recommended."

A frown crosses my face for a moment. I haven't even heard of that book. It's been such a short time since I let my focus on the core business slip, but already there are things I'm missing. Do I want to focus on those things? Do I want to take some of the work back from Sera? Or should I just jump in and help when I have time?

"I'll get them done," I say, not letting any of my worries show other than that little bit of a frown. "You know, you're doing a hell of a job for a woman with no training."

She shrugs. "Like you said, most of it is automated. I'm just checking over everything. The core business is a well-oiled machine, and Vanguard is on its way to machine status, so it's not as bad as I'd expected."

All of that is why I thought it was possible for anyone to step in and do the job at all. If it were like running New York, she'd never have been able to get up to speed quickly enough. That doesn't mean that it's anything to blow off as "a simple thing".

"Well, you're still doing a hell of a job. I don't know anyone else who could do this well with as little time behind the driver's seat as you've had."

She smiles. "I'm trying, but I appreciate the pat on the back, Andrew. It was scary trying to figure it all out. Especially when it came to making decisions with Vanguard. I appreciate all the one-on-one stuff."

I can't help but smirk. Sure, I feel like a fourteen-year-old boy sometimes, but she makes it too easy. "I enjoy our one-on-one stuff, too. Maybe we can get out of here at a reasonable hour, and then we can have a little more one-on-one time."

"Funny," she says, but she's grinning. "Go do some work for once, boss."

I give her a nod and walk out of the office. As soon as I'm in my chair behind my desk, I lean back. I pick up my letter opener and slowly rotate it in my fingers, a fidget I've come to do more and more since Sera started working with me.

Those comments she made to her mom keep ringing in my head. Sure, I sidestepped them while I was in her office talking to her, but now that I'm alone, they're back again. What is it that's frustrating me so much about her description of us? *Just blowing off some steam…* I clench my teeth, and my finger presses a little too hard against the edge of the not-very-sharp letter opener.

A sting shoots up my arm, and I look down to see the thin stream of blood running along the silver edge. Instead of moving or jerking, I just watch it. Crimson on silver. *Drip. Drip. Drip.* Drops of blood fall from the hilt to the table below.

It's completely random where they fall, each drop separated from the others, but then two fall a little too close to each other. And they touch. The two drops become one. They don't even leave a mark where they initially landed. Every bit of the red coalesces into that single, larger drop, and it's like there was never a time where they were separated.

Something about that image pulls at me. Yanks me away from thoughts of business, thoughts of my family, and even thoughts about Sera's warm skin under my hard fingers.

It makes me think that maybe I've been looking at everything wrong…

Thirty-Two

SERA

DINNER HAS BEEN STRANGE. FOR ONE, WE WENT OUT. After Andrew decided to knock out a bunch of the tasks on my to-do list, we left the office at five instead of seven, like normal. A ten-hour day. The first in three months.

"This was nice," I say as I put my napkin on the table and smile at Andrew. He doesn't respond, though. Instead, he returns my smile and nods. That's the other thing. Like the morning after we went to my dad's house, he seems lost in thought.

I'd expected him to be flaunting the fact that we're eating on the top floor of The Shard, the tallest skyscraper in London. We ordered fancy food for the first time in at least a month. We had wine. It should have been a lively evening, especially with how early we left work. But it's not.

Andrew doesn't even finish his food before he waves our waiter over to us. "Can you bring the check and get the maître d'?"

The waiter frowns. "Was there something wrong with your meal?"

Andrew shakes his head. "No. I just need to speak to the maître d'. The meal and service was excellent, as always."

That seems to give the waiter some relief, and he goes to do what Andrew asked, but I'm left very confused as well. "What do you need the maître d' for?"

Andrew chuckles. "I want to see London."

What the hell does that mean? I've learned to accept the mysterious statements that Andrew makes at this point. He'll explain when he gets around to it.

The waiter comes back with the check and the maître d' who looks very concerned. "Is there something I can help you with?" he asks.

Andrew turns his chair to face him, and he smiles. "I'd like to rent the key to the roof for the next hour or so."

"Sir, I can't let you have the key. It's against the rules, and…"

Andrew interrupts him. "Then who do I call so that I can get the key? I know people go up there occasionally, and I'd like to do so tonight."

The man in a tux frowns for a moment and then says, "Let me make a phone call. I'll be right back."

Andrew smiles and nods to him before he slips his credit card into the little black book holding the check. The waiter picks it up and walks away with it.

"We're going onto the roof?" I ask, fully expecting one of Andrew's normal excited bits of banter.

Instead, he seems to look past me and simply says, "Yes."

An entire city stretches out below us. Millions upon millions of people are going about their lives. Some are going to work. Others are leaving. Some kissing their spouses, and others going out to find their first love.

A world of life sits below us as we stand at the top of The Shard, the tallest building in London. It's nothing compared to a mid-sized skyscraper in New York, but there's something about the view from here.

The world here differs from New York. The people are different. There's not as much hustle and bustle. The business world is slower. The stress is lower. Yet, while we look down at the world, it's hard to believe any of that.

The wind gusts around us, the misty evening leaving our hair damp. Sharp steel and glass blades rise around us as though they're trying to pierce the sky. Being up here makes me feel like we're back home in New York.

"Why'd you want to come up here?" I ask. Nearly yelling since the wind is loud enough that it seems to be trying to steal my words from Andrew's ears. "I know we got off work early, but…"

He interrupts me. "I wanted to know what you wanted from all of this."

All of what?

"What do you mean?" I turn away from the cityscape below us and look at the man with piercing green eyes. The man who knows how to tease my body and tempt me in ways no one else ever has.

"What do you want? Why are you here? What makes you work so damn hard and ignore everything that feels so obvious?"

A shiver runs through me, and I don't think it's the cold. Is he really talking about what I think he is? Not the business I'm planning to start up. Not the business I'm currently spending twelve hours a day on. No, not business at all.

"Andrew, you're being very obtuse." I try not to let him know all the possibilities that are running through my head. Maybe I'm wrong about what he's thinking. Maybe I'm in so much lust that I can't see through that haze when he's around.

He takes my hand in his and squeezes it. Then he sighs. Low and exhausted, I know that sound. The ragged breath of a man who's fought himself for too long.

"It would be so easy to let this thing between us turn into something more than just a good time. *More than just blowing off steam.*" The way he says that sentence clicks in my mind. I said that today. When I was talking to my mom. "I know we're supposed to keep emotions out of it. We need each other, and the possibility of us fucking that up is far more likely if we let emotions get in the way. My dad would tell me I'm an idiot. The job comes first. Always."

He sighs again, and this time, it's somehow even more exhausted. I give his hand a squeeze, and he steels himself, standing up a little straighter. "But Sera, every moment I've been with you has made me want to be with you more. Like a drug that I can't walk away from. I see the little marks on your body, the love-bites that you cover up with makeup, and it makes me happier than anything else I've ever done.

"More than breaking record sales. More than beating my family's expectations. Hell, more than finding Luciano's. Sera, when I look at you and think that you're mine, I feel something different than I'm used to. The night we shared all those years ago was something I fantasized about ever since then. The workdays don't feel like work when you're there."

He turns around, pulling his hand away from me. That shiver was right. He's not talking about work. But he is, at the same time.

I move to stand beside him, feeling every bit of the battle he's waging inside himself and understanding every blow he's taken because it's my battle, too. "What are you trying to tell me?"

"How do you keep from wanting more, Sera? How am I supposed to keep my nose to the grindstone when the only thing I want is you?"

I turn to him. Damn him for saying those words. No different than when he whispers dirty, filthy things in my ear while he's inside me, these words work their hooks into me, forcing the thoughts to the surface. Thoughts I've pushed deep down.

"Because I don't have a choice, Andrew. You're doing all this for what? To impress your brothers? To be a hero instead of the little brother? Andrew, without this, I would *never…*" I stop. No, I can't say the words that would push him away permanently. I can't tell him the truth. *I would never be able to start my own publishing business.*

"Sera, you don't understand. Hell, my brothers don't even understand. I've been looked down on since I was born. I was the baby. The one who had no expectations. No one taught me. No one pushed me. No one fought me. They just ignored me. Now, I'm a grown man, having trained myself to run an entire branch of Loughton House, and they don't even acknowledge me when I walk in the room."

I chuckle. "You know what, why don't you go make covers every day for the next three years. Get ignored by literally everyone above you unless there's a problem. Not do anything that matters. Just be a machine for three years, churning covers out every day for people who don't have any desire to talk to you. Do that, and then we can talk about being looked down on."

His jaw is clenching. I guess I struck a nerve. I've gotten good at that, it seems. "So, you think that working with me will open up a new world for you?"

I nod. "You'll open it for me at the very least, and not because I'm blackmailing you. I'm good at what I do, Andrew. I devote myself to everything I do, and you know that now. But no one becomes a part of upper management with a background in covers. It's always one of the other groups that move up. Sales or marketing or finance. Now you know that I'd be able to do the job in most of the management positions, and you're going to get me there, right?"

He turns back to the city view. "Probably." It's barely loud enough over the wind to hear, but a wave of anger and frustration wash over me.

"Probably? What the hell, Andrew?"

He shakes his head. "You have three years of experience, Sera. There's some bit of hierarchy and diplomacy at work, especially here in London. I told you I've done a lot of hard work to make this place run the way it does, and that's mostly because I don't have any bullshit issues. Politics, Sera. That's the part of the equation you're missing. And you don't have to worry about it in your current position because I'm the political figure. You're the one doing the work."

"Fine. I quit. Send me home. I'm not working fourteen hours a fucking day just to learn stuff, Andrew."

He turns to me, confusion all over his face. "I didn't say no. I just can't promise that I'll set you up with an upper management position. There aren't a ton of them. To get one of those positions, I'd either have to demote a whole slew of people or I'd have to create a new position just for you. It's not that easy. I can promise that you'll *eventually* move up much higher than any other cover manager has."

I laugh. It's ludicrous. "Hear me out, Andrew. Would you take this agreement? Come, do some shady shit with your boss. Work fourteen hours a day, six days a week. Live with him. Learn how to run a fucking company in less than a month. For ninety-thousand dollars a year. Would you take that deal?"

He chews his lip. "I'll give you a raise tomorrow," he says.

I slap his chest as I turn to him. "It's not a fucking raise that I want." Staring him in the eye, I shake my head. Turning away from him, I feel as lost as he was at the beginning of this conversation. "I want the same thing you do. I want to do something beyond a day job. I want my work to be more important than painting over fonts and changing hair color. I want what you have, Andrew."

He puts his hand on my back, and I don't push it away. "So that's why you keep your nose down and do your work." He says it as though it's some kind of revelation.

"Yeah, and this is the chance of a lifetime for me. For you, though? You could try another thing in a month to impress your family. The only reason this is complicated for you is that you want to hide it from them."

I feel deflated. Damn near broken. I've spent my life looking up to two people who broke the mold in their careers. They both came from nothing and are unbelievably successful. But me? The daughter they've given every opportunity to. I'm just a simple cover artist.

The rain starts to pour down on us as if on cue. Brief flashes of lightning fill the sky in the distance, and Andrew steps in front of me, blocking the wind. In the shelter under his body, I look up at him. He puts his hand under my chin as gently as if he were holding a piece of porcelain.

"You're the only person I've ever met that could do what you've done," he says. "I trust you to make decisions as much as my brothers. I put all my faith in you, and I know you won't let me down, Sera. I won't let you down, either. I promise you that you don't have to worry about where you'll end up."

Looking into his eyes, I could swear that tears were rolling down his cheeks. No, it's the rain. The storm that's swirling around us. Not him. Not us.

"You want to know how I can push myself this hard when I want more than anything to be more than coworkers?" I ask. "Because no one else can take care of me, Andrew. No one else can give me what I want. You promise me you'll make sure that I end up with everything I want, but what if we fall in love, and that love spirals out of control? What if it crashes and burns, Andrew? Are you still going to let me be a VP of something when you hate me? Will I want to work for a man that broke my heart?"

He clenches his jaw, and his gaze hardens. "I know your worth. I wouldn't let my emotions ruin your prospects, and I wouldn't let them ruin my chance to use your skills. I won't let you go, even if I can't have you for myself."

His fingers move to my cheek, and his thumb continues to rest under my chin. "I want more, Sera. I want you. I'm not in the business of giving up anything I want, and I have wanted nothing as much as you. I *will* make this work. I promise you that there's nothing in the world that will stop me."

But will he still want me if I don't stay with Loughton House? What if I become his competition? That was my plan from the beginning. A plan I haven't forgotten.

I can feel the rain pattering against my skin. Cold little shocks that I ignore. The wind whips my hair as it sneaks between Andrew and me. "What if you're wrong this time?" I ask. "What if you don't have all the information?"

His grip hardens. Those smooth hands tighten around the back of my neck. Just like when he fucks me and makes me moan his name. "I don't care if I'm missing something. I'm making a promise, and I don't break promises."

The only reason I'm arguing with him is because *I want to work with him.* This arrangement we have is perfect, but it won't last. There's no way that his brothers will let me continue running the London branch when they find out.

Can I really trust his promise? Can I believe that no matter what happens, he'll make sure I'm in a proper position at Loughton House? Or is this all his way of wooing me?

"Maybe," I whisper. "Maybe I can trust you."

He doesn't let me finish the rest of what I was going to say. Instead, he presses his lips against mine in the pouring rain. And I taste salt on those lips. *You can't see the tears in the rain.* A lyric from Sweet Delusions.

I succumb to the kiss; no different than I did the first time I tasted those lips. Those powerful hands and heady sensations pull me away from my thoughts, and I don't fight them. He asked me to trust him, to believe his promises, and I'm going to.

Inside me, the war continues to rage. Watch out for yourself because no one else will. Let's have some fun. Two opposing pieces of advice from my parents. The two pieces of advice that I've basically lived by my entire life.

And for the first time since I can remember, they directly oppose each other. I can't depend on the advice of my parents right now. Deep down, though, I know that Andrew's right. I've wanted no one as bad as I want him.

And I remember the thing my parents *both* told me before I started working for Loughton House. *Trust yourself.*

So, I let the sensations wash through me. The ones that have pulled me to him since the beginning. His touch. His kiss. His very breath. I don't fight the desires. I know that he's right. Deep down, I knew this was the way things would go. From the moment I saw him at that Christmas party, I knew that there was something special about Andrew Loughton.

Something that would make me ignore the rules I'd laid out for myself.

When he pulls away from the kiss, he's smiling. "Let's get you out of the rain. And those clothes."

I smile back, but that war inside me hasn't gone away. I still feel my stomach churning with worry about what this means. But I can't let it stop me from trusting myself. If I'm wrong, then the bad thing will happen whether or not I worry. I might as well enjoy the time between now and then as best I can. At least that's a truth I can cling to.

"Only if you promise to make it worthwhile. I happen to enjoy being kissed while I'm all wet."

His smile turns into a smirk. "I didn't say I'd stop you from being wet. I simply think you'll be happier to be naked and wet."

Thirty-Three

ANDREW

My finger traces the lines of Sera's stomach as she sleeps. Sprawled out on my bed, her naked body is beautiful. Passed out after hours of sex, sweat still clings to her skin and hair. She's gorgeous, but it's more than that, and it took hearing her talk about our arrangement for me to understand how much more.

As my finger moves down to the soft hair between her legs, she sighs, and her legs spread a little. She fell asleep to me touching her like this, just moments after her last orgasm, and I haven't stopped even though it's been thirty minutes.

I feel like I can't stop, like breaking this physical contact will break the reality of what happened this evening on top of The Shard. My fingers brush against her swollen lips, and she lets out a little moan before my hands move to her inner thigh. I know I need to stop touching her, that I need to pull the blanket over us and try to get some sleep.

I know I won't be able to sleep, though. Today at the office when I heard her talking to her mom, the cracks in all my logic started to show. Or maybe they'd been there since the beginning, and that was the light shining on them. Whatever it was, I realized my priorities aren't the same as they were when we first came to London.

It's been such a short time, but this woman, this gorgeous, funny, and incredibly smart woman, has become the priority. Sure, I still want to make a name for myself within my family, but maybe it doesn't matter quite as much as it once did.

As my finger brushes against her nipple, she smiles, and her eyes open enough that I notice that she's awake. "Mmm, that feels good," she whispers in the silence. "Is it morning already?"

I shake my head, and her hand moves between her legs. "Are you ready for another round?" The corner of her lip curls up before she lets out a soft moan. "I'm so sore, I don't think I've ever been this swollen."

God, she knows how to turn me on. This crazy, amazing woman knows how to do everything that drives me crazy. Even when she doesn't realize it. My cock is already swelling in anticipation, but I ignore it. Instead, I pull the blanket over us, and Sera smiles at me.

"I've never seen you turn down a chance to be inside me before. Are you out of condoms or something?"

I chuckle as I lay on my back, my body pressed against hers, and I wedge my arm under her pillow. "No, we've got plenty of condoms. We need to get some sleep, though, and if we start up again, I don't know if we'll finish before dawn."

"You aren't quick about things, are you," she says as she rolls onto her side to face away from me. My hand instinctively moves to her stomach, my fingers lightly roaming over her body as they did before. I turn onto my side, wedging my body tightly against hers, and she presses back against me. My cock's hard, and it's difficult to fight the urge to want to slide inside her. Especially when she grabs my hand and pulls it to her breast.

"Stay still, mister. You need to sleep as much as I do, and if you can't stop that, I'm going to have to go back to my room. So, grab my boob and dream of doing dirty things to me. I'll take it as a personal offense if you aren't humping me when I wake up."

I chuckle, but as the rhythm of her breathing settles in the silence, I feel myself being lulled to sleep by it. The soft snores and the slow throb of her heartbeat pull me toward sleep.

Because, for the first time, I finally understand what it's like to have someone. Since my mother died, I've always been the forgotten one. Even my dad ignored me, unless he needed something. But right at this moment, I feel like there's no one Sera wants more than me. For once in my life, there's someone who cares about *me*.

Thirty-Four

SERA

My body feels damn near broken after last night, but that's not what I'm worried about. My finger hovers over the delete button on my company phone. The secret file I've been building of how to start my own publishing business. A conglomeration of things I've learned while running Loughton House in London and a whole slew of things I've researched with Loughton House's network.

Could it be considered some kind of corporate espionage? Very possibly. Do I feel like it is? Not really. Hell, I wouldn't be able to really compete with them for years, if ever. It was never my plan to hurt them at all.

I'm just wanting something of my own. I wanted some kind of work that fed my soul. Work that meant something. That would compare to what my mom and dad accomplished.

It's all sitting right here in a file on my phone. The framework of a business plan built with my trust fund as my foundation. A trust fund I've never touched since I never needed it. My entire life, I've stayed away from using my parents' success. I could have been a musician or a lawyer. Those were my parents' paths, not mine. All I've wanted was to pave my own, to prove myself as capable as them, and I couldn't do that with them helping me on every step of the road.

This business I've been planning is exactly the thing I'd hoped for. But it would break every bit of trust that Andrew has in me. It would break any kind of relationship we build.

That's why I'm tempted to delete it. More than tempted. I know that it's the right thing to do, but I've spent every day adding to that plan. Every evening, I put a little more information into the file.

I've checked in on Andrew's progress with Loughton Media. It's coming together. There are dozens of major writers, storytellers, journalists, and artists signing contracts with him. It won't be long until the whole thing is ready to be shown to his brothers, and then he won't need me here. He won't have any real reason to keep me in a position where I have access to this kind of information.

It won't be possible to rebuild this file at that point.

My finger moves away from the little trashcan icon, and I let out a sigh. When I know where things are going with us, when I know that he's going to deliver on his promise, I'll delete it. Until then, I'll keep it in my back pocket in case things go poorly with us. With my future.

He promised me security within Loughton House regardless of what happens between us, but I've never seen his promises put to the fire. I don't know what he'll do if it comes down to his heart or his word.

Leaning back in the black leather office chair, I try to relax. I trust Andrew, but trusting someone and leaving yourself no way out are two different things. That's no different from signing a prenup, something I'd assume that Andrew would insist on.

No, there's nothing wrong with what I'm doing. Any rational person would leave themselves a way out.

The door to my office opens, and Andrew walks in with a grin on his face. I glance at the phone, the screen still on with my file front and center, and my heart races a mile a minute. Before I've moved a muscle, he says, "You won't believe what we're going to do in two weeks."

Leaning forward, as casually as I can, I put my arms on the desk and grin back at him. My hand finds my phone and discreetly turns the screen off. "We're going to Bermuda to investigate the Amelia Earhart disappearance. No, we're going to watch British people try to play American football." Andrew's grin turns to laughter at that, and I keep going. "Oh, no. Here's an even better idea. We're going to fly a plane over London filled with sparkly American sprinkles and dump them out, covering the entire city in them. We'll probably get some jail time for it, but it'd be worth it to give the British people some sparkles."

Andrew goes from laughing into cackling, and I feel pretty good about myself. When he finally calms down, he sits in the chair across from me. "No, though we might have to consider that last one. A bit of jail time would be worth it for a prank on that level." He pauses, and I don't interrupt his timing. "We're going to a Christmas party. And I'm going to be Santa. Guess what you're going as?"

Flashbacks of our night together all those years ago run through my mind. The night that started everything. "Is it going to include male stripping and tear-away pants?"

He gives me a terrible attempt at a seductive wink and says, "Maybe if you play your cards right."

I can't help but grin at the idea. With how much time we've spent together, memories of that night don't come as often as they once did. It's almost like our new memories are wiping out the old ones. "Well, if I get any choice in the matter, I'd prefer an elf costume that doesn't double as your stripper assistant. You know, a bit more leg coverage and a lot more cleavage coverage. I'm a professional now, not some fresh out of college twenty-two-year-old." I don't leave out the reminder of his promise, either. "Plus, I could be all their official bosses in a few months."

And he ignores it. Completely. "You'll get a respectable costume. Don't worry. The last thing I want is for a bunch of guys gawking at you all night. I'm the only one allowed to do that anymore."

The way he says it is so freaking possessive. I feel like the room got very warm. "Do I get to make sure none of the twenty-two-year-old college grads get to gawk at you? You have a history of leading them down terrible paths, you know. I wouldn't want them to end up impersonating the owner of the company in a few years…"

Andrew laughs again, and my mind goes back to the way it was between us that night. All fun and games. Chaos. God, we were young back then.

Would I want to go back to that? If I could reverse time, would I have done something different? Would he have? Could I have convinced him to stay, to be young and dumb with me? We both have plenty of money. We could have run away and had adventures forever instead of sitting in offices, worrying about our futures. Worrying about whether we'll ever do enough.

"Well, I hope we have at least as much fun as the last Christmas party we went to," I say. "We can't let our younger selves have all the fun."

He chuckles and stands up. "I'm pretty sure that you'll have plenty of fun. Especially when we make a daring escape…"

Thirty-Five

ANDREW

I CAN'T HIDE MY GRIN AS I LOOK AT THE TWO OUTFITS side by side. A Santa costume that's made *exactly* like the one I wore almost four years ago, and an elf costume that's decidedly less slutty. But under that costume is a much sexier set of lingerie than I've ever seen Sera wear before.

A week from now, we're going to be reliving the night we met, and I can't help but be excited about it.

"You're going to make it home for Christmas, right?" I haven't heard Phillip sound this excited since he and Addison made up. "Mason won't be back until the first, but man, we haven't spent a Christmas together in what seems like forever."

Even after all these months, it makes me laugh a little to hear Phillip get sentimental. What a change a girl and a little perspective shift can make. "Yeah. We're going to the company Christmas party, but after that, we'll be down there."

"Good." The voice coming from the speakerphone sounds relieved. Like he needs me there. "Addison's going to want her friend there, too. I may have a special surprise…"

There's only one surprise he could mean, and it's going to involve a little box with a ring in it. "We'll be there, Phillip. Calm down, okay."

Phillip huffs as I continue to smile at the costumes hanging on the door. I should care more. I know I should. He's my oldest brother, but part of me can't get over the thing I've been wrestling with for weeks.

How the hell I'm going to convince my brothers that Sera needs to be promoted all the way to upper management. Maybe once I can show them all the things she's done over the past months, they'll agree. No, there's no way they'll believe me. Or they'll say it's only because it's the London branch.

"Anyway," I continue, "I've got to go. I've got a meeting with Sera to finalize a few end of the year marketing agreements that'll start on the first."

"Okay. Let me know when you're getting into town, and we can get some food and catch up."

"Sounds good. Talk to you then." I turn around and end the call. How the hell am I supposed to convince them that Sera has earned her place at the big kid's table? Truthfully, I didn't expect her to be as much of an asset as she's become. I could take a vacation, and I wouldn't worry about her managing this place without me.

Yet, Phillip and Mason are going to fight me every step of the way if I push for her to get the place she deserves. If it were anyone other than my brothers I was talking to, they'd trust me. I deserve respect. I deserve to run my side of the company however I damn well please, but they'd throw a shit fit if I tried to do it without mentioning it. The only reason they suggested I bring her is because I made it seem like I was already dating her.

If I can't convince them, though, that'll break her trust with me, and I can't have that happen. Fuck. I'm stuck between a rock and a hard place, and truthfully, the only way I see this working out is by showing them Loughton Media. I need them to see that I'm not just running this stuff on autopilot. That I'm doing everything they're doing and more.

That's when Sera walks in. God, she looks good wearing that little pencil skirt. Her blouse is professional, but there's no way I'd miss the way it makes her tits stretch the fabric just a little. That sexy little valley between them. How is it that after all these months, my cock still gets hard seeing her?

"Hey, if you've got a minute, can you run through the presentations I sent you? It's the ones we'll be showing for Vanguard and the core assets of the London branch on the second. I need you to make sure that all the data looks good and is clear. I don't want them to think we're hiding shit because we aren't. Our Vanguard profit margins are already beating theirs, so they're going to look closely at it."

I cock my head. I knew we'd been doing well, but better than New York? That's impressive. "You don't think they'll believe us?" I ask.

"Absolutely not. They're going to think we've been twiddling our thumbs this entire time, doing the minimum. It's like they assume we're both lazy idiots. Do they understand how much you work, Andrew? I guess they don't know that I'm doing anything at all, but you've been running this place for years by yourself. Even your dad didn't really touch it."

I shrug. "They know they don't have to worry about London, but they also think they could do better. Maybe they could. Phillip knows the business better than anyone, and Mason makes fantastic leaps sometimes. I know one thing, though. Together, we're better than either of them."

I can see the way my words impact her. A bit more redness on her cheeks. Her frustration washes away, and she gets a grin on her face. "Well, let's show them just how good we are. I don't want questions about the accuracy of our data since you have a big enough bombshell to drop afterward. We need them to be impressed."

I nod to her, and I only glance at the costumes one more time before I walk back to my computer to pull up the presentations.

"Run through them with me," I say and turn the monitor to where she can see it.

That grin gets wider. "This I like, Andrew. I enjoy working with you. I don't know why, but I've never worked as well with anyone else."

We complement each other better than I'd ever expected. Sure, I had strong suspicions that she could do the job, but we're doing better than the minimum. Especially with how well Vanguard is doing.

"I couldn't have picked a better partner in crime." *Or a better partner in bed...* I don't say that, though.

We run through the presentation, and as we get to the actual charts, I ask her all those little questions I know my brothers will ask. The specifics of where the data comes from, how it might have been manipulated to look better than it is. I take notes on it so we can insert slides explaining all those points. Phillip and Mason may not be paying very much attention to the introductory slides, but when they see numbers like this, they're going to sit up and take notice.

"We need to put the details of how we hit these numbers," I say. "The nitty gritty parts. Genres and niches we exploited. The ideology of our decisions. That'll be what Phillip, especially, will home in on. They're going to want to exploit the same weaknesses in the market. New York and London aren't very different, and they've got a much bigger pool to play in as far as author choices are concerned. When they win big, it's ten times as big of a win as we get."

Sera nods, just as seriously as ever. This is her ticket to landing where she wants, and she knows it. When I drop the bomb about Loughton Media and how she's the one who started and run Vanguard, Phillip and Mason will decide where she goes based on her presentation.

I just want to hold her and tell her it'll be fine. That there's no reason to worry about any of this. But truthfully, that's just not the reality. I may be equal partners with my brothers, but there are two of them and one of me. If they both go against my decision, then I can't promise shit.

"Okay, I think I can get that stuff together. Want me to make another presentation about how I made those decisions? Or just tack it onto the end of this one?"

"Tack it on. It's a guarantee that they're going to want that information, so you might as well just keep it all in one file."

She gives me a nod and stands up. "We've done pretty damn well, haven't we?" she asks.

"Better than anyone expected. Me included. Maybe working fourteen-hour days was worth it."

She chuckles. "You worked fourteen-hour days. I worked seventeen-hour days. And yeah, I'd say it was worth it. I just hope your brothers agree."

The unsaid question lingers in the air. *And if they don't agree? What happens then?* "Well, all we can do is show them what we've done. They're not ones to ignore ways to increase earnings, and they aren't the kind of people to discard anyone that's obviously valuable."

She nods. "I'll get the second half of the presentation figured out." When she turns around, she finally sees our costumes and pauses for a moment. Then she glances back at me. "Is it weird that the thought of you in a Santa suit turns me on a little? Is that a weird thing?"

"Not weird at all. Why do you think I've got an elf kink?" I give her a wink before looking around the elf-filled room, and she grins back. Then she walks out the door.

I'm left in silence again, and when I look at the numbers on the screen, I can't help but hope that my brothers recognize just how important Sera is to the future of our company. She's a fucking genius with absolutely no experience. No real training. Just inspired understanding and a work ethic that blows all of ours out of the water.

But it's more than that. Even if she wasn't everything she is for the company, she's important to me. That, more than anything else, is why I'm going to do everything I can to give her what she wants and deserves.

Thirty-Six

SERA

My second Christmas party ever, and I'm a freaking elf. But I've got a smile on my face a mile wide. This is not a brand-new position at a brand-new company. I'm not outside my comfort zone. This is where I freaking belong, and I'm living it up.

Andrew hands me a glass of champagne, gives me a grin, and says, "To the most unexpected genius I've ever met."

God, every time he says stuff like that, it makes me shiver a little. This is a man who could do anything, have anyone, *choose* anyone to work with. And he, without a doubt, wants me at his side. Not just for sex. Not just because he trusts me not to rat him out to his brothers. No, he wants my ideas and thoughts. He wants me.

I'm important in this position, and it's everything I've ever wanted. All the months and years of feeling like I didn't live up to what my parents have done with their lives feels like it's culminating in this moment. Like I was born to do exactly this. Creative business decisions that no one has thought of. Seeing what other people have missed. Hard work and long hours that end with changes in the very fabric of how an industry works.

It is exactly what I want.

Christine, the Director of Marketing, comes up to me in a sparkling silver gown. So like the one I wore years ago. "It's a beautiful party, Sera," she says. Those eyes tell me she's surprised to see someone else acting like Andrew at a formal event. He's literally the only guy not dressed in a tux tonight.

"It is, isn't it? The last Christmas party I went to was when I hired on with Loughton House three years ago. I can't believe how long ago that feels."

She gives me a look that could set someone on fire. She's been in the publishing business for twenty-something years and was one of the first people hired when Loughton House London opened three years ago. As of last week, Andrew told her and the other directors that they needed to follow my directions. It was the first time he recognized my position in front of anyone other than Marie, his secretary, who's known the whole time. Maybe I shouldn't have mentioned my limited amount of experience. Oops.

"Well, most years it's a little less… impressive. This year, I think Andrew's trying to inspire some confidence from our new authors. Everybody likes a little glitz and glam."

I look around the room. It's more than "a little glitz and glam". More like a snowy forest captured inside a hotel. Crystal snowflakes dangle from the ceiling, shimmering in the soft blue light of thousands of tiny bulbs hanging above them. Like stars in the night sky. The clear glass tables look like ice. Little "snowdrifts" made of faux snow are piling up against the walls. Fake trees hug the walls and brush up against the ceiling, making it feel like we're in a clearing in the woods. Everyone's wearing fancy clothes, making it feel so much like something out of a fairy tale.

But I don't feel like I'm in a fairy tale right now. I'm getting a taste of the real corporate world for the first time. Christine has a look in her eyes that tells me just how little she enjoys my presence, much less the fact that I'm kind of her boss. She's smiling, though. Being the perfect upper management employee. She knows the corporate game, and she knows that the best thing she can do is play politics and figure out why I'm there and how I found myself in my position. Whatever that position may be.

"I certainly don't. The New York branch never had this kind of party. Maybe there'd be a bigger turnout if Phillip put a little more effort into the décor."

She gives me a confused look. Did she think I had come from the London branch? "Do you like it here? I've never worked with the New York teams before. Rumor has it Phillip can be a little tough to work with."

She's giving me an opening to expose myself. She's prying without asking pointed questions. Instead of telling her I was just a cover artist, I say, "Phillip's never been hard to work with. If you were good at your job and made sure you screwed nothing up, he just let you do your thing. His only focuses were productivity and efficiency. No different from his father."

I may not have twenty years of experience working for Loughton House, but my mother trained me from a young age to win in this kind of arena. Now that I recognize that I'm in the arena, I let the old training set in.

Christine asks, "You worked with Russel?"

I give her a little shake of the head. "No, I never worked directly with Russel. Phillip's run the New York branch since before they hired me on. Russel didn't interact with anyone but upper management and his sons."

That's when Andrew walks over, a drink in hand, and says, "Is the party better than last year?"

Christine chuckles, and when she smiles at Andrew, it's obvious that she looks at him as more than a boss.

Which I can understand. He's gorgeous, rich, and hilarious. But he's also mine. The office doesn't know that, though. Nobody does.

"You outdid yourself this year, Andrew. Much better than last year's Casino Night." He grins at her, but then he turns to me.

"Are you ready to give out awards?"

I nod, and Christine frowns. "This year, we're trying something special," I say, reinforcing my station above her. "But as for the specifics, you'll just have to wait and see."

She's still frowning when I walk with Andrew toward the stage. A Christmas tree stands high above everyone here, the only tree with decorations. Really, the only thing that distinguishes the room from anything other than a Winter Wonderland.

And in front of it is the podium and a table of awards behind it, covered in a silk sheet. "Are we really giving out all of them?" I whisper.

"Every. Single. One." This is Andrew's plan, and I'm still a little confused why we're putting so much effort into it with how much else is going on.

Andrew stands behind the podium and begins to speak as I pull the sheet away from the awards. They're not expensive awards, just tiny little trophies like kids get in sports. Each one's different. One has a shoe on top, another has a coffee pot, and one of the more bizarre ones is the Excel symbol.

"Ladies and gentlemen," Andrew begins. "Can I have your attention for a short while? Pull up a chair because I think you're going to want to pay attention. This is *very* important."

There's murmuring in the crowd. We've kept this idea top secret for almost two weeks. Andrew waits for everyone to quiet down, and he starts back up.

"This year, to show our appreciation to everyone who has worked so hard during this transition period, we're going to be giving out some very prestigious awards. I'd really appreciate it if the recipients keep them in their office so that we can all gaze upon them. And for those of you who work from home, if you could have it handy for Zoom calls, that'd be great. We want everyone to know just how amazing you are."

More murmuring, and I can't help but grin as Andrew stares seriously at the crowd. It almost makes it seem like more of a joke since he's never this serious. I don't know if I've ever seen Andrew in a work environment without a grin plastered across his face.

He pulls a folded-up piece of paper from a pocket on his Santa coat and begins reading. "Loughton House would like to thank Justin Ford for his undying dedication to high-quality memes. For giving us laughter during these trying times with just a silly picture and a few words. And he does it all, pissing no one off. Come on up, Justin. Take this trophy, along with my deepest appreciation."

The crowd erupts with laughter, and a guy in his early thirties stands up and walks up to the stage. I pick up the trophy with a goofy cat face on top and hand it to Justin after Andrew shakes his hand. The entire time, Andrew is doing his best impersonation of Phillip as he can.

"The next outstanding team member is Agatha Davis." A woman in her late sixties stands up, and she's already grinning and shaking her head. Her table is laughing so hard they're almost falling out of their seats. "Miss Agatha," Andrew says, as he gives the older woman a wide smile, "you've earned the widely coveted award for the best birthday cakes. We've all experienced the terror of shop-made birthday cakes, and I think I speak for the entire company when I say that ever since you took over as resident birthday cake maker, our lives are much better. Thank you, from the bottom of my heart. And stomach."

Several people stand up to applaud as she walks up the steps. When I hand her the little trophy with a birthday candle on the top, she leans forward and says, "I bought every one of those cakes."

She shakes her head as she walks back down the steps, and I glance up at Andrew. Dressed in his Santa outfit, he continues down his very long list of awards, each of them more ridiculous than the last. He's good at this. No, more than that, he's great at this. I may help him run the company, but I could never make an entire crowd smile and laugh like this. I couldn't make people love me like he does.

"Jennifer, we have awarded you the best in show of purse puppies. Brutus is adorable, and we might even replace the Loughton House logo with a picture of him in the future. Don't quote me on that, but we might be in talks about it already."

Pure chaos from a company that's known for its seriousness. And it all stems from Andrew. This would never happen in New York. Even though London has its own share of corporate politicking, there's a different feel to the atmosphere.

It's the same reason I've fallen for Andrew. Quick with a smile, dangerous with a laugh, and underneath it all, he's so damned clever. No one's going to be talking about me being recognized as an untitled upper manager. The recent changes, including Loughton Media, aren't going to be at the forefront of conversation. They're going to be too worried about these stupid trophies, this beautiful party, and that everyone got very nice Christmas bonuses. Throw in actual Christmas, and we don't have to worry about any news getting back to New York before New Year's.

I do my part, handing out each trophy for all the stupid little things we could come up with. Best movie recommendation. Best chocolate chip cookie recipe. Most cups of coffee drank. Best accent. Most pairs of shoes. They're ridiculous, but this is the first time I've watched hundreds of people laughing about every award for more than half an hour.

The people that work for Loughton House in London are happy in a way that New York's employees aren't. When I first sat on Andrew's balcony, I marveled at how different it was here. How the sounds, smells, and atmosphere of London are so strange. Yet, none of those compare Andrew's effect on it all. He sets the tone, and unlike Phillip and Russel, he's a boss that his employees love.

How can watching him be so silly give me the same strange sensation in my chest that watching him be brilliant does? It's like my heart's swelling. Is this what the Grinch felt like?

When all the awards are handed out, and my smile is so wide it's almost hurting, Andrew closes the awards ceremony. "Thanks everybody for having a bit of fun with me. I feel like I just pranked the entire company, but you'd better keep those awards on your desks because next Christmas, you're going to have competition. Agnes, I can't wait for someone to step up and try to take away the Best Birthday Cake baker next year."

"They can have it! I just want wonderful cake!" she yells from the back of the room, and everyone erupts in laughter again.

"Well, I want you all to have a wonderful night, a fantastic holiday with your families, and then an even better New Year because when we come back to work, it's going to be fast-paced. We're going to be breaking some records next year, and I want you well rested to spend those big Christmas bonuses. And for work, of course."

There are some snickers, but everyone's having a good time. When Andrew steps toward me, I fall into step beside him. Everyone at the party, for the first time, sees us walking together. There's no doubt that there'll be questions. Maybe even a few accusations. Part of me fears that. What would it mean to my career if people thought I got to where I was by fucking the boss?

Does it matter, though? No, I don't think so. I've done a hell of a lot of work, and I deserve to stand next to Andrew here. If there are accusations, then we can deal with them after the holidays.

"Phase One is complete. On to Phase Two." He whispers it in my ear, and it sounds like he's working on either a CIA mission or a bank heist. I'm kind of hoping for the first option, but more than likely, it's the second.

"What are you talking about?" I whisper back. Christine sees me, and there's no lack of fury in her eyes. Well, I guess even Andrew can't make everyone in a company this big happy.

He grins at me before he says, "Now it's time to reenact the more important pieces of our first night together."

That night flashes through my mind, and somehow, the first thing I say is, "Andrew, I'm not helping you do any stripping tonight."

"You can't help when you're the audience…"

Oh, this ought to be entertaining.

Thirty-Seven

ANDREW

Sera's standing there gawking when I take her hand in mine and speed walk, not to the door. No, we're playing that first night on repeat, and we absolutely did not just walk out the door last time. "Where are we going?" she asks as I drag her toward the restrooms.

"You've got to change. Everyone will recognize you in that outfit. You're literally the only person here dressed like an elf."

She plants her feet and refuses to budge, her brows furrowed as she tries to understand what's going on. "But we can leave, Andrew. You're the boss. You did the thing. Everyone's seen you and talked to you, and you were wonderful. Now we can be like normal people and leave whenever we want."

And I smirk.

"Maybe we could do that. This is better, though. Just stop trying to make this logical, Sera. We've been logical and rational for months. Let's have a little adventure."

Her face turns thoughtful until she finally shrugs. "Okay, Andrew. Wisk me away."

I nod and continue to drag her toward the restroom, but when we get there, I stop. I look around us to make sure no one's looking, and I pick up the little steel trashcan next to the door.

"What the hell?" Sera's not expecting me to do this, and she's definitely not expecting me to hand her a small white trash bag that's tied at the top.

"Quick, put it on. All of it." Then I push her toward the door. She turns, gives me a confused look, and then goes inside. I wait, which is harder than I'd have expected. Especially with the little remote in my pocket that's begging me to press it.

I just lean against the wall, my hands in my pockets. People pass me by, each of them giving me a grin like they're my friend.

When Sera walks out of the bathroom, she's wearing the same elf costume, but she's got a very knowing smile on her face. "You're about to embarrass the crap out of me, aren't you?" she whispers. "At a company party."

I wink at her and take her arm in mine. "I'd never embarrass you here. But elsewhere? Maybe."

"I'm going to regret this," she mutters, but I pretend like I don't hear her. Instead, I click the button on the remote, and Sera's entire body tenses for a second. Her breathing hitches, and she looks at me with an anxious expression.

"You're going to love it." Then I lead her out of the party. Out of the hotel. When we sit down in the car, she whispers in my ear, "This is a very…" She pauses for a second, her body tensing again before finishing, "Very powerful little vibrator."

"It is. I didn't want you to get annoyed with it. There's still so much adventuring to do before we go back home."

Her eyes get wide, her mouth opening slightly. "You expect me to wear this on an adventure? I thought you were just bringing me home."

I chuckle and put my hand on her thigh, giving it a good squeeze. "Oh no, Sera. You need more experiences that you'll never forget. Preferably ones with you moaning out my name. A swollen pussy and shaking legs. I've fucked you in every possible way at the office, but now I want to do the same everywhere else. But first, I need you so desperate you won't care where we are when I pull up that dress."

Her body tenses up even more, and she just stares at me. I say nothing to the driver. He knows where we're going, and letting Sera know would just make her even more nervous. There's no reason for that. Nothing about tonight is going to be even close to pushing her boundaries. But the fear and apprehension are going to turn her on more than anything that vibrator could do.

Already, her legs are spreading ever so slightly. Her breath's coming out in a soft pant as she stares out the window, leaving the window foggy. The night's quiet compared to most. When the car finally pulls over, we both stare at the building in front of us. Hampton Court Palace, one of the most historic buildings in London, is having a Christmas party tonight. And we're not going, even though I have tickets.

"We're going to another party? Are you really stripping in a castle?" Sera asks. Her eyes have that slightly hazy look to them, and when I run my hand over her ass, she lets out a soft moan.

"No, but we are going to do some dancing."

My hand moves up her back, and when they touch her neck, she shivers. "Dancing? But we're wearing these costumes, and I feel like I'm about to explode."

I can't help but grin. She's so turned on that she's not even processing the fact that we're about be in a literal castle. "We're replaying that first night together. We both danced wearing these costumes then, and I'm feeling generous enough to skip the stripping part tonight."

I feel for the little remote control in my pocket. The little button that will make the vibrator pressing between her lips move faster or slower. Like a magic wand that controls how badly she gets lost in need. The longer I've been with Sera, the more I've realized that deep down, the one thing she truly craves is giving up her control. At first, she was hesitant, but each time that I took her in the office, her resistance cracked a little more.

She's not putting up a fight. She wants to give into those feelings. Her body knows them well enough to let go.

"Andrew," she says and looks up at me, "I hope you know that I'm really glad you kidnapped me."

I lean down and press my lips to hers. Soft. Gentle. The kind of kiss that doesn't agree with how much my cock is straining against my pants. The kind that whispers of things more than lust, more than physical need.

"It was the best decision I ever made." A simple statement that doesn't express the way I feel about the woman who's become the sun I orbit around. I don't even want to think about what my life would be like right now if I hadn't forced her to hear me out.

Her hand moves to my cheek, and her nails scratch against the stubble with a rasping sound. "You've shown me a different world. And a different side of myself. Thank you."

I give her a smile and take her hand. How do you put the feelings I have for her into words? What words would express how much I think about her? I rack my mind for some way to explain just how much she means to me, but the words elude me.

Instead, I presses the button. "Andrew…" she moans. And I lead her to the front door of Hampton Court Palace. A place I'll never forget.

I've only been to Hampton Court Palace once before, and it was to meet with several members of Parliament to discuss the nationwide reading campaign several years ago.

It's beautiful, not all that different from our own Christmas party. Then again, most Christmas parties are pretty similar.

This one's just a little more expensive, and the people here have a hell of a lot more money.

"Aren't we going to be a little conspicuous?" Sera whispers as we step onto the dance floor. People swirl around us in tuxes and gorgeous ball gowns. Everything is a mix of sparkling silver and black coat tails, something you'd never see in the states. Everyone but us. Even at an event like this, money talks, and I have more than most of the people here.

"Definitely. Every single person will be looking at us, just like the night I stripped. I suggest you keep from orgasming until we leave. We might make national news."

She whispers, "Please don't make the vibrator any faster," as she grips my hand tighter. I smile down at her. God, she's something special, and I want this night to be memorable for more than just the sex. I want her to remember this forever. The night that she danced with me with literal Princes beside her. The night she wore an elf costume in a room full of the most important people in England.

This is not a night anyone could forget, but I hope it's only the first of many insane adventures I take her on.

The orchestra was playing *The First Noel* when we walked in, and the song is ending. "You do know how to waltz, don't you?" I ask, only now realizing that I'd never asked that before. I may be willing to look a little silly for a song, but I don't want Sera to feel like a fool just for an adventure.

She chuckles. "Definitely. This isn't the first time I've been to a formal ball before."

I nod to her, and as the orchestra begins to play *Silent Night*, I sweep her into the dance. And almost like we're at Luciano's, there's no need for us to talk. Yes, there are hundreds of people around us, but as the violinists begin to play, it feels like they all melt away.

She's smiling as I twirl her, and when I pull her back to me, she's laughing. It's wonderful and a completely different vibe than I'd expected. It was supposed to be funny, to be a story we told and another way to extend her teasing.

But seeing her like this and knowing that she's still desperate for me makes me feel like there's something more to tonight than a silly adventure. This is not like the time I took her to Luciano's or The Shard. This is more than that. Even more than that first Christmas party.

When she looks into my eyes, it feels like we really are in a magical wonderland. Or at least that there's something magical between us.

Her skirt twirls around her as I send her into another spin, and when she comes back, she presses herself against me a little tighter. "Thank you," she whispers as we cross the dance floor, our eyes on each other the entire time.

Her hand squeezes mine as we twirl around. We stick out like a sore thumb, and I'd expected to be at least a little aware of the people around us staring. She certainly was. But now that we're dancing, it really is like we're the only people in the world.

And as fast as it'd begun, the music ends, and we're left standing still in the middle of a group of people trying to pretend like they're not staring at us. "Holy crap, you were right. They're literally all looking at us," Sera whispers as I pull her away from the dance floor.

She's giggling, and I'm pretty sure I let out a few giggles as well. When we step away from the crowd, I whisper, "Now we run. Just like last time. The only difference is that no one's chasing us now, so we don't have to run quite as fast."

I put my hand in my pocket and click the vibrator button again. She shivers and smiles up at me. "There is not another man in the world like you," she says again. I don't know what to say, but I do know what comes next.

"I hope you're ready for the rest of the night."

She swallows, and I see her body tense, but then she nods. "We'd better get to the room pretty quickly or we might still make national news."

Thirty-Eight

SERA

I'M IN A CASTLE. A LITERAL CASTLE, BUILT HUNDREDS of years ago. The most important people in England's history have walked these halls. People planned wars. Treaties have been signed. The world has held its breath while people in these very walls have talked.

And a man in a Santa costume danced a waltz with a woman in an elf costume while literal royalty watched.

Right now, I don't give a damn about any of it, though. He has not gotten us to the room nearly fast enough. The buzzing between my legs and the touch of Andrew's hand on my lower back are all that I can think about. That and I know my mind is about to be blown.

Andrew's hand slides down my lower back until it's resting on my ass. Occasionally, he'll give it a little pat. A reminder of the times he's slapped my ass at the office. Or even louder in his bed.

I can feel my heart beating through my whole body. Yet Andrew seems completely at ease. Like, nothing at all out of the ordinary is happening. He's just walking at his normal pace down the hallway in his Santa costume.

Then he stops, presses me against a wood-paneled wall, and kisses me like he's been desperate to do this for days. His fake beard tickles my chin, but I barely notice. His hand moves from my ass to my breast, squeezing it hard as he tries to kiss me hard enough to bruise.

"You're driving me fucking crazy," he whispers. "You smell like sex, Sera. Your little pussy must be drenched. I bet if I ran my finger between your thighs, I'd find a river running down your leg, wouldn't I?"

Oh God. I can't answer him. Instead, I just nod. I expect him to just accept that, but he doesn't. His fingers trail from my breast down to the bottom of the skirt. He reaches under it, and his hand slides across my inner thigh.

"You little slut," he whispers. "I was right. You're so wet that I bet your feet are slick." His hand moves to my pussy, and he presses against it, forcing the vibrator against my clit even harder. It's like lightning exploding through me, and I try to escape it, try to wiggle away from his grip, but he holds me still. He forces my body to accept it.

"It's too much," I whisper, but he doesn't let up.

He moves his lips to my ear, and he whispers, "If you come for me, I'll turn off the vibrator until we get to the room. I'll let you breathe for a few minutes before I make you scream."

Fuck. It's too much. His lips press against my neck, his teeth finding their place against my skin. I feel too constricted. Every move makes my clothes brush against my oversensitive skin. The lightning flows through me, setting every inch of my body on edge.

And then he whispers, "Be my good girl, Sera. Come for me. Don't make me turn you around and spank that ass in this hallway."

Somehow, as insane as it sounds, those words push me toward orgasm. The vibrator may have my body going crazy, but it's his words that turn me on, that let me relax enough for the waves of bliss to wash over me. Every freaking time.

"Yes, sir," I whisper back. "I'm trying." How does it always feel like this when he takes control? How do I go from terrified and over-stimulated to desperate for more?

"I know you are. You're such a good little slut, but I think you need a little help." He reaches under my skirt, and with no discretion, pulls it up, wedging it between our bodies. Anyone walking down the hall would see me, and Andrew doesn't give a damn. He grabs my ass, while the other hand pressing the vibrator against me makes circles.

I'm left gasping, and the pressure inside me is building. I don't try to escape it, though. My hands go to my breasts, wishing that I wasn't wearing a bra, and I squeeze.

Then Andrew talks to me again, and the dam inside of me explodes. "When we get into that room, I'm going to tie you to the bed. I'm going to make you come so many times that you don't know if what we're doing is real or a dream. I'm going to show you what it really means to be my little slut."

My legs shake, and if Andrew wasn't holding me up, I'd probably collapse, but his hands hold me tight against the paneling. "That's it, Sera. Come for me."

Waves of pleasure roll through me. For a moment, in the middle of a hallway in a castle I don't even know the name of, I feel completely free. Like, nothing in the world could even come close to being important. Not business. Not my family. Nothing. All that matters is Andrew and those waves of perfection.

Like all good things, they fade, though, and I'm left breathing heavily. It's only then that I realize what just happened. "We could have been arrested," I say. "They might have cameras or something."

Andrew just grins at me, and the vibrator turns off. "If someone comes knocking on my door, I'll pay the fine, and you'll never know."

He slowly lets my body relax. His hand moves away from the throbbing between my legs, and when I've proven that I'm steady on my feet, he walks a foot away to the nearest door. And slides his card into the slot.

"We're here," he says with a smirk.

That son of-a… "I thought you'd said I'd get a breather before you made me scream."

"You will. I still need to strip you down and tie you up. Plenty of time to breathe while I'm doing that."

I follow him into the most luxurious room I have ever been in. It's literally a room from a fairy tale. A marble fireplace is inset into one wall, a slow fire burning in it. Paintings from centuries ago hang from the intricately carved wood paneling. A mural has been painted on the ceiling of a ship on the ocean.

And against one wall is a bed that will forever be lodged in my memory as what a king would sleep on. Spiral shaped posters rise from the enormous frame. It looks like it must have taken a crane to move the thing into the room. Made of solid dark woods, it's embellished in gold along the edges of the spirals and the trim of the frame.

At first, I'm just in awe of the room, but then Andrew wraps his arms around my waist. The coat's gone, along with his shirt. His naked arms pull me to him, and my entire body feels like it could melt into his touch. "You're the most wonderful woman I've ever met," he whispers.

Even though I can feel his cock pressing through his pants against my back, I feel so freaking loved right now. Yes, nearly every piece of our relationship has been filled with crazy sex, but maybe that's not a bad thing. It certainly hasn't hurt that he can turn me on like no one else ever has.

"You're not too bad yourself," I say back, no longer worrying about whispering. "Are you serious about tying me up?"

He lets go of me and walks over to the Santa coat. Digging into one of the ridiculously large pockets, he pulls out several bundles of rope. "Absolutely."

I chuckle at the look on his face. The almost childish excitement. "What do I get out of this? I'm pretty sure most women would balk at the thought of being tied up by their boss."

The curl of his lip makes me shiver. The way he looks at me like he's going to destroy me makes me want to beg him to hurry. Maybe I don't need a breather.

"You get hours of orgasms, little slut," he says as he steps in front of me. His hands go to the buttons that run up the front of the silly little elf costume. "And you know how much you enjoy it when I don't give you any options. Just think, you won't be able to pull away even if you wanted to. You're going to come so many times the thought of another orgasm will be almost terrifying."

He licks his lips as the last button comes undone. Fuck. The way he's looking at me makes me a little worried that I'm not ready. That everything that we've done previously is just a tease compared to this. That time in the office where he handcuffed me? He had time limits. I couldn't get too loud. There weren't a thousand unique positions he could put me in.

There are no limits to what he could do tonight.

"Think about how vulnerable you'll be spread out, your hands and legs held in place. You won't be able to squirm away or push back. You won't even be able to push yourself toward me if I decide to tease you. That's your fantasy, isn't it? Giving up all that control."

As if my body needed any more temptation to fall into this. "Yes," I whisper.

He smirks at me, but those eyes still look ready to devour me. "Good. Now it won't just be a fantasy. Now it's something you'll be able to beg me for."

This is not exactly what I'd expected from tonight. He removes my top, and then the bra comes off. I should be worried about being naked while he's looking at me like that, but I know nothing is going to happen until I lay down in that bed. The bed being surrounded by heavy pillars of wood that I could never hope to break.

What could he do to me he hasn't before? I don't know. Probably nothing. He's spanked me. He's fucked me and teased me and pushed me in ways I never imagined. What could he do that's different this time?

If he were anyone else, I'd say nothing. But I never imagined this or the remote-controlled vibrator. I never imagined him forcing me to come in a hallway or in the office.

He's going to break me tonight. And I can't wait.

My skirt falls around my feet, and Andrew's hand runs over my naked ass. "You have the most beautiful body in the world, Sera," he says. He's not whispering now. There's no one to hear him. His lips press against my lower back, and as he pulls my thong down achingly slowly, he leaves a trail of kisses down to my calf.

Compared to how intense he was only moments ago; this almost makes me want to relax. Almost. I know that as soon as I climb into that bed, the soft kisses and gentle caresses will end, and I'll be left with the ravenous man that knows exactly how to push me past any limit I've ever thought I had.

I still step out of my underwear, and when he stands up, his fingers glide over my skin. "Get into bed now. I want you to try to calm down. I know you just came, and that you're more than a little nervous, but this is something you've fantasized about, right?"

Nodding even though he's behind me. He'll see it. He'll know that I'm agreeing to this. I take a deep breath and before I crawl onto the oversized bed. I stop and turn around and face the man that I'm willing to trust in ways I'd never trust anyone else.

"Andrew, I need you to listen to me." He cocks his head, but he nods. "Andrew, don't wear a condom. Tonight, I don't want anything separating us. I've been on the pill this whole time."

He sucks in a breath, and I can see those eyes get even harder, even more ravenous. He's thinking, trying to decide if he can trust me, and I don't wait for an answer. I decided to put my trust in him tonight, and I just hope that he'll do the same.

I crawl onto the bed, his eyes never leaving me. "How do you want me?" I ask when I'm laying in the middle.

"I'll position you. Don't worry."

I'm supposed to relax, to let go of everything and just exist. To not think about the bomb, I just dropped on him or whether he'll take me up on my offer. I know that I'm not supposed to control things, but even now, after months of him playing with me, it's more difficult than I ever expected. How do you just let someone control your body like this?

But I take another deep breath and try to settle the panic rising inside me. It's fine. I'm going to love it. My body wants it, and deep down, I know I crave it. Maybe fear is part of it. Just like with the vibrator, it's like every time I get scared, my body goes into overdrive, and I get to feel new heights of bliss.

When it's all done, I'm always glad that he's played with me. Especially when I start out terrified. Instead of trying to fight it, I put my arms at my sides and close my eyes. As soon as they're closed, I see him. I imagine what he's going to do. The way he'll tease my body with his fingers and his mouth. Kisses everywhere. Rough fingers will dig into my skin. The rope will tear at my ankles and wrists. Tight against my flesh, they'll hold me still even when I'm writhing on the bed.

My eyes flash open when I feel Andrew's hand on my wrist. He takes a short strand of rope and winds it around my wrist in a simple knot. Then he runs the rope to the pillar at the foot of the bed and pulls it tight, forcing my arm in that direction. There's no pressure on my wrist as he ties the rope around the pillar, but when I test it, my hand can barely move. It's locked in place.

I swallow. Hard. Andrew walks around the bed to take my other arm and do the same thing. I feel like I'm about to be tortured, and maybe I am. But maybe my body craves that, too. Truthfully, I think Andrew knows me better than I know myself. If it really becomes too much, all I have to do is tell him to stop. He's reminded me of that so many times.

But I've never needed to. Never wanted to.

Andrew smiles down at me, and his finger runs over my breast and up to my throat. His fingers constrict just enough that I feel the pressure. And for the first time, a bit of panic runs through me. I tug on the ropes that hold me to the bed, but I'd have had a better shot at getting out of the handcuffs. My breath comes out quicker as the panic grows inside me.

His smile widens as he releases my throat. I expect him to tie my foot just like my wrists, but he doesn't. Instead, he grabs a pillow and wedges it under my ass, something he's never done before.

"If anything tingles, you'd better let me know," he says seriously. I nod, and his words have a soothing effect on me. I can trust him not to let anything happen to me. At first, that animal instinct inside me had wanted to escape the cage he was putting me in, but as I look up at him, I recognize that this is for me as much as him.

That nod is all it takes for him to go back to tying me up. He makes a knot around my ankle and pulls my leg into the air. I have to shift my hips a bit as he runs the other side of the rope to the *pillar by my head*. Oh, God. He's going to keep my legs spread and in the air, while he plays with me. It's almost like I'm in stirrups except the doctor's going to fuck me until I pass out.

That knowing smile just keeps growing as he does the same thing to my other leg. Then he stops and looks at me. My legs are spread wide, my hands are useless. When I pull on the ropes, I'm left feeling even more helpless. It's exactly like he said. I have absolutely no control right now. The most I can do is bend my knees a little.

Andrew slowly takes off the rest of the Santa outfit. The pants and boots. He sits down beside me as he takes off his socks. "You know, when we get back from New York, I think I'm going to have to buy a new bed. I haven't even started to play with that sexy little body, and I already know that it'll be worth it. Hell, just seeing you like this would be worth it. Even if I couldn't have my way with you."

There are no words to say. I'm past the point of dirty talk, and I haven't gotten lost in the sensations yet, so it's all just kind of terrifying still. I may have fantasized about someone doing this, but I never expected it to happen.

When he stands up, he pulls his boxers down. His cock is standing tall, and I'd swear it's bigger than normal. Is that possible? Or is it just my very addled brain playing tricks on me?

I don't have time to think very hard about it because he gets onto the bed. On top of me, his face between my legs and his cock squarely over my mouth. His tongue dips between my lips, and I give into the sensations. That's the point, right? Let it all happen to me. Be a fuck toy for him to play with.

His arms wrap around my hips and squeeze my thighs as his tongue finds my clit. Fuck, it feels so good. I'd thought it'd be too much with how hard I'd come earlier, but it's glorious. His hands on my thighs feel like fucking heaven.

And I keep staring up at his cock, and I could swear that I can see it throbbing. Hard and desperate to be inside me. I know what I want to do. Pushing off the bed as much as I can, I stick my tongue out and slowly run it along the underside of his shaft. Andrew's entire body quivers, and his mouth leaves my pussy.

"Is that what you want, little slut? Do you want my cock in your mouth?" Instead of answering, I just keep licking. My neck is aching already with how hard it is to reach like this, but it's not something I can ignore. I *need* to taste his cock. I need it inside of me.

Shifting his weight, Andrew bends his cock down toward my mouth. "Open up," he commands, and I do exactly as he says. Letting my muscles relax, I lay down, my mouth open, and he pushes past my lips.

He doesn't move, though. Not letting me have anything more than the tip. Then he goes right back to licking my pussy. Each lick goes from my entrance to my clit. Slow and steady, it's wonderful, but it's not the same intensity that we had in the hallway. Not the same desperation. He's teasing me. Just like that time in the chair.

I want to wrap my hands around his ass and pull him to me. I want him to be rough and forceful and really use me, but I literally have my hands tied. Andrew's fingers move down my thighs until he's caressing my lips, and it's wonderful. I just need more. They slide between my lips, mimicking his tongue, but every time they get to my entrance, they press inside me just a little. Just for me to want more.

Fuck. It's all a tease. No different from that damned vibrator. I try to press my pussy harder against his lips, but with the angles I'm in, I don't have the leverage to force his face and fingers against me.

I try to make him just as desperate as I am. My tongue swirls around the tip, rough and needy for any taste of him I can get. It's like he's immune to my attempts, and so I finally arch my back, my shoulders screaming at the exertion, and I inhale more of his cock.

He lets out a soft moan, his body tightening, and I can feel him swell even more. "Is that what you really want?" he mutters. Then his body shifts, and he's pushing himself down on me. He pushes me back to the bed, his cock deep in my throat. “Fine. If you want my cock in your mouth that much, I’ll make sure it stays there.”

His mouth goes back between my legs, but this time, his hips thrust. Each time is harder than the last, and it’s everything I’d wanted. I can’t pay attention to the sensations flowing through me with how he’s using my mouth. Each time his cock hits the back of my throat, my body does its best to escape, but the ropes hold me tight.

Squirming all I want. I don’t have to hold back or “be a good girl”. It’s the most freeing feeling in the world. I can simply be. Nothing to think about. Nothing to worry about. Simply exist.

So that’s what I’ll do. Andrew’s body moves on top of me. His groans are muffled since he’s got his mouth between my legs, but he’s enjoying himself.

Then he stops. Slowly, pulling away from my mouth, I’m left gasping as he rolls off me. Even though there’s no stimulation, I still feel that calm filling me. When he picks up my underwear and rips the vibrator out of them, I should be nervous. But I’m not.

He walks around to the foot of the bed and crawls between my legs, his eyes on mine the entire time. Those damned ravenous eyes. And I want him to use me. To break me. To do whatever the hell he wants.

He presses the vibrator to my clit, and it’s like pure electricity is flowing through me. My entire body tenses. My arms and legs pull at their bonds, but nothing gives. My back arches, but even that is limited by the angle I’m in.

“That’s it. Struggle for me. Squeeze that little pussy so that when I fuck you, you’re even tighter than normal.”

Then he does exactly that. He positions himself against my entrance, and slams into me like he's trying to drive nails. Even with how soaking wet I am, I scream. The vibrator continues. It's almost angry, whirring against my overly stimulated clit, and his other hand goes to my breast. Using it as a handhold, he groans.

"God, you're fucking tight, Sera. Like a vice made of silk." He continues to thrust, but it's not like when he was using my mouth. No, this is almost uncontrolled. This is rough, it's passionate. This is Andrew when he takes off that fucking mask he's always wearing. It's like there's clarity between us for the first time.

And my heart soars. Maybe it's taken all of this for him to be real. Or for me to recognize it.

Then I feel my body shudder and contract. I let out a loud moan as all the muscles in my body tighten. "That's it, Sera. Come for me." I didn't know that the orgasm was coming, but just like with everything else that's happening, I'm not in control of my body. More than likely, Andrew had expected it more than I did.

I stare into his eyes as he thrusts. As he takes me to higher highs. As he uses me for both of our pleasure.

There's not another man like him. I've never had a bond like this with anyone. Every other partner I've had has been disposable. They were a passing thing, like leaves in the fall.

But Andrew… Andrew will always matter. Anyone who knows my body, and more importantly, my heart like this, can't be disposable. Until this moment, while tied to a bed in a castle, I'd tried to pretend that this thing between us was like any other relationship.

It's not.

I had liked those other boys. I'd had fun with them. Laughed, smiled, and had adventures with them. With Andrew, it's more. It's bigger. More real. There's only one word that encompasses these feelings, and it's a word I never thought was possible.

Love. I think that I'm in love with Andrew Loughton.

Thirty-Nine

ANDREW

Sera is a fucking goddess. A work of art that nothing and no one could replicate. Her body calls to me in a way that makes me question my sanity.

Bound, moaning, coming, and quivering for me, she's a gift that I can't ever appreciate enough.

Tonight, I'm worshipping at her altar. An altar to the goddess of madness and lust and… something else. Something less tangible. Something less comprehendible.

My cock slides in and out of her as she writhes in her bonds. She's come dozens of times. She's exhausted. Her body probably aches in so many ways, but she just keeps staring at me, begging me to keep going with her silent eyes.

Each orgasm has her squirming less, though. It's taken everything to hold myself back. Her core tightening around my cock is making it hard to control myself. Skin to skin for the first time feels different. It's not just the sensations, though. There's something more.

This is the first time I've ever felt like sex is something more than a good time. Even with Sera, it's been scratching an itch or just wanting some fun.

And these ropes are keeping me from truly embracing it. I need to be on top of her, my chest pressed against her breasts, my lips against hers. Without interrupting my thrusts, I undo the knots on her ankles. One at a time, I lower them to the bed beside me. Her hazy eyes change as she realizes what's happening.

My body crushes hers as I lean forward and wrap my arms under her back. I kiss her with all the passion I have in me. All the passion I've ever felt toward her. And she moans in return.

She's mine, and I'm never going to let her go. I may be worshipping at her altar tonight, but no one else will ever take my place.

My fingers dig into her back as I give into the pressure that's been building for what seems like hours. Through each of her orgasms, it's gotten harder and harder to hold back the inevitable, but I needed to push her to this place. I've known what she craves since the first time I held her arms above her head. Tonight, I needed to show her what it is to be free.

"I love you," she whispers. It's not even words. It's a wind. An exhale. But I know the sound as well as I know her.

Those are the words that I've held back for too long. The same ones I felt on top of the Shard. I didn't know it was those magic words then, but that was the feeling. The need to hold her to me, to keep her from the rest of the world.

Those gray eyes stare into mine, inches away, and a soft smile crosses her face as I finally give into my body's need for release. Clarity washes over me amidst the bliss. This is not a moment that I'll ever forget. This night matters, and this woman matters even more.

It's like my entire being shifts, like little pieces inside me are being shattered and remade into different shapes. I would do anything for her. Sera is not just a girl I'm having fun with. She is not a tool. She is… mine.

"I love you more than anything, Sera," I whisper back to her. Even in the room's silence, it feels like our words are breaking something. Like the tiny world we built tonight is slowly cracking with each sound we make.

And then her eyes close, the smile on her lips never changing as her body calms. For the first time since I met her, I feel like she's completely relaxed without a care in the world.

I quickly untie her wrists and check them and her ankles for bruises or injuries from the rope. There's nothing to be found, and I sigh with a little relief. I'd been worried that my first time tying her up would go horribly wrong. Luckily, that's not the case.

Just like so many nights in the past, I can't stop staring at her naked body on top of the covers. At first, I was attracted to all the parts of her that the world could see. Her tits. Her ass. The way she sways her hips when she walks. The way her eyes sparkle when she's telling you that you're an idiot. All the things that most men would comment on.

Now, those are nothing compared to the little things that make her uniquely Sera. The little scar along the top of her hip that I have no story for. Just a little white line. The little red birthmark on her ribs that I'd initially thought had been a sex injury. The little patches of freckles on her shoulder from a childhood sunburn.

No one else in the world would see a picture of those things and talk about how beautiful they are, but that's because they don't know how beautiful a person she is. And those are the things that are hers and hers alone. They all have stories. They all make up the girl that I've fallen in love with.

My finger runs along the little scar, and I take a deep breath. This is not what I'd expected to feel after an hour of crazy sex. I hadn't thought I'd be so emotional. Sitting here in the dark room with Sera softly snoring beside me, I should revel in the best orgasm of my life.

But I'm not. I'm thinking about what this all means. What does this change?

Because I didn't want to let her down before. Now I *can't*. And that makes all the difference. I need to find a way to make sure that she gets the position she deserves, whether or not my brothers agree. I have to do whatever it takes.

I can't lose her. Not now that I understand just how much she means to me. Just how much I love her.

Forty
SERA

Our trip back to New York may have been delayed for a few days. We'd meant to leave the day after the Christmas party, but after our night together, we needed some time before coming back to the normal world. It's too full of other people and responsibilities.

Even during the Christmas holidays, there are things to do, especially with our big presentation looming only a week away. Then there's the whole family get together for the Loughton's, which has Andrew a little nervous. I need to stop by my mom's house, too. I haven't seen her in months, and we've always been close.

The ocean below us feels like a million miles away as we soar across the Atlantic at five hundred miles per hour. Andrew is going through his files and trying to prepare for questions that his brothers may ask. They'll want proof of our success. And they'll want data on how he plans to push forward with Loughton Media.

I understand that it's necessary to not let things slip through the cracks in a company as large as Loughton House, but at a certain point, I wonder when it becomes too much. Andrew isn't a middle manager. He owns one third of the company. He shouldn't have to prove his decisions to his brothers. I didn't understand initially, but now I get it. Now I understand why it was so important that he do it all with no input from them.

While he's focused on everything that's about to happen, I have absolutely nothing to do. He doesn't want any help because he needs to know exactly what and why he has a copy of each file in this folder. He has to know where to find them.

It all reminds me far too much of my own file collection. The backup plan in case this all goes terribly wrong. I haven't changed my mind or my moral stance on the issue. I know how I feel about Andrew. Every time I see him, hear his voice, or feel his touch, my heart swells with love. People talk about getting butterflies when they talk to someone they're interested in, but it's different with me. I never had them when I talked to him before.

But now, I have to forcibly focus on our conversations so that I don't turn into a doe-eyed teenager with a crush. I don't know if it's because I've never felt this way before or if this change in our relationship is just new.

Or if it's because I'm still not sure that I believe in love.

My parents have proven that even the most amazing people in the world can't find it. They're both still friends. They have plenty of love in their hearts. For me, and me alone. My mom has been married three times. My dad has been married six times. They're still on such friendly terms. They showed up at each other's weddings and gave toasts to their success.

But they can't seem to love anyone except me. I'll never doubt the reality of a parent's love for a child, but for a partner? That still seems like a fairy tale.

Yet, I can't believe that what I feel toward him is anything else. I can imagine my life with this man. I can see us working together, living together, and maybe even having a family. We've spent damn near every moment together for months. We've seen the best and worst of each other.

"Sera, do you remember if I'm missing any books that have done better than expected? I've got the spreadsheet right here." He carries the laptop over to me, a list of indies that have outperformed on the screen.

I scan through the list, thinking back to the dozens of talks we've had about this topic. Granted, it's tough to catch a single missed book, but attention to detail is the reason both of us are good at this job. That and the fact that we both know all of these books like the back of our hands, a skill I learned on my first day in London.

"A Diary of a Drug Fiend. That's the only one I'm seeing missing."

He chuckles and shakes his head ever so slightly. "You don't know how much I appreciate having someone that's in it with me. I don't have to explain anything or hope that you did your part. You're just as invested, just as knowledgeable, and, at the same time, you're not a dick. You're not out to prove that you're better."

I frown. What did he expect when he brought me on as his partner in crime? "Have other people been anything else?"

He gives me one of those patented "are you serious?" looks. "Sera, the only people I've ever worked with as a partner are Phillip and my dad. Both can be super dicks. Anyone else… well, they just don't contribute the same. There's a reason I've micromanaged everything. It's always on me to make sure things run smoothly, even in London. Working with you has been so fucking nice. We've been leaving work at five regularly. Somehow, even with adding two new pieces of the business, we're leaving early. That's incredible."

We've been putting in the work and I wasn't doing any less than Andrew, but to hear him say it like this, it's like he's surprised I'm doing anything. "What did you expect when you brought me to London? Did you just want me to answer emails and sit on my thumbs all day?"

Andrew almost cackles. "No, you were supposed to do your job. I just didn't think you'd do it to the same level that I would. You were just supposed to make sure that nothing stupid happened and give me a bit of breathing room to work on Loughton Media. Sera, you outperformed Phillip. London has a record quarter because of you. There's no way I could have expected that."

He's right, and I hadn't thought about it quite like that. I mean, I feel accomplished, but wasn't that the goal the whole time? At least since I decide to stick it out with Loughton House instead of starting a company. "It's good that we worked well together. Maybe that will translate into working well together for the foreseeable future?" I say that last bit with more than a little smugness.

And I see the waver in Phillip's smile. Not a full change from playful grin to frown, but just a moment of hesitation. "Yeah. It's going to be great having you working on the team permanently." Not exactly the phrasing that makes me feel secure in what I expect after this meeting.

I keep my comments to myself and remember that he promised. I trust him. He gives me a big grin and picks up his computer. "*A Diary of a Drug Fiend*," he mutters as he goes back to the table.

It's like the conversation didn't happen, and he goes back to work. I take a deep breath and let it out slowly. I'm trusting him. No different from when I let him tie me up. Or play with me in the office. Or when I agreed to impersonate him after he kidnapped me and dragged me to London with no warning.

I've trusted him from the beginning. Now is not the time to stop. But if he breaks that trust, I do still have a backup plan. At least that's what I'd thought originally. Now, I know that using that backup plan will be the end of my relationship with Andrew.

The only man I've ever loved.

Forty-One

ANDREW

Christmas was nice. There was an official rule agreed on by everyone: no talking about work. We didn't say even one word about Loughton House, even though Dad seemed to want to hear about it. He kept hinting at it, at least.

But Phillip wasn't having any of that. After the engagement was announced there was plenty to talk about, though, so it ended up being a good time. And only slightly nerve-wracking. I've got too many secrets hidden away from my brothers right now, and the more time I spent with them before I made the big reveal, the more likely it'd be for them to catch me.

I give Sera a grin as she puts her company phone into her pocket. I close my laptop and slide it under my arm. "Time to lay all our cards on the table," I say, and Sera nods to me.

We both stand up, and I lead the way out of the little office we've commandeered for the day. It's strange how much the New York offices have changed since we left.

There's not the same amount of hustle and bustle as there was before. It almost feels like London.

Sera makes a weird noise as we approach a corner, and I glance behind me at the same time that I walk into the hallway intersection. "Stop!" she says, and I whirl around just as the coffee cart slams into my hip. A metal bar on the bottom connects with my knee, and I collapse. I catch myself, but my laptop crashes to the ground with a sickening crunch.

"Fuck," I mutter as I stand up. A woman in a catering outfit is standing with a look of shock on her face, her hands over her mouth.

It's not her fault. I should have been paying attention, and I probably would have been if I wasn't so stressed about this goddamned meeting. I look down at the laptop, and my heart sinks. All my files. All the preparation. It's fucked. I heard that crunch, and it's not a sound that means good things.

"You're fine," I tell the caterer. "It was my fault. Not yours."

"I'm so sorry," she mutters, but she realizes that I'm not worried about her at all, and she quickly gets the hell out of Dodge.

I pick up the laptop and notice that it doesn't close correctly anymore. Maybe it'll work? I hit the power button, but there's nothing. Absolutely no response. I hit it again. And again. Nope, something broke on the inside, and there's no fixing it. At least not before this meeting.

"Hey," Sera says. "I've got the Core and Vanguard presentations on my laptop. You emailed me the Loughton Media one. We can just run it from there. You'll have to get back to them with charts and figures if they want the ones we haven't into the actual presentation, but Andrew, that presentation is fucking solid. You can send them documentation afterward."

I sigh and nod. "You're right. Let's just do the thing." I hate the idea of going into a meeting with my brothers without being completely prepared for everything. Every single thing is going to be scrutinized. They're going to be pissed when they find out what I did, but if the results prove I made the right decision, they'll understand. If I can't convince them of that, then I'm going to have hell to pay. But Sera's going to have even more.

Which isn't going to fucking happen.

She pats me on the shoulder and says, "Don't worry, Andrew. This is a slam dunk. We outperformed every expectation. We're coming off a slow quarter. No one expects anything from you, right? Let's show them exactly how well we did, and then, when they're done questioning our legitimacy, they can beg us to show them how we did it."

I take a deep breath and nod again. She's right. We have nothing to worry about. "Yeah. We already won. Now we just have to tell Phillip and Mason just how badly we beat them."

She grins, and I lead the way to the conference room. My knee fucking hurts, but it barely registers. My head's buzzing with nerves and excitement.

When we walk in, Sera unzips her laptop bag. Phillip and Mason are leaning back in their leather office chairs, looking as lazy as I can remember them. "We're going to use Sera's computer because I had a bit of technical difficulties a few minutes ago." I toss the busted laptop on the table, and Mason chuckles.

"Numbers didn't add up the way you wanted them to?" he asks.

"Oh no, the numbers are great. The coffee cart had a short-lived romance with my kneecap that ended with me and the laptop on the ground." Phillip grins but stays silent.

I haven't ever felt this nervous around my brothers, and seeing them acting like cats on a sunny windowsill doesn't help. Because when I show them what we've done, they're going to be shocked. They won't want to believe it. It'll break the ideas they already have in their heads.

As soon as Sera pulls up the slideshow, I start the presentation. This is the straightforward part, I remind myself. Just run through it and then their questions will get into the nitty gritty of the data.

"These are our core authors and releases. As you can see, they track similarly to what was expected. Slightly higher than projected because of a better than expected release in October."

I give them a chance to look at each of the charts before I scroll through. They don't have any questions. This is what they'd expected. Typical trajectories. Typical earnings.

"There's not much else to say about the core business, but now we'll get into Vanguard. We copied the model that you set up here in New York, Phillip. We already went over the plan for which agency we wanted to go with, and as Sera explained, we needed Sharon and Sullivan's manpower."

The slide changes and the most basic chart is shown. Expected profit versus actual profit. Not revenue. Profit.

"We doubled expectations for profit." I let the words hang in the air, and both Andrew and Mason sit up straight, their eyes going to the chart. I flip to the next page. "We tripled the profit margin that New York has. Tripled."

"That data's wrong," Phillip says. "There's no way in hell you managed tripled profit margins. Just basic printing costs are going to break that number."

Sera speaks up then. "Part of the reason we used the agency we did was because of their track record with small budget books. None of these books will break any records, but they're solid. The authors won't be fully traditionally published. They're not looking to make a ton of money. They want the notoriety that we bring to the table for their self-published books. We gave them lower percentage rates and focused on eBook sales, which have minimal costs associated with them. These are authors who are used to making minimum wage money and are now making six-figures. They're happy, and it cost us very little other than royalties."

I take over. "We wanted to replicate what independent eBook publishers are doing. Instead of trying to turn self-published authors into traditionally published authors, we're becoming the ultimate in independent publishing. And those numbers don't lie. Triple the profit margins, Phillip. Double the profit. Minimal investment since the print runs are barely even noticeable. This is a fucking money grab that's never ending."

Phillip glances at Mason, who shrugs. There's no way he's had enough experience to know whether or not this would work. But Phillip knows.

"It worked," he says softly. "It's repeatable?" This is a question, not a statement.

"Endlessly repeatable. This is the new business model. We outpaced our core business in three months of work."

I glance at Sera, who's waiting impatiently for what comes next. "And it's all because of Sera," I say.

Phillip and Mason both look at her sharply as she stands on the opposite side of the table. "What are you talking about?" Mason asks. He's searching our faces, trying to ferret out what the truth is.

"She's run Vanguard basically on her own. I was there to help her. I taught her and answered questions, but she made probably ninety percent of the decisions. Including bringing this idea to the table."

"What?" Mason exclaims. "Maybe I'm misunderstanding, Andrew. You let a cover artist set up and run an entire division? Is it just me that thinks that sounds like the worst decision possible?" He glances at Phillip, who looks just as confused.

Sera's smiling. A good sign. I say, "Maybe we should let some other cover artists run things since she outperformed you and Phillip." I give them a quick grin to tell them I'm just joking. Spoiler alert, I'm not joking at all.

"It's luck that she outperformed us. There's no other explanation. Even the worst gambler gets a few lucky dice rolls," he continues, his voice nearly cracking. "I've spent my whole life running businesses, and I'm still getting the hang of things after six months."

Sera doesn't let me defend her anymore. "I took the Phillip approach, which I doubt you did. I worked, on average, a hundred hours a week from the moment I arrived in London. You've spent the last three years playing on an island while I was in the business. Maybe I wasn't running anything, and maybe I don't have anything on my resume about learning the industry, but I've done plenty of research prior to this position."

She pauses for a moment before giving Mason a grin that would rival mine and then continues, "Of course, if you really don't want me to explain how I doubled the profits and tripled the profit margins, you can continue to degrade my results. Results which you and Phillip weren't able to manage."

Phillip has stayed quiet this whole time. He's ignoring Mason completely. His eyes stay focused on Sera as she stands tall and takes on a part-owner of the company. He's judging her. He's trying to understand whether it's possible for her to have done what she's suggesting. Then he looks at me and says, "Sit down, Andrew. I'd like to hear the rest of the presentation from Sera."

Sera nods to me, not at all afraid of Phillip. Or at least not obviously afraid. I have to remind myself that they know each other. She's his fiancée's best friend. She knows him better than I do, more than likely.

So I sit down and listen to Sera give the rest of the presentation. Mason's hackles are up, and there's no way in hell he's going to support Sera in anything, while I'm definitely supporting her. It all comes down to Phillip, and he hasn't made up his mind.

I see Mason's anger creeping up just as bad as it did when we were kids. Unlike then, he doesn't lash out, keeping it tightly leashed, but his nails are still digging gouges into the armrest of his chair. Sera ignores him completely.

She picks up the pen to control the presentation and moves to the next slide. One by one, she shows the books' profits and expenses. No travel. Half the books don't even have print runs. The other half are barely even enough to count. She walks Mason and Phillip through why she decided which contracts would get be eBook only contracts and which would get other published in other forms. She goes through it all line by line, and Phillip doesn't say a word.

When she gets to the last book on the list, she flips to the final chart. Next year's initial expectations. This is the one thing that Sera and I bickered about. She wanted to show our actual expectations based on calculated trajectories and longevities, but I disagreed. I said that we needed to sandbag our expectations. Nothing would be gained by showing our entire hand. Why not give ourselves some leniency next year?

"Next year, we hope to grow London's profits each quarter to the point where we perform similarly to New York's core business this past quarter. That's while continuing to maintain our current profit margins. These are initial expectations, and no one can be certain of how a new division will do a year from now. That's 1000% growth."

Phillip's been paying close attention this entire time. He's not the fun-loving guy who plays board games with employees right now. No, this is the man that I was sure was a robot when we were kids, and he's doing the thing he's best at. Seeing in between all the lines. Putting all the things together to see if it makes sense.

"Those numbers don't work," he says after almost three minutes of silence while we wait. Just like I knew he would. "If I'm to believe your trajectories and even taking explosive growth into account, those numbers simply don't work. You'd be at *maybe* seventy-five percent of New York. Maybe. Where is the rest of the income supposed to be coming from?"

Sera looks him dead in the eye and says, "Loughton Media."

Phillip frowns, confusion written all over his face. "What are you talking about?"

That's my cue to stand up. "Loughton Media is why I needed Sera to come to London. It's why I let her run Vanguard."

"More surprises?" Masons says incredulously. "Did you forget that you're still working for Loughton House? That we're supposed to be partners? Why are we just now hearing about this?"

"Why don't you just listen?" Sera asks, more surprised at his response to this than the way he'd reacted to her.

I give her a "shut up" look, and she looks just as pissed as Mason was. "I am thirty-three percent owner of Loughton House and was told to run London. That branch is mine, and I've always run it as I saw fit. No one knows it as well as I do, and I decided that it needed another expansion as well. I do not require permission to spend company funds that are allocated to my branch, and I certainly have not lost money this quarter."

"Explain yourself," Phillip says. "You may be allowed to do what you please with your budget, but we're not just partners, Andrew. We're family. Loughton House is supposed to be run by the three of us together. This isn't the company Father ran. If you'd wanted to open a new division, you should have talked to us."

I shake my head. "No, Phillip. You started Vanguard without talking to anyone. You changed the way the offices worked on your own. Yes, you told me what you were doing, but you didn't get my advice. You didn't hold my opinion at the same level as your own. You ran the company the way you saw fit, and that's what I'm doing. If you want me to run the only branch across the world from everyone and everything I care about, then I should get to do exactly that."

Phillip chews his lip. For once, I'm truly grateful that he's not my dad. He's not taking this personally. He's spent his whole life listening first, then forming an opinion, and finally reacting. Mason is about to come undone beside him, but we all know the pecking order around here.

Phillip may have given us all a piece of the company, but for the foreseeable future, he's still the boss.

"Fine. We'll discuss how our partnership works this afternoon, but right now, let's see the presentation I assume you have for Loughton *Media*." He says the word like he's tasting it for the first time and isn't sure if he likes the taste of it.

I nod to him and gesture to Sera to open the next presentation. She doesn't say anything, but I can see that the anger she'd had at me has faded to some degree after witnessing the way Phillip acted. The way I'd stood up to him and made sure that we reduced the tensions rather than inflamed them.

She pulls up her email, and Outlook crashes immediately. She frowns and tries it again, but it crashes again.

"What the…" she mutters, and Phillip notices the little symbol in the corner first.

"You have an update pending, so that may be what's keeping Outlook from working. Do you have it anywhere else? A backup on the cloud?"

Sera thinks for a minute. "I've got it on my phone. It'll be a little wonky, but I should be able to pull it up through Bluetooth."

Phillip nods, and Sera fiddles with her company phone while I close her computer to disconnect it from the projector.

"There we go," she says as the wall is lit up with an image of her phone's screen. She glances at it and goes back to looking at her phone.

But Phillip interrupts her before she opens her email. "Stop," he commands. I've never heard his tone get that sharp before. He's always been the most calm and collected person I know. An entire lifetime of working beside my father will do that to you. But this isn't calm and collected. This is pissed and riding on the edge of absolute fury.

"What. The fuck. Is that?" he growls as he stands up and walks toward the projector screen. "This, right here." His finger is pointing toward a file labeled "Wylder Bus Plan".

I frown at him and glance at Sera. I'm sure it's just a backup of the Vanguard files she needed at some point. People have plenty of random files on their work phones. You never know when you're going to need something.

Sera freezes, though. She doesn't explain herself. She doesn't say a word, and my stomach sinks as I realize what she could be doing. It was months before we ever talked about what she wanted from our deal other than training. I'd assumed that she was trying to ingratiate herself with me and learn from someone running a successful part of the company. I'd thought she was trying to move up the ranks.

But what if she wasn't? What if she was going to take insider information from us? She's not any old employee with no capital. I know who her parents are now, even though I didn't initially. I know the kind of money she has. No, she may not have enough to start up a billion-dollar business, but she could certainly start up a multi-million dollar one. She even suggested it all those months ago, but I'd thought she was joking…

"Open the file," I say.

She shakes her head slowly. "No."

"Open the goddamned file, Sera," I say. The words come out of my mouth like they're meant to wound. Still, she shakes her head.

My entire body feels like I'm on fire. I snatch her phone out of her hand and open the file. Right there, on a ten-foot-wide screen, we see exactly why she'd been willing to work seventeen hours a day for months at a time.

The first file is titled *Wylder House Publishing Business Plan*. How much more proof do I need to realize how badly I misplaced my trust in her? I scroll down through the list of files. Each one cutting my heart like a knife. *Procedure for Bringing on New Authors, Average Income Based on Genre, Expected Returns Based on Marketing Budget.* The list of damning files goes on and on. Months of data that could only be built from a position like she'd had.

"Why?" I ask. "I offered you a position to work beside me, Sera. You saw how well we worked together. We could have changed the fucking world together. Instead, you stole my secrets to start a competitor? What the fuck is wrong with you?"

I see the tears begin to fall. "It's not like that, Andrew. It was a backup plan just in case you didn't give me a good job. Just in case you used me and threw me away. I was only trying to make sure I got what I deserved. I didn't want to end up fired with nothing to show for all that work."

The anger inside me rages to the surface even more. "I promised you, Sera. I trusted you, and you… You were planning to become my fucking competitor. I told you everything. Everything."

"Only if you broke your promise, Andrew. I swear."

I'm lost for words. My hands are shaking as I stare at her. Hell, my whole body's shaking. Still, she's standing tall, though.

Phillip steps in. "You're fired, Sera. Whether you were going to go through with this or not is not the issue. You're lucky that we don't press charges for corporate espionage, and that's only because you're my fiancee's best friend. Get out, and do not come back, Sera. If you do, I will have you arrested."

She closes her eyes and takes a deep breath before nodding. "That's fine. I always knew that I shouldn't trust you. I knew that there was no such thing as love. No such thing as trust. Thank you, Andrew, for reminding me I should never worry about anyone except myself."

She shouldn't trust me? How the hell did I ever fall for her? Was it really just the sex? No. It wasn't. It couldn't be. There was so much more than sex between the two of us.

She turns her back on me and walks out of the room. Leaving Loughton House behind. Leaving me behind.

Forty-Two

SERA

It's been a long time since I felt like this. Truth be told, I don't know if I've ever felt this crushed. I can't tell if I'm mad at Andrew or myself or just mad at the whole freaking world. Or even if I'm mad. All I'm sure of is that I understand the meaning of *crushed* now.

I feel like an elephant stepped on my chest. Like the entire world fell down on top of me, and the pain is too much to bear. It's aching and sharp at the same time. The tears won't stop falling. No matter what I do, no matter how many times I wipe my eyes, they just keep running down my cheeks, onto the pavement.

The man I fell in love with hates me. My job is gone. I have nothing in my life now. That singular moment turned into a black hole, sucking away everything I cared about. And that vacuum resides in my chest, the cause of all the pain I feel.

It just keeps trying to take more from me. The pain writhes in my chest, a living thing, and every step away from Loughton House makes me hurt even more. This morning, I was the most confident woman you could ever meet. I had my future set. That meeting was going to put me in the place I've been trying to go. A seat at the table with Andrew beside me.

We were going to change the fucking world. We were going to revolutionize Loughton House. We were going to be important. Together.

And then they saw my stupid backup plan. A plan I put together before I'd even talked to Andrew about what kind of position he could get me. A plan I wanted to use to keep from being in this very position.

Now I'm alone, looking at the city that I loved, and feeling very desperate for anything that could make me feel even the slightest bit less broken. I pull out my personal phone, and text Trish.

Sera Wylder: Any chance you could take the afternoon off?

Trish Hayes: Maybe? What are we doing?

Sera Wylder: Karaoke bar. An hour from now. It's been a really shit day.

Trish Hayes: I'll be there. And I'll get the drinks.

I take a deep breath, and then something snaps in my brain. A song from my childhood. One of my dad's songs. *Slivers of Joy.* The words reverberate in my mind. The rhythm flows like water. Little tapping drops against a silvery bass. The harsh sting of the lead guitar against that steady flow. *Slivers of Joy* was his first big hit, a song I'll never forget since he sang it at every concert he ever performed. The one song that never got old.

I need to be with my friend, but I need something else too.

"You brought a guitar?" Trish asks, her eyes going to the instrument in the case next to my seat. "To karaoke?"

"It's a bass," I say as I take my first sip of the Cosmo.

"Same difference. Why'd you bring an instrument for karaoke? Is the rest of the band showing up, Paul McCartney?"

With a smirk, I say, "Funny. No, I just needed to play a song. I haven't played in a long time, but I don't think I could forget this song even if I never heard it again for the rest of my life."

Trish seems confused, but I'm sure that's to be expected. It's not like I've ever been open about my past or my parents. Nobody knows about them. Except Andrew. I learned that lesson in college. Just because my parents are rich and my dad's famous doesn't mean that I want to buy everyone's drinks. Hell, I don't even spend the money they've left me. It just sits in an account collecting interest.

But today, I think I might just tell Trish. Or maybe I won't. Who knows? I just know that I need someone else here because being with her makes that black hole in my chest hurt just a little less.

"Well, start talking. What's going on? I thought you were living it up in London. Pulling a reverse Addison and living with your boss."

I take a deep breath and let it out slowly. I don't know why I should be nervous about telling Trish anything. It's over. There's no way in hell that Andrew and I will be anything at this point. I'm not getting my job back, and I refuse to be a cover artist at some other publishing company. That leaves me with my backup plan. Starting my own publishing house. I may not have any of my files, but I know most of it. Starting Vanguard was basically a practice run for me.

"I got fired today, and tomorrow, I'm starting a publishing house." The look on Trish's face is pure shock. "And I think I'm experiencing my first broken heart." The first statement wasn't hard, but saying the second makes that black hole pull at me even harder.

She blinks a few times like she's not sure what she's hearing. "Wait. One thing at a time. You're starting a publishing company? All by yourself? Do you even know how to do that? And where are you going to get the startup money? It's not a simple thing, you know?"

I chuckle. That's the easiest part. "You know how Loughton House started the indie publishing side of things? I did that in London, and I was fucking good at it. So yes, I know how to start and run a publishing house. And well, I might have a multi-million dollar trust fund in my name that I've never touched. A few million should definitely be good enough to start a small publishing company."

The punches keep coming, and Trish probably feels like she never even knew me. To be honest, she didn't. "You have millions of dollars? And I didn't know? Are you a Rockafeller heiress or something?"

"More like Rock and Roll heiress. My dad is the lead singer of Sweet Delusions, and my mom was a partner at one of the biggest law firms in the country."

She squints at me like she thinks I'm lying to her. She scrunches up her nose with a very skeptical look and finally sighs. "Okay, so you're a Rock and Roll princess who was baptized in hundred-dollar bills. And you're doing your own thing because the Three Amigos running Loughton House…?"

"Saw that I might have been planning to become competition..." No skepticism there. Just cackling.

"Oh, that's fucking rich, Sera. Woo boy, I bet that punched them in the dick. I'd have paid money to see that madness. How'd you escape with your life?"

"Well, I…" I have to look at the table as I try to blink away tears. A vision of that moment in the office races through my mind. The look of betrayal on Andrew's face. The way his eyes burned into me in all the wrong ways.

And more than anything, the way I knew his chest was hurting just as much as mine did.

We share this wound. I know we do because the thing I feel for him was real.

"Sera…?" Trish asks. She puts her hand on mine. "What's wrong?"

"I fell for Andrew. Hard. And…"

Trish sighs and shakes her head. "And now that's not a thing anymore. He can't fire you and still fuck you like nothing happened. Okay, you're right. Today was a really shitty day."

I nod to her, and we sit there for a few minutes as the tears run down my cheek. Not as many as earlier, but just as painful.

She takes a deep breath and asks, "What song are you going to play?"

A subject I can manage words for. "*Slivers of Joy.*"

She cocks her head. "Well, that's a fucking song I haven't heard in a minute. I won a karaoke contest with it back in the day. Mind if I join?"

Of course she did. "I'd love it. Songs are always better with someone else."

She nods and goes to talk to the DJ. I'm left alone with my thoughts, and that song plays in the back of my mind all over again. It's been on repeat ever since I remembered it, but now that I'm alone again, it's like that's the only thing I can think about.

Those gentle tapping chords. That screeching guitar. The chaotic melody that weaves with the words.

I think I understand it now. And maybe I understand my dad a little better, too.

Forty-Three

ANDREW

"I CAN'T FUCKING BELIEVE YOU LET HER HAVE ACCESS to everything," Mason snarls. "Is this your first day, or what?"

"Mason," Phillip warns. Once again, Phillip is controlling the situation. And I want to punch him in the mouth. Maybe I want Mason to lash out at me. Maybe I want someone that I can be pissed at. Other than myself. Other than Sera.

Because I know why Sera had that file. I've worried I couldn't fulfill my promise since the moment I made it. That night on The Shard…

She didn't trust me, and maybe she was right not to. After everything we've done together… But she trusted me enough to fall in love with me, and I don't doubt her feelings at all. At one point, she'd planned to become our competition, but I don't think that was her plan anymore.

"Andrew," Phillip says slowly. "Was this all so you could start this other division? Or was there something else?"

His eyes burn into me, asking things I don't want to answer. *Were you fucking her?* I'd gone to London with both of them thinking that I was dating her when she would barely give me the time of day outside of work situations.

"I brought her to London to run the company while I worked on Loughton Media. At the time, there was nothing between us. Then we…" I take a deep breath and finish, "fell for each other."

"That wasn't love. That was a girl trying to commit a felony." He's calming down, and that's even worse.

Phillip glares at Mason, but he doesn't say anything which means he doesn't disagree with the words. Only the phrasing.

She was, or maybe still is, in love with me. I'm sure of it. The way things felt between us couldn't be anything else. But my brothers are right. She did try to steal from us. Even more than that, she ruined every bit of respect I could have gained from my brothers. All that work we did…

He sighs again as he leans forward, his elbows on the desk, as he steeples his hands. "Now, I won't judge you for making decisions because of a girl, but Andrew, you know as well as I do that in this business, we have to keep our secrets. You can't let just anyone have access to all the information we've gathered over the years."

I nod. "She wasn't going to use that information, Phillip. She didn't need to. I'd promised her a seat at the table. Not as a partner like the three of us, but as an upper manager. Why would she need to start her own company when she could help run ours?"

Phillip shakes his head. "It doesn't matter what you promised her, Andrew. That information is worth millions. What would have stopped her from selling it? Even now, I'm going to have to pay extra close attention to our competitors to make sure that there's no data leaks. I've already sent the phone to a technical forensic analysist to see if the data has been transferred anywhere.

"She was in the process of committing one of the biggest data breaches in publishing history, and the only reason I haven't filed a police report already is because there's a chance that she hasn't actually transferred any of the information. She's Addison's best friend, and I happen to like her. If nothing was transferred, then I will leave it with her being fired, but Andrew, she's not coming back to Loughton House."

I glare at him. She wasn't going to use that information. It hasn't been transferred. I'm sure of it. I'd stake my reputation on it. I'd wager the entire fucking company on it.

"You're not going to listen to anything else, are you?" I ask. "You've made up your mind?"

Phillip leans back in his chair. "You were the first to fire shots at her, Andrew. You're the one who took her phone and were just as pissed as the rest of us. Why aren't you still pissed at her?"

Because she didn't trust me. And maybe she was right not to. No, I can't say that. "Because this conversation is why she had that file. She made us a stupid amount of money. She revolutionized our business strategy. And none of that matters to you at all. I think she should be brought back and given an upper management role, but if you disagree, that's it. Mason won't listen to me. The two of you outvote me, and now I can't give her what she deserves."

"She deserves an orange jumpsuit and some prison time," Mason says. "Look Andrew, I know you think you and her were in love, but she was using you. Trust me. It happens to the best of us. Sure, she did some incredible things, but she wanted the information. What did you offer her when you convinced her to help you? Why'd she agree to move across the world and work as much as she did to begin with?"

Fuck. "Information," I whisper. "That's all she wanted."

Mason nods. "I think we helped you dodge a bullet, little brother. Hopefully we all did by catching that file in the presentation. Kudos on that, Phillip."

They keep talking, and as I go through the months of time we spent together, a part of me wants to believe that she really was just after the information. But so much of me rejects the idea that I can't help but think that they're missing something.

We were in love. More than anything else, I know that. No amount of logic will ever change my view of that. I saw what was in her heart. On The Shard. In that dance at the castle. When she was working with me every fucking day in that office.

We were in love. And nothing else really matters.

Forty-Four

SERA

I SIT DOWN WITH THE BASS ON MY LAP WHILE TRISH picks up the mic. As soon as I hear the first chord, I follow along, closing my eyes as I do. Imagining the concerts I watched as a kid. I've played this song so many times, but I never understood it. I never grasped what it was saying.

A light beat which sets the pace for the guitar. Slow and steady and in harmony with me. I can imagine my dad smiling at me as I played this song. The look in his eyes. It was just a song to me then. It didn't speak to me because I'd never been broken.

Shards of Joy is the best song my dad ever wrote.

"My father told me. To find a girl," Trish sings, starting low and slow. It's spot on. Damn near a reproduction of my dad's voice. "Buy a house. Have a family." The guitar beat sharpens. Skewing away from my steady rhythm, setting the stage for the pain.

"He said there'd be time for work. And time for play." I shift the pace of my rhythm, speeding up to try to catch the guitar.

Andrew was my ball of joy. A light in my life like no other. A fire where the rest of the world was cold. "She'll show you love. You'll show her laughter."

The guitar slows down, going back to the original pace, but I keep steady with mine. Once again, we're fighting for control of the words, and they bounce between us. A dance that's never quite right.

"Light of my life, tears of my soul, you were my everything."

"The sun when it rained, the fire in the cold, you healed my pain."

Another shift as I try to catch the guitar, but it pauses. It stops playing completely.

"But now you're gone. Now I've nothing."

"Except shards of joy."

The guitar starts up again, much faster now as we finish the refrain. We dance together, back and forth in speeds and pitch, and I'm always one step behind it. I know this song like the back of my hand.

I know that this song does not end the way I want it to end.

"Lost in a haze with no sun to shine."

"Never again will I find."

"Anything but shards of joy."

It hits me like a fucking stone to the chest. Pure anguish. I close my eyes, and I don't see my dad. There are no images of concerts or my fingers strumming. All I see is Andrew.

I see him leaning back in that stupid chair laughing at me while I'm learning the basics of the business. I see him touching my cheek; leaning in for a kiss. I see him staring at me while I sleep on the car ride home, that goofy smile on his face. I see him loving me.

"Never again will I find."

"Anything but shards of joy."

My fingers strum harder. Louder. The anger and loss build inside me like a hurricane ready to burst. The black hole in my chest just keeps growing. I love him. I can't give him up.

I'm chasing that fucking guitar, and it only makes me angrier. Why won't it slow down? Why won't it let me touch it even for a moment? I can't keep playing this fast. Basses weren't meant for this.

"I'm numb. Broken. Shaking. The memories bring me home."

And then the guitar stops. The drums stop. And the refrain plays once more. And the tears stream down my face.

Those memories of our time together, those perfect, unimaginably wonderful memories, fill my mind. My own shards of joy. I sing the words right alongside Trish. Alongside half the crowd. But I'm not there. I'm not in a karaoke bar as I sing the words.

And I strum the last few notes.

"Lost in a haze with no sun to shine."

"Never again will I find."

"Anything but shards of joy."

This is my dad's song. He wrote it right after they divorced. This is why I can't believe in love. Why I was a fool to think that me and Andrew were any different from my parents. Love is a fairy tale told to children. The hard reality is that anyone who thinks otherwise is just delusional.

And that pain in my chest hurts just a little less. The anger inside me softens just a little more.

I stand up and walk down the steps to where we were sitting. Andrew and I could never work. We were lust-filled, overworked, and delusional. We saw love in a sexual frenzy. But that lust wasn't real or permanent or something you can latch onto.

It wasn't blood.

The ache in my chest fades even more. I was an idiot, and the best thing I can do is walk away, my head held high, and start my publishing company. There'll be more fun. There'll be more laughter. I'll have plenty more sex.

Everything will be simpler without Andrew involved. Everything with him was far too complicated. I know the smart decision is to break away from Loughton House and trust myself instead of a family of men who care more about politics than about my worth. Instead of making the smart decision, I'd truly considered staying there just for Andrew. No, this is better. Simpler. Less painful.

I take a deep breath and let it out as I put the bass in the case again. I won't need to play any more songs tonight.

"Girl, you can fucking murder with that thing. I thought you'd be screwing up every other line. I mean, that's a tough song for anybody, but you're not even a musician."

I chuckle. No, I'm not a musician. Or a cover artist. I'm about to be a publisher. "I've practiced it a few times."

Forty-Five

ANDREW

I LET HER CALM DOWN OVERNIGHT, BUT I CAN'T WAIT any longer. The need to see Sera is too much to ignore for longer than that. I bang on her door like cops in the movies do. There's no way she's sleeping through this. She can't ignore it. I *need* to talk to her.

"Just a minute," she yells from inside as I knock again.

I hear her walking through her living room, and then there's a sigh from the other side as she cracks the door, the chain still connecting it to the frame. "Need to yell at me again? You can't fire me twice, you know."

"Did you manage to take that information off the phone?" I ask. I do my absolute best not to have any kind of accusatory tone, but the question itself accuses her.

She shakes her head and sighs again. "I wish I had since I'm starting the publishing house tomorrow. But no, your precious information is safe and sound on the company phone you confiscated."

I breathe a sigh of relief. "Good. Because if you'd transferred anything, you'd have worse problems than me yelling at you. Phillip would have filled a police report for several million dollars' worth of data theft."

That wakes Sera up in a hurry. "I didn't take anything, Andrew. I didn't do anything illegal. My job was to start a publishing division, and almost all of that information was used directly for that job. Yes, the name was… suggestive. But I didn't break any laws."

"I didn't think you did," I say softly. God, how do I do this? How do I put my fears to rest? How do I ask her all the questions that have filled my mind for the last twenty-four hours without pushing her further away?

Because I still love the girl looking through the crack at me. "Can I come in? I feel like we should talk."

She frowns and shakes her head, the messy bun she always has shifts just like always. She has a hairclip around it today instead of a pencil like normal. "No, I think it's better this way. Maybe it'd be better if you just left."

"Why are you acting like this? You're really going to throw away everything we have, everything we are, because of a misunderstanding? I don't want to fire you, Sera. I'll fight to get you back into Loughton House. You were trying to commit a felony, though. You have to understand where my brothers are coming from. They're trying to protect Loughton House."

"I don't have to understand anything, Andrew. I didn't break any laws. You obviously aren't here to offer me an upper management position, so I'm going to go ahead and start my own publishing company. You promised me on The Shard that you'd make sure that I was taken care of no matter what. We're sitting squarely at "no matter what" right now, and what's happening? You're backing your brothers. You're worrying about the people who have shit on you for years instead of the girl who was willing to do anything for you. I trusted you, Andrew, but I shouldn't have. I'm glad I got to work with you. Now I'm accomplishing my dreams."

I run my hand through my hair. "You're putting me in a hard place, Sera. I want you back at Loughton House. I want you back in my life."

She gives me a grim smile. "You put me in a hard place when you attacked me in that presentation. Sleep in the bed you made, Andrew." She pauses for a moment before sighing. For just a moment, I think I glimpse a tear welling up, but then it's gone. "I don't regret our time in London, but I can't go back to being a cover artist, Andrew. You have to know that."

"What are you saying?" She can't be suggesting what I think she is.

"Accept that I'm going to start a publishing company, and we can go back to what we had before. Even though you fired me, I can understand why you did it. But I have to keep moving forward. If you can do that, I would love to…" The way she says it has the slightest bit of pleading in it. Just enough to know that I'm right. She does still care about me. This wasn't all a lie.

"I can't do that, Sera. I've worked my entire life to try to gain some bit of respect from my family. Can you imagine how it'd look if I stayed with you? They'd constantly be worried I was helping you, funneling person assets and information to a competitor. There's no way that'd work. It'd be a disaster."

She shrugs. "I had to take the shot. Have a good life, Andrew. I enjoyed London, but sooner or later, it all had to end. We both knew that. At least we both got what we wanted out of it. You got Loughton Media, and they aren't going to stop that. I have a purpose now. Good luck with it all, but I think it's time for you to go."

Without waiting for a response, she pushes the door shut, and I move to let her. I don't know what to do. Is there any answer that works here? What does she expect me to do? I can't force my brothers to let her back into the company, especially at the position she probably deserves and definitely wants. And I don't really blame them for wanting to keep her out of Loughton House. She fucked up, and if she were anyone else, I'd have fired her myself.

If she were someone else threatening to start up a competitor, we'd figure out what she was doing, and we'd crush her. We're the thousand-pound gorilla in the room, and she's a fucking mouse. No way she wins that fight.

But she's not someone else. She's the girl I'm in love with.

Even if she pissed me off. Even if she's threatening my company. Even if she's smart enough to compete with Loughton House, I can't crush her. I can't let my brothers crush her. Something inside me is forcing me to protect her, even if she doesn't want me anywhere near her.

I just don't know how to do that.

But maybe there's someone who might be smart enough to help me. The one person I never expected to ask for advice.

Forty-Six

SERA

As soon as I close the door, the waterworks start. When I hear Andrew's footsteps leaving my door, I swallow to keep the sobs away as I lean against the wall. It took everything in me not to let him convince me that going back to Loughton House, back to him, was the right decision. God, everything in me craves him. Or do I crave what we had in London?

That beautiful little bubble we lived in for those six months? The excitement of learning something new, of doing something important?

Or was it really just the man I was doing it all with? My heart aches for him. I remind myself that there's no such thing as love. Only memories of happiness. That man was no different from the rest, and the thing I thought of as love was merely lust. The most lust I've ever felt in my life, but lust, nonetheless.

I am not a fairy tale princess. I will not find my "one true love" who will be with me forever. No, the best I can hope for is wonderful memories of a man that made me soar. Shards of joy.

I slide down the wall until I'm sitting with my arms around my knees, the tears running down both my cheeks and splashing onto my t-shirt. But if that's the case, then why does this hurt so much? Why can't I just let go like I'd wanted to last night?

He's just a man. Just a stubbornly arrogant man. That makes me feel like I'm flying. That makes me care so much less about my dreams and goals. He is the only person in the world that could make me want to go back to being a nobody at Loughton House instead of the owner of a publishing company.

He's the only one that could make my heart ache like this.

I can't stay here. That crushing feeling in my chest is already growing again. I can't work, and I can't think. The only answer I can come up with is that I need to go somewhere; I need to talk to someone. Talking to Trish didn't help nearly as much as I'd hoped. I need someone who knows what I'm feeling. Someone who understands what it feels like to have your heart ripped apart.

It's time I talked to my mom.

My mom's house is an older townhouse in the heart of the Upper Eastside. Not the nicest home in the area, but definitely more than I could afford as a cover designer. I fish the key out of my purse, the same one she gave me when I left for college, and I unlock the door.

The day she gave me my key, she told me that this would always be my house just as much as it is hers. The first time I came home, I knocked on the door, and she seemed bothered by it, so I haven't knocked since.

"Hey mom," I call as I open the door. Just in case she's not decent, but it's afternoon, so that's pretty unlikely for a woman who still wakes up at five in the morning.

"I'm in the kitchen," she yells back.

The scent of coffee is in the air as I walk through the house. Strange. She's strictly a tea drinker after noon. When I walk into the kitchen, I understand why.

She's sitting on a barstool in her robe. With my dad sitting next to her. Also in a robe. What the hell?

"Oh," I say as I stop in surprise.

Dad grins at me. "Afternoon, sweetheart."

I blink. This is not normal. "What are you doing here?"

He gives me a grin, and Mom chimes in. "We've been… talking." Her fingers move on the island, and I see a very sparkly, very new ring on her ring finger. One that wasn't there at Christmas.

Her thumb rubs it absentmindedly, and I glance at Dad, who's grinning from ear to ear. "You want to be on the bride or groom's side of the wedding?" he asks. A non sequitur for sure if he hadn't seen me looking at the ring.

"What? You're getting married?" I can't believe this. After everything that's been happening with me and Andrew, and now the two people I look up to the most in the world are proving me wrong. "Didn't you two already try that, and it didn't work?"

Dad runs his hand over my mom's lower back, and she glances at him with a wide smile before answering me. "Honey, we've always loved each other. We just… had different dreams. Your father wanted to travel the world with his band. I wanted to climb the ladder at the law firm. We couldn't do both together, and so we decided to be friends instead of married. It was simpler that way. The expectations of each other were better that way."

"But you both remarried. Multiple times." My voice rises, and my body's shaking. No. They cannot be happily remarrying after all these years. I love them both, but they don't love each other. They can't. It'd break everything I think I know about the world.

Dad says, "I think we both liked the idea of sharing our lives with someone, but there was always something holding us back from ever truly embracing that other person."

"I was in love with another man," my mom says with a grin and puts her hand on my dad's thigh.

This is too much to take in right now. I was coming over here to understand how I can get over Andrew. Now I have to handle my parents proclaiming their undying love and that they're remarrying?

"I just… I don't understand. If you two loved each other, then why wouldn't you have stayed together? Why were you okay with the other one dating and *getting married?*"

They look at each other, and it's impossible to miss the sparkle in their eyes. My mom turns to me and says, "I loved your dad enough that I wanted what was best for him. I wasn't willing to give up on my dreams, but I couldn't force him to miss out on his either. And he deserved someone in his life. I couldn't have gone on tour with him. I couldn't have been okay with him partying and doing all the things that went along with being a professional musician if we'd been married. But I didn't want him to be miserable, either. I divorced your dad *because* I love him."

"But those parts of our lives are over," Dad says. "Your mom's retired. I tour, but it's old man tours. Not like when I was younger. And the tours are short. Really, we only do them because we enjoy playing, and it's nice to remember the old days."

"Wait…" I'm really struggling with this. I've never heard of anything as crazy as "We got a divorce because we loved each other". "You're telling me that this whole time, you've both loved each other as much as when you got together?"

They both nod. "Yes. Absolutely. Our dreams and goals just weren't something we could give up." Mom's got a smile on her face that I only remember when I was a kid. That same look she used to give my dad when he was doing dishes after dinner and singing to the radio. Back before we had much money. I was so young then, but I remember the way she used to watch him.

"Sweetheart," she says, "your dad is my soul mate. That's never changed. I think we both knew that eventually we'd remarry. Your dad even joked about it when you were younger. He'd take me out when he was in town and do his absolute best to woo me. But he never succeeded."

The corner of Dad's lip curls up a little higher. "I might not have gotten into your pants any of those nights, but I certainly wooed you. You wouldn't be wearing my ring if I hadn't."

"Or did I play hard to get well enough that you finally had to settle down?" she asks, just as playfully as him.

Seeing them is so hard on my resolve. No, they never told me that love wasn't real. They never explicitly told me not to trust another person to stay with you. But I watched them. It felt like every year one of them was getting married to someone new or divorcing the one they were with. How could I not think that they didn't believe in love?

"Okay, I'm just going to ignore this whole thing right now. I'm in crisis mode, and this is all really confusing. As long as you're both happy, then I wish you the best. But I just got fired, and I don't even really care. But I think... I think I might be in love, and that does matter."

They both look at each other, and my dad gets up and gets a coffee mug out of the cabinet. "Well, sit down and let's talk about your love life for, literally, the first time ever." The coffee's still steaming as he pours it into the mug and adds a teaspoon of sugar and a splash of milk. Just like I like it. Just like I've had it since I was a teenager.

Mom and I are quiet until he slides it across the island to me and sits down. Dad asks, "Now, I assume this is about your boss?"

Mom nods, a grim smile on her face. "Definitely about her boss. She hasn't had time to fall for anyone else. And you know how office romances happen..."

"Yeah, Randy was a wild time for you..."

Oh my God, this is not what I wanted. "Guys, focus. Yes, I fell for my boss. Yes, that was probably dumb of me. But he's amazing. Funny, gorgeous, and I've never met a cleverer guy."

They're both looking expectantly at me, waiting for the "but". "But I didn't trust him. For good reason, mind you. So while I was helping him to expand Loughton House, I also did all the research I would need to start my own publishing house. And he and the other owners of Loughton House found out. I got fired, which doesn't matter since I'd prepared for that exact issue. But..."

"But your boss doesn't want you to start a competing company," Mom says slowly. "Which is understandable."

I nod. "They're not leaving me any options. I don't want to start a company, either. That's been my backup plan for months, and now I just want to help Andrew run Loughton House. More than anything, though, I want Andrew. What am I supposed to do? I can't go back to being a cover designer. I just can't. I need more."

"You've given him the two options you're okay with?" Mom asks.

I nod, and Dad sips his coffee. "What were you thinking would happen after that meeting?"

"That I'd help run the company," I say. And as I say it, I realize just how ridiculous it sounds. Did I really think that? My two skills are cover designer and… running a billion dollar company? It sounds insane, but I was good at it. I was really, really good at it.

"Why did you think that?" she continues to ask, not being judgmental at all. "That sounds like a stretch, doesn't it?"

"I don't know." My doubts race through me. "Look, I set up a system that would make their expansion twice as profitable. Millions of dollars in profit are going to be because of me. I can do these other jobs if they let me. They just don't want to let me. Maybe they did before they found out, but part of me doesn't think that's true. Andrew said he'd convince them, but I don't know if even he believed he could. Which was the whole point of the backup plan."

Finally, Dad speaks up. "Make the company, Sera. It was a long shot before they got angry. Now they won't trust you, and you seem to know what you're doing. If you're successful, which I fully believe you will be, then you get to decide your own fate. If you're not, then all that happens is you go back to your old job with experience on your resume."

"But what about the fact I'm in love with my competition?" I say, more than a little exasperated.

"Who cares? Fall in love with him. Marry him. Talk about your businesses together. Help each other when you can. It's not like a billion-dollar business is worried about you. And even if you do everything right, and you're married in twenty years when you're finally an actual competitor, then let Loughton House buy you out so that you can run it under their name."

It seems so clear the way he says it. The most logical answer to a completely illogical question. "He won't accept me taking their secrets and making a competitor," I say softly.

"If he loves you like you seem to love him, then he will do whatever it takes to keep you. Whether that's convincing his brothers in a week to let you work with him or just accepting your business as a good thing. It doesn't matter. Leave it in his court. At least for a little while."

A sigh escapes my lips as I look down at my coffee cup. That's not even what I was coming here to talk about. The question on my mind wasn't how I should move forward. It was… It was about whether love is real.

But looking at my parents, I don't feel like I need to even ask it. They've been friends since I was born. Regardless of who they were married to or with, they were always there for each other. They weren't just friends, though. They were in love. In love enough to let each other be free to live their lives. To trust that they'd come back. That they'd never leave.

And neither one of them did. Not really.

"Didn't it hurt?" I finally ask.

My mom frowns. "Did what hurt?"

How do you explain the ache in my chest? The feeling that nothing is ever going to be okay again. That all I want is being in Andrew's arms again?

"When you split up. Didn't it hurt?"

She sighs and stands up to walk around the island. "Oh, sweetheart. I thought it would kill me," she says as she wraps her arms around me. "I didn't know how I was going to survive living without your dad. The pain was excruciating. I'd wake up in the middle of the night trying to find him. He left his pillow with me, and I'd cry myself to sleep against it. Truthfully, if it weren't for the fact that I couldn't leave you alone all those nights, I'd probably have run off to wherever he was playing and watched his show. Just to see him again. To remember why I was doing it."

"I wish I had one of his pillows," I say as tears threaten to well up. "It's so hard to be away from him."

Dad says, "It gets better, Sera. I know it's hard to believe, but even a week from now, that heartache won't be so bad."

I don't want to hear about what's going to happen in a week. I want the pain to go away right now. Because I don't know if I'm going to make it until next week with the way I feel. I'd thought I'd survive without him when I could tell myself it wasn't love. The pain had faded so fast.

But when I saw him, when I looked into those green eyes of his, I couldn't ignore the emotions that I'd bottled up. They exploded inside of me, and the pain was so much worse than before. And I don't think I can bottle them up again.

"How about we open some wine?" Mom asks. "Then we can put on some music and talk about all the stuff you've been doing. I haven't gotten to hear much about your trip to London except how drunk you got when you visited your dad."

I don't know what else to do. But some wine sounds good. "I guess so."

She smiles at me, and I try to relax. Of all the people in the world, my parents are probably the only ones that I've never doubted. They've always had everything they've ever wanted. Maybe they're right. Maybe I just need to let Andrew have time to think and get his thoughts in order.

But the other part of me, the part that could create a plan that would beat Phillip in profit, isn't capable of letting go of things. That side needs to force the issue and act. Not wait around and hope for the best.

If there were any answers that made sense, I'd have already made them, though. Unless I'm willing to give up on my dreams, there's no possibility of me fixing things between Andrew and me.

And the pain doesn't go away. Even as the wine is poured and I talk about my months in London. Because each of those memories is another memory of Andrew.

Another memory of perfection that I don't think I'll ever have again.

Another shard of joy.

Forty-Seven

ANDREW

My dad, the creator of Loughton House Publishing, the emperor of the publishing world, is currently playing online poker. In a pair of shorts. What the hell has happened to the world?

As soon as I walk into his townhouse, he gives me a hug. And I am absolutely positive that the man I grew up being terrified of has been replaced by an alien. "Andrew, it's been a long time. Come in. Let me quit this game, and then I'll pour us some whiskey."

Whiskey? My dad doesn't drink. He's literally only drank one time in my entire life. The night he found out my mom died. I barely even remember it, but Phillip's talked about it. "What's going on, Dad? You're playing poker online?"

He chuckles and shrugs. "What else am I supposed to do? I keep up with what's happening with the business, but truthfully, I kind of feel like I'm out of the loop. You started *another* division? Loughton Media? It seems like a bit of a waste, don't you think?"

Alright, Russel Loughton and the man standing in front of me are not the same people. "Dad, you seem… *different*. What's going on?"

He picks up a crystal decanter and pours two glasses, one for me and one for him. "I've spent a lot of time thinking, Andrew. Retirement does that to you. There's nothing to worry about other than my health. For the first few weeks, maybe even the first few months, I was constantly logging into the business to check on what's happened. I tried to keep up to date on everything in case someone needed my advice, but when no one called or asked me anything, I realized that maybe it's time that I let go. So I did. I still check up on you and your brothers' plans, but that's just because I don't know how else to keep up with you boys."

Fuck. For a man that's never given a damn about any of us, he sure seems sentimental in his retirement. "You know, you could always call us. We have phones. You have a phone. It's not like you ever wanted to hear from us when you were working. How are we supposed to know that you want to hear from us now?"

Dad takes a sip of the whiskey and sighs. "You're right, son. I guess, well, I didn't think that any of you had any interest in spending time with me. Phillip certainly didn't seem to be interested in it. And Mason…" He doesn't finish that thought, but he doesn't need to.

Not surprising with how he raised Phillip. Or with how he literally disowned Mason. I probably shouldn't be interested in talking to him, either. It's not like he showed me an ounce of affection, even though he's the only parent I remember.

But right now, I need someone who isn't my brothers and won't sugarcoat things for me. I need honesty, and if there's anything my dad is, it's honest.

"Maybe we take it one day at a time? I need your help with something, Dad."

He frowns at me and sits down. "Something that you and Phillip can't figure out on your own? That's surprising seeing the numbers from the fourth quarter. I'd have thought you had it all figured out. Beat the tar out of anything I ever managed, that's for sure."

I shake my head. "It's not about business. It's about a girl."

He frowns again and takes a sip of the whiskey as I explain what had happened. When I finish, he's still wearing the frown. "She was prepared to start up a competing company if you didn't give her what she wanted? And she's that good?"

I nod. "She's the first person other than Phillip that I would be worried about competing against."

"I'd either hire her or crush her, maybe the second and then the first. But Phillip and Mason aren't on board with that, so what do you do? How do you convince them?" He drums his fingers on the edge of the crystal glass as he stares off into the distance. It's strange seeing my dad work that genius mind of his on something other than business. But I guess this is business. Manipulating people is what he was the best at, after all.

"Do the one thing that will force their hands. Hold the only thing they've ever cared about for ransom. It may not work, though. They may never forgive you for it. It may ruin everything you have going for you, so you have to ask yourself one question. Is she worth risking everything for?"

There's no doubt in my mind. "More than anyone I've ever met."

Forty-Eight

SERA

I STUCK TO MY GUNS. JUST LIKE MY PARENTS suggested. After tapping into my trust fund, I've already rented a set of offices. It's not anything expensive or large, but it's enough. That's all I'm looking for right now. Just enough space to do the job.

There needs to be space for enough people to work here when needed, but most of them will work off-site from their houses. My team is going to be small, but I need to give myself the space to grow. It's going to take several months to go from spending money to making money, but I won't have time to move everything to a new location when that happens.

The first step is getting my system in place, though. It's going to be a lot of long days in my future, but that's fine with me. The office is strangely quiet, and as I work, it's hard to ignore it. Even in London, when I was on a floor with only a few other people, there was always some kind of movement. More than anything, there was always Andrew.

I curse the fact that I never transferred those files from my company phone. I could have spent my first week looking for clients and contacting freelance editors and cover designers. Now, I have to squeeze that into the space between building the foundation of Wylder Publishing. I'd felt like I was on a deadline when I was working with Andrew, but that was nothing compared to this.

This is like a sprint for my life while that was a leisurely jog through the park. Sure, they're both tiring, but failing here means I have to go back to being a cover artist, and that's not going to fucking happen.

Hours pass as I rebuild the spreadsheets from memory. Finally, I have to get up and stretch. "I need some coffee," I mutter just to hear something and walk across the office to the brand new coffee pot.

I keep expecting to hear Andrew's voice joking with me. "What you really need is an espresso machine," he says in the back of my mind. "Or you could be a real boot-strapper and just snort coffee grounds."

"Shut up," I whisper back. The ache in my chest is better. It's been almost a week since I decided to continue on with my plans, to ignore the desire to go running back to Andrew. I spent the whole next day in bed. If I tried to do anything else, I'd have gone straight to Andrew's arms. I needed to purge my system of him. Like a drug addict in rehab.

But I don't think it's ever going to really work. An addict has to want to quit. That's what everybody says, isn't it? And I don't want to quit Andrew. All I can do is fill my day with work and let myself cry at night. But it's getting harder. His voice is constantly in the back of my mind, teasing me and reminding me of things.

"You know, there's one good thing about having no one else in the office," he'd have said. "You don't have a reason to wear that bra. I could bend you over that desk, and you could scream as loud as you want. No one would hear you."

There's that familiar throbbing between my legs. Separating Andrew from sex is impossible. Every thought of him turns me on, and every time I get turned on, I think of him. A vicious, smutty spiral that only gets worse the longer I'm alone.

He's inseparable from the work, too. Now that I'm doing all the things that we did together, it's like he's right here with me, talking me through the steps all over again. I'm sure it's keeping me from missing any of the important things I might have forgotten, but it only makes the ache in my chest hurt a thousand times worse. "Remember to account for unexpected sales in your spreadsheets. You don't want to have to rebuild them ever again. Now, give me your underwear. I bet they're soaked, aren't they…"

The coffee maker clicks over to warm as it finishes, and I fill up my cup. "It's almost lunchtime. Why don't we get some Pad Thai today? Your favorite is the shrimp, right?"

"I don't have time for lunch," I mutter to the voice in my head. "There's too much to do."

"There's always time for lunch. You eat food, and I'll eat you."

God, why can't his voice just go away? Why can't I just quit thinking about that smile or him kicking his feet up on the desk? We spent so much time together. Every moment of every day for months. I don't think I've ever been as close to another person as I was to him. We knew everything about each other.

I could have picked out his clothes for him or ordered his lunch. I even knew odd things like that his favorite cookie is oatmeal chocolate chip. Without raisins because "they remind him of what a bug probably tastes like". He knew my favorite music and could have bought me a wardrobe that fit my tastes perfectly. He knew I didn't believe dishwashers could clean dishes as well as I could, so I handwash everything.

Yet, here I am. Doing everything I can to forget him, even if that's the last thing I want. I'm fighting myself. I'm doing the only thing I can think of to keep from crawling back to him, my tail between my legs. Everything in me wants to beg him for my old job back just so I can be near him again.

The memory of that first day in London floods my mind. Him sitting in the chair like a lazy teenager, his computer in his lap, and me thinking about him falling over. The way he'd pushed me. The way he'd done everything he could to help me be the best I could ever be. I'm not the same woman I was back then. I could never have started a company even if I'd had all those files. I wasn't strong enough.

And something shifts inside me. A realization. *Trust yourself.* Not my parents.

I don't regret falling in love with Andrew. Those two words led me down the right path. Even if it hurts more than anything I've ever felt. My parents felt like following their dreams was more important than staying with their soul mate, but I am not my parents.

A vision of Andrew sitting in a chair, his feet up on the desk with that arrogant smile on his face, seems to materialize in front of me. "Let go of control, Sera. I'll never let anything bad happen to you," he whispers to me.

I trusted him with my body. I always trusted him. *Let go of control.*

I can't just forget him and move on. I can't let him go and hope he comes back to me like my dad suggested. I have to let him have control because I trust him to always think about me first. Even if he enjoys himself, he'll never let me fall.

Andrew Loughton is the only person in the world that I trust as much as I trust myself. And it's time that I tell him. It's time that I actually give up control.

Forty-Nine

ANDREW

I GLANCE AT MY PHONE ONE MORE TIME. FIVE minutes until the biggest meeting of my life. So much bigger than the Q4 review for London. Because this one has to do with Sera.

As I put my phone on the desk beside me, it vibrates as an email comes through. I'm tempted to ignore it, but there's nothing else to do for the next five minutes, and the efficiency I've forced myself to learn begs me not to waste time. Even if I probably won't have an email address at Loughton House after today.

An email from S.Wylder@WylderPublishing.com. My breath catches in my throat for a second as I reread the email address again to make sure I'm not crazy. I don't know what to expect as I click the notification.

Andrew,

I'm sorry about all of this. It's not your fault, and I know you've done everything you can to fulfill your promise to me. I was angry at your brothers. And myself. I've told myself that my dreams were more important than what we had, but every day we're apart, I feel more and more like a ghost of who I was.

I have a publishing company now. All of my dreams are coming true. There's no reason I won't be successful. I should be happy. But I won't have you. I won't see your face in the morning or hear your laughter when I eat dinner.

I only have one dream anymore, Andrew. I dream of you. Every night. If I can't have you, then I don't know if any of this matters. I wanted to live up to my parents. I wanted to be as great and as successful as them.

But they weren't happy because they were successful. They were happy because they had what they wanted. And the only thing I want is you. I'm sitting in my new office right now making spreadsheets, but I'd gladly give it all up to have you back.

It's my fault that everything fell apart. I'm the one that made that stupid backup plan. I didn't trust you, and that's why everything's ruined.

I'm trusting you now, Andrew. Just like all those times in the office. At the castle. I'm trusting you to keep me safe. I know you won't let me fall now just like you didn't let me fall when I got too drunk. Tell me what to do, and I'll do it. Whatever it is. You're my only dream, and I'll do whatever it takes to get you back.

I love you.

Forever yours,

Sera

Will I accept her apology? Absolutely not. She was right to have a backup plan because I wouldn't have ever given her what she deserved. No matter how much we'd accomplished in those six months, no matter how genius she is, my brothers would never have allowed me to give her the position she deserves.

I turn off my phone without replying to the email and stand up to go into the conference room, a freshly printed piece of paper in my hand. Phillip and Mason are early, both of them looking confused at me as I walk into the room and don't sit down.

"I want you to give Sera Wylder a position in upper management starting tomorrow," I say, not even giving them a greeting.

They look even more confused. "That's what you called this meeting for?" Mason asks. "I thought this was covered. She's a security risk without enough experience to do that job."

Phillip nods. "I agree. I thought this was all cleared up. Why are you bringing it up again?"

I ignore them both. They've given me their answer. "I just wanted to make sure that's the way you felt. I wanted to give you another chance before I did something drastic."

I slide the paper across the table to them. "This is my resignation. I want nothing to do with Loughton House if my opinion is given so little weight."

They get up and say words, but I ignore them, my mind set on a single thing. A single person. And I smile as I get into the elevator to go downstairs. Sera sent me her address by accident. I get to see her now.

I get to hold her now.

And I don't give a damn whether Phillip and Mason let me walk away. Like Sera said in her email, "I only have one dream anymore", and that dream doesn't require my brothers be a part of it. I don't give two shits what they think about me.

As long as Sera loves me, that's all I care about.

Fifty

SERA

I STARE AT THE WALL ACROSS FROM ME. EMPTY. LIKE the rest of the office. The coffee pot makes little noises occasionally, but otherwise, it's all still silent. A ghost of a memory of that happiness.

I click the mouse to refresh my inbox again, the twentieth time since it showed read. Still nothing. He's always so fast at responding to things. Maybe he was in a meeting? Maybe he clicked it accidentally?

My computer dings, and a new email pops up at the top of the list from an email address I don't know. Who the hell is ElfLover69er@gmail.com? Could it be him?

Before I can open the email, the door to the office swings open, and I whirl around. Standing there with that ridiculous grin on his face is Andrew. "I thought you were going to run a publishing company, not *be* a publishing company."

I chuckle and stand up. "I've had the place for three days, asshole. And I might have to *be* the publishing company until I get a little cash flow. What are you doing here? Did you read my message?"

"For someone just starting a business, you sure are bad at checking your email."

I frown and turn around to look at the only message in my inbox. Clicking on it, my jaw drops. It's a resume. Andrew's resume.

I turn back to look at him as he crosses the space between us, the door shutting behind him. "Why are you sending me your resume?"

"Because that's part of looking for a job, Sera. I know you're a big shot now, but you should know what it takes to get a job in these trying times."

"What are you talking about, Andrew? You're not trying to get a job."

He finally is within arm's reach of me, and he says, "I actually am. I let my brothers know I was resigning from my position about thirty minutes ago and came straight here. Thanks for having your address in your email signature, by the way. That saved me a ton of time trying to find you."

I'm still really confused. "Why did you resign?"

"Because they wouldn't give you an upper management position. Obviously. I figured that one of two things would happen. Either they give in to my ransom demands and give you whatever job I want you for, or they don't. If that happens, I just have to convince you to hire me and we'll conquer the world together. Though you might have to let me buy into the business. I have a feeling Wylder Publishing is a pretty solid investment."

It's hard to believe that this is real with how I've felt all day. I reach out and touch his cheek. The soft stubble that I remember so well makes the ache in my chest fade almost immediately. By the time that my thumb runs along his lip, it's completely gone, and I feel like everything could be right again.

It's a fragile feeling, though, like when you glue two pieces of ceramic back together, but the glue hasn't dried yet. It *could* be right, but it isn't assured. If you let go even for a moment, it could all fall apart again.

"Is this real?" I whisper. "I… I think I was going crazy, Andrew. I was hearing your voice in my head. When I went to make the forms for project reporting, I heard you whispering in my ear what I needed to do."

He smiles down at me. "It's real, Sera. I'm sorry it took this long. I needed to move some money around to make sure that it wasn't connected to Loughton House anymore so my brothers couldn't somehow claim it as part of the business."

He leans forward and whispers, "This is real. Everything between us has been real from the beginning, and there's no way in hell I'll let it go. The past week has been the hardest week of my life. I couldn't come to you with promises since I broke my last one. I had to have proof. Well, I'm here. And I'll be here until you decide you want to do something different."

The silence of the office doesn't matter anymore. I can hear Andrew's heart beating, can touch his face, and smell that light hint of spice and musk. "Then kiss me and make the pain go away."

Those green eyes flash for a second, and then his hands are on my cheeks, holding me in place as he kisses me like there's nothing else in the world. God, it's like I never felt any pain at all. Almost as if we had never left London. My hands move through his hair, my nails scratching against his scalp as his hand moves to my throat. I remember the way he'd hold me like this. The way I'd felt so safe and loved from that touch.

My hands move to the silk shirt covering his chest, and I wish it was gone. When he finally pulls away, he sighs. "It's like I can breathe again. You make me feel this way. Like I've been a fish out of water my entire life, but when you're near, I can breathe."

"I know," I whisper back. "I'm sorry, Andrew. I shouldn't have made that backup plan. I nearly ruined everything."

He shakes his head. "You were right to make it. I couldn't have convinced them to give you the position you deserve. Regardless of the backup plan, they wouldn't have listened to me."

I kiss him again, and he runs his fingers over my cheek. "But none of that matters now."

His finger tickles my nose, and I shake my head, feeling very much like a teenager with a crush. Andrew steps back and grins before he looks around the room again. "So am I hired?" he asks. "Or do I need to start pounding the pavement looking for another job?"

It's my turn to smirk. "Maybe. It depends on what you're willing to do to get the job. There are certain…" I lick my lips and glance at the bulge in his slacks, "duties that aren't typical of most assistants."

He chuckles and grins from ear to ear. "Oh Miss Wylder, I'm desperate. I'll do whatever it takes. You can count on me to be… up to the task."

Fifty-One

ANDREW

Sera is a force of nature. Even when we were spending every minute at the office in London, she was never this focused. Always two steps ahead of me, she's got a list of things we have to make before we can even start hunting down authors to contract. She's moving like a woman possessed as she closes one spreadsheet only to open the next.

She's making forms I've never even seen before. Ones that she says she took from the agency we bought in London. Then there are others that our legal team had in their files. And the ones that my dad had put together for the Bangkok expansion that fell through last year when Phillip took over.

There are no files to copy or tweak. All of this is straight from memory. How many times did she look over all of them? Is this how she understood how to run Loughton House so quickly?

And at the same time, she keeps looking over at me and grinning like she's a kid in a candy store. I understand that feeling at least. It's so hard to focus on work with her this close to me. Our week apart was pure torture.

Now she's right here. My cock is straining at my slacks even though we christened her back office just a few hours ago. "Stop," I finally say, and her fingers freeze over the keyboard.

"What?" The wild look in her eyes makes me wonder if she really is possessed. "Do you need something?"

I chuckle and stand up. "No, but we need to take a break." I don't know if I've ever seen someone so annoyed at the thought of taking a minute to freaking breathe. "Look, we didn't work on Sundays in London for a reason. You're going to burn yourself out on your first week at this rate. Calm down and remember that nothing's going to fail just because you didn't get literally everything done in your very first week in the office."

She opens her mouth like she's going to argue, but then she sighs and leans back in her chair. Her fingers flex as she stretches them. "How long of a break?" she finally asks.

"Just like twenty minutes. Enough time for your brain to rest. The last thing you want is to make a stupid mistake."

She closes her eyes and lays her head back against her chair. "There was a reason I wanted to take all those files with me," she says without opening her eyes.

I walk over to one of the windows and look out at the street below us. It's not quite the view that we had at either Loughton House office, but a fifth-floor view is better than the second floor. "Why a publishing house?" I ask.

I hear her moving in her chair, and I'm sure she's looking at me. "What do you mean?"

"Why did you decide to start a publishing house? You said you're bankrolling this thing with your trust fund, so why didn't you just start another smaller business before? You could have opened that as soon as you graduated from college and never worked for another human being. That's what most people with money would have done."

I can see Sera's face in my mind, can imagine the shrug of her shoulders and the way her hair would shift just a little, even though it's in that messy bun. "Because running a laundromat wouldn't matter. That's just a job, no different from making covers. And I never set out to start a business. I just wanted to do something that mattered, and running a publishing company matters. Do you know how many people I gave brand new hope to when I offered them contracts? Our business plan changed lives for the better. That's what I want to do. Not just make money."

I nod my head and watch as five o'clock sends thousands of people onto the streets. Like the chime of a school bell, people step out of the offices in a wave. All of them trying to get home as fast as possible. Here we are, nowhere near finished with our day.

"So you decided that you'd rather work harder than anyone you've ever known so that you can do something special. You're willing to trade your hours and energy to help a bunch of people you never met."

"My parents spent as much time working as you do." I turn around at that. She's staring at me, a smile on her face. "My dad lived his job for nine months out of the year, every year. My mom worked seven days a week. You normally work ten to twelve-hour days. My parents worked just as much, if not more."

She stands up and crosses the room. "I spent time at their work so I could spend time with them. My mom had me going through files at ten o'clock at night. I learned to play bass so my dad could try out new guitar riffs for his songs. My childhood was being my parents' friend and coworker. The one they trusted and loved. Sure, I did kid stuff, and they showed up, but if I didn't have anything special, they were always working."

Her hand runs over my chest as she smiles up at me. "I enjoy working hard, Andrew. That's just who I am. I think the only time I haven't worked hard is when I was a cover artist. At least after I got comfortable with it. Maybe that's why I got bored?"

It's so strange to hear her talk like this. I'd thought I was alone in the fact that my dad was always working. I guess I was wrong. The only difference is that Sera's parents cared about her enough to involve her in a good way. In a fun way.

"Well, I don't want to work ourselves to death. And I definitely don't want to miss anything if I ever have kids. I enjoy working, but I'd hate to spend my entire life doing it, if that makes sense."

She nods and presses her palm flat against my chest. "I know exactly what you mean, but it's a new idea for me. You're the reason I want to take time away from work. Our little adventures in London are the instances I've thought that having time off would be nice."

"Good. Because I want this to work between us," I say. "I enjoyed what we had in London, but when we came back to New York, the thing that I wanted more than anything was time for us. Away from the office."

She smiles and takes a deep breath before nodding. "Me too. But I also want all of *this* to work, too." She looks around the room. She wants me, but she also wants to have a job that she can be proud of. It makes sense. Then her smile turns into a grin. "But if I can only have one or the other, I pick you, Andrew. I already told you I'd go back to making covers if it meant that we could be together. I'd prefer to have everything I want, but you're the priority."

My arms wrap around her, and I inhale her scent. That soft almond and lilies that I've come to associate with her. "Don't worry, Sera. You'll have everything you want and more. I made a promise once before, and I couldn't keep it. This time, you don't have to doubt my word. Or have a backup plan."

"I know," she whispers. "Nothing that happened was your fault. What I wanted was impossible."

At that moment, the door to the office opens, and I smile. "No. It just took longer than either of us was willing to give it," I say before pulling away from her.

"Wylder Publishing," Phillip says as he walks into the silent office. "Not a bad starter office."

Sera whirls around to face him, and I can see her pulling herself together, making herself into the impenetrable businesswoman that she becomes in times like these. It's unnecessary. If they're here, then my ransom's already worked just like Dad said it would.

"What are you doing here?" I ask, as though I don't already know.

Mason walks in behind Phillip and says, "Bringing you home. Obviously." I shoot Sera a quick glance, but from the look in her eye, I know she's not going to say a word.

"Well, unless you're giving me free rein to place Sera where I want her within Loughton House, then you might not want to hold your breath."

Phillip sighs and looks around the room as he walks through it. Mason seems to wait for him to talk while Sera and I just watch him. "Do you like it here?" he finally asks.

"It's a little quiet, but yes." I don't know what Phillip's doing, but I'm reminded of how much he learned from Dad. All the little theatrics were so common when Russel Loughton wanted to win over his employees. It was how he dominated a room without saying a word.

"I can't let you place Sera wherever you want. There are too many people that have worked their asses off to get where they are. I can't just ignore that, Andrew. You know I can't."

"Then you might as well go home because Sera and I have work to do." I'm not backing down, but Phillip wouldn't have found us if he hadn't been willing to do whatever it took to get me back. He knows that I'm not going back to Loughton House without her.

Phillip finally turns around and rubs his chin, looking just as tired as Dad did at times. He ignores my comment and continues what he was saying. "But if we changed things around…"

It clicks. The subtle difference between shifting departments around to give Sera control of things instead of simply placing her in a position. It's the political side of things that I've never been all that good at.

"What would you shift?" I ask.

"Loughton Media is yours, and it's still in the building stages. Why don't you two run it together? From here?" I glance at Sera again, silently questioning if that would work for her. I didn't need to, though. It's not hers. It's mine, and it has absolutely nothing to do with anything she wants.

I shake my head. "No. She's going to do the thing she's best at. Running a company that's built on giving unknown authors a chance. Either here or Loughton House."

Phillip sighs again, and I can tell that he's frustrated, but he's trying to listen. Trying to make sure that everything plays out how he wants it to. "Okay. You're stuck on Vanguard." He sits down on a desk and looks up at the ceiling. I know that I've won the ransom, but I also know that he's got to figure out how to work within the boundaries of Loughton House's politics.

"I'm trying to work with you on this," he says. "Vanguard is still new, and though I'm sure people have settled into their roles, there may be some ways to convince them to move. What if we shifted them to Loughton Media? I looked through your files after the meeting, and I think we should keep moving forward with it."

He frowns and turns to look at Sera. "What do you want? I want my brother working with me again. He seems to care more about his relationship with you than he cares about his position in the family business. A multi-billion dollar business doing cutting-edge things. The best publishing house in the world. If he's willing to give all that up for you and…" he looks around the room, "this, then I guess we're going to have to trust you not to sell us out the first chance you get. We want our brother back."

Sera's jaw loosens a little. "I'm not going to sell you out, Phillip. All I wanted to do was protect myself in case Andrew's plan ended up with me getting fired. I'm replaceable. He's not. I understood that from the beginning."

Phillip nods, and, surprisingly, I see Mason nodding as well. Even more surprising, Mason says, "Truthfully, we were a little hasty to fire you, Sera. Both of us were angry with Andrew for hiding things, and then we saw that file and went a little overboard. We've had time to think, and we'd like you to come back, but we'd like to do it without having half the administration mutiny."

Sera takes a deep breath and says, "I'd like to do what I was doing in London. Dealing with new authors and agents. Deciding who we keep and who we drop. Making and maintaining budgets for marketing campaigns."

Phillip chuckles. "Well, there's not a position for all of that in New York. It's a little too big for one person to handle all of that."

I speak up. "But one person can oversee it in London…"

She grins at me. "That's true."

"You'd really want to move to London permanently?" Phillip asks, completely surprised at the thought.

She shrugs. "It could be fun. Plus, Phillip is usually the one who goes over there, right? If you moved some people around *there* to Loughton Media, then Phillip and I could manage all of it easily. By the time we came back to New York, we were only working fifty-hour weeks, and Loughton Media was still brand new. And everybody there loves him. Even if he did something crazy like hire a cover artist to run things, they'd get over it."

Everything she wants and more. The words I told her only a few moments ago race through my mind. She could have asked to stay in New York, but no. She took the easy option. The one where we would have plenty of time together. Away from the rest of the world.

It's exactly what I want. Low stress. Managing the sides of things that we both care about without as much extra.

Phillip looks at Mason, and they both shrug. "That could work," he says. "We had an agreement to share the responsibilities of the entire company, though. Nobody was supposed to be swamped while the other two weren't busy."

I frown. But that hasn't been the case at all for months. I went and did a thing while they managed the New York branch. "Because we were supposed to share the company, so all our opinions counted the same. Except that isn't the way things have gone so far. You two ran New York, and I ran London. Why don't we continue to do that except maybe keep in touch a little more? Maybe have a few more quick chats between those quarterly meetings? It's not like I can't weigh in on things from overseas. I'll just have to do it in the afternoon instead of the morning, London time."

Phillip smiles. "That could work. We need someone watching London, and you're literally the only person to have ever run it. I guess that makes more sense than anything else."

I smile and say, "Excellent. We'll pack our things and head to London as soon as we figure out Sera's compensation."

She looks around the room and sighs. "What am I supposed to do with this place? I got a year lease on it…"

Fifty-Two

SERA

"THAT'S RIGHT. THE LAST ONE IS RELEASING IN ALL formats on February 17th. We'll have all the promotional graphics sent with the inventory."

"That should work on our end. We're really excited to try out this new small author push that Loughton House is doing. I didn't think we'd witness this big of a shift in the industry in my lifetime."

I can't help but smile as I say, "Me neither, Mr. Parker. It's a good time to be in the business. Just wait until we get these authors doing some signing tours. I think you're going to be very surprised at the crowds these no-name authors will bring."

"It's an exciting prospect. Have a great evening, Ms. Wylder." I hang up the phone and lean back in my chair. The familiar tingling runs through me like lightning. I run my hand through Andrew's hair, and he looks up at me, his tongue still flicking across my clit.

He pulls away, a faint sheen on his chin, and asks, "We got the window displays?"

I nod to him, enjoying the way my body feels. "We sure did. None of our authors could have pulled that on their own, but when we marketed all twenty of them as a set, Parker went crazy for them. His only stipulation is that he wants them to do signings together. A small price to pay for nailing the biggest independent bookstores in England."

This is exactly what I wanted. Twenty no-name authors who are now about to go on signing tours throughout London. One is a lifelong fantasy reader who became a teacher. Another is a stay-at-home mom who was trying to bring in a little extra money when her husband got laid off during the last recession. Another is a lawyer who's burned out on the legal system. All of them wanted something other than their current position in life.

And now, they're all about to have their lives changed forever. We did that. We gave them a life that makes them smile every day. They get to tell stories instead of feel trapped by debt or a job that they hate.

Andrew sits down on the desk in front of me and gives me one of those smiles that I fell in love with. "You know, you're kind of a genius, Sera. How'd I get lucky enough to meet you all those years ago at that Christmas party?"

It's been a long time since I thought about that Christmas party. "If I remember correctly, it had something to do with you being the most charming liar I'd ever met. Well, that and the fact that you look absolutely dashing in a Santa outfit."

He runs his hand through his hair and says, "So you're saying that you'll like me even when I have gray hair and a big gray beard? Or that you'll still like me when I gain forty pounds?"

"I mean that you look good in a red stripper outfit. Obviously."

Inside, though, I'm thinking that he'd probably look dashing with gray hair. Or with a few extra pounds. Because I know that there's a difference between falling in lust with someone and falling in love. Lust is what we started with. The excitement, the attraction, and maybe the way my body yearned for the way it felt when he touched me.

I already knew all about lust. But love is something new, something that I'm exploring with him. I'd thought that love was something between a parent and a child, but there's more to it. Even if Andrew couldn't bend me over the desk in the office or make my body quiver with his touch, I'd still feel compelled to be near him.

My parents may have been in love for years while they were apart, but I don't understand it. The thought of being away from Andrew hurts me. It makes my chest ache thinking about it. Can I handle it? Yes, but only because I know that he'll be back soon.

"Are you still planning to go on the tour with them?" I ask.

He nods. "I need to. They don't know what they're doing, and I'm the only person in upper management that doesn't have very much going on right now. I'd bring you along, but…"

"But I have to make sure that the place doesn't burn down," I say with a sigh. "I know. It's what I wanted, though. You know I require a certain something before you go. Right?"

He nods, the grin crossing his face again. "I would be remiss in my duties if I didn't make sure you were completely satisfied before I left you for a few weeks."

"Good. I'm probably going to need it at least a few times."

He stands up and licks his lips. "Well, who am I to refuse you something only I can provide? We can go to Luciano's every day if that's what you want."

I give him a grin. "You know me so well."

I stand up and wrap my arms around him. God, it feels good to know he's all mine. The man that showed me what love is. The man who taught me what it was to trust someone completely. "I'm going to miss you so much," I say.

He runs his hand through my hair, and this time, he doesn't even pull it a little. "I know. I'm going to miss you, too, Sera. But this is how our lives have to be. We could always leave it all behind if you wanted. We could go move to some island in the middle of nowhere and drink ourselves silly on a white sand beach for the next fifty years."

I shake my head. "No. I could have done that before. Hell, I thought about it. We both want this, and we're damned good at it. I can handle you going on business trips as long as I know you're coming home to me. And you'd better come home to me, mister. Because I will show you a whole other side of me if you don't."

He chuckles and pulls me closer to him. "Don't you worry. There's not a Luciano's in Manchester."

"Well, go get your wallet, Mr. Billionaire, because we're going there for lunch in about fifteen minutes."

He steps away, gives me another grin, and goes back to his office. I'm left staring at the door. Anyone else would see this as an issue, but not me. Yes, him leaving is going to be hard, but this is what I wanted. I love Andrew Loughton with all my heart.

And I love my job, just as he does. As he said, we could ride away into the sunset and spend our lives on a beach somewhere. We could wake up to margaritas and go to sleep with bellinis. We could do absolutely nothing of note for the rest of our lives except love each other. That's the dream of so many people, but we're not those people.

In our fairy tale, he didn't save me, and I didn't save him. We aren't riding off into the sunset. We're sitting down and changing the world. Together. And sometimes that means that we can't spend every moment together, but that's okay.

Because no matter how far away he is, he's still mine, and I'm still his. That won't ever change. Every moment away from each other only makes the moments together even better. Maybe I didn't find a white knight on a white steed. Maybe I just found the man I want to spend the rest of my life with.

And I think that's so much more magical.

Epilogue

ANDREW

I don't think I've ever been this nervous. Not even six months ago when Sera and I were about to present Vanguard and Loughton Media to Phillip and Mason. Now, after six months of working together in London, we're back in New York in the same conference room.

This time, there aren't any hidden business ventures or shady partnerships. No lies or business futures on the line. We're just informing each other of the details of each of the divisions.

Mason says, "Thank you, Sera, for walking me through your decision-making process back in January regarding Vanguard. Comparing last year's numbers with this year's shows how effective your approach is."

"It won't be long until other businesses catch onto what we're doing," Phillip reminds everyone. "By this time next year, we're going to have competition, and our early adoption of this process won't give us that much lead time. We need to keep re-assessing our approaches and optimizing. Right now, it may give us an advantage over everyone, but the smaller, agile companies will be nipping at our heels."

Sera chuckles. "You mean like my company would have done?"

Phillip and Mason grin. It's good that we can all laugh about the near catastrophe of last January. All four of us have been working very closely over the past six months, and I feel like Sera's fitting in better than anyone expected. Even Mason has given her the respect she deserves. He's still an ass, but he's family. And they're all looking at Sera more like family than an employee at this point.

Which is important.

Mason unplugs his computer and brings it back to his spot at the table, and my heart skips a beat. It's Sera's turn to present her numbers and projections. Unlike January, some of these numbers will be news to me, but I'm not all that worried about them.

There are more important questions at stake right now.

Like whether my ruse will work out the way it needs to. Sera stands up and carries her laptop to the projector hookup. Her screen pops up on the projector, and when she clicks the file, her screen goes to the blue screen of death with a note about some kind of corruption. I breathe a sigh of relief. Phase One of the plan worked.

"What the hell?" Sera says with more than a little frustration.

I can't help but put my hand in my pocket to feel the little box. I say, "You sent it to me, so it's probably in your email."

It took me a long time to plan out how to do this. I had to call the IT guy in and get him to show me how to set it all up. Then I had to be ridiculously sneaky right before the presentation.

Sera sighs and pulls out her phone. It's damn near an exact repeat of that meeting in January. She connects her phone to the Bluetooth, and her screen comes up on the wall behind her. On cue, Phillip stands up. "Stop," he says. Just like I asked him to.

"What is that?" he says in that dramatic tone. He walks around the table toward the wall, his finger pointing at a little icon in the middle. The place on her screen she'd pay the least attention to when she was focused on opening her email.

She looks at the little file he's pointing at, her frustration turning first to fear as the memory of this happening before flashes through her mind. Until she sees what he's pointing at.

"What the… Wylder Bus Plan…" She's never seen that file before, but I have.

I stand up with my most serious look. "Open it," I say, and she hesitates. This is so similar to that moment six months ago.

"I've never seen that before," she says, more confused than afraid, and I can't keep the serious look on my face anymore. A smile cracks through, and I take her phone to click the icon.

And right there, front and center, there's a single file. Sera Loughton's Prenuptial Agreement. She's still confused, like I expected. "Sera," I say. "When I stole you away to London, you agreed to work with me. You agreed to spend every moment with me for months hoping I could give you want you wanted. A chance to change your life. A chance at doing something that would matter."

She nods, still not sure what all this means. "Even though you trusted me, you needed a backup plan. Just in case everything went wrong."

I give her the phone back and reach into my pocket. When I pull out the little velvet box, I get down on one knee. "I'm asking you to trust me again, Sera. And I don't expect you to do that without a backup plan. That prenup is for us to work out so that we're both protected in case things go wrong. Marry me, Sera Wylder. Marry me and let me prove to you that you won't ever need your backup plan. Let me prove that no matter what, I will love you and you will come first."

I open the little box and show her the ring. She drops her phone as she puts her hands over her mouth. "Yes," she whispers.

I take the ring out of the box, and when she puts her hand out, I slide it onto her finger. In a flash, I remember all the moments that set us on this path. The crazy ones. The steamy ones. The ones that had me crying in the rain on The Shard.

A rollercoaster of emotions, but in the end, every step of the way was important. We've grown and changed and sacrificed. We are not the same two people who stepped onto that jet going to London.

"I love you, Andrew," she whispers as I pull my hand away. Those gray eyes flash with happiness. Not the wild and carefree kind she had at a Christmas party four years ago. No, that was fun and lust and excitement. This is the kind that comes when you have everything you want.

I stand up, and as I pull her in for a kiss, I hear someone clapping. But I don't care. I need to kiss the woman I love more than anything in the world. And for a moment, we're in a magic bubble. There's nothing important outside of the two of us.

"I don't want another day where you're not mine," I whisper.

"Never again. I don't need a backup plan, Andrew. You're mine, no matter what happens." I remember the day that I accidentally cut myself with that letter opener. The way the blood had dripped onto the desk.

And the way those little drops of crimson had found each other. What had once been two drops became one, and it was as though they'd never been separated. I can barely remember a time without Sera. I can't imagine a future without her.

You cannot separate two drops once they've found each other, once they've become one. I don't think there's anything in the world that could break us apart. We've rebuilt ourselves to fit with each other.

Maybe we can't always live in our little bubble, but we don't have to anymore. Because it will always be us against the world. We became the bubble, and even if we're a thousand miles away from each other, there's nothing between us.

"Congratulations," Phillip says, and it pulls us from the moment.

Mason's grinning when he says, "We scheduled an early lunch, but when we get back, I'd like to see your presentation."

Sera cocks her head at Mason and then at Phillip before turning to me. "You got both of them in on this, didn't you?"

I shrug and give her a grin. "It was the only way to pull it off. But there are other people involved too. Like the place we're going to go eat."

She frowns. "Why…?"

"Well, London's not the only place in the world with secret places to eat lunch…" I wave at my brothers and pull her out of the conference room. She gives me a grin, the same kind that she's given me each time I take her on an adventure.

That's our life now. Work hard and play harder. We found our purposes. Each other and making a mark on the world. Together.

And now there's nothing that will keep us apart.

Bonus

Subscribe to Sylvia's newsletter to find out more about her upcoming books, deals, and why exactly she tends to write about trouble-making cats.

As a thank you, you'll get exclusive access to two bonus chapters about the wedding and honeymoon. Expect sand, sea, and plenty of steam! And some very heartfelt marriage vows, obviously.

https://dl.bookfunnel.com/9eqkts2vk8

Sylvia Hart

Sylvia Hart Sylvia Hart fell in love with romance books at a young age (along with Richard Gere). She is decidedly against the daily wearing of corsets (bedroom wear is a totally different story), so she's decided to settle for a billionaire instead of a prince.

But not just any billionaire will do. This girl needs one that looks good in a suit and in the sheets.

Since she hasn't found said billionaire, she's decided to write about them. Cold and brooding or fiery and fierce, she's willing to explore the possibilities. But, behind every silk tie, there will always be a heart of gold. Even if he doesn't realize it from the beginning.

Join her newsletter and find out about new books first:

https://www.subscribepage.com/sh_signup1

Also by Sylvia Hart

Boss Agreement

Ruthless businessman, heir to a publishing empire... and my new roommate?

Two hours after meeting my new boss, I share his bed. *Not that way!* A hotel room ceiling collapses on top of me, and he's the handsome stranger who saves me. I'm left without a place to sleep and look like I was in a wet t-shirt contest.

Finding out later that he's my boss is *mildly* humiliating. It also means I owe him one…

Phillip Loughton is determined, demanding, and competitive to a fault. He makes a stupid bet with his dad to try out life as the other 99% for a month… and I offer him my couch.

I know, I'm an idiot. But I need help with rent, and he needs a place to stay, so here we are. Just thirty days of living with my billionaire boss as my roommate. What could go wrong?

Nothing at all, as long as we follow the roommate agreement. The first rule? No kissing the boss. Except I'm learning more about Phillip by living with him than I ever would over caviar. Like how good he looks with a towel around his waist…

I broke the first rule. Now I'm breaking the second: don't fall for him.

But what happens when he goes back to being my boss?

Boss Agreement is a steamy standalone romance that's perfect for fans of Olivia Hayle, Nicole Snow, and Penelope Bloom. With a feisty heroine and cinnamon roll hero, there's plenty of laughs, steam, and swoon.

Tricky Business

My new boss? A billionaire marketing genius known for charming the pants off women. Me? I'm just trying to learn from him while keeping my pants on, thank you very much.

Except the elevator has other ideas, because within five minutes of meeting my new boss, it eats my skirt. Doing an interview in granny panties wasn't my idea of a perfect meet-cute… and yet Emery Brooks offers me the job.

I'm a pro at selling steamy romance books on ChitChat, the hottest social media app, and he needs me to join his advertising business. It's only a little embarrassing that he's seen my videos on #BookChat detailing exactly how I like my spice…

But I prefer book boyfriends to real ones, and Emery doesn't do "dating." We're strictly business. Honestly, really really strict (my private fantasies don't count!).

Until he catches me with my pants down. Again. And I discover that Emery might be the world's biggest liar… in all the right ways. He acts like Prince Charming, but there's nothing polite about what he does behind closed office doors. Or on a hotel balcony.

But I've read too many romance novels. There's always a shoe waiting to drop… and happily-ever-afters only exist on the page.

https://www.amazon.com/dp/B0B6HFPYT5

The Billionaire Bet

I didn't leave any glass slippers behind after our one-night stand, so why is the masquerade ball billionaire back in my life pretending to be Prince Charming?

A fancy Halloween ball with New York City's elite wasn't in my planner, but somehow that's where I find myself, surrounded by deal-seeking billionaires and drowning in expensive perfumes. Yeah. I know.

But the real surprise is the masked stranger I meet. He's tall and well-built with a voice as deep and rich as the coffee I sell, and he only has one rule: The masks stay on.

The night we spend together is incredible. Mad and passionate, and worlds apart from my normal, boring life. Before I leave, he breaks his own rule… and the masks slip.

I never expected him to show up at my failing coffee shop three weeks later.

Eli Harris, my beautiful masked stranger, just happens to be a billionaire businessman who spends his days turning loss into profit. A coincidence?

It can't be. An offer this perfect is literally too good to be true, and I'm not naive enough to believe billionaires have hearts of gold.

But I'm out of options.

Protecting my business and my heart is impossible with Eli this close to me. He keeps reminding me of the passion we shared that night and making me daydream about how it would feel to repeat it.

Just when I think my one-night-stand could be Mr. Right, I find out about a bet that only a billionaire would make. I guess he was wearing an extra mask all along.

The Billionaire Bet is an 88,000 word, standalone romance with an HEA and all the feels.

https://www.amazon.com/dp/B09NNBTQXK

Printed in Great Britain
by Amazon

40097263R00245